The Colonel's Renegade

By the same author

The Viceroy's Captain
The General's Envoy

Anthony Conway

The Colonel's Renegade

Hodder & Stoughton

First published in Great Britain in 2002 by Hodder and Stoughton
A division of Hodder Headline

The right of Anthony Conway to be identified as the Author
of the Work has been asserted by him in accordance with the
Copyright, Designs and Patents Act 1988.

2 4 6 8 10 9 7 5 3 1

A CIP catalogue record for this title
is available from the British Library

ISBN 0 340 82208 2

Typeset in Sabon by Hewer Text Ltd, Edinburgh
Printed and bound in Great Britain by
Clays Ltd, St Ives plc

Hodder and Stoughton
A division of Hodder Headline
338 Euston Road
London NW1 3BH

PROLOGUE

The man moved quickly through the darkened narrow streets, looking backwards over his shoulder as much as he looked ahead. You could not be too careful. Not with something like this. His loose-fitting sandals slapped on the uneven dirt surface as he hurried along. He had tried lifting his feet higher to muffle the sound but it slowed his pace and he could ill afford the time. Nor could he go barefoot. It had been many years since that had been an option. A measure of success in business and the more comfortable way of life had softened him. This ungainliness was the price.

He reached up and straightened the crimson tarboosh which kept slipping from his head and as the lane began to ascend in a series of broad uneven steps he clutched at the folds of his voluminous ankle-length galabeiah lest in his haste he might trip.

Pausing for breath, he once again glanced back. Now that he had climbed to a certain height he found he had reached a vantage point that afforded a modest sliver of view back between the tall dilapidated buildings which crowded in from every side. Silhouetted against the night sky the towering battlements of the Citadel could be seen, rearing on top of the hill where Saladin had established it in the twelfth century as part of his successful defence of Cairo from the crusaders. It was ironic, the man thought, that the great general's fortifications should now be occupied by descendants of those same murderous crusaders. Eight hundred years on, the Citadel had become home to the troops of the British garrison.

The thought of it made him pause, questioning what he was about to do. Unpleasant images appeared of the pink-faced foreign soldiers, their arrogance and their transparent contempt. His mind was suddenly a turmoil once again. He cursed under his breath, mopping the sweat which ran into his eyes. Involuntarily his hand moved to the cloth bag he carried slung from his shoulder. His moist plump fingers kneaded it until he felt for the hundredth time the shape of the bulging envelope within. The touch of it acted like a stiff wind on fog, clearing his mind, restoring order, strengthening resolve.

He set off again, pushing himself forward, his breath coming in great heaving gasps. He no longer looked back now, the renewed clarity of purpose dispersing his fears along with his doubts. It was as if the mission, in achieving clarity, had cocooned him with a protective shield. Somewhere at the very back of his tired mind he knew it was an illusion, but he had been in the game too long. The ardour and intensity of youth had left him many years ago and with them had gone the greater part of caution, the very thing that had kept him alive through all the intrigues and the dangers. Now all he wanted was escape, an exit from the awful world he had grown weary of inhabiting. The contents of the envelope would buy him exactly that. History, politics and all the messy murderous detritus that clung to its corrupted fringes could go to hell.

He was nearly there now. Ahead of him he could see the outline of the house that was to be the rendezvous. He had selected it himself. He slowed his pace to catch his breath in readiness for the coming meeting. Checking his watch, he saw that there were still some minutes to go before he could expect to be relieved of his burden. Once again he fingered the envelope through the thick grubby cotton of the bag.

He quickly studied the layout of his surroundings. Never use the same site twice when making an exchange. That had been one of his guiding principles throughout his career. Old locations such as this littered the city, places where he had done his deals across the years, stretching back into the early days when he had been new to the trade. Each location told a story, but only to him. To anyone else they were just another street corner, cafe, bazaar. To him they were the composite elements of an autobiography. Markers picking out the line of his success as the best in the business, like a dog's piss points staking out territory.

He moved aside into the deepest of the shadows. Now there was nothing to do but wait. He had time to catch his breath. Harry Ghazali would be here very soon. Then it would all be over. Everything. The anticipation washed through him with an overpowering sense of relief. This was the one. This was the big one and he was so very close. He knew he had been right to choose the Tombs of the Caliphs for the exchange. If anything went wrong it would be the easiest place to escape. It was a maze, a city within a city with its own streets, squares, houses, shops and piles of rubbish. For centuries the cemetery of Moslems, among the countless thousands of tombs were countless thousands of dwellings. It was less a cemetery than a sprawling desert town. By day it was a cacophony of Arab street life. Only now, at this latest hour where night hinged with the pre-dawn, were the lanes emptied of people, quiet and deathly still. With a shudder he pushed from his mind the place's more usual name. The City of the Dead.

From a short distance away he heard the footfall of someone approaching, the steps clipping smartly. It was someone coming towards him with a purpose. The man shrank back into the darkness, flattening his awkward shape against a wall as best he could and swinging the cotton bag across his chest, gripping it to him fiercely. The heat of the day was still radiating from the plaster-covered brickwork. He could feel it through his sweat-damp galabeiah.

Then all of a sudden he could see Harry Ghazali at the end of the lane opposite his hiding place. He had just rounded the corner and was pausing to get his bearings. Harry Ghazali in a

3

trim western suit. The man had selected him for the contact because of his reputation throughout the city as someone who could be trusted. That counted for everything in this business. You did not get a reputation like that without justification. Although he had not met Ghazali before, the man felt himself starting to relax. The tension drained from him. He even smiled.

He pulled away from the wall, edging out of the shadows. He raised one hand to signal. Fifty yards away Harry Ghazali looked up and saw him. Ghazali froze on the spot. His mouth opened and he shouted, the words blasting through silence. Corrupted by echoes from the surrounding walls, the clarity was lost. But not the meaning. The man read it in the alarm on Ghazali's face as his fist dug into his jacket and pulled out a gun.

The instant the hand clamped across the man's mouth from behind, he knew that everything was lost. Animal instinct caused his body to convulse in an attempt at escape, while the vestiges of his terrified reason stepped to one side, acknowledging defeat. Immobilise and silence the target, then kill with a knife thrust to the kidneys. He knew it all. And he knew there was nothing he could do to stop it. Ghazali was running towards him, the pistol raised and firing. The man could hear the bullets smacking into the plaster beside him as clearly as he heard the grunt from the assassin who drove in the blade, hard and deep, as the dogs began to whoop and howl like desert jackals throughout the City of the Dead.

I

The rage inside him was a silent thing. It was a thing to be appeased, contained, harnessed even to some greater purpose, but he feared it would never be completely assuaged. Not until his last breath left him.

His horse pounded across the packed sand. The air was still pleasantly cool at that early hour, immediately after sunrise. Eight miles from the city he had mounted the plateau at Giza, passing the Great Pyramid of King Cheops and heading westwards into the desert. In front of him was nothing all the way to the Qattara Depression and the vastness of the western desert. It stretched the entire breadth of the country into and clear across Libya, Algeria, rising into the Atlas mountains of Morocco, expanding ever westwards until dropping at last into the Atlantic Ocean on the far side of the continent. It was difficult to imagine a greater, emptier and more inhospitable space. Yet, with all of that lying before him, John Caspasian felt enclosed.

As he rode out across the level sand, he struggled to regain the sense of freedom that he had felt when first leaving the stables. It had lasted until the moment the land had opened before him. At that point, with nothing to stop him, with the vast spectacle of the desert in front of him, the futility of the exercise had struck home. For when the running was over, where was there to go except back? Back to the city, the barracks, the officers' mess, and to his rooms and his life within it.

Slowly he reined the horse to a walk. The animal was confused. It was an athletic hunter, a mare standing some fifteen hands. He had borrowed her from Captain Tremain, the Adjutant. Used to being given her head, she exulted in the unrestrained exercise of her physical power and resented this interruption from the stranger who had taken to riding her in recent days.

With a last look at the desert, Caspasian turned back to the pyramids, wondering, as he set his mark on the Great Pyramid of Cheops and rode slowly towards it, whether he would have time to climb to the top before he had to be back at camp. He had done it before, leaving his horse in the care of a Bedouin to whom he had paid several piastres. The climb had been arduous. Each of the stone blocks composing the pyramid was a three-foot ragged cube, steps for a giant. His effort had been rewarded by a spectacular view of the distant city with its citadel and minarets, the Nile, palm groves and other more remote pyramids. Nothing now remained of the pyramid's outer casing stones which originally would have made it an unclimbable, smooth-sided glacis. They had been carried away in medieval times to build the new city of Cairo long after the ancient capital of Memphis had sunk beneath the sand and dirt.

He flicked back the sleeve of his jacket and glanced at his watch. There was barely enough time to make it back for first parade, but he was not overly concerned. On arrival back in the regiment after his last posting, he had been appointed as Quartermaster. Him. John Caspasian. A shelf-stacker. A counter of blankets, boots and bullets. He had been appalled. The Colonel had made a cursory attempt to console him, saying that it was only a temporary arrangement until some younger officer could arrive from England and take over the post. For Caspasian it would not be a moment too soon. Until then he had to try and resign himself to a life of ledgers, stores and interminable stock checks. The role encompassed everything from rations to bedding stores, accommodation to uniforms, rifles and ammunition to pencils and typewriter ribbons.

As he wiped the thought of a pyramid climb from his mind

and headed for the road that led back into the city, Caspasian wondered if some inscrutable Egyptian god of destiny was toying with him, amused by this eventual return to a role he had played in boyhood. Then, in the years before the Great War, he had worked in his grandfather's ship's chandler business in the port city of Yokohama, the place of his birth.

The steady pace of the mare lulled him into a pleasant reverie. It had been a good time, not exactly carefree, but with that generally benign and comfortable simplicity that he felt should be the hallmark of every childhood. The nature of his grandfather's business and the ports of Asia in which it operated had ensured that the young Caspasian's boundaries had been stretched further and faster than might reasonably be expected for a boy of his age. Yet he had kept pace. Watched over from a tactful distance by his grandfather, who had taken pains to remain simultaneously both available and remote, John Caspasian had achieved one by one the little triumphs that – in his grandfather's words – lead a boy out of the women's quarters and into the place where the wide wind blows.

It had been no surprise to the youngster that his mother had taken exception to her father's choice of words. Yet she had colluded, though it had cost her dearly. For his part, Caspasian had accepted his extraordinary lifestyle as the norm, being the only experience he had ever known and having no friends of similar age or situation with whom to compare his state. He grew used to the sea voyages, the storms and the adventures. It was only later that he understood the reason for it all. The reason his grandfather had been so anxious to inject into the youngster such a concentration of experience which, to any other boy possessing more normal roots, would have been extended over a much greater period of years. In the fullness of time the strengthening had served its intended purpose, as a bolster against the assaults of the world.

By the time Caspasian reached the outskirts of the city, heat was pouring back into the day with the same merciless claustrophobia of water flooding a sinking ship. In places, pockets of air would remain, in cafes, hotel rooms and offices, bravely defended by overworked ceiling fans. Elsewhere, people would be stifled like yawns, punched back into chairs from where they would observe the day's comings and goings, the only movement apart from their dust-rimmed eyes being the flicker of fingers through a string of bright worry-beads.

Caspasian swept off his hat and mopped his brow, blinking away the perspiration that soaked his untidy sandy-coloured hair. His sharp blue eyes narrowed against the glare. He arched his back and stretched, feeling his spine and joints crack pleasantly as he twisted in the saddle, working from waist to shoulders and neck. He stood momentarily in the stirrups, smiling at the mare's outraged glance back at him. With suppleness returned to his long athletic limbs, he repositioned the hat on his head, brim pulled low, and looked to left and right, absorbing the intensifying sights of the thickening city.

On either side the road was flanked by an unbroken line of old buildings, each some three or four storeys high. At pavement level, shops sprouted from the ground floors, opening onto the road and topped with awnings protecting the displayed wares. Overhead, intricately carved wooden balconies projected from the second and third storeys. At the very top, on the flat roofs, canopies provided a valuable shade for the buildings' occupants.

At street level business was already well under way. An old man propelled himself through the hot dusty air like a deep sea diver in weighted boots. He looked up and his eyes met Caspasian's. They stared at each other with cautious interest, creatures of a different species meeting on the brink of a waterhole.

As the road approached the banks of the Nile it opened into a square. A sudden breath of air washed over Caspasian, bringing the smell of strong coffee. After his long ride it was more than he could resist. He sought out the cafe from which it had come and turned towards it, slipping out of the saddle as the mare slowed to a bored amble. A scattering of tables and chairs covered the broad pavement, thankfully still protected by shadow. Later in the day it would disappear, but for now it served as bait, attracting customers.

Caspasian selected a table by the roadside where he could secure the mare nearby at a water trough. He nodded a greeting at two men who occupied the next-door table. They returned it half-heartedly. One of them was drinking a glass of sahlab, a thick milky drink of arrowroot and cinnamon. The other idly stirred a glass of shay, heavily sugared tea. A plate stood between them piled high with sweet pastries. Basbusa, baklawa and kunafa, all of them glued together by a sticky coating of honey and nuts. The proprietor came across, wiping his hands on a fold of his galabeiah.

'*Salam alekum.*'

Caspasian nodded. '*Wa alekum es salam.*'

The proprietor smiled, pleasantly surprised that this new customer had taken the trouble to respond in kind, each of them wishing peace upon the other. However, not wishing to press his luck and cause embarrassment, the proprietor broke into English when he asked the tall Englishman what he might serve him.

'A cup of coffee, please. *Qahwa,*' Caspasian answered, indicating the strong black Turkish coffee whose distinctive smell had caught his attention moments earlier.

The proprietor nodded. 'Sweet?'

'*Ziyada,*' Caspasian said. After the desert ride he felt he could handle the shot of syrup to his system.

When the cup was placed before him a couple of minutes later, Caspasian lifted it to his lips and tried the coffee. It hit him like a slap on the back of the head. He turned to see his neighbours grinning at him. They raised their glasses and nodded. Caspasian knew it would have been a rare sight for them, seeing an Englishman like him at their regular morning haunt. British officers would more usually be seen on the terrace of Shepheard's Hotel on Shari Ibrahim Pasha opposite Ezbekieh Gardens in the city centre. But then Egyptians of their class would not have been there to observe them, although they might have caught a glimpse as they passed quickly by on the pavement below.

In such respects as this Cairo reminded Caspasian so much of British India, with many of the same social distinctions and cultural barriers. In other respects it was a wholly different world. Snatched from the disintegrating Ottoman Empire in 1882, its annexation by the British had never been as complete as the occupation of India. By one stratagem or another the British had nevertheless managed to hang on to the country against the will of the great majority of its people. After all, straddling the Suez Canal, it was perceived as being of vital strategic interest. Not only was it located at the crossroads of North Africa and the Levant, but the shipping route to British India passed right through it. Whoever controlled Egypt had their hand on the jugular of the Raj and, indeed, on all trade between Europe and the Far East. It was a stranglehold that Caspasian knew Britain had no intention of relinquishing.

A British Protectorate throughout the Great War, in order to silence mounting Egyptian political opposition the country had been granted a limited independence in 1922. Nevertheless, Britain reserved the right to garrison it with troops and to maintain full control of the Suez Canal. The Sudan remained completely under British rule and was administered by a Governor General. In addition, foreign nationals in Egypt enjoyed the status and privileges of a *corps diplomatique*.

While such a heavily qualified independence did little to satisfy the hard-line Egyptian opposition, sufficient sections of society were appeased in order for it to work. The British aim had been cleverly achieved. For the moment. The opposition had been split asunder. The King, the land-owning gentry and a few other groupings accepted the new state of affairs, but elsewhere discontent remained. Egyptian ministers played at parliamentary democracy and carried on the work of running the country, although everyone knew that behind each one of them was a British civil servant pulling the strings. King Fuad inhabited his palace as Head of State, while real power was exercised by the British High Commissioner from the grand colonial-style edifice of the British Residency on the eastern banks of the Nile.

Caspasian looked around the square and soon spied a cluster of torn posters plastered to a wall. They were admonitions from the Wafd opposition party, advertising a rally. For the last four years, ever since the assassination by nationalists in 1924 of the Sirdar, the British Commander-in-Chief of the Egyptian Army, and since the clampdown of the political opposition that had followed, the situation had been relatively calm. But pressure was beginning to mount again and to Caspasian, used to the sensitivities of the Raj and the growing Indian independence movement there, it was all too familiar.

He finished his coffee, careful to avoid the thick layer of gritty sediment coagulating in the bottom of his cup, and got shakily to his feet, caffeine drumming in his head. From the square it was a relatively short ride northwards to Kitchener Barracks. The camp, not too dissimilar from an average military cantonment in India, lay on the west bank of the Nile, opposite the southern end of Gezira Island, the large strip of land that bisected the river as it passed through the heart of Cairo. The famous Gezira Sporting Club occupied the southern part of the island, while the northern half was covered by the smart residential area of Zamalek where a great number of the westerners chose to live.

As he approached the open gates, Caspasian straightened his jacket, slapping off the worst of the dust. The sentry slammed smartly to attention and presented arms. Caspasian braced in the saddle and acknowledged. Behind the sentry a large signboard announced to the world in tall highly polished brass letters that this was the home of the Twelfth Gurkha Rifles. Immediately through the gates stood the guard room, flanked by a pair of Turkish guns captured by the regiment in Mesopotamia a dozen years earlier during the Great War.

The front of the single-storey building was shaded by a veranda, beneath which was a display of other military paraphernalia, more captured firearms, swords, banners and trinkets, each telling a tale of its own. Like any officer or soldier of the regiment Caspasian was familiar with every detail of each of them. While a small silver plaque attached to each one told the bare facts of place and date, the stories behind them were required knowledge for anyone joining the regiment. Caspasian still remembered the unforgiving test he had endured from the Adjutant when he had first arrived in the Twelfth Gurkhas as a subaltern. But it was all part of the regimental tradition and lore, a slice of everything that made this particular military grouping unique, just as every such regiment was unique. The Gurkhas had their own word for it. It was the *Kaida*. Difficult to translate, the word implied more than simply a body of lore, of customs and of rules, although it was all of these. It was the way things were done. It encapsulated a world view. It indicated a way of being. The only problem that Caspasian had with it was that, to some of his less imaginative colleagues, it had become a way of being that excluded all others. With such men as these it was not a guide but, rather, a mental straitjacket.

From the guard room, Caspasian swung left and followed the road around the periphery of the lines towards the stables. A groom ran to meet him, accepting the mare from him as he dismounted, leading her away to tend to. It was a long walk to the officers' mess and Caspasian could feel his limbs stiff and aching after the ride. Most of his fellow officers had already breakfasted and were at work on their various duties about the busy camp. Caspasian was grateful that he was spared the need to exchange small talk. He was not in the mood for it.

His rooms occupied part of a large bungalow that he shared with two others. It was just one of several such bungalows grouped around the main mess building where all the single officers came together to take their meals. Married officers lived further afield within the cantonment, enjoying a fiction of normal married life. Caspasian had once likened it to the illusory sense of freedom enjoyed by a free-ranging hen, its captivity masked by the remoteness of the wire. The battalion second-in-command, a good-natured major, had pleasantly chided the young officer, accusing him of envy. Caspasian had promptly shut up, stung by a recognition of the truth.

His own segment of the bungalow occupied the western end and consisted of three separate rooms and a veranda. There was a bedroom, a bathroom and a large sitting room. Adjacent to the bungalow was a separate building housing the servants' quarters. In the evenings, Caspasian enjoyed sitting on the western-facing veranda to watch the sun go down before dinner in the mess. It was a peaceful time in which to gather thoughts and reflect upon the day. Sometimes he would read a few pages of a book and there was always a ready pile of them on the wicker table that stood beside his chair. Markers protruded from each of them as it had never been his habit to finish one book before starting the next. Several would be read in tandem as the mood took him.

But at other times Caspasian would sit there simply staring into space, his thoughts far away from the hot dusty city. He was ill at ease with his present role as Quartermaster and longed for an escape from it. How such an escape might come, or in what form, he had no idea.

When he had bathed away the dust of his early morning ride and changed into fresh clothes, Caspasian made his way to the Quartermaster's department. Occupying a large sprawling complex of buildings, Caspasian's office was at the far end.

It was bright and spacious and for this he was thankful. But that was where the mercies ended. The rest was a warren of shelves, stores, pantries and warehouses, stuffed with boxes and materials of every shape and size.

To assist him in his task of keeping the regiment supplied with everything it needed in order to live and operate, Caspasian had a staff of clerks and storemen, headed by a Viceroy Commissioned Officer, a VCO Subedar known as the Gurkha Quartermaster. Beneath the GQM, as he was known, in the descending chain of command was the Regimental Quartermaster Havildar. It was a branch of the regiment with which Caspasian had not before been closely involved. Indeed, when he had been a young officer he and his contemporaries had viewed it with disdain, having little appreciation that, without the QM's department, the rest of the regiment would be wholly unable to do anything. Nevertheless, Caspasian's grudging acknowledgement of the department's importance did nothing to dispel his feeling that he would really rather not be obliged to run it. The Colonel had sidelined him, removing him from an operational command, and Caspasian bitterly resented it.

This morning Caspasian managed an entire hour of paperwork before exasperation got the better of him. He finished drafting a memo to the second-in-command notifying him of the poor state in which a consignment of tartan cloth for the Pipes and Drums platoon had arrived, screwed the cap onto his fountain pen and tossed it aside. Through the open door, the GQM looked up from his desk in the outer office and grinned knowingly at the havildar who stood before him with a sheaf of delivery notes detailing the fresh rations that had just been delivered to the cookhouse.

'I'm off for a ghum, saheb,' Caspasian snapped as he strode briskly past and headed for the door.

'Where to, saheb?' the GQM called after him. 'Just in case anyone calls for you.'

'A nice little stroll across to the arms kotes, I think,' Caspasian said over his shoulder. 'I haven't visited the armouries recently.'

'No, saheb. Not for at least a day.'

Caspasian scowled at him and slammed the door.

From the ranges on the far side of the camp the crack of rifle fire struck Caspasian with the force of a finely chosen insult. The rifle companies were honing their skills in the run-up to the inter-company shooting competition. Caspasian's role extended to ensuring the ammunition was at hand when required. It was galling in the extreme.

Suddenly he knew where he had to go. The A Company arms kote. There at least he would find someone with whom he could commiserate, a man similarly exiled from the real business of soldiering. Havildar Gangabahadur Limbu. Sergeant Ganga.

Normally, the job of minding the company arms kote was given to a corporal, a naik in Indian Army terms. But in Ganga's case the Colonel had made an exception, for Ganga was a man in Caspasian's own mould, effective when there was lead in the air, but otherwise wholly unsuited to peacetime garrison soldiering.

Finding Ganga present in the regiment had been a great consolation to Caspasian when he himself had arrived back from his last posting in China. It was almost three years since the two had seen each other. They had been involved in an operation in the wild tribal areas beyond India's North-West Frontier Province and had been lucky to escape with their lives. From there Caspasian had proceeded to China where he had greatly missed the assistance and expertise of his old friend, Ganga. One of the best marksmen in the entire Gurkha Brigade, Ganga would have been invaluable on more than one occasion.

The A Company arms kote was round the back of the main armoury, separated from the others as if in reflection of its caretaker's own state of partial disgrace. As Caspasian rounded the corner he saw that the door stood open. After the glare of the mid-morning sun, the Stygian gloom of the dark interior yawned like an unused side entrance to Hades.

There was a sudden burst of invective from within and the next moment Sergeant Ganga plunged out into the dazzling light, colliding headlong into Caspasian. The two men rebounded off one another in surprise and in that split second as Caspasian caught the look of shock in Ganga's eye, he felt a shiver down the length of his spine. It was an instant of assessment, immeasurably slim, as the instincts of the old Gurkha soldier weighed the man before him in the balance of friend or foe. The next moment, Caspasian saw Ganga's mental safety catch flick from Fire to Safe. Caspasian exhaled with relief.

'Ganga, whatever's the matter?'

Hatless and unable to salute, the sergeant braced to attention, as rigid as an iron bar. 'Sorry, saheb. The Havildar Major told me to count the drill rounds and I keep losing count.'

Caspasian could imagine the vindictive pleasure with which the Havildar Major had given the order. The inert drill rounds were used for basic weapon-handling practice such as loading, unloading and stoppage drills. Every company kept an enormous box of them, the jumbled, loose rounds piled high to the rim. For someone like Ganga, counting them was as difficult an exercise as counting the motes of dust in a shaft of sunlight, and as pointless. In Ganga's face Caspasian could read the same sense of bitter frustration that was consuming himself. As if in confirmation, a volley of distant fire from the range caused them both to look up.

'Peacetime soldiering, eh?' Caspasian said. 'Don't you just love it?'

Ganga relaxed, scratching the savagely close-cropped hair on his head. Perspiration glistened on his round face.

'Come on. Let me help,' Caspasian said. 'I am the Quartermaster after all. I'm supposed to be good at this sort of thing.'

Far from protesting, Ganga led the way into the dark musty room, kicking the box vengefully when he located it. 'There.' He indicated his stool to Caspasian and broke into a broad grin. 'Over to you, saheb. Now I can get on with the arms inspection.'

Before Caspasian could protest, Ganga stepped quickly across to the rifle racks that disappeared into the bowels of the windowless armoury. With the company on the ranges, most of the racks were empty. In one portion however, a row of Mark IV Lee-Enfield rifles rested on their brass butt plates, leaning snugly in the rack's deep wooden grooves. Ganga reached up and took out one of the rifles. He hefted it in his hands, sensing the weapon, getting a feel for it. All of them had been reported as having faults, but Caspasian knew that before Ganga sent any rifle to the armourers for their professional attention, he always liked to tinker with it himself. As often as not he managed to solve the problem. None of the other company kote corporals ever soiled their hands with such a task, for the armourers were all low-caste Kamis. To the largely Hindu Gurkhas, metalwork was like tailoring or shoemaking, a task reserved for untouchables. Specialists in these skills were recruited from the relevant castes quite separately from the recruitment of Gurkha riflemen. Kamis for metalwork, Sarkis for leatherwork and Damais for tailoring, all of them serving in the Quartermaster's department, distinguishing it still further from the mainstream life of the regiment.

By the time Caspasian had counted to a hundred he had already had enough. He scooped up the loose rounds from the neat little piles on the concrete floor and poured them back into the box. Ganga looked up in surprise and smiled. 'That was quick, saheb.'

Caspasian dropped shut the heavy lid and fastened the catch. 'Two thousand, five hundred and sixty-three,' he said definitively. 'Where's the ledger? I'll make the entry myself.'

Ganga frowned doubtfully, to which Caspasian replied,

'Well do you really think the Havildar Major's going to count them to check it's right?'

Ganga beamed. 'That's why you're a captain and I'm only a poor ignorant sergeant. I would never have thought of that.'

Caspasian stood up and stretched. 'Like hell you wouldn't.'

Caspasian entered the figure in the relevant column, in-itialled it in the margin as having been verified by himself, and closed the ledger. 'Let's go to the ranges.'

With a sigh of relief, Ganga replaced the rifle in the rack, picked up his hat and sought out a large bundle of keys. Out in the sunshine once again, he swung the solid iron door shut, clamped on the three padlocks and checked that each was secure.

Falling naturally into step, the two men made their way through the camp. They picked up the road that led to the ranges on the far side of the parade ground and followed it down a long winding avenue of thin trees that provided the poorest of shade to marching troops. Little by little the sound of rifle fire grew louder. Just by listening to it, Caspasian and Ganga could read exactly what was happening. The company that was firing at that moment was practising snap shooting during the advance. Starting from the three hundred yard firing point, there had first been a thunderous volley of fire as the soldiers on duty in the butts had raised the hand-held targets high above their heads, exposing them above the parapets. Each target consisted of a flat cardboard figure secured to a long pole.

Targets would be exposed three times and at each exposure the firers would engage the target directly to their front with a single shot. After the third exposure, the firers had only a few seconds to sprint the hundred yards down to the two hundred yard firing point before the targets would again be raised into view three times. Then again down to the one hundred yard firing point and the next three exposures. At the three hundred yard firing point the firers would have to fire from the prone firing position, at the two hundred yard firing point they would fire kneeling, and at the one hundred yard firing point they would fire standing. By that time they would be breathing heavily from the exertion of running, making it all the more difficult to maintain a steady aim at the targets.

With the last shots fired, the firers would unload and then move forward to the butts to inspect their targets, having to endure the jibes and insults of the butt party who would have been detailed from one of the other rifle companies awaiting their own turn to fire. Then, with the practice completed and scores noted, the companies would change over and the whole process would begin again. A meal would be brought up at midday and everyone would break for half an hour, seeking out whatever shade might be found to eat their curry and rice from mess tins heaped to the brim.

As Caspasian rounded the last bend in the road and the ranges came into view, he was met by the familiar cry from the firing point officer.

'Watch and shoot! Watch and shoot!'

The firers had just changed over and it was now the previous butt party's turn. Standing at the three hundred yard firing point, a score of riflemen waited, eyes riveted to the empty butts. Suddenly the targets appeared and the firers dropped to their stomachs and wriggled quickly into a firm firing position, with only seconds to get off their first rounds before the targets disappeared from view. Shots rang out, but here and there some young soldier had taken a second too long and his target disappeared before he could fire. Curses and hoots of derision exploded from the watching Gurkha officers and NCOs, the subedars, jemadars and havildars standing to the rear.

'Ah, there you are, Caspasian! I might have guessed you'd try to escape from your duties.'

Caspasian turned to see the Colonel marching towards him, smiling broadly. Beside him, Captain Tremain the Adjutant was, as ever, the image of the perfectly dressed officer, every surface polished that could be polished and every crease ironed and pressed to a razor's edge. He seemed to be impervious to the heat which quickly reduced everyone else's uniforms to damp rags.

Caspasian braced to attention and saluted. 'Good morning, sir.'

'I didn't see you at breakfast,' the Colonel observed.

'Caspasian's helping me exercise Jennifer,' Captain Tremain added helpfully.

The Colonel frowned. 'I take it Jennifer's a horse?'

'Quite so, sir.'

'Thank heavens for that.' He turned back to Caspasian. 'I hope you're going to behave yourself at the Residency do tonight, John?'

Caspasian winced without showing it. 'You know me, Colonel, the very incarnation of discretion.'

'Exactly. I do know you. All too well. And I don't want you going sick at the last moment and failing to appear, or disappearing after the first half hour and slinking off into town. There are going to be some very high calibre people there tonight and it's an honour for our mess to have received an invitation.'

Caspasian knew as well as the Colonel that the High Commissioner was simply doing the rounds, inviting the officers of the next regiment on his list, but if the Colonel chose to pretend the Twelfth Gurkhas were receiving some special attention that was his affair. Caspasian had known Colonel Gordon Humphreys for a long time and liked the man, even if he was capable of being a little pompous at times. His affectionate nickname amongst the officers was 'Old Queezy', dating from his first days in the regiment. During the long sea voyage out to India to join the regiment, Humphreys had spent the majority of the trip hanging over the railings vomiting. However, Caspasian had seen him in action and there was nothing queezy about the Colonel's nerve when it came to battle.

'We're meeting up at the Gezira Sporting Club beforehand and then we might go on somewhere afterwards,' Captain Tremain added with a malevolent grin. Caspasian's dislike of socialising was quietly renowed in the regiment and Tremain's delight at catching him with such an offer in front of the Colonel was evident.

Caspasian smiled icily. 'Well, thank you, Andy. You know me. Always one for a party.'

'That's the spirit, Caspasian,' the Colonel beamed. 'It's good to have you back in the regiment. It's been so . . . erm . . . well, you know . . . without you.'

A volley of rifle fire thundered across the range as the men on the firing point blazed away at their targets. Rifle bolts slammed back and forth and empty cartridge cases tinkled on the hard packed earth.

'Detail, unload!' screamed the firing point officer. 'For inspection, port arms!'

The Colonel raised his nose to the air, sniffing gently. 'Is that lunch I can smell, Caspasian? What have your boys in the catering platoon cooked up for us today?'

Captain Tremain stifled a snigger. 'Yes, John, do you plan the menus yourself?'

But Caspasian did not answer. He was staring fixedly out across the ranges, his solid jaw masking the depths of his misery.

2

Mehmet Baran Pasha lived in a villa on Gezira Island. Situated towards the northern end in Zamalek, it was a grand residence built in the Moorish style and had been in the Baran family for three generations. A high wall kept it comfortably segregated from the hubbub of the busy street that ran past outside, but once through the gates one entered another world.

The garden was intense rather than spacious, so heavily land-scaped as to give the impression that it had been distilled from something much greater. All the various elements were there, but stripped of the broader dimensions that would have caused them to make better sense. Fountains, statues, paths, lawns, flower beds, trees and summer house, everything was packed tightly together, the intervening spaces that would otherwise have maintained everything in proportion, truncated to the point where the atmosphere created was claustrophobic. While it was out of keeping with the character of the villa itself, the garden was one of Baran's great loves and as he sat on an upper floor balcony with his newspaper lowered, he surveyed it proudly.

A distinguished member of the Turco-Egyptian elite that had governed the country for over a hundred years, Baran enjoyed his place as a leading light in Circassian society. Together with his wife Simay and their four teenage children, he hosted a round of parties every year and his hospitality had become something of an institution in Cairo. Aside from his business interests and two minor government appointments, he sat on the boards of several charitable organisations from which he gained nothing except the respect of his peers. For Baran this was all that mattered.

Educated at the Sorbonne, he made a point of travelling to Paris at least every two years, taking his whole family with him so that the refinements of French culture that had so impressed him in his youth might also rub off on his offspring. In due course, finances allowing, it was his intention that his children would follow in his footsteps, similarly benefiting from the highest standards of western education. That was where he believed the future lay, and modern Turkey, freed of its exhausted Ottoman trappings, was well on the way to taking its rightful place as part of the new Europe. Its leader, Kemal Ataturk, was seeing to that. For Baran it was tempting to regard Turkey as synonymous with the small toehold of land at the eastern extremity of the European continent, ignoring the fact that by far the greater portion of the country lay east of the Bosporus, cheek by jowl with the Levant.

He had enjoyed a restful morning. A minor back injury had kept him at home. The office had telephoned twice, first to enquire about the pulled muscle, and then to refer some matter to him about a delayed shipment. Baran had answered both queries irritably. He was relishing the peace and quiet and resented having them interrupted. The children were at school, Simay had gone round to a friend's for lunch, the house servants were all out on lengthy errands of one sort or another, and the villa's rare emptiness was having a wonderfully soothing effect on him.

He flicked the newspaper back into shape and started to scan for something worth reading. From the garden below the restful sound of water playing in the fountain rose up to him, filling him with a sense of well-being. An article on the Wafd momentarily drew his attention but he found himself unable to get into it. Political intrigue was not for a day like this.

With sudden resolution he folded the paper abruptly, tossed it onto the small coffee table at his side, and eased himself warily out of his chair, pleased to find that he could now do so without the discomfort of the previous day. A bath would do very nicely. Very nicely indeed.

Humming to himself, he walked slowly through into his bedroom. He undressed gingerly, careful not to overtax his injured muscle, and laid each item of clothing fastidiously on the bed. The bathroom adjoined the master bedroom and once he had set the water running, he returned to the bedroom and busied himself with some gentle exercises that the doctor had shown him. Unprepared, he caught sight of himself in the full-length mirror on one of the cupboard doors. Abruptly he stopped humming, his good mood mildly dented by the spectacle before him. Slight of build and grey-haired, Baran had always flattered himself that he had aged gracefully. Confronting his reflection unawares gave the lie to his cherished illusion. He wondered if there was any such thing as growing old with grace.

He quickly adjusted his pose but it was already too late. The damage to his pride had been done. He felt as he imagined a hot air balloonist must feel whose canopy has just been severely perforated. Struggle though he might to effect the repair, he could feel himself descending rapidly from the height that he had occupied all morning.

With a sigh he turned away from the image of his sunken chest, scrawny legs and pot belly, and went through to the bathroom and turned off the taps. He stooped to test the temperature and was not surprised to feel that the pain had returned. The relationship between pain and morale was a close one. Wincing, he stepped into the bath and lowered himself down into the hot water. With a deep sigh he leaned back, sliding deeper until his feet met the end and the water had risen up to his chin. He closed his eyes, feeling contentment return as the warmth soaked away the pain.

The noises from outside retreated until the only sound of which Baran was aware was his own breathing and the last few drops from the taps. Each one fell with a deep resonance.

Liking the sound, Baran moved a hand lazily in the bath water, hearing the agitated ripples slap against the enamel sides. He felt himself starting to doze. His breathing became deeper the more he relaxed. He found himself thinking about . . .

His head was thrust so violently under the water that the momentum almost slid him clean out of the tap end of the bath, feet first. Only the firm grip on his hair held him in place. Water had shot up Baran's nose the second it had been propelled beneath the surface. Instinctively he opened his mouth and gulped. Reason caught up a full second or two later as he gagged on the water that his clenched lungs fought to expel. His whole frame convulsed, legs thrashing wildly, hands grasping at air.

Wide open now, his eyes stared up through the disturbed water and saw the dark quivering outline of a figure. A man. Baran's hands closed upon the arm that was holding him down. His fingers felt the rough woollen cloth, enviably dry above his own watery hell. The moment his fingers closed upon the forearm, Baran was struck by the hopelessness of his efforts, for the muscles were as solid as rock, wholly unaffected by the greatest force Baran himself could muster. One hand, one arm. That was all that the man needed to fix Baran in place.

Involuntarily Baran gulped a second time, his lungs raging for air. A panic greater than terror absorbed his whole being. This could not be happening. Not to him. It was simply impossible. For a second Baran wondered whether perhaps he had fallen asleep. He tried to wake himself but to no avail. This nightmare was his only reality. There was nothing else outside it. Nowhere else for his conscious mind to flee. This was it.

The pain ended as suddenly as it had begun. The grip on Baran's hair was released and he pushed himself above the surface, gasping and retching at the same time. He scrabbled for the sides of the bath to pull himself clear but received a punitive rap on the top of the head with something hard. Dazed, he sank back, eyes blinking furiously to get sight of his tormentor.

'Mehmet Baran Pasha,' the man said contemptuously.

Baran saw him clearly now for the first time. The man sat on the edge of the bath, legs crossed. One hand rested on his knee, the other, still wet, drummed fingers on the dripping enamel. He was a big man and powerfully built. A thick vigorous moustache hid his mouth completely so that when he spoke all Baran could see were slight undulations in the dark bristly hair.

'You have betrayed us,' the man said, and before Baran could respond or even register the meaning of the statement, he was thrust again beneath the surface.

Panic raced back, but this time he was released almost immediately. His lungs, braced for endurance, gasped while still full of air and Baran choked.

'You have forgotten who we are.'

'Who the devil are you?' Baran managed to splutter between coughs.

The man looked at Baran curiously. The next second he grabbed Baran's penis in one hand and lifted him out of the bath. Baran screamed. As he struggled half in and half out of the water, the man let go and Baran fell back in a cascade of water, hands clutching his injured groin.

'What do you want?' Baran yelled in agony.

The man sighed and looked around the bathroom. 'Nice fittings. Where are they from?'

'What? Where's what from?'

'The bathroom fittings,' the man prompted earnestly.

'What the devil . . .'

Before he could finish Baran had been grabbed by the penis again and hauled out of the water. Again the man let go. As Baran sank back he screamed, 'From Paris! They're from Paris, for God's sake! What the hell does it matter?'

The man smiled. 'You still don't get it, do you?' he said, adding 'Baran Pasha,' stressing the final word.

Baran stared at him, eyes narrowed. 'Look, if it's money you want . . .'

A dangerous look in the man's eyes stopped Baran in mid-sentence. 'Information then?'

The man chuckled, rocking backwards. 'What can you possibly think you could tell me that I don't already know?'

Baran struggled for composure, realising how absurd his predicament made him appear. He was a man of influence, accustomed to deference. Physical violence had played no part in his life for a very long time.

'All right, all right. Let's just calm down, shall we?' Baran said.

The man smiled pleasantly, humouring him.

'Obviously I've got something you want,' Baran continued, growing in confidence. 'All we have to do is establish what that is and take it from there. Whatever it is, it's yours.'

The man nodded. 'That sounds very reasonable. How can I not agree.'

Baran risked a smile of his own, though a nervous one. 'Good. Excellent. What is it?'

Without answering his question the man rose from the side of the bath and walked away into the bedroom. Caught completely off guard, Baran was astonished. His eyes hunted around desperately for a weapon.

From the bedroom the man's disembodied voice called, 'Your house really is splendid. Quite remarkable.'

Baran scrambled painfully out of the bath, his earlier back pain now reduced to an insignificant twinge in comparison with the threat posed by the intruder. He quietly opened the bathroom cabinet, not seriously expecting to find a weapon inside, but cursing nonetheless when he was disappointed.

'Aren't you coming?' the man called out.

'Er . . . Be right there.' Baran snatched a bath robe from a hanger and slipped it on. Knotting the cord he went reluctantly through to the bedroom. The man was busying himself leafing through the contents of Baran's bedside table drawer.

Suppressing his sense of outrage, Baran said, 'So tell me, what is it you want?'

Without looking up the man replied, 'Your life.'

Baran paused, then tittered. He jerked a thumb in the direction of the bathroom. 'But you could have taken it in there.'

'Yes, I could have, couldn't I?' the man said, giving the impression that he was only half-listening.

'Then why didn't you?'

The man finished whatever he had been doing and slammed the drawer shut. He turned and smiled radiantly. 'Who can say?' He looked towards the bedroom door. 'On second thoughts I don't like this room. Let's go.'

Taking Baran firmly by the arm, the man led the way out into the corridor. Marching briskly past the other bedrooms, they reached the top of the grand marble staircase that swept in a dramatic curve down to the ground floor and the large impressive entrance hall, paved with a chequered pattern of black and white tiles.

The man peered over the edge of the top step. 'This will do,' he said. 'By the way, my name's Kalkan. Do forgive my lack of manners. I should have introduced myself earlier.' And taking hold of Baran's shoulders from behind, threw him down the stairs as hard and as fast as he could.

Baran tumbled down head over heels in a mess of limbs. His initial scream was quickly cut short as his face crashed into one of the marble steps. Thereafter, as Kalkan monitored Baran's rapid progress from above, moving slowly down in his wake, only grunts and gasps escaped Baran. Kalkan winced instinctively as he heard a bone crack. He stepped gingerly over a patch of blood and hair stuck to the sharp hard edge of a stair. Finally, when Baran came to rest at the bottom of the staircase, his broken frame emitting one long diminishing exhalation of air, Kalkan jogged the last few steps and crouched down to inspect his victim.

'Still with us?' Kalkan observed, his voice heavy with false admiration.

Baran's eyes rolled in their sockets, slowly coming to focus on the face peering interestedly into them. He opened his mouth to speak but nothing came through the broken teeth except a trickle of bright red blood, frothy from Baran's rib-pierced lungs. One side of Baran's skull was dark and mis-shapen from a blow that Kalkan judged would prove to have been the fatal one.

He stared hard into Baran's dimming eyes, and before the last flicker of life petrified, he leaned close to Baran's ear and spoke softly.

'The Bey sends his regards.'

Baran was beyond terror. Beyond pain even. But on the brink of extinction, he at last registered understanding.

3

By the time Caspasian made it to the British Residency he was already regretting not having ignored Old Queezy's directive and simply absenting himself from the whole wretched business. Enduring the discomfort of his formal regimental mess dress in the heat was bad enough, but having to suffer the chatter of some of his brother officers was almost more than he could bear. Nevertheless, he had resolved to try his hardest. He really was attempting to do as Colonel Humphreys had said when he had interviewed Caspasian on arrival back in the regiment.

'Put the past behind you, Caspasian,' the Colonel had urged brightly. How on earth could a person do anything else? It hardly required any effort to put the past where it already was! Still, Caspasian knew what his well-intentioned commanding officer had meant and he was determined to give it a shot, if only because there was little else he could do. And an escape from the confines of the QM's department was worth any amount of effort.

In consequence, throughout the painful drinks at the Gezira Sporting Club, Caspasian had smiled earnestly until his face ached. When the party left the club and got into cars to make their way on to the Residency, Caspasian moved to one side in the shadows and rubbed a hand roughly across his cheeks, massaging the strained flesh. He wondered idly whether it was possible to sprain a face muscle. How would the regimental medical officer treat it? It could hardly be put in a splint.

Once across Khedive Ismail Bridge, the small convoy turned south and headed alongside the Nile towards the British

Residency where guards checked their names on the guest lists before admitting them into the compound. They parked the cars before falling in loosely behind the Colonel who led the way round the back of the main building to the grand sweeping lawns where the reception was being held.

Lights had been strung from the surrounding trees and, together with lanterns planted at intervals throughout the gardens, provided just enough light for socialising to take place, but also sufficient patches of shadow where Caspasian felt he would later be able to hide away. If it all became too painful he did not care what the Colonel had said. He would make his departure prematurely and face the consequences.

While the Colonel led the way towards the High Commissioner, followed by those officers with an eye on protocol and promotion prospects, Caspasian slunk away in search of a drink. He found an orderly in spotless white galabeiah and smart crimson tarboosh standing primly beside a potted palm, a silver tray balanced on one gloved hand. Caspasian helped himself to a glass of beer, utterly ignored by the orderly who might have been made of plaster. The beer was warm and Caspasian grimaced in disgust.

'I don't believe my eyes.'

At the sound of the voice Caspasian turned round. There was something about the gravelly voice and the French accent that was familiar. Secreted in a shadow even deeper than his own, the tall bulky figure of a man moved slowly forward.

'John Caspasian?' the man ventured again.

A smile spread across Caspasian's face, this time without effort or discomfort. 'Paul? Paul Béranger?'

In response there was a deep growling chuckle followed by a few badly sung bars of a song, the tone dark and threatening.

'*Tiens, voilà du boudin, voilà du boudin, voilà du boudin.*'

It had been many a year since Caspasian had heard the terrifying pulse of the French Foreign Legion's most famous marching song.

Paul Béranger strode towards Caspasian and clasped him warmly by the hand. 'But what are you doing here, *mon brave*?'

Caspasian stared back at him, thunderstruck. 'I could ask you the same question. Me, I'm here with my regiment. They've been part of the garrison since last spring. We're out at Kitchener Barracks.'

'You are still with the Gurkhas?'

Caspasian smiled. 'Of course.'

Béranger gave a big Gallic shrug. 'But of course. How stupid of me to ask!'

'And you? Still with that awful mouthful? The Régiment de Marche de la Légion Étrangère?'

Béranger smiled. 'No. We've reorganised. I'm now with the First Régiment Étranger d'Infantrie. The first REI. The RMLE is no more.'

'Here in Cairo?'

'Ah, there is no problem telling you, my friend. I have become involved in this stupid expedition.' He surveyed the crowded lawns until his eyes set upon a clutch of earnest people around the High Commissioner. 'Archaeologists,' he said contemptuously.

Caspasian felt himself about to laugh. 'You don't mean this idiotic business about the tomb of King Menes?'

Béranger's face turned scarlet. 'Please, Caspasian, don't make me feel even more stupid than I already do. If our friendship means anything to you, please leave it alone.'

But Caspasian had been feeling bad enough himself all evening and relished the chance to pass some of it on to someone else, especially an old friend and sometimes rival who he knew would take it in the spirit in which it was intended. Pure evil malice.

'The secret tomb of the legendary King Menes,' Caspasian enthused. 'Aren't they also talking about a lost city?' His eyes widened. 'Lost in the desert sands and the mountainous jebel.

It's the stuff of legend all right, Paul.' He chuckled. 'The stuff of fantasy more likely.'

'All right, all right. You've had your fun. I never realised you could be so cruel.' But then a thought occurred to Béranger and he studied Caspasian thoughtfully. 'But you haven't yet told me exactly what you are doing here.'

Instantly Caspasian regretted his goading. He took a sip of his beer which tasted even more unpleasant than before. 'I told you, I am back with my regiment.'

'As a company commander?'

'No,' Caspasian replied peremptorily.

'Oh. As second-in-command then?'

'Not yet.'

'If I remember correctly, a Gurkha regiment only has a handful of British officers.' A light slowly dawned in Béranger's eye. Caspasian watched with mounting horror as delight spread across Béranger's features. He should have known better than to try and tease such a man as Capitaine Paul Béranger of the 1st REI.

In sudden disgust Caspasian tossed his beer into a nearby shrub and placed the glass back on the orderly's tray. 'OK. So I'm the Quartermaster,' he announced defiantly.

Once again, Béranger shrugged innocently, the gesture saying all he needed to say.

'Just for now, you understand.'

'Of course. But let's get this straight. While I am going to be out in the desert with the expedition, engaged on a fruitless quest I grant you, but while I am out in the open air almost doing a soldier's job, you are going to be . . . what? . . . auditing your stores?'

He leaned closer to Caspasian and sniffed. 'I can even smell the dust of the shelves, my friend.'

Caspasian was now more miserable than ever. Béranger saw it and relented. His face was suddenly kind. 'What happened?' he asked sympathetically.

Caspasian shook his head. 'One thing and another. You know how it is.'

Béranger nodded, understanding. He had first come across Caspasian on the Western Front when the RMLE had found itself serving in the trenches at the juncture of the French Army and the British Expeditionary Force. The first unit of the BEF beyond the boundary had been the Twelfth Gurkhas. He had seen the young Caspasian in action. The two of them had fought side by side when a German assault had penetrated the Allied lines. Having identified the boundary between the two armies, the Germans had thrown everything they had got at the precise location where the boundary lay, identifying any such juncture as a weak point. Liaison was always weakest at such places and any success could rapidly be exploited while the two allies argued over which of them should allocate their precious resources to seal the breach.

What the Germans had not counted on was finding two such extraordinary units side by side. Both of them shared a common sense of professionalism that rose above national differences, partly because both of them were composed of men from a spread of nations. Denied the narrow confines of nationalism, they sought their identity in professional pride. When the Germans attacked, the momentum and ferocity of the unexpected assault carried them deep into the Allied lines. The moment the two regiments recovered their balance however the game was up for their common enemy. Legionnaire and Gurkha had surged forward together, pursuing the dazed enemy all the way back across no-man's-land.

What Béranger had also predicted however was that Caspasian was the sort of man who would always find existing in a peacetime army difficult. Caspasian's present demeanour said everything that needed to be said. To Béranger it was obvious that the man was in trouble.

Béranger suddenly had an idea and scanned the sea of heads around the ample gardens. 'Come with me,' he said, spotting the person he had been searching for. 'There's someone I want you to meet.'

He led the way across the lawn, weaving through the clusters of people grouped like atolls. As he followed his friend, Caspasian noticed how few of the people engaged in the many conversations were actually listening to anyone else. Most people were not talking with those around them, so much as addressing them. Everyone had a point to make, regardless of its relevance to the conversation in which they were supposedly participating. Everyone was speaking and no one was listening, not even those who were silent. The silent ones were consumed with the effort of thinking what they were going to say next, as well as glancing in every direction except that of the current speaker, seeking out their next opportunity. The only exceptions occurred where the speaker was of such exalted rank that the act of being seen to hang acquiescently on their every word outweighed even the need to say something mildly intelligent oneself.

Béranger stopped abruptly behind a short man in late middle age, wearing a grubby Norfolk jacket that was starkly out of place in the setting of a Residency reception. Béranger coughed politely and the moment the man turned Caspasian was struck by the expression in his eyes. There was a twinkle in them that was as much in contrast to the surroundings as his jacket. He stared amusedly first at Béranger and then peered inquisitively at Caspasian beyond the big Frenchman.

'Professor, I would like you to meet a good friend of mine, Captain John Caspasian of the Twelfth Gurkhas.' Béranger turned to Caspasian. 'John, this is Professor Miles Fenwick. He is one of the leaders of the British expedition.'

Caspasian shook hands, aware all the while that he was under intense scrutiny. 'I am glad to see members of the two rival expeditions still on talking terms,' he said.

The Professor laughed. 'The rivalry has been grossly exaggerated by the press.'

'Not as far as my boss is concerned,' Béranger sighed. He nodded in the direction of another small clutch of people. 'Monsieur Simonin,' he said, indicating the broad back of a short fat individual in a light-coloured suit with sweat stains starting to appear under the armpits and between the shoulder blades.

'Another ex-legionnaire?' Caspasian suggested.

Béranger glared at him. 'It's all Monsieur Simonin can do to lift his own backside off a chair, let alone pick up a rifle and pack.'

Professor Fenwick coughed lightly. 'I'm not sure I should be hearing this.'

'Forgive me,' Béranger said quickly. 'I must learn to keep my trials and tribulations to myself.'

Changing the subject, Caspasian said to the Professor, 'Paul mentioned you were one of the leaders. Who's the other?'

'Sir Hubert Mansfield,' the Professor replied.

Caspasian smiled. 'And together the two of you are going to outshine Lord Carnarvon and Howard Carter.'

'That's hardly our prime aim.'

'Just as well,' Caspasian goaded. 'I should think the whole thing will turn out to be some fantastical confidence trick or a mirage.'

Once again the Professor studied him. 'That is strange, Captain. I would not have taken you for a cynic. Worldly wise perhaps, but not . . .'

'Aren't they the same thing?' Caspasian cut in, more rudely than he had intended.

'Not in the least. In fact it has been my experience that a degree of worldly wisdom leads one in exactly the opposite direction. Cynicism is the refuge of the ignorant. It is where people hide who have closed their minds to experience.'

Caspasian felt himself go suddenly very cold. Not just the Professor's words, but also his tone closely echoed Caspasian's grandfather.

'Scratch a cynic,' the Professor said staring hard at Caspasian who shifted with discomfort under the hard gaze, 'and you will often find a failed romantic. An idealist even. They are a hair's breadth apart and yet they are a world apart. It is what a person does with the experience the world throws at them that determines on which side of the division they alight.'

Caspasian almost choked. He cleared his throat and said, 'Then I wish you the best of luck with your endeavour.'

The Professor smiled. 'I hope we can do better than luck.'

'Everyone needs luck if they're going out into the desert.'

'Amen to that,' agreed Béranger. 'Luck and a plentiful supply of ammunition.'

'I would have thought water was a more important commodity,' the Professor said.

The big Frenchman shook his head defiantly. 'You can always find water at an oasis, but you won't find a case of rifle bullets at the bottom of a well. And without them the tribesmen will hang you out to dry.'

The Professor smiled. 'I am rather hoping Sir Hubert will take care of that. He's been trying to buttonhole the High Commissioner all evening. So far without success.' He looked around for his colleague. 'I think he's given up and left it to me.'

'As regards what?' Caspasian asked.

'An escort.'

'Ah.'

'You sound doubtful, Captain?'

'I hope you're successful,' Caspasian said. 'But it's my understanding that all troops are committed to preparations for his birthday parade and other duties.'

'So everyone at GHQ has been telling us all week. Hence my attendance here this evening. An attempt to bypass the system,' the Professor said with a mischievous twinkle in his eye. He looked at Béranger. 'But Monsieur Simonin will become suspicious if he sees you talking to me.' Then, as an afterthought, he said, 'Why not introduce the Captain to him? I'm sure they will both enjoy the experience.'

Béranger raised his eyebrows.

'Well?' Caspasian said.

'So long as you promise to be polite.'

'Paul! I'm an Indian Army officer. How could I be anything but polite?'

Béranger took hold of his elbow and led him across the lawn to where a lively conversation had just ensued as two groups had merged like two small pools of mercury finding each other on a smooth surface.

'Monsieur Simonin,' Béranger said. Caspasian noted that his old friend wore deference with as much discomfort as if it had been a German Iron Cross.

In response the fat individual standing with his back to them held up an impatient hand and waved it while he listened to the end of some story or other. When it had finished some little while later, concluded with hoots of laughter, Monsieur Simonin turned to Béranger, his smile fading as he turned.

'What is it now, Capitaine?'

'Can I introduce a friend of mine? Captain John Caspasian. He was eager to meet you.'

Simonin held out his moist pudgy hand for Caspasian to shake. 'English?'

'Yes,' Béranger answered for Caspasian.

Simonin sighed. 'I hope you are not another spy, trying to foil the success of our expedition?'

'Another?'

Simonin glanced slyly around the crowded gardens. 'You English have been such wonderful hosts to us while we have been here, but don't think I don't know what's going on. You are desperate to get to the tomb before we do.'

Caspasian smiled, retrieving his hand and resisting the urge to wipe it. 'You have nothing to fear from me, Monsieur. Personally I think you're all wasting your time.'

'Oh, so you're an archaeologist as well are you, Captain?' Simonin asked sarcastically.

'Not I, sir. Just a humble soldier, and happy to be so.'

'Then you will forgive me if I ignore your scorn.'

'I do not scorn, Monsieur, only doubt.'

Simonin eyed Caspasian suspiciously as if trying to gauge the man. Unable to penetrate Caspasian's icy smile, he turned to Béranger while still keeping his eyes on Caspasian as if he expected the tall Captain to assault him when he was not looking.

'Where is Michelle?' he said.

Béranger glanced around the gardens and shrugged. 'I have no idea. She was over by the steps when I last saw her.'

By the tone of his voice Caspasian could tell that Béranger did not like having to act as minder for Michelle, whoever she was.

'Well be a good fellow and go and find her, will you? Tell her I will be leaving in a few minutes.'

Béranger glowered at Simonin but the Frenchman was already in conversation with someone else. His tame legionnaire had been dismissed.

'Come on,' Béranger said sourly.

Together with his friend, Caspasian walked across the Embassy gardens looking for someone he had never seen before.

'Who's Michelle?' he asked.

In reply Béranger simply glanced at him out of the corner of his eye, but it was not the sort of glance Caspasian would have expected. 'Michelle is a mystery, my friend.'

'Oh?' Caspasian said, intrigued.

'You'll see.'

Caspasian searched idly on all sides, looking for the sort of uncomplicated female companion that he could imagine at Simonin's side. Suddenly Béranger stopped.

'There,' he said, indicating the steps leading into the Residency.

Caspasian followed the direction and saw a group of men gathered around someone. There was a call from the left and Béranger turned to see who had hailed him.

'*Merde*. Look, Caspasian, can you tell Michelle that Simonin wants her. I've got to have a word with this cretin. He's been after me all evening. Some blasted journalist.'

Before Caspasian could reply Béranger had gone, leaving him to carry out the simple task. As he approached the group there was a burst of laughter as one young officer cracked a joke, but the laughter was forced, overly hearty and designed to impress. Interesting, Caspasian thought. Not a wife, but a daughter perhaps. And judging by the attention she was receiving, an attractive one. He closed up behind the group and, peering through the tight press, saw Michelle for the first time. The spectacle that confronted him left him numb with shock.

At the same moment that Caspasian had arrived, the woman turned in his direction. For Caspasian, all other sounds died away. All other people too. Michelle was one of the most beautiful girls he had ever seen. How on earth she could be the offspring of the hideous Monsieur Simonin, he could not imagine. Adopted perhaps. In long black slim-fitting evening dress, with long shining raven-coloured hair to match, loose about her slender bare shoulders, she gave the impression of a young doe that was startled to find itself in the middle of rooting swine. She appeared confused by their attention, alarmed even, and yet Caspasian could see that she was putting a brave face on it, although it was costing her. She had forced a kind smile at the jest, but awkwardly, not understanding, longing to be elsewhere.

Caspasian eased his way through the wall of backs that had excluded him, keeping him from her. Reluctant to admit a newcomer, the others tried to close ranks but Caspasian was in. Michelle turned and raised her eyes to him and Caspasian felt his heart stop. His mouth went dry and he felt reduced to the level of tongue-tied schoolboy.

'Mademoiselle Simonin?' he ventured, 'I am sorry to interrupt but I have a message from your father.'

The girl frowned and in her bright hazel brown eyes Caspasian saw the flash of some deep hurt. Someone in the crowd sniggered.

'Madame Simonin,' the girl corrected. 'What did my husband say?'

For a full two seconds Caspasian could only stare dumbfounded. Then, aware of the hurt in Michelle's eyes and of the excruciating embarrassment he had just caused her, he coughed and blurted out, 'Just that he has to leave soon. I think he needs you to join him.'

From the other members of the crowd there were expressions of regret, not one of them selfless. Michelle murmured her thanks to Caspasian, said a quick farewell to everyone and no one, the crowd parted for her and she left.

As she walked away and the crowd dispersed, Caspasian could only stand and stare after her. He felt rooted to the spot. Someone approached from behind and the next moment Béranger spoke. 'Good, you found her.'

Caspasian shook his head. 'Why didn't you tell me she was his wife?'

Béranger saw Caspasian's scarlet cheeks and guessed. 'Oh, *mon Dieu*! You didn't . . . ?'

Caspasian nodded miserably. 'How in the name of God does a girl like her end up married to a man like that?'

'I do not know, my friend. I do not know. In fact, no one seems to know anything about her. When I was briefed by Simonin for the mission, he simply mentioned that his wife would be attending also. Naturally I expected some haggard old dairy cow and instead I find myself confronted with Aphrodite.'

'No, not Aphrodite,' Caspasian said. 'This one's real, not some myth.'

'Well, myth or not, as Simonin's wife she's as far removed

from the likes of you and me as if she was on the moon. And I
don't mind telling you that I'm not at all happy about a young
girl like that coming on an expedition like this. The desert is no
place for the likes of her. It is a harsh and hostile place.'

There was a voice from behind them. 'I'm glad that someone
recognises that.'

Béranger and Caspasian turned to find an Egyptian
man standing behind them. Béranger smiled and wel-
comed him.

'But here's the man who started the whole business. I think
you are the only one here, John, who has not already met the
famous Chief Superintendent Harry Ghazali of the Cairo police
force.'

Caspasian shook the man's hand. He had indeed heard of
Chief Superintendent Ghazali. The papers had been full of his
name when the story had broken about the mysterious segment
of papyrus that he had recovered from the murdered dealer.
Caspasian remembered sitting in the mess over breakfast one
Sunday morning, reading how Ghazali had struggled with the
murderer who had been attempting to secure the papyrus for
himself, and how Ghazali had been wounded in the struggle.
His life had only been saved by the chance intervention of a
British military police patrol that had been scouring the City of
the Dead in search of a deserter. Coming upon the struggle,
they had chased off Ghazali's assailant who had made good his
escape in the warren of alleyways.

The murdered dealer had contacted Ghazali the previous
week intending to sell the scroll to the Egyptian Museum. With
the discovery of the tomb of Tutankhamen six years before,
there was a desperate hunger for such artefacts and treasures.
The last room of Tutankhamen's tomb had only been opened
the year before, last November, shortly before Caspasian had
arrived in Cairo. Lord Carnarvon and Howard Carter, the
tomb's discoverers, had, until recently, still been at work in the
Valley of the Kings. The whole field of Egyptology had received

a vigorous new lease of life, and the scroll was the latest dynamic twist in the tale.

Harry Ghazali was a trim cultured man, well dressed in a smart cotton suit. Wearing a delicate tortoiseshell pince-nez balanced precariously halfway down the bridge of his nose, he smoked a brand of strong Turkish cigarettes unknown to Caspasian. Caspasian liked the man and listened to his account of the find with interest.

'Naturally I am delighted that the British and French governments are mounting their expeditions,' Ghazali concluded after some minutes. 'But I must confess that I tend to agree with the sceptics. I view the whole enterprise with a certain degree of humour. The whole history of such relic discoveries has been riddled with fakes and forgeries. Still,' he conceded, 'if other governments apart from my own and if other learned bodies apart from the Egyptian Museum are prepared to hazard their money on such an enterprise, then good luck to them I say.'

He raised his glass to Béranger. 'May your journey into the desert not be a futile waste of time,' he said pleasantly. He turned to Caspasian. 'At least the French are taking it seriously enough to appoint this brute as escort to their expedition.'

Béranger smiled. 'My men and I are simply there to protect Simonin from the heathens, Chief Superintendent.'

'Your men?' Caspasian asked.

Béranger shrugged. 'Barely a section. It is nothing.'

Ghazali laughed. 'Yes, and armed to the teeth like Ali Baba's thieves, no doubt. The English, on the other hand, are doing things as they always do. As gifted amateurs.'

'Professor Fenwick was just telling us that he has been trying to get hold of the High Commissioner but his staff have been ensuring he remains at arm's length. Apparently everyone in the garrison's involved with preparations for his birthday parade. Then there's this demonstration march by the Wafd that is due to take place, and his ADC tells me that the canal needs extra reinforcement because a troop convoy is due to pass through bound for Bombay,' Caspasian said.

Ghazali smiled. 'I believe they are going to hire some local fellow to pull together some porters and co-ordinate everything for them. No escort, nothing. They see it as an interesting opportunity to see something more of my fascinating country.' Ghazali frowned. 'They should not underestimate the difficulty of what they are undertaking. No one should venture away from the Nile valley without the healthiest respect for the desert.'

'Do not worry,' Béranger said. 'I will see that no harm comes to our expedition.'

'For that I am grateful,' Ghazali replied. 'I do not want to have to conduct the inquiry into the death or disappearance of anyone.' He sighed, his face worn and tired behind the small glasses and the wreaths of cigarette smoke. 'I have more than enough on my plate as it is. Cairo is a turbulent place these days.' He looked at Béranger. 'Please, come back safely, lost city or no lost city. If only to spare me the extra paperwork.'

Béranger laughed. 'I fully intend to, Chief Superintendent. Personally I don't care whether Simonin finds the lost city and the tomb of King Menes or not.'

Béranger and Ghazali became engaged closely in conversation and Caspasian began to feel uncomfortable clinging to the fringe. He therefore made his excuses and left, the last overheard threads of their talk concerning King Menes and the likelihood or not of him having been a real historical character.

His fellow officers from the Twelfth seemed to have disappeared, but Caspasian suspected they might have moved inside the main building from where he could hear strains of music emanating. Someone was playing a piano, rather well by the sound of it, and Caspasian decided to go and listen. There was nothing else to do. He would try to locate Béranger again before it was time to leave and perhaps they could arrange to meet up before Béranger departed on his ridiculous mission into the desert. Nevertheless, the Frenchman had struck a raw nerve. It might indeed be a fruitless journey, but it would undoubtedly be preferable to Caspasian's own QM duties.

He stopped on one of the few unoccupied patches of lawn and looked up at the night sky. There was nothing to see, just an opaque sheet, all stars drowned out by the lights and dust of the city. He sighed deeply. It was like living inside a goldfish bowl, or underneath a huge pudding basin where people went round and round in pointless little circles, bumping into each other every so often and, each time, repeating the same stupid conversation as if they had never met before.

Between the passage of assembled guests, he caught sight of Monsieur Simonin. The man had obviously said his farewells and was taking his leave, Michelle at his side. She was only a little taller than her husband but Caspasian noticed how she still had to slow her step to allow Simonin to keep up. He appeared to be quite angry and was talking to her quietly but urgently as if taking her to task over something, one wagging finger inches in front of her face. Michelle was looking down, saying nothing. To Caspasian she looked like a princess from the sack of Troy being led away into slavery.

Suddenly angry, Caspasian turned away from the ghastly spectacle and pushed his way towards the steps leading into the Embassy building. His attention was so occupied that he walked headlong into Colonel Humphreys. He looked up abruptly. The Colonel was red in the face, though whether because he had been drinking too freely or because the wing collar of his mess kit was a size too small, Caspasian was unable to tell.

'Colonel, I'm sorry. I didn't see y . . .'

'Don't you come the contrite apologetic young officer with me!' he stormed. Here and there faces turned towards the confrontation. With an enormous shock Caspasian realised that the Colonel's red face was due to pure rage. And Caspasian himself appeared to be the cause of it.

The Colonel also noticed the turning heads. He gripped the shoulder of Caspasian's mess jacket and steered him to one side. He lowered his voice but glared harshly at Caspasian.

'You little weasel. I accept you back into the regiment, fully prepared to let bygones be bygones. I give you a responsible appointment, determined to let you prove yourself a reformed character, and how do you repay my trust?'

'Colonel . . . I . . .' Caspasian stammered, completely at a loss.

'Don't you bloody Colonel me, Captain!'

'But I . . .'

'You what? You didn't mean to? You didn't intend to throw all my good graces and good intentions back at me?' He jammed his face an inch in front of Caspasian's. To Caspasian's surprise there was not the slightest hint of alcohol. What he was witnessing was red hot anger, wholly uncomplicated by the bottle.

'I need you, you great runt. The birthday parade's going to be the highest profile event for the regiment in ages.'

'But you said you didn't want me near it?'

'Not in it, you blithering idiot. I'm not totally mad. Not yet, although you'll put me there soon enough. And the demonstration. Where am I going to be without my Quartermaster?'

From far, far away, a tiny fragile light of understanding blossomed in Caspasian's mind. In perfect synchronicity with it, from behind the Colonel the High Commissioner himself appeared, Professor Miles Fenwick beside him chattering contentedly. Both of them looked up suddenly when they came upon the Colonel and Caspasian.

'Gordon, is this the young fellow then?' the High Commissioner boomed. He turned to the Professor. 'Miles?'

The Professor left it for Colonel Humphreys to respond. The Colonel pulled himself together, his wing collar fit to burst with the effort. 'This is Captain Caspasian, sir, yes,' he said stonily.

The High Commissioner stepped forward and grasped Caspasian's hand, shaking it vigorously. 'Professor Fenwick assures me you're just the right man for the job. Isn't that so, Miles?'

The Professor inclined his head, saying nothing.

'Well now, listen here, Caspasian,' the High Commissioner said conspiratorially. 'Just you ensure the Professor finds this blasted tomb before the damned Frenchies, is that clear? We can't have the damned frog pinching the limelight, can we? Not after the British triumph of Tutankhamen.'

Caspasian could only stare back at him, dumbfounded.

'I'm sure Colonel Humphreys will give you all the help you need, won't you, Gordon?'

A choked gurgle escaped from the Colonel's throat.

'That's the spirit,' the High Commissioner barked merrily. 'Any problems, you just come straight to me.' He turned to his ADC who glared daggers at both Caspasian and the Professor for having outflanked him, gaining access to his boss without his permission.

When the High Commissioner had gone, leading the Professor with him, Caspasian prepared himself for a fresh onslaught from his commanding officer. Instead Colonel Humphreys just stared at him, shaking his head.

'I assure you, Colonel,' Caspasian quickly said. 'I had nothing to do with this.' He knew however that his protestation of innocence was falling on deaf ears even as he uttered it.

'What have you done this time, Caspasian?' the Colonel said savagely. 'I'll tell you one thing though. I don't care what the High Commissioner said, you'll get fuck all help out of me. Big fat zero, is that clear.'

Caspasian struggled to keep his joy from showing. If he smiled he was certain the Colonel would punch him full in the face, and if he were to defend himself he would end up in the guard room or, worse, back in his office.

The Colonel took a step backwards, as if himself fearing that he might lay hands on Caspasian. As he turned to walk away he shook his head sadly. 'What have you done?'

I'll tell you what I've done, Caspasian thought to himself. I've bloody well escaped! That's what I've done!

4

It was a further two days before Caspasian was able to engineer a second meeting with Professor Miles Fenwick. Colonel Humphreys did everything in his power to obstruct it, sending Caspasian instant demands for audits, reports and briefs, all of which had to be attended to immediately. For the first time since taking up his post, Caspasian threw himself into his work with a will, realising that he would not otherwise be allowed to leave.

Finally, when the last report had been signed off and delivered by runner to Battalion Headquarters for the Colonel's perusal, Caspasian pushed back his chair, stretched his arms until he felt the joints crack, stood up and walked out of the office. He had arranged to meet Professor Fenwick at Shepheards Hotel. The Professor had been staying there since arriving in Cairo two weeks before.

He had just reached the guard room and was already scanning the road outside for a taxi, when the Adjutant, Captain Tremain, hailed him from behind. Caspasian turned irritably, wondering what new delaying tactic the Colonel had decided upon. Captain Tremain hurried towards him, a broad smile lighting the angular features of his thin tanned face.

'What is it now?' Caspasian sighed, squaring up to the approaching figure, ready for a confrontation. He had had enough. If he encountered one more obstacle he was going to take the High Commissioner at his word and appeal direct to him for help, whatever the consequences for his career in the regiment.

Tremain chuckled pleasantly. 'Really, John, I don't know what you mean.'

'Look, I'm going into town to meet the Professor. There are things we have to sort out. If the Colonel still objects, tell him to speak to the High Commissioner.' He stared hard at Tremain. 'And if he won't, I will.'

'There's no need for that, Caspasian. I've just come to let you have a list of the men we can spare for your expedition.'

Caspasian looked suspiciously at the slip of paper in the Adjutant's hand.

'I'm afraid there aren't many, but what with the parade, the demonstration and the canal security duties, I'm afraid it's all we can spare.'

Tentatively Caspasian reached out for the paper. Halfway there his hand stopped. 'Do you mean to tell me the Colonel's changed his mind?'

'Not in the least. Your name's mud as far as he's concerned, but he's not stupid. He heard the High Commissioner as well as you did.' He waved the paper in mid-air. 'This is just his recognition of the state of affairs. Take them and be grateful you've got such an understanding boss.'

With that, he thrust the list at Caspasian. While Tremain stood back with arms folded across his chest, Caspasian read the list of names. There were eight of them. As his eyes ran down the names he felt as if he could hear the Colonel laughing in his office.

'You have to be joking!'

Tremain stared back innocently. 'What do you mean?'

'This is the biggest bunch of troublemakers, malingerers and rogues in the entire regiment!' He stabbed his finger at the top of the list. 'Rifleman Bharatmani Limbu. The only parade he ever attends is sick parade. And him,' he said, selecting another name, 'Harkabahadur. Isn't he still under close arrest? I saw him yesterday in the middle of the parade ground being drilled under armed guard, doubling up and down with a pack full of rocks on his back.'

He moved down the list. 'And these two are cooks. They

haven't fired a rifle since before the regiment left Rajasthan, and even then they couldn't hit a target at thirty yards. And who's this? Indrabahadur, one of the mess bloody orderlies! Caught drunk on duty last year.'

'That's the man,' Tremain said pleasantly. 'He'd been fiddling the mess accounts too, don't forget that.'

Caspasian eyed him suspiciously. 'Why wasn't he given a dishonourable discharge?'

Tremain shrugged. 'I couldn't say. But it had absolutely nothing to do with him being related to the Subedar Major. That was just a nasty rumour.'

'Naturally.' Caspasian crumpled the list and stuffed it back in Tremain's hand. 'I'm afraid you'll have to do a lot better than that.'

He started to walk out of the camp but Tremain caught up with him and barred his way. 'It's all you're going to get, Caspasian. Believe me. You're lucky to get anyone at all.'

Caspasian stopped. A thought suddenly occurred to him. 'If I do take them I'll need someone to hold them together.' He smiled.

'Go on,' Tremain said slowly.

'Release Sergeant Ganga Limbu from the A Company kote and you've got a deal.'

'Ganga?' Tremain asked, genuinely surprised. 'Whatever do you want an old soldier like him for? I know he was a good shot in his day . . .'

'He was the best. Still is.'

Tremain thought about it for a moment. 'I'm not sure. I'll have to check with the Colonel first.'

'For goodness sake, Tremain. Make a decision for yourself for once. You know what the Colonel thinks of Ganga. He wouldn't have him any nearer the High Commissioner's parade than he would have me there.'

Tremain paused for a second. 'All right then. But that's it. You're not getting anyone else.'

Caspasian smiled. 'I won't need anyone else. Just Ganga and this bunch,' he said, taking back the list of names and smoothing out the creases.

Tremain turned to go. 'You really are an odd one, John. What the devil do you want to go wandering about in the desert for anyway? If you'd kept your nose clean and done your job, you'd have been given a rifle company in a year or two. As it is now, the Colonel would rather disband the regiment than let you have a command.' He slapped Caspasian on the back and walked away. 'You've done it this time, old man. You've done it this time. And there's no going back.'

All the more reason to make the most of it then, Caspasian thought as he climbed into the back of a taxi and set off into town.

He found Professor Fenwick waiting for him on the hotel terrace, sitting at one of the glass-topped coffee tables, reading the morning paper.

'Ah, there you are!' he said jovially when he saw Caspasian coming up the steps. 'I wondered where you'd got to.'

They shook hands. Caspasian pulled up a chair and sank into it with a deep sigh.

'Oh dear,' the Professor observed. 'I hope I haven't caused you any trouble?'

Caspasian laughed out loud. 'About as much as is humanly possible,' he said harshly. Then, seeing the look of concern on the Professor's face he added quickly, 'But no more than I would have caused for myself had I continued in that job one minute longer.'

The Professor still looked doubtful and Caspasian was worried for a moment that he might be about to retract his offer of a place on the expedition.

'Look, Professor,' he said, 'you have done me a great service, whatever the consequences. It was my call as to whether I accepted the offer or not.' He held up his hands. 'As you see, I am here,' he said looking around for the waiter. 'And ready for some tea.'

The Professor's expression lightened. He caught the attention of a waiter and ordered a pot of tea for the two of them and some honey cakes.

'The Egyptian Museum's recommended a guide to me but I'm not convinced. I had a chat with him and frankly I think we'd be better off arranging our own porters. We have the map. We just need to get there.'

The Professor worried at the flap of his brief case lying beside his chair and, locating a map, spread it out on the table.

'I've gone over the ground with Sir Hubert and we've marked the route on here.' The Professor indicated markings in red pencil on the map. 'We'll go by boat up the Nile as far as the village of Agadir. That's about two days south of Aswan. We'll disembark there and head south-east on a compass bearing.'

Caspasian studied the map carefully.

'As I'm sure you already know, Captain, unlike the territory to the west of the Nile which is undulating sandy desert, the eastern desert is far more mountainous.'

Caspasian nodded, tracing the route with his finger. 'Yes, the Nubian desert. I see that this line runs all the way to the Sudanese border.'

'And beyond,' the Professor said. 'The fragment of papyrus spoke of the city and tomb of King Menes as being three days' march south-east of a mountain called Jebel Hashmir. I've identified that as being here,' he said, pointing out a feature on the map. 'And I know that Monsieur Simonin believes the same.'

'You've discussed it with him?' Caspasian said with some surprise.

The Professor looked shocked. 'Certainly not. However, I did get some information out of one of their escort party. All quite innocent, I assure you. With the aid of a certain amount of local beverage the fellow spilled the beans, so to speak.' He searched the map. 'However, they are apparently going to disembark somewhat further north than I am. About here,' he said, pointing out the location. 'So, although they are planning to leave before us, once we're ashore the route that I have selected will save us several days overland march, and bring us to the site of the lost city before Simonin and his party.'

'Or so you hope,' Caspasian said smiling.

The Professor sat back and surveyed him, his face serious. 'Captain Caspasian, this expedition means a lot to me, as well as to the British government. All my life I've dreamed of making a find like this. It's not about wealth, reputation or anything as vainglorious as that . . .'

He paused as the tea arrived, waiting while it was poured and served. When the waiter had left he offered Caspasian a honey cake and then placed one on his own side plate. When he was ready he continued, staring out across the rooftops as if watching something no one else could see. 'Imagine discovering a tomb that was last sealed over five thousand years ago. King Menes, if he really did exist – and I firmly believe that he did – was the first of all the Pharaohs. He founded the first dynasty. After that there were over thirty dynasties, each of numerous kings. But he was the first one ever. Just think of it!'

Caspasian could feel the Professor's enthusiasm taking hold of him.

'What is more, his tomb has never been discovered. One or two scripts have hinted at a secret capital, away from the Nile valley, but none has ever been as specific as this, or given us a possible location for it, as this fragment has done. I have spoken with Howard Carter about the moment he and Lord Carnarvon opened the tomb of Tutankhamen six years ago. The first instant the torch beam shone upon the treasures. But compared to Menes, Tutankhamen was a complete newcomer. Menes was as remote in time to Tutankhamen as Alexander the Great is to us. At least two thousand years before him!'

Caspasian was impressed, feeling as if a great void of time was opening beneath him.

'Our civilisation has been going for, what, several hundred years? It depends on where you date it from, but even if we start with the end of the Dark Ages, we're barely a thousand years old. And if you went back to the start you wouldn't find much in common with the folks around at the time. They'd be speaking completely different languages, and you'd find their level of sophistication quite shocking. But the Egyptians! By the time it ended with the coming of the Romans, their civilisation was well over three thousand years old, and because it had largely been confined to the Nile valley and thereabouts, protected by deserts on every side, it had been fairly homogenous throughout. Just think of it! All that time for a people to come to grips with the mysteries of existence! Look at the depth of wisdom hidden in the stories of their gods, astronomy, science, their accounts of the afterlife even. And Menes was the founder of it all.'

He leaned closer. 'What is more, when Carter went into Tutankhamen's tomb, he had been preceded by several generations of tomb-robbers. There was nothing that had not already been fingered and discarded. The stuff that was left was the material the grave-robbers had rejected. It was all jumbled up, stacked in great piles. But there has never been anything on the illegal antiquities market even remotely mentioning King Menes.'

'Meaning?'

'Meaning that it has never been robbed. Nothing has been taken from it to circulate around the markets of the world. Because it has never been found! So if we find it we will be entering a chamber no one has entered since the day King Menes was laid to rest. Imagine it! Touching articles that were last touched by people who lived over five thousand years ago. It will be like going down a tunnel through time, reaching right back to the very beginning of human civilisation. That's why I want to find it. Not the value of the treasure in crude monetary terms. To me that is a complete irrelevance. But the greater meaning of it all. To reach back and touch the past, the beginning of this whole great adventure called civilisation.'

He slumped back in his chair, his face ablaze with excitement.

Caspasian took a long sip of his tea, replacing the cup on the saucer as quietly as he could so as not to disturb the moment. After a while he said, 'Aren't you overlooking one thing?'

'What?'

'That there might be nothing there.'

The Professor smiled, as if at a child, though not unkindly. 'Captain, you surprise me. I would almost say you disappoint me. And I know now that you need more than ever to come on this expedition. Quickly, before your heart and soul go to sleep forever. When I saw you at the Residency reception I had not seen a man look so transparently miserable in ages. But yours was a misery with something concealed behind it. Disenchantment. When most men are miserable it is because they lack something. Money, success, love. You, on the other hand, had something too much. An extra element of character. That's what was causing your misery. Tell me, is money or career success of any worth to you?'

Caspasian smiled. 'No. But I notice you've dropped out love.'

The Professor sighed. 'Love is always a complication. It matters to all of us, but not always in the same way. You, however, were not simply miserable, you were disenchanted.'

'Is there really such a difference?' Caspasian asked, intrigued.

'Of course. A pig can be miserable because his trough is empty. Only a person can be disenchanted. And, I would argue, only certain people. To be disenchanted you have to possess an extra element. Think about the word carefully. An enchanter was a magician. A person who moved freely between two worlds. I myself believe that the disenchanted are as they are because they can no longer do so. Though they perhaps do not actually know it with their conscious minds, they feel that there is another realm from which they are barred entry. The disenchanted, if they are truly so in my own interpretation of the word, have been undone, disempowered, sapped of their magical powers. Hermes with clipped wings, no longer able to venture at will between the realms of gods and men.'

Caspasian laughed, feeling a little awkward. 'That's a very grand notion, Professor, but I am sorry to disappoint you. I was simply looking miserable because I loathe my present job.'

The Professor smiled kindly and leaned forward to refill their cups. 'Then I apologise. I have embarrassed you. It is a failing of mine. We will speak no more of it for now.' He sat back, his eyes twinkling and mischievous. 'We can discuss the weather instead if you like, or the polo at Gezira.'

He helped himself to a cake, bit into it and luxuriated in the sweet taste of the thick honey. 'But of one thing I am certain. I have picked the right man for this job.'

Caspasian raised his cup in a toast. 'Whether you have or not, I am delighted to be coming along for the ride. It has saved me from endless hours of tedium.'

The Professor smiled enigmatically. 'I think you will find that it has saved you from more than just that.'

He looked across the terrace and waved at someone. 'Here's Sir Hubert. How opportune. Now you can meet the other key member of the team.' He glanced sidelong at Caspasian and, after a second's hesitation, leaned across and said, 'A word of warning . . .'

But it was too late. Sir Hubert had arrived. Caspasian swivelled in his chair, rising to meet the newcomer. To his surprise, Sir Hubert was a young man in his early thirties, like Caspasian himself. Tall, slim and dapper, he stood eye to eye with Caspasian, transparently measuring the man as he greeted him.

'So you're Caspasian,' Sir Hubert said, not unpleasantly.

Caspasian returned the smile, uncertain as to how to take the comment.

Sir Hubert's handshake was vigorous and firmer than necessary. Proving a point. 'Good to have you aboard. I believe GHQ were about to assign us an escort, but then the Professor short-circuited the system and acquired you.' He broadened his smile to show more of his perfect white teeth. 'No matter. You're all much of a muchness, I suppose.'

Caspasian recovered his hand and moved his chair to one side to allow Sir Hubert to insert his own between him and the Professor. For a second Caspasian thought that Sir Hubert was going to address him again, but then, as if he had suddenly remembered something of greater importance, he turned abruptly to the Professor and began to talk hurriedly to him about various administrative arrangements for the expedition, none of which involved Caspasian.

With sinking heart, Caspasian picked up his tea cup and sat back in his chair as if waiting for a rain shower to pass. Exclusion from the conversation gave him an opportunity to observe Sir Hubert more closely. There was a fastidiousness about his dress that was exacerbated by obvious wealth. Everything about it was little short of perfect. Collar studs and cuff links were of gold, and in the centre of an ornate tie pin, a small diamond winked immodestly in the sunlight. Creases were sharply displayed only where they were intended, the high quality cloth seeming to reject the dishevelling effect of the heat and humidity with disdain.

While Sir Hubert himself appeared to be in good physical shape, Caspasian could tell that it was the manicured fitness of the tennis court rather than the natural result of a hard rugged lifestyle. He carried himself with an awareness that eyes might be upon him and, though fully engaged in conversation with the Professor, nevertheless gave the impression that at least half his attention was still with Caspasian, ensuring his poise remained impeccable.

Eventually growing tired of his exclusion from the conversation, Caspasian noisily replaced his cup and saucer on the table and prepared to take his leave. Sir Hubert turned to survey him with apparent surprise that he should not have felt party to their talk, and a sudden effusive show of remorse that left Caspasian feeling even more socially inept than usual and questioning whether he had been unreasonable, all of which had been precisely calculated by Sir Hubert.

'No, really, it's time I was going,' Caspasian lied, regretting the premature end to his meeting with the Professor.

'Oh, well, if you must,' Sir Hubert said, but when Caspasian rose to go only the Professor stood up to shake hands with him.

Once out in the street, Caspasian heaved a gigantic sigh of both relief and regret. Relief to be out of Sir Hubert's company, regret that the man should be on the expedition in the first place. He remained stock still for several moments, allowing the passing crowd to break upon him like a wave across rock. Immobile, he divided it, ignoring the resentful stares while he contemplated the morning, considering what now to do. His mind made up, he turned in the direction of the Opera House and made for the Derby Club, stepping out at a brisk pace, his pent-up energy anticipating release.

The club stood close by Ezbekieh Gardens, a narrow flight of steps mounting to a column-flanked portal where a doorman stood watch. Caspasian returned the man's greeting equally cursorily and strode across to the reception desk.

'Good morning. Any squash courts free?'

'Just a moment, sir.' The clerk consulted a ledger and shrugged. 'Actually, all of them,' he said. 'Which would you like, sir? Any preferences?'

Caspasian shook his head and the clerk proffered a key. 'Do you need a locker?'

Caspasian took the key. 'I've already got one, thank you.'

The changing rooms and squash courts were below ground level and had the pleasant still coolness of a wine cellar. Locating his locker, Caspasian unlocked it and opened the door. Two items of loose clothing were draped over a hook, a long cloth belt with them. Caspasian stripped out of his suit and put on the karate gi, looping the belt twice around his waist and tying it with a knot at the front. It was a heavy duty cotton suit that he had purchased in Shanghai and which had been sent on to him with the rest of his belongings at the termination of his last posting there. The baggy trousers and jacket were already well worn, the cloth faded from numerous washings, the edges of the belt frayed and colourless.

Barefoot, he made his way to the squash court, turned on the light, unlocked the door and went in. With the door closed behind him, he moved to the centre of the court, sliding his feet across the bare wooden floorboards to get a feel for the degree of purchase. It was perfect.

Facing the far wall, he knelt down adopting the seiza position, knees a fist's width apart, open hands palm-down on thighs, shoulders comfortably back, spine and neck straight, eyes closed. He breathed evenly, emptying his mind of thoughts and, as the memory of Sir Hubert receded, Caspasian's practice of zanshin deepened.

With no one else using the adjacent courts and with the sounds of the outside world excluded from the basement, it was not difficult to achieve the state of calm contemplation that Caspasian sought. In the cool silence time slowed its pace, and again the image of a wine cellar occurred to Caspasian, the setting where the immeasurably slow maturing of one thing into another could took place. It was an almost alchemical process in which time, moving indiscernibly, co-operated with physical elements, enabling them to achieve a new state beyond themselves, a process wholly invisible because happening within. When Caspasian opened his eyes, the process had been effected and he rose the same man, but transformed. His mind was clear, his senses alert, his body ready.

After loosening his muscles and joints with a series of gentle stretching exercises he practised movement, his feet gliding across the cool wooden surface as he slipped from one stance into another, working his way through his favoured repertoire. When he had done this to his satisfaction, he worked through a long series of blocks and parries. His forearms and hands pushed aside imaginary blows, the speed intensifying as he worked.

By now, in spite of the pleasant temperature, beads of perspiration pricked at his skin, the heavy cotton of his jacket starting to cling to the taut muscles of his shoulders and back. He limited his kicks to the most commonly employed, the mae geri front kick and the mawashi geri roundhouse kick, confining both to the chudan middle level. Use in combat above this height merely invited an opponent's foot sweep and disaster, especially outside the training dojo where tighter clothing and footwear slowed one's speed. It might look impressive but in reality it was wholly impractical.

Next he worked on his hand blows, and here again he focused his attention on the practical, the small number of punches and strikes that his considerable experience had identified as realistically useful. The chudan and jodan tsuki, the forefist punch at middle and face levels. The ago uchi snap punch. The shuto-uchi-komi forward thrust with the edge of the open hand. The two other main shuto open-hand blows, the shuto-yoko-uchi to the side of the neck or head, and the shuto-sakotsu-uchi axe blow, delivered as if felling a tree. There were numerous others, like arrows in a quiver, but few of them were needed except when executing kata, the pre-arranged routines that exercised a practitioner in the combination of movement, attack and defence against an imaginary opponent. And it was into these that Caspasian progressed after a thorough practice of the basics.

Each kata was preceded by a moment of zanshin meditation, a simultaneous emptying of the mind and focusing of the will. This accomplished, Caspasian burst into action, his moves dictated by the requirements of the particular kata being delivered. Hand and foot strikes were executed with tightly controlled power. The breath remained even, flowing from deep in the lungs, while Caspasian kept his centre of gravity located solidly in his lower abdomen, the tanden, ensuring balance whether stationary or on the move.

His favourite kata completed to his satisfaction, he returned to the fudo dachi beginning stance, upright, hands at his sides, ready. He estimated that he had been at work for approximately one hour. It would do.

Having performed his warming-down exercises, he knelt once more at the conclusion of the session. Again he closed his eyes, his breathing returning to normal and, as he drew the practice to a close, he allowed the outside world to re-enter his mind, only now he viewed it with equanimity. Sir Hubert could go hang.

5

Standing uncertainly in the bright sunlight, the wobbly line of eight Gurkha soldiers reminded Sergeant Gangabahadur Limbu of a mouthful of broken teeth. Surveying them, his mood swung between exultation and despair. His delight at the prospect of escape from the routines of barrack existence was muted by the anticipation of a potentially hazardous desert expedition in the company of such unpromising creatures as these.

He shook his head slowly, tongue clicking. He opened his mouth to speak, struggling for something suitably scathing with which to admonish them, but let it fall shut, lost for words. Instead he pushed back his broad-brimmed felt hat and scratched his forehead where the sweat ran down into his eyes.

At one end of the line, Naik Indrabahadur Limbu giggled nervously under Ganga's uncompromising scrutiny. Prised from the officers' mess where he had narrowly survived an investigation into the accuracy of his accounts, in front of Ganga he exhibited the discomfort of a nocturnal animal surprised in broad daylight by a predator.

Ganga moved silently towards him until they stood face-to-face, fixing the lesser individual with an unforgiving stare. Indra tried a smile. 'So here we are, guruji,' he said pleasantly.

'Be quiet,' Ganga hissed, struggling for self-control.

'I just thought . . .'

'Quiet.'

'But . . .'

'Quiet.'

Like a fish, Indra opened his mouth and shut it one last time.

At his side, the two cooks expelled from the catering platoon, Riflemen Dhanprasad Rai and Akalbahadur Limbu made attempts at standing rigidly to attention. While their bodies succeeded, their heads failed miserably. Eyes blinking, they looked down at their feet as if to check they were still attached to their legs. They inspected their own dress and each others. They scanned their comrades elsewhere in the line and lastly they scoured Sergeant Ganga's face to spy out the impact they were having upon him. His eyes swept coldly over them and passed on, not trusting himself to speak.

Next in line were two riflemen detached from A Company. One glance at them told Ganga all he needed to know. One was too old and the other too young, the two extreme frayed ends of an otherwise serviceable piece of rope. Rifleman Birbahadur Rai was only weeks away from departing on pension. An old dog who clearly had no interest in learning new tricks, he stared fixedly ahead, marking time until his discharge and pension. Beside him, young Rifleman Anand Sherpa, a recent arrival in the regiment, appeared transfixed in terror, eyes as wide as saucers when confronted by the fearsome sergeant with a reputation that was secretly the envy of every other NCO in the sergeants' mess. For Ganga, the pursuit of professional excellence had always come first. On more than one occasion in the past he had been unable to stop himself from criticising a bad tactical decision of a superior, whereas someone with a keener eye on promotion prospects might have bitten their lip and remained silent. Nor was it just a matter of personal pride with Ganga; on operations a bad decision invariably resulted in the unnecessary loss of lives. By speaking his mind Ganga had put paid to a promising career, although it had marked him out as someone who had managed to remain his own man while yet being commanded by others in the military hierarchy.

Rifleman Bharatmani Limbu looked glumly up at Sergeant Ganga, watery eyes appealing for clemency even before Ganga had uttered a word.

'Not on sick parade today?' Ganga asked sarcastically.

Bharatmani shook his head. 'I am not a well man, guruji. There has been some mistake. I should not be here.'

'At least we agree on one thing,' Ganga said.

'It's my feet, you see. These boots aggravate the blisters.'

'Nothing a good route march can't solve,' Ganga said.

Next to him, Lance Naik Ramprasad Lama of the signal platoon chuckled. 'Don't worry, guruji. I'm a trained medic. I'll look after him.'

'Then good luck to you.' Ganga's eyes narrowed. 'But why are you here?' He jerked his chin at the rest of the assembly. 'Do you think you deserve to be grouped with this bunch of rotting bananas?'

Ramprasad smiled. 'I volunteered. When I heard Caspasian saheb was taking an expedition into the desert I told my Jemadar that I wanted to go too.'

'And he let you?' Ganga asked incredulous.

'He is a gaunle. From the same village.'

'I get the picture,' Ganga said smiling wryly. Their wives were probably sisters or they were related in some other way, however tenuous, the unofficial network of bhai-bando connections extending insidiously into regimental life. Ganga did not doubt that Ramprasad had some ulterior motive for wanting to be out of the regiment, but if the man preferred the desert to a parade then Ganga felt he could not be all bad.

Last in line stood Rifleman Harkabahadur Limbu. Ganga planted himself squarely in front of him. 'So. You're out of the guard room again. What was it this time? Shafting another man's wife or just the usual brawling?'

Harkabahadur stared fixedly ahead. His posture was faultless. Long hours under close arrest on the parade ground with pack weighted with rocks had perfected his drill beyond the standard set by the manual. Harkabahadur said nothing. Ganga moved his face closer until he was only inches away, but even then Harkabahadur remained staring rigidly at a point in the middle of the sergeant's forehead.

'There will not be any trouble from you on this trip, Harka, do you hear me?'

'Yes, Sergeant guruji,' Harkabahadur stated.

Ganga held his position a moment longer for emphasis and then drew back. Deciding to leave it there, he turned swiftly on his heel and marched away from the line, spinning to face the assembled men when he was a few yards away.

'You are a pathetic excuse for soldiers but you're all I've been given so I've got to make the best of you. The Adjutant likes his little joke. You're the joke. Not a very funny one.'

Someone smirked.

'Go ahead. Laugh. Enjoy my discomfort while you can. But just wait until we're out in the desert.' A smile spread across Ganga's broad face. 'We'll see who's laughing then.'

From behind him he heard the approach of footsteps and turned to see Caspasian walking briskly towards him. Bracing himself, he called the parade to attention, wincing at the sloppy drill movements. Only Harkabahadur was perfect, but for all the wrong reasons.

Ganga spun about and saluted Caspasian smartly.

'This is it, is it?' Caspasian asked.

'I'm afraid so, saheb. Not much to look at, are they?'

'They'll have to do. Remind me who we've got.' He drew Ganga to one side, out of earshot of the others. Noticing them strain to overhear, Ganga barked, 'I didn't tell you to stand at ease!'

He ran through the list one by one for Caspasian's benefit. While Caspasian knew most of them from previous time spent in the regiment, having recently arrived back from his last posting Ganga's brief recap was a useful reminder.

'What do you want me to do with them, saheb?' Ganga asked when he had finished the summary.

Caspasian pondered. 'Don't worry about fitness. We can

sort that out on the march once we disembark from the steamer upriver. But I do want rifles zeroed and a thorough check of all equipment. Once we leave Cairo there'll be no coming back to fetch things we've forgotten.'

'No, saheb.'

'You've seen the list of weapons and equipment I drew up?'

'Yes, saheb,' Ganga replied, then added doubtfully, 'but do you really believe we'll get it?'

Caspasian smiled. 'If we don't, I'm going straight to the High Commissioner.'

Ganga grimaced.

'I know, I know. I'm supposed to watch out for my career,' Caspasian said.

Ganga nodded. 'It wouldn't do you any harm, just once in a while.'

'Look who's talking! When did you last compromise your principles?'

'That's different. I was never headed anywhere. You were. You could have been a general. Still could be.'

'And you'd make the best damned Subedar Major this Regiment's ever had.'

Ganga smiled. 'You've been out in the sun too long, saheb.'

'Nonsense,' Caspasian said, his eyes deadly earnest. 'If I could do one thing it would be to see you on the road to that promotion.'

'We'd make quite a team,' Ganga said, allowing himself a moment's reverie. 'You as the Commanding Saheb and me as your Subedar Major.'

'Quite a team indeed,' Caspasian agreed.

There was a shuffling from the men in line. Ganga turned and glared at them until they were still.

'Not much chance of that so long as we have this maila to deal with,' Ganga said.

'They're not rubbish,' Caspasian said smiling. 'They've just been lacking the right hand in command. A bit of remedial leadership is all that's needed.'

Ganga noticed the glint in Caspasian's eye and grinned. 'Then God help them.'

'Not at all. You'll see. They'll make out.'

Ganga looked over his shoulder to where Harkabahadur was standing ramrod straight, eyes still fixed on some invisible point ahead of him. 'Watch that one though, saheb. He's dangerous.'

'Harka?

'Yes.'

'Oddly enough it's him I've got the greatest hopes for.'

Ganga stared at him amazed.

'You wait. His discipline's bad but in the right circumstances I'd rather have him at my side than Ramprasad.'

'The signaller? But he's supposed to be one of the Colonel's bright-eyed boys, bound for the top.'

'Then why's he coming on this expedition?'

'You think he's lazy?'

'I'm sure of it. He's used his connections to get out of things before. The High Commissioner's birthday parade's going to place a heavy load on the signal platoon and Ramprasad wants no part of it. He thinks a nice little cruise down the Nile's just the ticket. We'll see about that.'

'And Bharatmani?'

'Old SC? Sick Chit? All he needs is a good kick up the arse. First time he tries it on, he'll get one!'

When they had drawn rifles from the armoury, the little group fell in again at the edge of the parade square. From elsewhere around the camp, passers-by looked at them and smirked. Word had spread quickly that the wild Captain Caspasian was off on another escapade. The contrast between the various members of the disparate assembly provided ample cause for merriment. One or two of the bolder ones shouted out taunts. In response Harkabahadur glared murderously at the various callers and at one point responded in kind with a comment about the man's wife and what she got up to when he was away.

Seeing a fight brewing, Sergeant Ganga called them to attention and marched them briskly away in the direction of the ranges. Once out of the camp, he ordered them to port arms and then broke into double time, jogging all the way to the ranges. After only a few yards Bharatmani was trying to attract Ganga's attention, gesturing to his feet. Ganga studiously ignored him.

Soft and overweight from his life in the officers' mess, Indrabahadur quickly succumbed to a combination of exhaustion and the heat, falling back through the ranks until he was lumbering some distance behind the rest of the group. Bharat soon saw fit to join him.

When they eventually arrived at the ranges, strung out over some considerable distance, Ganga issued the ammunition and placed them on the one hundred yard firing point at the start of the zeroing procedure whereby each firer would adjust his sights to ensure they were correctly set and aligned to the weapon. He took his position centre rear and gave the order to open fire. Lying on their stomachs, the firers engaged the targets as best they could while Ganga and Caspasian looked on disbelievingly through binoculars, studying the effects of the fire and the paucity of holes appearing in the targets.

'Pathetic,' Caspasian murmured. 'When the devil were they last on the range?'

Ganga shrugged, hopefully inspecting the eyepieces of his binoculars for smears that might be obscuring his view and making the firing seem worse than it actually was. His binoculars were dust-free and spotless. 'It's always the same. Companies concentrate ammunition on the rifle platoons. Bharat probably misses range days due to sickness, Harka will have been in the guard room, Indra fiddling the books, the cooks . . .'

'I get the picture,' Caspasian said miserably, cutting him short.

When each firer had fired a five-round group it was time to move from the firing point down to the butts and inspect the targets. Sergeant Ganga would then go to each target in turn, identify the approximate centre point of the five-round group, and note its position in relation to the firer's point of aim on the target's centre. He would then adjust the rifle's sights with a small screwdriver to bring the group onto the point of aim, whereupon the firers would then fire a further five rounds to see if the adjustment had done the trick. It was often necessary to go through the whole procedure of firing, inspection and sight adjustment two or three times, as the grouping was tweaked to the left or right, and up or down. When successfully completed, the rounds would fall exactly on and around the centre of the target where the firer was aiming and the rifle could then be said to have been zeroed. Later, in contact with the enemy, so long as the rifle was correctly aimed the rounds would strike the opponent. But, as Ganga knew all too well, numerous other factors would then come into play, such as the strength and direction of the wind, the state of the light, whether it was raining or dry, whether or not the firer was firing uphill or downhill using plunging fire, and whether the firer was engaging a moving target, either coming towards or going away from him, or traversing either to left or right. Most important of all would be the firer's position and his hold of the weapon. This would take long hours of training, first of all dry training in the classroom using the inert drill rounds that Caspasian had assisted Ganga to count, and finally live firing on the ranges. Without first having zeroed the sights, however, all the training would be wasted. The rifle's aim would be faulty, the target would be missed and the enemy would live to fight another day.

As the last man completed his five-round group Ganga barked out the order to unload. Rifle bolts snapped back and empty brass cases sprung out of the hot smoking breeches. One by one the men stood up, awaiting Ganga's next order.

'Move forward and inspect targets,' he shouted.

The line of firers ambled away from the firing point, enjoying the warmth of the day.

'On your bellies!' Ganga shouted.

The men looked at each other.

'Down! Now!'

'But, guruji, my knees . . .' Bharat started to protest.

'Down I say!' Ganga screamed.

Flinging themselves into the dust, the men started to crawl. When they had gone a few yards, one of them started to get up.

'All the way!' Ganga shouted, rushing up to the offender and thrusting him face-down into the dirt. 'And when we've adjusted the sights you'll crawl back again. And so on until you can fire a decent tight group and hit the blasted point of aim. I don't care where you've been hiding away these past months and years. You're under my command now, and by all the gods you're going to know it!'

With only two days to go before the scheduled departure upriver, Caspasian went into town for a further meeting with the Professor and Sir Hubert. They met for lunch at Winders, a fashionable restaurant near the Opera House, but the event only served to confirm Caspasian's low opinion of Sir Hubert. Throughout the meal the man was taciturn and dismissive. Once or twice Caspasian caught the Professor's eye and thought he could read an apology there.

Final co-ordinating details were covered and they parted. While disappointed that the expedition was not simply to be led by the Professor and himself, Caspasian nevertheless resolved to make the most of it. He would be out of his office for several weeks so if the price to pay was the discomfort of having to tolerate Sir Hubert, then so be it. Caspasian would keep his head down, do his job, and try to enjoy the experience as best he could.

Leaving the restaurant, Caspasian checked his watch. It was early afternoon. There was little point in returning immediately to camp. Ganga had the administrative arrangements under tight control and it was seldom that Caspasian found himself in town with time on his hands. With the prospect of the expedition before him he felt a sense of relief and of joyful anticipation. He set off walking with nothing else in mind but the killing of time. Heading west in the direction of the Egyptian Museum and the Nile, he thought he might even walk all the way back to barracks. Should he grow bored with the walk, then he could always hop into a taxi and complete the journey that way.

He had not gone far when the clean smell of cumin cut a path through the dust and heat. An instant later it was complicated by cinnamon and saffron, heralding the proximity of a spice market. Caspasian stopped and turned slowly, tracking it with his nose until he was confident he had the direction. Heading towards it, he smiled to himself, revelling in the luxury of free time. He decided to let the city lead him wherever it willed and with every step, as the flavoursome scents grew stronger, Caspasian's step lightened.

After a short distance he found himself in a narrow street bordered on either side by open-fronted houses, all of which appeared to be selling rugs. For the moment the scent of spices had vanished and he was starting to fear that he had imagined it, but a moment later the street finished as suddenly as it had begun and to his delight Caspasian was tumbled out into a large but crowded square. In all directions brightly coloured awnings shielded from the direct sunlight a vast range of heaped spices. Some were piled in straw baskets. Others were stacked on sheets that had been especially spread out on the ground. Amongst the spices all manner of other goods ranging from trinkets to clothing were strewn in varying degrees of order.

Caspasian sunk his hands deep in his pockets and meandered

through the busy marketplace, allowing himself to be guided by nothing more substantial than impulse. As conscious will retreated into the background, a new form of alertness surged forward to take its place, amplifying colours, sounds and smells, blending them together with something else. His sensei had once told him it was called mu-shin, the state of no mind. Although the years had blurred that original teaching with other concepts these had somehow clarified rather than concealed the original. Ideas from other cultures and from other forms of thought had acted as a scouring wind, rather than clutter, leaving Caspasian with access to a quality beyond words and outside any single body of lore. It was personal to him, unique and yet, in its simplicity, wholly unremarkable.

Although his path through the jumble of the marketplace was unplanned, to Caspasian it felt as if he was following a marked route, walking on a long but narrow carpet that had been unfurled in serpentine fashion and visible to him alone. It therefore came as no surprise when he raised his eyes and found himself looking at the figure of Michelle Simonin.

She had not seen him. She stood on the far side of three confused stalls whose sagging awnings, jumbled goods and noisy occupants acted as a barrier through which Caspasian had spied her. Viewed in profile, she presented Caspasian with an image on which he would happily have feasted all day. Her close-fitting white dress was matched by a large white hat with an exotic brim that swept low over her eyes, shielding her from the sun's glare. In the context of the market she was somehow both conspicuous and wholly suited, like a lone tree outstanding on otherwise unbroken savannah.

Several agitated merchants were worrying at her, various garments draped over their arms which they thrust imploringly before her. Michelle appeared neither bothered nor interested. She cast her eyes equally over everything and then turned away to consider some other portion of the market. Caspasian could see that her mind was elsewhere.

Being removed from her by some distance, Caspasian was able to take in the larger picture of which she was his centrepiece. Even so, the thief was so skilled that he almost escaped Caspasian's attention. Almost but not quite, for the man's disinterest in Michelle was too extraordinary to be wholly innocent. Sidling towards her through the press, his eyes busy with everything but Michelle, the man closed stealthily upon her.

Having spotted the thief, Caspasian scanned for the most direct route to take him to Michelle. Identifying a narrow space between the intervening stalls, he moved slowly forward, easing himself sideways into the gap and keeping his eyes fixed on the thief. Then everything happened at once. The man turned in his direction and for a second their eyes locked. In that moment Caspasian read the instantaneous mental evaluation taking place in the thief's mind. The man saw that his intentions had been discovered, he noted Caspasian's distance from his target and the difficulty of his route, and compared it with his own range to the victim. He gauged his chances, weighed the risks against possible rewards, and acted with a speed that took Caspasian by surprise.

Spurting the last few paces to Michelle, the thief snatched at the small white leather bag hanging from her shoulder and tore it free. The slender strap securing it gave way and he was off, tearing through the crowds. At the same moment Caspasian lunged forward through the stalls upsetting two of them and sending their contents tumbling noisily in all directions. To his dismay, instead of turning on the thief, the stallholders and merchants shrieked in alarm and closed upon him. With one mighty heave, Caspasian hoisted clear the last stall, ignoring the cries of its owner, and found himself confronted with a wall of furious men. Beyond them, he could just see Michelle. She glanced once in his direction, alerted by the outburst of noise, but her attention was on the thief who was making good his escape through the market. Caspasian heard her shout after the man. Then to his dismay he saw her set off alone in pursuit.

With shouted apologies, all of them ignored, Caspasian turned his shoulder and pushed forward. The wall of men held for a moment and then gave way, propelling Caspasian free as if from a slingshot. He steadied himself, regained his balance, and searched urgently for Michelle. There was no sign of her. Then, across the jumble of heads and market stalls, he glimpsed her hat and set off after her. Behind him he could hear a number of the merchants following, shouting abuse, commanding him to stop and pay for the damage he had caused.

He ran after Michelle as fast as he could, losing her track every few paces but then catching sight of her again as she tracked the thief who was zigzagging through the crowd. Amidst all the greater noise of the market, her own shouts were lost and eventually the thief, reaching the borders of the square, disappeared up a narrow winding street that climbed away from the market, Michelle only paces behind. By the time Caspasian arrived at the same point moments later, Michelle and the thief had disappeared from view around a corner some thirty paces in front. Caspasian shouted after her but there was no reply.

He sprinted up the street, taking the steps four at a time, bouncing off the wall as he hurtled round the first tight corner. Another stretch opened in front of him but there was still no sign of Michelle. Then, from further on he heard the sound of a woman's scream. He cried out, propelling his voice forward as he ran in the hope that, if Michelle was in danger, the thief might hear him and hesitate. Moments later he rounded a bend and almost tumbled headlong into the two of them. Michelle had her back to him and beyond her the thief had turned for a confrontation. In one hand Michelle's bag dangled by its broken strap from his fist. In the other, a long-bladed knife glinted dangerously, the point aimed at Michelle's throat barely two feet away.

Caspasian grasped her by the shoulder and thrust her aside. To his amazement she violently shrugged off his hand and lunged for her bag, ignoring the thief, the knife and Caspasian's own shouted warning. Nothing else mattered to her. Not even her own life.

Unprepared for the move, the thief was caught off balance and before he could snatch the bag out of her reach, Michelle had laid hold of it. As Caspasian watched in stupefied wonder an absurd tug of war developed, Michelle yanking wildly at the bag and shouting for the man to let go, the thief pulling at the strap which was still wound round his fist. Suddenly, remembering the knife in his other hand, he lashed out at her, the point grazing her left cheek. Another backhanded swipe caught the neck of her dress, tearing the fine cloth.

Prepared for her resistance this time, Caspasian gripped Michelle from behind by both shoulders and lifted her bodily out of the way, throwing her roughly to one side, clear of the lethal knife that was already lunging at her again. She went down on all fours, momentarily stunned as the breath was knocked from her.

In an attempt to take advantage of Caspasian's unguarded flank, the thief leapt forward, drawing back the knife ready to sink it into his new opponent. Instead, as the knife thrust forward, Caspasian's right arm swept downwards in an arc, palming the blade harmlessly to one side with the flat of his hand. As the mawashi-uke block reached completion, the same hand closed into a solid fist and shot upwards catching the thief under the base of the nose and driving upwards. His head was jerked sharply backwards by the force of the blow and blood exploded from the ruptured cartilage. The man shrieked in agony, dropped the knife and clutched his face with both hands.

There was no room in Caspasian's heart for clemency. The thief had been going to kill first Michelle and then Caspasian himself. Turning square-on to his target, Caspasian grasped him by both shoulders and brought his knee up hard between the man's legs. He felt the wind go out of the body in his hands and repeated the blow for good measure. It would be some time before this particular pickpocket moved quite so stealthily again.

Releasing his grip, Caspasian stood back as the thief crumpled to the floor, curling into a semi-conscious ball. Michelle was getting to her feet, clutching her bag to her as she rose. Caspasian took her elbow and helped her. He lightly took hold of her chin and turned her head so he could inspect the cut on her cheek. Apart from that, she seemed to be physically unhurt.

'We'd better find somewhere to clean this,' he said, gently touching one finger to the wound to coax away a speck of dirt that had fastened onto it.

Michelle started, turning quickly away from him as if his finger itself had caused the wound. 'I'll be fine,' she said hurriedly, gathering up her hat and preparing to go.

'Just a minute,' Caspasian said, going to hold her back. 'You can't just walk away like that. It's not safe.'

'I said I'll be fine.'

'OK, but I'll come with you.'

She spun on him, alarm in her eyes. 'No, you mustn't!'

Caspasian was stung by the consternation he could see on her face. 'Why ever not?'

'You just mustn't, that's all.' She looked at him, seeing him properly for the first time. 'Don't I know you?'

Caspasian smiled. 'Yes. I'm afraid I was the idiot who told you your father was waiting for you at the British Residency reception the other night. I'm sorry if I caused you embarrassment.'

She seemed only vaguely to recall the incident, making Caspasian wonder whether the slip was a common occurrence.

'Look,' he persevered, 'at least let me buy you a cup of coffee.'

To his surprise his suggestion really seemed to frighten her. She blanched and started to walk away, her bag still clutched tightly to her. Caspasian followed a couple of steps behind her.

'What was in the bag that was worth dying for in any case?' he asked crossly, beginning to realise that his own life had been risked because of the pursuit. 'There'd better be a hell of a lot of money for that.'

She glanced back over her shoulder and stared at him as if he had just issued the ugliest insult possible. 'I don't have any money.'

'What then?' Caspasian said, puzzled, thinking there must be some valuable jewel, priceless heirloom or something of great worth that had provoked her extreme reaction to the theft.

'How could I expect you to understand?' Michelle said, almost whispering, quickening her step as if Caspasian himself was the thief.

He was about to make one last attempt but thought better of it and let her go. Without another backward glance, Michelle Simonin walked away. To be sure that she made it home safely, Caspasian decided to follow her at a distance. As he watched her, he was amazed how quickly she regained command of herself, making her way back through the marketplace and on towards Kasr el Nil. She plucked a small handkerchief from a sleeve and held it to her cheek, correcting the set of her hat as she went. By the time she reached the front steps to the Chester Hotel, it would have been impossible for any casual observer to guess that just a short time ago she had faced death for the sake of a small white handbag.

Seeing her mount the steps at a sprightly jog, Caspasian stopped where he was, some fifty yards behind, and leaned against the wall pondering. To his amazement, the second before she disappeared into the atrium she turned and looked directly at him. From that distance it was hard to gauge her expression beneath the brim of her hat. To Caspasian, embarrassed and surprised that she had so easily taken note of his shadowing, it looked ever so slightly like the hint of a smile.

*   *   *

Guler Yurcu lay back and let her lover's hands move freely across her naked body. He bent low and kissed her breasts, warm from the sunlight streaming into the room and from their recent lovemaking. Guler marvelled that he seemed to know so much about her. It was as if he could read her mind, intuiting exactly what she wanted at the exact moment that the desire took shape in her. She was no longer young, but having a lover who visited her when her husband was away at work somehow made her feel young. It created a delicious tension, the danger of discovery only adding to the considerable pleasures of the flesh.

She looked down at her lover's bare shoulders. They were beautifully defined and muscular. She reached out and ran her hands across them, smiling at him as he raised his face for a moment.

'Oh my dear, what am I going to do with you?' she remarked lazily.

He chuckled and bent again to his task, sucking a nipple between his lips and toying with it delicately. Guler threw back her head and writhed, her nails digging into his shoulders.

'You're like a big cat,' she hissed, losing control of her voice as she felt his tongue flickering. She enfolded him with her legs, grasping his body to hers, her heels crossed below his buttocks.

'What if my husband should come home now?'

'I thought you said he was not due back until this evening?'

Guler smiled to herself, enjoying the playful taunt. 'Don't sound so alarmed, my dear. I was just thinking aloud.'

Understanding, her lover paused, his face drawing back from her breasts. 'Do you think he might want to watch us?'

Guler thrilled at the image that had been conjured before her. Her lover detected it and continued. 'He might want to pull up a chair.' He glanced across the room. 'He'd set it right there, in the window, so the light could shine over his shoulder and illuminate our play.'

'Yes!' Guler enthused, her body unable to keep still. She

bucked her hips gently upwards, pressing into her lover's hard stomach muscles. He bore down, restricting her movement knowing it would arouse her all the more.

'Do you think he would pass comment?' he continued, 'or would he watch in silence?'

Guler ran her tongue across her lips and swallowed hard, unable any longer to respond.

'Perhaps he would want to join in,' her lover mused.

Guler rolled her head from side to side.

'Hm,' her lover considered. 'He would just watch then. And what would he see? A stranger taking his wife in his own bed. How do you think he would react?'

With one hand Guler brushed back a strand of hair from her face. She was tiring of the word play, her body aroused to the pitch where it craved release. Once again her lover sensed it and slid along her body until he was able to cradle her shoulders beneath his forearms, gathering her to him. Guler planted her feet firmly and arched her back, seeking him. Together they found each other and then he too was unable to speak, the two of them locked together like dogs coupling.

Guler's eyes were tightly closed and her lover observed her as he worked, studying the loose skin of her face as he might scrutinise an object in a gallery, dispassionately, part of his mind elsewhere. It was stifling in the room. The bed stank of her sweat and he longed to be gone. Still, so long as the opportunity existed it was no great inconvenience to slake his thirst like this. At least he imagined she was clean, unlike the whores in the city who were apt to leave a client with all manner of complications.

A deep moan beneath him told him that his job was nearly done. True to form, Guler cried out a moment later, the muscles of her body going as rigid as age allowed them to. Satisfied, she attempted to release herself from her lover's embrace and was flattered when she understood that he wanted some pleasure himself now. She opened her eyes and found his warm smile upon her. He buried his face in her neck as his hips convulsed. Guler opened her arms wide, stretching them above her head and stifling a yawn as she luxuriated in the feel of her lover's increasingly urgent ministrations.

A minute later it was over. She heard him gasp and then his whole body melted across her, firm limbs subsiding into suppleness.

From somewhere deep within the large house, the tiniest of noises heralded the unforeseen. Guler was instantly alert, her body tense. She forced herself up onto her elbows.

'What is it?' her lover asked sleepily, shifting with reluctance as Guler struggled free.

'Ssh!'

The noise came again. Someone was softly whistling.

Now her lover could hear it, but to Guler's surprise he smiled. 'One of the servants?' he asked.

In an instant Guler had gone cold. 'Oh, my God, no,' she whispered, her voice so urgent she might as well have spoken aloud. 'It's him!'

Her lover chuckled. 'The ever watchful husband, eh? Now we will see how he reacts after all!'

'Don't jest!' she hissed at him, anger and terror vying for supremacy. She struggled free of his limbs and rushed across the room to snatch up a gown that lay draped over the back of an armchair. When she looked back at the bed she stared in horror to see her lover still lying there unmoving, regarding her stonily.

'What are you thinking of?' she said wildly, hands imploring him. 'Get out! Use the back stairs down to the kitchen. Go! Now!'

From the main hallway a voice called out pleasantly. 'Guler, is that you?'

Guler steadied her voice as best she could and answered. 'I'll be down in a minute. Stay there.' She turned back to her lover. 'Go!'

Slowly, he shifted his legs off the bed and stood up. He stretched, luxuriating in the feel of it. He could go now. His task was over. But instead of dressing in the clothes that he had discarded all around the room some two hours previously, and instead of making for the back stairs as requested, he strolled smilingly out of the room past Guler, heading in the direction of the main hall.

'What are you doing?' Guler asked, staring at him with horror. 'Please, the back stairs!' she implored him.

But her lover was following his own agenda now and continued out of the room.

'What do you think you're doing?'

'I'm going to have a little chat with your husband,' he replied evenly. 'I think it's time I made his acquaintance, don't you?'

Terrified, Guler gaped at him, the full horror of the situation impacting upon her. 'Don't! I beg you. Please, Kalkan, don't!'

Kalkan turned briefly. 'Don't worry, my dear. I'll be back upstairs in just a moment. Then we can conclude our unfinished business here.'

Stark naked, Kalkan strode out of the room in search of Guler's husband, his hands flexing at his sides as he prepared himself.

6

The vessel, belonging to the IDK Nile Steamer Company, was an old two-wheeler, the two huge paddle-wheels straddling the steamer, one midway along either flank of the fat lozenge-shaped body. Two long thin funnels thrust upwards from the broad flat roof, and a wooden promenade deck circuited the entire upper level.

Moored alongside Gordon Quay, two gangplanks connected the boat to the shore, one fore and one aft, both the focus of frenzied activity by the labourers who were busy conveying on board the myriad stores belonging to the French expedition. Overseeing the loading, Capitaine Paul Béranger stood at the side of the vessel's railing, checking on his clipboard as each load was carried aboard.

'How much more of this interminable activity do we have to suffer?'

Without looking at Monsieur Simonin, Béranger smiled a hard long-suffering smile. 'At least another four hours, Monsieur. We can't afford to leave anything behind.'

Simonin swatted at a fly that had plastered itself to the side of his face, its wings fouled with Simonin's sweat. Instead of being driven away as intended, it was slapped into a bloody paste. Simonin cursed, scraping off the residue and wiping it down the side of his vast shapeless trousers.

'What kind of a godforsaken country is this?'

'I would have thought you'd be used to such places?' Béranger answered bemusedly.

Simonin snorted. 'I am, but it doesn't make me like them any more.'

'No, Monsieur,' Béranger said, hoping to leave it at that. He had already guessed that while Monsieur Simonin liked whatever fame and fortune might sometimes accrue from his archaeological activities, he had no stomach for the more rigorous discomforts of the task.

He felt Simonin's eyes upon him, evaluating from head to toe and back again. Béranger did not have to look to know the expression. Midway between sneer and envy. He could also predict what was coming next.

'I suppose you like it?' The question was loaded with scorn.

Béranger shrugged, just his mouth and one eyebrow. 'It doesn't much matter whether I do or not.'

'What the devil's that supposed to mean?'

'A job's a job. If it has to be done, and if it's me who has to do it, the Legion's taught me to get on with it.' He paused a second. 'And to shut up.'

Unsure whether he had just been insulted, Simonin confined his response to a dismissive grunt.

Béranger was thankful when, a moment later, a carriage drew up on the quayside and Michelle Simonin alighted. Monsieur Simonin left his side without further comment and forced his way along the deck to the gangway where Michelle was coming aboard. Shoving the last of the porters aside, Simonin went to greet his wife.

'And what have you been up to all morning, my pretty?' He reached for her cheek which she had to lower towards his lips that were puckering expectantly. The spectacle revolted Béranger, glancing discreetly at the extraordinary couple. It reminded him of a jackal he had once seen dragging down a gazelle, its fangs deep in the throat of the panic-stricken animal.

Michelle smiled painfully, glancing around to see who else was about, blushing with shame when she caught sight of Béranger. She gave no answer, knowing that had her husband wanted one he would have couched his question in an altogether different tone.

'We sail tomorrow morning, my dear.'

'Do you want me to move our things out of the hotel this evening?' Michelle asked.

'Good Lord, no!' Simonin shrieked. 'I don't want to spend one day more on this tub than I have to.' He leaned close to her, smiling. 'And if I stay in the hotel, so do you.' He suddenly stared at her, frowning. 'What have you done to your cheek?'

Michelle's hand shot up to conceal the cut. She had made an attempt to conceal it with makeup, but sparingly for in the normal course of events she hardly used any. Too great an effort would only serve to draw attention to the small wound.

She laughed. 'You know how clumsy I am. I caught it on the edge of that bathroom window, the one that opens inwards.'

Simonin scowled savagely. 'I'll have it out with the manager. It's outrageous.'

'No, please don't, my dear. You know how I hate a fuss.'

But Simonin was not listening. 'I am paying a small fortune for that suite. The facilities and service are abominable. Quite despicable. I've a good mind to tell Béranger to let his men get drunk in the bar and take the place apart.'

On cue there was a burst of abuse from the quayside and Simonin looked down to see two of the legionnaires simultaneously snatching at each other's lapels and slapping the other's hands off. It was impossible to tell what had sparked the confrontation but Simonin knew where it was leading.

He spat in disgust. 'Filth and offal. The scum of the Marseilles sewer.' He glared along the deck. 'Béranger! Sort it out.'

His order had been unnecessary, for Béranger was already striding down the gangplank nearest the soldiers, an ice cold glint in his narrowed eyes. Reaching the quayside, he covered the ground to the two men in four overlong strides. But now they had each got a firm one-handed grip on the other's shirt and were both swinging wildly with the free fist. It was messy and ugly.

Béranger swung with the clipboard and caught the nearest

85

soldier a glancing blow across the back of the head. The man blinked, barely registering the swipe. Without pausing, Béranger reversed his hold on the board and swung it backhanded against the other man's skull. The impact was similarly unimpressive. But that had not been Béranger's point.

Tossing the clipboard to one side, he took hold of the two combatants and dragged them apart.

'Stand there,' he commanded, positioning them face to face, barely one step apart. One of them turned to go.

'Stand, I said!' Béranger screamed at him.

From their tasks around the cargo strewn alongside the quay, the remainder of the legionnaires gathered ponderously like interested cattle, knowing what was to come. The two separated men started to look regretful.

'OK,' Béranger began, stepping back from the men and planting himself with hands on hips. 'If you're going to fight, you'll do it properly. You'll fight like legionnaires, not like girls.'

'We were just . . .' one of them tried.

'Shut up,' Béranger snarled. 'Now then, when I say, you each get one punch. At the same time. Usual rules apply. No dodging, ducking or blocking. Straight in. Is that understood?'

The men's faces set like stone, realisation dawning.

'Is that understood?' Béranger shouted.

'Yes, Capitaine!' they shouted in response.

'Right then. On my command.'

The two soldiers prepared themselves, setting their feet in the best stance possible, clenching jaws for the pounding to come.

'Now!'

They swung, the two punches landing simultaneously. Watching mesmerised from the deck, with a mixture of horror and excitement, Simonin was struck by the sound of the blows, one pitched higher than the other. It was wholly unspectacular. The visual effect was far from disappointing however. Blood spurted from a vicious cut that had been opened above an eye,

while the other man spat teeth and red foaming saliva. Both of
them staggered, spinning away from each other, hands clutching their damaged faces.

Béranger grunted with satisfaction and retrieved his clipboard. 'Now brace up to attention,' he ordered.

The men painfully complied. 'If I catch you brawling again
it'll be Sergeant Kraus who swings the punches. You know
what that means.'

They nodded earnestly. They did know. Very well.

'Back to your duties then.'

With the fight prematurely concluded, Simonin heaved a big
sigh. A thought occurred to him. 'Michelle my dove, would you
like to see our cabin?'

Once again, Michelle knew that an answer was not required
of her. Her husband was already walking away from her down
the deck. He stopped outside a door and waved her forward
impatiently. She complied.

Inside, the cabin was spacious but gloomy. The shutters were
lowered and the wooden slats closed in a futile effort to exclude
the heat. Simonin noticed an electric ceiling fan and hunted
noisily for the switch. He found it but the fan refused to work.
He worried at the switch until it came loose in his hand and fell
off the wall.

'This piece of rubbish. How on earth is it going to get us
upriver? We'll all drown.'

Michelle moved to the centre of the room, hands clasping a
small bag the same size as the one the thief had attempted to
snatch. Simonin caught sight of it and glared. 'Are you always
going to carry that thing around with you?'

She ignored the comment, but carefully, the slightest of
conciliatory smiles playing at the corners of her mouth to
defuse the anger that would otherwise burst from her husband.

He shook his head vigorously. 'You will not learn, will you?
The old days are over for you. Gone.' He snapped his plump
fingers as best he could to emphasise finality. His arms en-

compassed the misery of the cabin. 'This is where you belong now. At my side.'

In their sweep his arms had included the bed. Simonin cocked his head on one side. 'Is your situation really so bad?'

Michelle knew she was helpless. Her husband knew it too.

'Come,' he said placatingly. He moved across to the bed and lowered himself onto the edge. The wooden frame groaned but held. Simonin pulled up his jacket sleeves like a magician about to perform a trick. The shirt cuffs underneath were stained. He patted the mattress at his side. 'Come,' he repeated, his voice soft.

Unable to do otherwise, Michelle walked slowly across and sat down as far away as she dared.

Simonin sighed loudly. 'Poor Michelle. Do I not match up to your aspirations?' Simonin leaned back, planting both palms behind him for support. With difficulty he crossed his legs, the supported foot wagging in mid-air as if ticking off a wayward child.

'Am I not the man of your dreams?'

She detected the cruel edge and knew that she had to exercise extreme caution. She smiled at him. 'You are playing with me, Émile. What do you want me to say?'

Simonin's expression hardened. 'I'll tell you what I want you to say. I want you to say you love me. Is that such a terrible thing for a husband to ask from his wife?'

'No, Émile,' Michelle answered, feeling exhausted and a hundred years old. 'Of course it is not. But you know . . .'

'Stop!' Simonin shouted. 'I don't need your love. You can keep it. Lock it away and see where it gets you.' He sat up and spun towards her with surprising speed, one hand grasping her shoulder roughly. 'I'll tell you where it'll get you. It'll decay inside. It'll rot, and at the end of it you'll still be left with me. So the sooner you accept the fact the better for you.'

'Émile, don't!' Michelle doubled over, burying her face in her hands.

He pushed his face close beside hers and spoke as if injecting his words into her with a syringe. 'But never forget that you are my wife, whatever you may feel. And a wife has certain duties. Do I make myself clear?' When she failed to respond he shook her and hissed, 'Do I make myself clear?'

In tears now, she nodded. 'Yes,' she whispered into her hands.

Appeased, Simonin sat back and wiped his hands, turning one over to inspect the nails. 'Come, come, my pretty. It's not as bad as all that, surely? Just think. After I've found the tomb of Menes I'll be rich beyond imagining. Famous too. Won't that make you happy?'

Michelle did not reply.

'I'll be feted everywhere I go and you will be at my side. Always.' Simonin thrilled at the prospect of his future state. He nudged Michelle. 'Imagine it! Paris, Monte Carlo, Capri. We will go wherever I want. The fun we will have!'

He turned and looked at her, his smile fading. 'Come, Michelle. You really will have to do better than that. You are making me cross now.' He took her by the shoulders and turned her towards him, shaking her, gently at first, becoming rougher. 'Michelle,' he said severely. 'I am talking to you.'

She let herself rock loosely in his grip, uncaring, only her hands on the small bag clenched tight. Simonin noticed.

'Give me that,' he commanded. 'I've had enough of that pathetic talisman.'

He tried to lay hold of the bag but Michelle wrestled it free. In panic, she tossed it to the far end of the mattress. To Simonin's amazement she then seized his face between her hands and kissed him on the lips. He hung there, immobilised, as she had intended. When she broke free she sat back and stared at him.

'There,' she said bitterly. 'How was that? Is that what you want?' Kicking her shoes across the floor, she reached behind her neck and unfastened the catch of her dress. 'Is this what you want? Like this? Do you even care how it is given?'

Simonin could feel her resentment and it startled him. But his own was the greater, having grown through longer practice. Nor did he care how she gave herself to him. In fact, he knew that he had never cared.

He watched her until he saw her falter, the realisation of what she was doing dawning on her at last. When she hesitated he laid hold of her. 'But don't stop there, my pretty,' he said through clenched teeth. 'Let me help you.'

Simonin seized the opened neckline of her loosened dress and tried to pull it down, but Michelle had only been able to undo the topmost buttons and the dress snagged when barely off her shoulders. In frustration he grabbed her to him and began to kiss her. She resisted, as she always did, but it never lasted. It could not, for he was the stronger of the two and they both knew it. Nevertheless, the fact there was always resistance annoyed him. It was stubbornness, pure and simple, and he resolved once again to crush it.

He waited until he felt her arms tire, forcing his kisses upon her all the while, and then thrust her back onto the mattress.

'Michelle,' he said softly, his lips nuzzling the mess of hair matted against her ear. 'Why must you always . . . ?'

The explosion in the bowels of the steamer sent shock waves throughout the vessel. In the cabin where Simonin and Michelle reclined on the bed it was as if a giant had suddenly swatted the underside of the floor with the palm of his enormous hand. Everything rose into the air, the bed included. Lights shook, bulbs bursting, the shards of glass exploding across the room, showering across the two stunned people. Chairs were overturned, drawers fell out of wardrobes and desk, and a large full-length mirror cracked diagonally from one corner to the other.

Simonin was rolled onto the floor and scuttled away sideways like a crab. 'What the devil was that?'

Outside they could hear the shouts and screams of the porters and sailors. From the sound of it, some of them had obviously been injured by the blast. Rising above the clamour, they heard Béranger and Sergeant Kraus barking out orders, calm but urgent.

Michelle was on her feet before her husband, quickly stooping to retrieve her handbag. She slipped her shoes on and pulled her dress up onto her shoulders, not bothering to refasten the catch.

'Michelle, where are you going?' Simonin called out to her as she made for the door. 'Don't go outside. It might not be safe.' He found himself talking to empty space. Cursing her, he struggled to his feet and followed her out onto the deck.

The scene outside had been transformed from one of quiet industry to panicked chaos. The steamer had been skewed round by the force of the explosion and was starting to list to port, leaning heavily on the quay like a drunkard collapsing against a bar. Packing cases, chests and bundles had been scattered everywhere, either by the blast or else by the porters who had dropped them before fleeing.

'There's a fire below deck. I think one of the boilers must have exploded,' Béranger called from further along the promenade deck where he was directing legionnaires carrying buckets of water. 'Best get off.'

Simonin did not need urging and ran towards the gangplank. Michelle hesitated. 'Capitaine, is there anything I can do to help?'

Béranger looked from the fleeing Simonin to her and smiled kindly. 'No, Madame. But thank you for asking.'

She calmly left the steamer to join her husband who, now that he had reached the safety of the quayside, was trying not to look shamefaced at the speed with which he had abandoned ship. He chastised Michelle petulantly when she joined him.

Sergeant Kraus emerged from the engine room, his face blackened with oil and soot. 'Capitaine, I think you should come and look at this. Quickly. We don't have much time.'

Béranger jogged across to him and together they disappeared into the smoke billowing from the hatchway. With the porters having fled, the legionnaires had been left to unload their stores alone. They were frantically trying to save as much as they could but, as the smoke belching from the portholes and hatches increased in intensity and blackness, it was becoming obvious that the steamer would not be spared.

A few moments later Béranger and Kraus staggered out onto the promenade deck again, doubled over and coughing. Béranger violently waved his men away. 'Get off! Now! She's going to blow!'

Simonin stared at him in astonishment. 'But you said it was a boiler?' he shouted. 'What about the stores? The expedition?'

'Fuck the stores!' Béranger shouted back. 'The steamer's been sabotaged.' He choked, coughing out the smoke and spitting. 'Explosives. And there's more strapped to the second boiler. The detonator misfired but the heat from the fire could trigger it at any second.'

Simonin's mouth fell open. He turned and fled away from the stricken vessel, now keeling over at a forty-five degree angle. 'Come, Michelle, come! Don't just stand there and stare!'

'Capitaine Béranger,' Michelle called up at the steamer. 'Hadn't you better get your men off the ship?'

Béranger waved her away. 'Don't worry. We're right behind you, Madame. Please move to safety.'

Reluctantly Michelle followed her husband, moving to one side of him when she reached the vantage point he had located some distance away from the stricken vessel. Béranger, Sergeant Kraus and the legionnaires tumbled down the gangplanks, arms laden with as much of the weapons and stores as they could manhandle ashore. Fortunately a number of the chests and bundles had yet to be carried aboard, so the moment Béranger and his men were themselves safe, they set to work shifting these as far away from the steamer as possible.

'That's enough!' Béranger shouted when he judged they had pressed their luck as far as they reasonably dared. He shooed his men back to join Simonin and Michelle, bringing up the rear himself. No sooner had he done so than an almighty explosion ripped through the heart of the vessel. It rocked and tore at its moorings, heaving great swathes of water over the quayside, before sinking back, flames engulfing it, working from the engine room outwards. Black smoke billowed through every porthole, hatch and doorway, while yellow tongues of fire erupted from the funnels.

Simonin stood transfixed by the spectacle. 'Mon Dieu,' he mouthed quietly. Instinctively he reached for Michelle's hand like a small boy needing reassurance. She folded her arms, hugging her bag safely to her and stared into the wreckage before them.

Harry Ghazali dusted the top of an iron mooring post before settling himself on it like a wiry seabird to observe the desolation at the quayside. He slid one hand inside his linen jacket and withdrew a silver cigarette case. Cracking it open, he removed a long slender Turkish cheroot, tapped it heartily several times on the lid of the closed case, and then simultaneously placed the cheroot between his lips and returned the case to his inside pocket. With the cheroot alight, he folded his arms and stared hard at the wrecked steamer. Overnight the fires had expended themselves, assisted by the fire service, and as Ghazali's men now crawled over the site inspecting and assessing the damage, only the vaguest wreaths of smoke still issued into the bright morning sky.

'Damnable business, Ghazali,' a voice heralded from a flank.

Ghazali recognised the visitor and reluctantly straightened up in time to greet Horace Blythe, head of security at the British Residency.

'Any idea who's behind it? Not that blasted Wafd lot?'

Ghazali shrugged. 'Too early to tell. If I had to hazard a guess I'd say it was one of the nationalist movements.'

'Forgive me if I'm less than impressed,' Blythe replied.

Ghazali frowned. 'What's your interest in this? Don't tell me the High Commissioner's sorry the French expedition's been thwarted! It gives the British a clear run at the search.'

'Far from it, old boy. The High Commissioner's positively mortified by it all. Embarrassment coming out of his gills. The fact it should happen on his patch, as he calls it, is bad enough. But imagine the public perception! Exactly as you say. He's afraid everyone'll be thinking the British are behind it. You know, knock out the frog and take the spoils for ourselves.'

Ghazali smiled happily, sank back onto his seat and folded his arms again. 'Surely no one would think such a thing of the British?' he asked mischievously.

Never one for subtleties or sarcasm, Blythe shook his head in earnest. 'You might well ask, but apparently there are those who would try to make mileage out of all this.'

'So what's to be done?'

'Solve the bloody crime, Ghazali. That's what. The High Commissioner wants to know who's behind it and why.' He kicked angrily at the iron ring fastened to the quayside, the steamer's mooring rope looped through it redundantly. 'In the meantime an offer's been made to the French Embassy that their expedition is welcome to share our own team's transport upriver as far as their drop-off point.'

'That is exactly the sort of generous gesture I would have expected from the High Commissioner.' He wagged a playful finger under Blythe's nose. 'You British excel at such things. It has made you into the world power you are today.' He shook his head sadly, thumb and forefinger adjusting his pince-nez. 'We poor natives still have much to learn.'

Missing the point, Blythe replied, 'Don't be too hard on yourself, old man. As a Copt you're almost one of us. Certainly a cut above the fellahin.'

Ghazali bowed his head, amused rather than insulted.

'That is very gracious of you, Horace. I am moved beyond words.'

Blythe grinned proudly, plucking at his wing collar. Aggravated by the heat, the stud was digging into his neck which, in the months since his promotion and consequent arrival in Cairo, had fattened like a turkey being force fed for Christmas. A thought occurred to him. 'Tell me, have you had anything to do with these murders in the Turkish community?'

'Quite a lot actually,' Ghazali replied warily. 'I'm heading the team set up to investigate them.'

Blythe was impressed. 'You don't say?' He leaned closer. 'What's the story?'

Ghazali shrugged apologetically. 'I'm afraid I'm really not at liberty to say.'

'Of course, dear chap. I wouldn't want you to breach any confidences. I was just wondering whether they were connected in any way.'

'You mean in so far as all the victims are of Turkish origin?'

'Yes.'

'It's still too early to say. I mean, yes, they're all members of the Turkish community, but beyond that there seems to be nothing linking the murders.'

'Extraordinary,' Blythe marvelled.

'Indeed,' Ghazali conceded. 'We've looked into various rackets and corruption allegations but so far nothing of any substance has emerged.'

'Just plain coincidence then?' Blythe offered helpfully.

Ghazali smiled. 'Stranger things have happened. The Turkish community in Cairo is enormous, after all.'

'I know, but the murder of . . . what is it now? . . . four of its most prominent members in as many months!'

'More. We found the body of Yurcu Pasha yesterday.'

'Of course. I read the report. Wasn't his wife killed too?'

'Sadly, yes. From the evidence she and her husband had been

enjoying a few moments of intimacy upstairs which is where the intruder found them.'

Blythe sniggered. 'So it's true? They were both absolutely starkers.'

Ghazali suppressed his revulsion at Blythe's coarseness. 'I knew them both personally.'

Blythe noted the mild rebuke and cleared his throat. 'Of course, dear fellow. Most unsettling for you. Let's just hope you can catch the villain soon, before he kills anyone else.'

'Which is exactly why we remain vigilant.' Ghazali looked at Blythe shrewdly as if about to divulge something, but then thought better of it and turned his attention to his cheroot instead. 'I have some theories, but all so far unproven.' He reached across and poked Blythe playfully in the chest. 'And as policemen we cannot allow ourselves the luxury of acting on the strength of mere suspicion alone, can we?'

'Indeed not,' Blythe agreed without really understanding why. In his experience of colonial policing little else was required. Generally the chain of events ran from suspicion to robust interrogation, followed inevitably by conviction and punishment. It was as simple as that.

Ghazali pondered a moment. 'Do you really think the French will accept the offer of shared transport? I mean, they're a competitive lot. I wouldn't be surprised if they preferred to sulk rather than appear beholden to the British.'

'That might be true of that toad Simonin, but he's not being given the luxury of free choice. The French Ambassador's already accepted. He and the High Commissioner are old friends. Get on like a house on fire. He's told Simonin to share the British steamer and like it.'

'And will he? Like it, I mean?'

Blythe guffawed. 'He certainly won't but he hasn't got any choice in the matter. The steamer leaves tomorrow morning and both teams will be on it.'

Ghazali smiled. 'You imperial powers do so love your little rivalries. But I must say, that's one journey I would not like to be on. With all those fragile egos thrown together it promises to be highly unpleasant. Highly unpleasant indeed.'

7

Some days before the scheduled departure of the British expedition, the High Commissioner had idly remarked to one of
his aides that he thought he might take some time out of the
office and pop down to the quayside and see them off. The aide,
deciding it would be appropriate to accompany him, had
mentioned this snippet in conversation to the First Secretary
who had been entertaining similar ideas. He in turn passed it on
to his friend in Chancery, who had spoken to the Consul who
was down from Alexandria for a few days, both of them
reckoning that it would hardly do their careers any harm to
be seen there too.

Word continued to pass from mouth to mouth until the
morning of departure arrived and, with it, a convoy of cars and
carriages bearing virtually the entire staff of the Residency,
together with their wives and children. At the last moment,
word of the impromptu send-off reached Colonel Humphreys.
He slammed down the telephone and bellowed for the Adjutant. Captain Tremain looked cautiously round the door from
his adjacent office in Battalion Headquarters.

'Get your hat. We're going out.'

'Erm . . . where to, Colonel?'

'We're going to see off Caspasian.'

Tremain blinked.

'And don't look so bloody confused!'

'I'm not, Colonel,' Tremain stammered, trying to make sense
of this latest directive. 'But I thought . . .'

'Don't think. Obey,' the Colonel said, coming round from
behind his desk and slapping his hat aggressively on his head.

'That's Caspasian's problem. He thinks too much. For God's sake don't you go the same way.' He stopped, planted his hands on his hips and heaved an immense sigh. 'It seems every other bugger in Cairo is going to see him off, so how do you think it would look if his own CO ignored the occasion?'

'Ah,' Tremain said, light dawning.

'That officer will be the death of me. Come on.'

The journey across town was particularly fraught, Colonel Humphreys casting frequent glances at his watch while his other hand drummed impatiently on the dashboard. Sensing his commanding officer's irritation with the unusually heavy traffic, the Gurkha driver started to perspire, his driving skills deteriorating proportionately. After the fourth near miss, the Colonel banished the driver to the back seat alongside Captain Tremain and took the wheel himself. When he eventually drew to a halt at the quayside, heads turned to regard the spectacle of the regimental staff car being driven by the Colonel, the Gurkha driver looking sheepish in the rear.

From the promenade deck of the steamer, Caspasian looked across the heads of the crowd lining the quayside, spied his commanding officer and swore quietly.

'This is getting more like a bloody circus by the minute.'

At his side, Sergeant Ganga noted the arrival of the Adjutant and fingered the chin strap of his broad-brimmed felt hat, setting it more properly in place. 'Do you want me to parade the men?'

'No. But you'd better do it.'

When Ganga remained uncertainly at his side, Caspasian suddenly realised the dilemma the two of them were facing. Failing to acknowledge the presence of so many notables with some sort of guard would risk bringing the regiment into disrepute. On the other hand, bearing in mind the quality of the men at Caspasian's disposal, that might be the lesser of the available evils.

'Do it,' he repeated with reluctance.

While Ganga marched away to muster his men on the quayside, Caspasian went in search of the Professor. He saw him buried deep in the crowd talking to the High Commissioner. Sir Hubert was with them and together they appeared to be enjoying a highly animated conversation. Making his way to the Professor's side, Caspasian discreetly drew his attention and mentioned that they were ready to get under way.

'Already? Goodness! Let's be off then.'

'That's the ticket,' the High Commissioner boomed merrily. 'Look after them, Caspasian.'

Caspasian smiled politely, taking his leave before Colonel Humphreys, fighting his way through the onlookers, could quite close the distance to them. Sir Hubert caught his eye and Caspasian returned the acknowledgement which was little more than cursory.

From the water's edge there was a cheer as the Gurkhas fell into line. Caspasian peered over the heads and winced at the appalling drill movements, even though to everyone except the Colonel and Tremain it looked immaculate. Scowling furiously, Tremain edged up beside Caspasian but before he could speak Caspasian held up his hand. 'Don't say anything. If you'd given me a half-decent detachment instead of this shower . . .' He concluded his sentence with a shrug and strode smartly away.

While the Gurkhas had been parading at the stern gangplank, the legionnaires under Sergeant Kraus had been falling in at the prow. In the absence of a band, both Sergeant Kraus and Sergeant Ganga were shouting out commands at twice their usual volume, each competing with the other and swapping irritated glances.

As Caspasian was making his way back to the gangplank in readiness to board, someone plucked at his sleeve. He looked round to see Harry Ghazali.

'Good luck, Captain.'

'Chief Superintendent, good of you to come,' Caspasian said.

He thought he could detect a glint of humour in the police-man's eye. 'It's turning into quite a social occasion.'

'But of course. It'll be the talk of the town for at least an hour.' He grinned. 'I thought I'd come to provide a bit of local colour.'

Caspasian laughed. 'Just ensure no one tapes anything to my boilers. That's all I ask.'

Serious for a moment Ghazali said, 'I assure you I have had my men go over every inch of the vessel. I can promise you that if anyone is going to sabotage your mission it is not going to be while you are on board.'

'That's a relief.' Caspasian stared the length of the steamer to where Simonin had arrived and was making heavy weather of transferring aboard his personal luggage which consisted mostly of two large well travelled portmanteaus. At the other end of the vessel, Sir Hubert was casting sullen glances in the direction of the French team. 'I fear there'll be more than enough to keep me occupied while we're in transit.'

'Well at least your respective masters appear happy with the arrangement,' Ghazali said as the French Ambassador and the British High Commissioner slapped each other on the back and guffawed at some jest or other. 'Let's hope their spirit of co-operation rubs off on the teams themselves.'

'In my experience, Chief Superintendent, hope by itself rarely bears an edible fruit.'

'Quite so, quite so.' Ghazali held out his hand which Caspasian shook firmly. 'I will follow your progress with interest. Do not keep us city dwellers starved of dispatches, Captain. Your expedition will lend colour to our tawdry little lives.'

With a wink and a throwaway wave, Ghazali loped off in the opposite direction from the crowd, choosing to avoid the hearty greetings that were springing up all over the quayside as the spectators enjoyed their office outing.

Sergeant Ganga clipped smartly to attention at Caspasian's side. 'The men are ready for your inspection, saheb.'

Caspasian glared at him. 'In front of all these laughing hyenas?'

Ganga grinned. 'Do you want me to fall them out?'

'Yes. Let's get on with this thing.'

They exchanged salutes and while Ganga barked commands at the men, Caspasian hauled himself briskly up the steep gangplank and stumbled into Michelle Simonin. Mumbling an apology, he tipped his hat and for a moment thought she was going to speak, but her husband was clucking at her elbow, shooing her along.

'Do stand aside, Monsieur, and be more watchful of Madame, if you please.' Simonin fixed Caspasian with his black beady eyes and pressed on, one arm shielding his wife as if she was in danger of falling in with bad company.

The Gurkhas trooped aboard in line, looking about them with interest like a school party entering a museum. At the far end of the deck, the legionnaires coagulated, studying the diminutive Nepalese hill men like connoisseurs. They noted the rifles, the webbing equipment and, above all, the large sheathed kukris hanging at their belts.

'Get below, the lot of you, and stop gawking!' Sergeant Kraus roared at his men. 'There'll be plenty of time for introductions later.'

Béranger came up beside Caspasian. 'Kraus is a good man.'

'German?' Caspasian asked.

'Yes. Ex-Stormtrooper.'

Caspasian nodded solemnly. 'I recognise the type.'

'Don't worry about him, John. He's all right. So what if he fought on the other side? In the Legion a man's past is his own affair. Kraus is a professional. Soldiering's his trade. It's in his blood.' He smiled at Caspasian. 'Not unlike the two of us.'

'That's fine by me, but what does Simonin think of it?'

'He was horrified,' Béranger said, chuckling. 'Said he wouldn't have him on the expedition, until I threatened to walk, taking my legionnaires with me. I said he could find someone else. He knows the Legion is the best in the French Army when it comes to desert operations, so he shut up.'

There was a cheer from the crowd on the quayside as the steamer's Captain signalled for the gangplanks to be retracted and the mooring ropes unfastened. The paddle steamer was an old sternwheeler and, as a plume of black smoke erupted from the funnel, the huge cylinder of blades at the rear slowly creaked and groaned into life as it began to rotate like an old village watermill, churning the dark green water into a turbid foul-smelling soup. The space between the quayside and the vessel inexorably widened and, staring down into the broadening swathe of agitated water, Caspasian felt suddenly the full impact of his liberation from the city and his desk-bound job there. He raised his face to the crowd and found himself staring at the distant pained gaze of Colonel Humphreys. The smile that had been dawning inside Caspasian was expertly choked and he straightened to attention and saluted sombrely instead. To his surprise the Colonel's cursory salute in return was complemented by a rueful smile and a sorry shake of the head that Caspasian thought might be verging on the good-natured.

When it was fifty yards out, the steamer let out a shrill whistle blast and turned towards midstream, the prow dipping gently, aiming upriver. On the quayside the crowd started to thin. With the High Commissioner departed, there was little cause for anyone else to remain and within a few minutes only the dockhands were left, moving about their business with a disinterested air.

With the steamer finally under way, Caspasian checked that Ganga and the rest of the men were settled into their accommodation for the trip. They would be on board for several days and he wanted to ensure that they were well rested before the hard overland journey began. The brief river voyage would be best used as an opportunity to gather strength for the tests of endurance that would undoubtedly come. Caspasian knew the desert and jebel and knew what a merciless environment it could be.

The men were quartered in two large cabins below decks. Ganga had originally been assigned a cabin to himself, but with the French expedition foisted upon them, he was now obliged to share with Sergeant Kraus. The prospect had not delighted him. Nevertheless, when Caspasian popped his head round the door to see how they were getting along, he found them sitting on the edge of their bunks deep in conversation. Ganga was explaining the logic behind the weight and balance of his kukri with Kraus nodding sagely, his own large sheath knife being held up alongside for comparison. Although English was not the mother tongue for either of them, using it as the medium of communication seemed to present little problem. Whenever a gulf was encountered in their understanding, mime stepped in to serve as a bridge until they once again set foot on firmer ground.

Content that for the moment everything was in hand, Caspasian located his cabin and set about unpacking his valise. A glance through the porthole showed that Cairo was fast receding. A native felucca swept past in the opposite direction, its high arching sails billowing strongly. It bounded over the wake thrown up by the paddle steamer, the crew clinging to the sides as the sleek vessel rocked and bucketed, corkscrewing through the suddenly turbulent water.

Caspasian collapsed back onto his bed with a slim volume of Coleridge and leafed through it until he reached his marker. Thumbing it open down the spine, he located the verse where he had previously abandoned it and began to read. He started awake a second later to find Paul Béranger standing over him grinning.

'You must be getting old. How else could I creep up on a Gurkha?'

Caspasian sat up. 'Nonsense,' he said crossly, irritated at having been caught out. 'How the devil did you get in? I just closed my eyes for a moment. That's all.'

'A moment? We've been under way for nearly two hours.'

Caspasian wrenched back his sleeve and stared at his watch with consternation. Béranger was right. He had dozed off and had been sleeping deeply. Béranger reached down and picked up the fallen copy of Coleridge from the floor.

'What is it that sent you to sleep?' He noted Caspasian's marker and read aloud.

> The many men, so beautiful!
> And they all dead did lie
> And a thousand thousand slimy things
> Lived on; and so did I.

He closed the book carefully and frowned. 'Do you think we are the slimy things that lived on after the war?'

Caspasian smiled. 'Of course not.' He retrieved the book and reopened it, looking fondly at one of his favourite texts. 'Do you know "The Rime of the Ancient Mariner"?'

Béranger pulled up a chair and settled down opposite his friend. 'No.'

'It's about a fall from grace.'

Béranger raised an eyebrow. 'Tell me more.'

'The mariner has embarked on a long and dangerous voyage. He slays an albatross, considered by his comrades to be a bird of good fortune. He does it without forethought, completely unpremeditated.'

Béranger looked puzzled. 'Then why did he do it?'

'Exactly. That's one of the great questions.'

'And the answer?'

'He is out of step with the pulse of life. He sees a bird and he shoots it, regardless of its beauty and grace. He is estranged from the world in which he lives and moves. But the point is, the world, as Coleridge sees it, is not a dead and spiritless thing. On the contrary. It is a coherent and interconnected whole. The mariner's crime is matched by consequences brought about by his callous and unthinking action. His shipmates anticipate this and in their terror at what is to come, they fasten the dead bird around the mariner's neck.'

'Like a millstone,' Béranger offered.

'Exactly. He must bear the weight of his sin, visibly for all to behold, but above all so that he himself might never forget what he has done. He must serve penance.'

'And?'

'And they all perish. All except the mariner himself.'

Béranger chuckled. 'Isn't that just the way! Some other swine provokes the killing but it is the innocent ones who suffer. Just like in the trenches. The generals ordered us forward, but we were the ones to march into the lead.'

'Ah, but once his shipmates are dead they can no longer suffer. The mariner on the other hand, has to endure all manner of tortures. Until he has been purified.'

Béranger shifted in his seat. 'Purified? That sounds uncomfortably religious.'

Caspasian shrugged. 'Not really. You see, his thoughtless act can only be redeemed by something equally spontaneous. Something similarly disconnected from rational thought. He can't bring about his salvation by an act of conscious will. That would be too easy, however sincere. No, he has to have changed inside. His soul has to have been reconstructed.'

'So what is this spontaneous thing?' Béranger laughed. 'Does he get drunk?'

Caspasian considered. 'Not quite. At least, not with alcohol.' He turned to the book in his hands and hunted busily until he found the passage he was looking for. 'In the moonlight he unexpectedly sees water snakes and the beauty of them touches him. Here, listen to this . . .

> O happy living things! no tongue
> Their beauty might declare:
> A spring of love gushed from my heart
> And I blessed them unaware.

The selfsame moment I could pray:
And from my neck so free
The Albatross fell off, and sank
Like lead into the sea.

Caspasian looked up. 'You see? The change that was needed inside him has finally taken place. Quite without his realising, and quite without any act of conscious will. His experiences have brought it about. Then, quite unbidden, when he beholds the sea serpents in the moonlight, he is overwhelmed spontaneously by . . .' Caspasian hunted for the word in mid-air. 'Compassion.'

'And that breaks the spell?'

'Yes. It lifts the curse imposed by his earlier crime.'

Béranger regarded his old companion seriously. At length, he reached forward and clasped Caspasian's wrist.

'*Mon ami*, we committed no crime.'

'I know that here,' Caspasian said tapping the side of his temple with his forefinger. He shrugged, a shy smile badly masking his discomfort.

Béranger eased himself back in his chair, elbows on the arm rests, steepling his fingers before him. He cocked his head to examine the way the light made its way through them. 'I understand,' he said. 'Perhaps we should have gone away somewhere to become mendicants, you and I. Instead we remained as soldiers. What does that say about us?'

Caspasian closed his book and skimmed it at the top of the bed where it lodged under the pillow like a knife in a tree. 'That our souls are a long way from reconstruction.'

Béranger smiled back, fingers interlocking to form closed fists, parallel thumb nails bouncing contemplatively on his lower lip. 'And we are far from salvation,' he added. He looked up as a small brass carriage clock chimed forlornly from the desk. His expression brightened. 'But not from tea, unless I'm mistaken. When I left the Professor he was trying to arrange some.'

Caspasian pushed himself to his feet, arching backwards until his spine cracked. 'I wonder what Monsieur Simonin will have to say about that?'

Béranger stood up. 'So long as there's some cake for him to cram in his fat mouth he wouldn't dream of boycotting even such a quintessentially English ceremony.'

They found the others at the prow of the steamer, sheltering out of the sun under a vast canvas awning. The Captain of the steamer, a Greek named Yassos, had joined his passengers and was regaling them gleefully with tales of the Nile's more treacherous currents and sand banks, recounting a recent disaster with expansive gestures that depicted the catastrophe.

'They were finding bodies washed up along the banks for months afterwards, each more bloated and rotten than the last. It was amazing the crocodiles had left anything at all. There was one corpse which had obviously been fought over . . .'

'*Mon Dieu*! Please desist, Captain, that will be quite enough!' Simonin exclaimed, stopping his mouth with the back of his hand whose fingers clutched a thick slice of Victoria sponge. 'Spare a thought for the ladies, please!'

Everyone looked around but could see only the one, Michelle, and she appeared not to be listening. She was leaning with folded arms on the rail, gazing across the broad river to the lush green swathes of cultivated land sweeping down to the water's edge. A broad-brimmed hat shielded her eyes from the dazzle, casting them in deep shade.

Sir Hubert looked up as Caspasian arrived and went to help himself to tea, first presenting Béranger with a cup and saucer.

'Don't trouble yourself with that, Caspasian. There's some bod around who will serve you. Just shout for him.'

'It's no trouble,' Caspasian replied pleasantly, handing Béranger a filled cup and following it with the milk and sugar. Sir Hubert observed his movements icily. 'Obviously not,' he said, not caring to mask his distaste. For a moment it seemed he had something additional to say but a friendly glance from Caspasian silenced him.

Professor Fenwick stormed in to conceal the breach. 'Well isn't this pleasant. Under way at last. Steaming up the Nile in the competent hands of Captain Yassos here, in search of treasure!'

Simonin scoffed, a fine spray of sponge and flecks of cream accompanying it.

The Professor chose to ignore it and beamed at Caspasian and Béranger. 'And just look at you two. The very spirit of co-operation.'

Béranger opened his mouth to answer but before he could speak Simonin interrupted, 'Only until we disembark and go our separate ways, Professor, so please don't try to influence Capitaine Béranger.' He eyed Béranger briefly. 'The Capitaine answers to me.'

Béranger closed his mouth and turned his attention to stirring his tea but the flickering muscle at his jaw line was visible to all.

Observing Béranger's discomfort, Sir Hubert added, 'I say, that sergeant fellow – he isn't a damned Hun, is he?'

'He is German, if that is what you mean, Monsieur,' Béranger answered.

Sir Hubert shook his head. 'Well I'll be blowed. I thought the name Kraus sounded like a Hun. Damned glad he's got nothing to do with our expedition. That's all I can say.'

'I hope it is, Monsieur,' Béranger replied.

Sir Hubert stopped in mid-sip uncertain whether he had heard correctly.

Simonin gobbled his last mouthful hurriedly in order to contribute his own portion of vitriol. 'Now there at least you and I are in agreement, Sir Hubert. I too do not hold with the employment of Boches. If it was up to me he would be on the scrap heap with the rest of them in Weimar rather than earning good French francs.'

As Béranger adopted a defensive stance Simonin quickly held up one hand in surrender. 'I know what you are going to say, Capitaine. The Legion does not enquire after a man's past, however steeped in blood.'

'If you want to talk about steeped in blood, Monsieur, I expect my own hands are dirtier than Kraus's,' Béranger replied.

'That's not what I mean,' Simonin defended. 'How can a French unit employ the enemy?'

'The Germans have not been the enemy for ten years.'

'You know what I mean. I remember Verdun,' Simonin said, as if mention of the name alone would be sufficient to prove his point.

'Were you there, Monsieur?' Béranger asked, unable to dull the twinkle in his eye.

'You know I was not.'

'I didn't think I remembered seeing you.'

Sir Hubert spoke up. 'But surely, if you were there yourself, Béranger, surely you must hate the bastards.'

'Were you a soldier, Sir Hubert?'

With difficulty Sir Hubert held Béranger's gaze as he replied. 'No. I was employed on other tasks vital to the war effort.'

'Which were?'

'I was running one of my father's businesses. The company produced tinned rations for use by our boys at the front.'

Caspasian tried to bite his lip and remain silent. He failed. 'What sort of rations would they have been?'

'My father had the idea of producing complete meals in a tin. Meat and vegetables together. Quite a new concept.'

Caspasian felt his mood darkening. 'Not Ready Rations?'

Sir Hubert almost choked on his tea. He suddenly seemed to shrink. 'I can't recall the exact name.'

'It was your own company and you can't remember the name?' Béranger asked incredulous.

Indignant, Sir Hubert rose out of his chair. 'Are you calling me a profiteer?'

Béranger stared dumbfounded. Everyone fell silent and looked at Sir Hubert. Aware that he had become the centre of attention, Sir Hubert slammed down his cup and saucer and stormed off. 'This is preposterous. I won't stand for it!'

When he had gone, Monsieur Simonin shrugged with disinterest and went across to engage his wife in conversation while the Professor and Captain Yassos returned quickly to their conversation.

Béranger came up to Caspasian. 'What the devil was all that about? I never mentioned profiteering!'

'I think you touched a raw nerve,' Caspasian said, his voice hard. 'That bastard!'

Béranger stared. 'You mean he *was* a profiteer?'

Caspasian stared hard into the middle distance, remembering. 'About as close as you can get. I well remember Ready Rations. A beautifully packaged tin with a colourful label announcing the contents. There was a choice of four; beef, lamb, pork and chicken. But they were all the same. A rock hard twist of some unidentifiable substance which was supposed to be meat, and a sodden mess of mushed-up vegetables. They were completely inedible. Anyone who persevered out of desperation usually ended up with gut rot. Eventually they were discontinued, but the army had been duped into buying hundreds of thousands of them and quartermasters, being the men they were, insisted on using them rather than destroying them as they should have done. I always swore that if I ever caught the bastard who had conned us I'd kill him.'

Béranger blanched. 'That's a little extreme, isn't it?'

'Not when you've seen men about to go over the top to die, first settling down to enjoy their last meal on this earth, only to find it inedible slop.' His expression softened, but into something only marginally less unpleasant. 'I think I will have to serve Sir Hubert with something he might recognise.'

8

The old man lay raving in his half-sleep. Lying on a straw mat on the floor of packed earth, the fetid darkness as tight about him as a shroud, his eyes, now open, now closed, stared into the brightness of visions. Those who tended him when Mahmud was away had long since departed in terror, unable to comprehend his jabbering. They had returned to their own dwellings throughout the isolated desert township to tell their families of his message. It was time to arm. The long period of waiting was over. The redcoats were coming.

Staring blind-eyed at the spectacle only he could see, old Yakub marvelled giggling at the breached walls of Khartoum. Gordon Pasha, the hated redcoat leader who had defied the Dervish army of Mohammed Ahmed Ibn Al-Sayid Abdullah, known as the Mahdi, the old man had seen him fall on the wall of spears, ending the siege that had endured for more than three hundred days.

Before that there had been the one they called Hicks. Yakub had not been there when the Mahdi had destroyed him, but he had heard how they had broken the British squares, and how General Hicks had died, fighting to the last. They were brave. Of that there could be no doubt. All the more reason for them to be destroyed. The brave always presented the greatest threat.

After Hicks and Gordon there had come Wolseley. He had been a much greater danger for he had been methodical. Assembling his great force at Wadi Halfa near the second cataract of the Nile, he had pressed on ever southwards. At Abu Klea his men had slaughtered thousands of the Mahdi's followers, but only after, once again, the Dervish army had broken into the British square. It was a formidable sight to behold, a British square advancing in full battle order. Yakub could well remember it. Each of the four sides could be as much as two whole battalions long. In the centre would be the baggage animals, perhaps a cavalry force or a detachment of the Camel Corps. Most feared of all would be the quick-firing Maxim-Nordenfeldt 9-pounders, the Krupp 12-pounders and the hated Gatling guns manned by the bluejackets, the men of the Naval Brigade. Yakub had witnessed them all and seen the devastation they wrought upon the charging Dervish ranks.

But worst of all was the Martini-Henry rifle in the hands of well drilled British infantry. Yakub had seen them volley fire at the packed Dervish masses, and down they had fallen like scythed corn, the Baggara tribesmen, the Taaishi warriors, the black-faced Jiadias, and of course the famous Hadendowahs, the fiercest tribe in all of Africa, with their terrifying aspect and long upstanding mass of hair. Seeing them for the first time, the redcoats had called them fuzzy-wuzzies because of it, but there was no doubting the terror in the redcoats' hearts when the Hadendowahs closed upon them wielding their cross-handled double-edged swords, a long heavy terrible weapon.

The square was the problem, a solid moving wall formation of Martini-Henrys, each muzzle carrying a long bladed sword-bayonet, a bristling fire-spitting hedge of razor-sharp steel. The trick, Yakub and his comrades had discovered, was to identify the weak points. Usually these were the corners. It all depended on three factors, the degree of training of the infantry forming the square, the quality of leadership exercised by its commanders, and the nature of the ground over which the square had to manoeuvre.

Old Yakub tossed and rolled on his mat. Perspiration beaded his brow as the fever soared. No one knew how old he was. Some said sixty, most reckoned on seventy. Everyone knew of the things he had witnessed. Amongst the tribe there were still several who could speak of those events from personal experience. Most of all though it was old Yakub, half senile as he was, and of course their leader Mahmud. Mahmud was younger than Yakub by nearly twenty years, but in ferocity and courage he had no equal within the tribe.

There was something about those men from the old days that stamped them out, setting them apart from all others. Some said it was the influence of the Mahdi whose hand lay upon them still and, after him, of his successor Abdullah, a chief of the Baggara tribe, known as the Khalifa. For the Mahdi had died only months after the death of Gordon Pasha. The Khalifa had taken over command of the great Dervish army thereafter, leading them for the next thirteen years until that fateful day outside the defences at Omdurman when the British had finally triumphed. That had been when the survivors of the tribe had taken to the desert wastes, and when Mahmud had wrested control, imposing order once again that they might survive and not succumb to foreign rule like the rest of the conquered peoples.

Omdurman. It was now exactly thirty years ago, but Yakub, turning in the furnace of his madness, could remember it still, his recollections garbled, confused with those of Khartoum and the earlier battles a dozen or more years before that.

In his mind's eye he could see it. The wells of Abu Klea. The forward ranks of the square had surged ahead. The ground, uneven and pocked with thorn bushes, had disturbed the parade dressing of the British infantry. At the rear of the formation the non-commissioned officers screamed for the men to catch up, but the foremost ranks had fired in a volley and the Dervish hordes were retreating before them. The British were eager for slaughter and were out for the chase.

The great mass of the Hadendowahs waiting in the sunken folds of ground off to the flank spied the widening rift. At the given signal they rose as if coming out of the earth itself and rushed forward, heading straight for the breach. Being at the corner of the square, the number of rifles that could be brought to bear on the charge by the British was limited. The next moment the tribesmen were in, hacking and slashing, screaming their war cries, unafraid of death. Had the Mahdi not said that they were immune to the enemies' bullets?

Yakub rose up on his mat and cried out. Leaning up on his elbows his face was a mask of ecstasy. He threw back his face and roared with laughter. In the huts below, neighbours glanced at one another fearfully. Even the old men, the ones who could also recall, turned to their fires and stared hard in the flames, longing to forget. If it was true, if the redcoats really were coming again, they feared for the lives of their sons and their grandsons.

But Yakub was in the thick of battle. Turning this way and that, he lashed out at invisible targets, exulting in the return of his youthful strength, however illusory. In one part, tightly grouped around their stricken comrades, a clutch of redcoats stood fast in the rout. The Hadendowahs were upon them, cutting and hacking. Elsewhere four bluejackets fought furiously with a jammed Gatling. Seeing the Hadendowahs close in, they drew cutlasses and hurled themselves upon the infiltrators with a will. On all sides the battle raged, but at last the redcoats regained the upper hand. Unlike Hick's column which had been cut to pieces at Kashgeil, the leadership and training of the British at Abu Klea stood the fiery test of battle. The breach had been sealed and every Dervish that had made it in through the breach was cut down.

Coming up the track, making his way quickly back towards the huts after the completion of his journey, Mahmud heard Yakub's ranting and broke into a run. As he neared the doorway, he noticed how his bodyguards had fallen back. They were still afraid of the old man. Good, Mahmud thought. That is how it should be. Fear him and fear me, for in fear lies respect, and in respect lies obedience.

He pounded through the door. Old Yakub, oblivious at first

to his presence, screamed out commands to rally fleeing comrades that had been dead some forty years.

'Steady, old friend,' Mahmud said, crouching down at the side of Yakub's mat. Behind him, standing fearfully out in the darkness, his guards cringed outside the doorway, peering in.

'Lie back and rest.' Mahmud stroked the old man's face and for the first time Yakub understood that he was there. Slowly his battle cries subsided into moans until at last he was silent. He let himself fall back, lying there exhausted. The fever would soon pass. Mahmud had seen it often enough to know this. The madness would never go, however. It was rooted too deeply in old Yakub's soul. The horrors he had seen had been too much for the poor fellow. Mahmud could understand this. Many of them he had seen himself, but in his own case experience had had cruder material to work with. It took imagination to corrupt the soul and destroy the mind as Yakub's mind had been destroyed. Mahmud, on the other hand, being intelligent but otherwise uncomplicated, was perfectly suited to war. The gore of battle was meat and drink to him. The tribesmen respected and followed Mahmud for his ferocity in battle. Yakub they venerated as a seer.

Mahmud turned to his men. 'Send the women with food and drink, and tell the elders to gather. I must inform them of what we are to do.'

One of his men dared to ask the question that was in all of their minds. 'Is it true then? Are they really coming back?'

Mahmud nodded. 'Yes. That is the news I was called to the river to receive.' He looked back at the old man who seemed to be sleeping peacefully once again. 'But how on earth he knew about it beforehand, I will never understand.'

Some of the younger guards looked excited, murmuring to one another 'Fighting! There's to be fighting!'

Overhearing, Mahmud turned to rebuke them but stopped himself. Let the young men rejoice in the prospect of combat, he reflected. They would learn soon enough that their dreams of glory had played them false. As such dreams always had. Since the earliest times when the unknown king of kings had laid the foundations of the city whose ruins lay less than a week's march from the village. The ruins that the tribe had been sworn to protect from intruders such as those who were even now making their way up the Nile.

Sir Hubert leaned over the lavatory and retched. His knuckles turned white as they clutched at the cool porcelain. Exhausted after an hour of this torture, he dropped to his knees, slumping forward until his forehead rested on the rear of the lavatory bowl. He gasped for breath, knowing that the respite would be short-lived, if the experience of the previous few days was anything to go by. The flesh had been falling off him and now when he observed himself in the mirror he was horrified by the gaunt spectre that returned his hollow-eyed stare. He had no idea how the food poisoning had occurred. He had been fastidious over his personal hygiene and had taken the greatest pains to ensure that the water he drank had first been boiled. Oddly, no one else on board had been similarly affected. Only him.

Feeling the tell-tale clenching of muscles deep in his abdomen, the familiar spasms, the waves of nausea that swept throughout his body and the prickling of a fresh outbreak of sweat on his dripping brow, Sir Hubert tightened his grip and arched his back in readiness for the next bout of vomiting.

When it came it was even more violent than the last. The whole business was aggravated by the motions of the vessel which had been negotiating a difficult complex of sand banks for the last hour. They were at a bend in the river where the currents were particularly disruptive. Everyone else was up on deck admiring the scenery. On one side of the river, sheer dun-coloured cliffs tumbled straight into the water, while on the opposite bank, a small settlement had disgorged its modest population of children who stood waving excitedly at the passing paddle steamer while their parents continued labouring stolidly in the fields just as the fellahin had been doing since the days of the pharaohs.

Wiping his mouth with a badly soiled towel, Sir Hubert rocked back on his heels and drew breath. In the background he was dimly aware that someone was rapping at his cabin door. He could not be bothered to respond. For all he cared they were welcome to come in and murder him.

'Anyone home?'

Sir Hubert's spirits sank even further. 'Go away, Caspasian.'

'Just thought I'd drop by to see how you are.'

'You mean you've come to gloat.'

'Nonsense. I've been afflicted like that myself in the past. You can't be too careful you know,' he said, his voice brimming with concern.

'I *was* bloody careful.' With that, Sir Hubert felt another wave of nausea approaching. His empty stomach clenched and he leaned forward, one hand miserably waving Caspasian from the room. Instead Caspasian stepped to his side, grasped the back of Sir Hubert's neck and thrust his face deeper into the bowl.

'Here, let me help.'

Sir Hubert toppled forward, hands scrabbling at Caspasian's trouser legs in a vain attempt to push him away, but vomiting got the better of him and he surrendered to the attack.

The second it had passed, he said, 'Just bugger off and leave me alone, will you?' His voice echoed strangely off the inside of the porcelain.

'Just trying to help,' Caspasian said innocently. 'Try this,' he concluded, holding out his open hand.

Sir Hubert craned his head round to inspect the offering. A small pile of black shavings lay in Caspasian's palm.

'I've already tried everything your medic had to offer. None of it did any good. What the devil's that?'

'Charcoal. I got it from the boiler room down below.'

'What am I supposed to do with it? Build a funeral pyre and throw myself on the top? You'd like that, wouldn't you?'

Caspasian chuckled pleasantly. 'Nonsense.' He squatted down beside Sir Hubert and held out the pile of charcoal, poking it with the finger of his other hand. 'They use it in Himalayan hill villages where there aren't any medicines. I've had to resort to it myself on more than one occasion. Never fails.'

'Never fails to what?' Sir Hubert asked sceptically. 'Never fails to bring about a slow and agonising death?' But his eyes were now fastened on the charcoal. Desperation had pushed him to an extreme where he was willing to believe in anything offered to him with at least a modicum of conviction. 'How do I take it?'

'Just chew it and swallow. Just a bit at a time. You can wash it down with a little water if it makes it any easier.'

Sir Hubert took a pinch of charcoal and did as he was told. Caspasian got to his feet and returned to the door.

'I'll pop in later to see how it's going.'

Sir Hubert did not reply. His face was scrunched up as he tried to force down the bitter shavings. As he did so he reflected on how much he hated Caspasian. The fellow simply was not to be trusted. How on earth he had ever managed to con someone into making him an officer was beyond Sir Hubert. To anyone of breeding it stood out a mile. Caspasian was not a gentleman. What kind of name was Caspasian anyway? To Sir Hubert it all sounded a bit dicey. It was the sort of name he would expect a tradesman to have. What was worse, the damned fellow had just witnessed Sir Hubert's humiliation. It was only as he mused upon this that it occurred to him that Caspasian had waited several days before offering the cure, if indeed it was a cure and not some further torment.

Amazingly, Sir Hubert found that he was indeed feeling a little better. Not much, but a little. With growing confidence he nibbled a few more charcoal shavings, grimacing as he crunched them between his teeth. Caspasian. Yes, some blasted tradesman. That must be it. Sir Hubert had a nose for such things. It was a wicked shame that a creature like him should be involved with such a prestigious expedition as this. That was the Professor's fault. He was the one who had insisted on Caspasian as their escort, but then as a dusty academic the Professor himself was little better. It was going to be up to Sir Hubert to maintain the tone of the expedition. And when they succeeded, as succeed they would, it would be up to him to front the numerous public appearances, interviews and newspaper articles. Caspasian could skulk back to whatever hole he had crawled out of. If he was still alive.

Up on deck, Caspasian had joined Béranger and Sergeant Kraus who were mustering the legionnaires and assembling their weapons, equipment and other stores in readiness for disembarkation the following morning. Machine guns had been stripped and the numerous individual parts laid out on canvas tarpaulins to be oiled before reassembly. Sergeant Ganga crouched down beside them inspecting the unfamiliar weaponry with rapt attention.

'So what did you give him?' Béranger asked nonchalantly as he leaned back against the rail beside Caspasian.

'Charcoal,' Caspasian replied.

Béranger smiled. 'No, I meant what did you give him before that?'

Caspasian was watching a legionnaire reassemble his M1892/16 carbine. 'I don't know what you're talking about.'

'A nice little dose of Nile river water?'

'Paul, what do you take me for?' Caspasian exclaimed with indignation. 'I wouldn't want to give Sir Hubert full blown amoebic dysentery, if only because I've got to take the bastard on a cross-desert march once we leave the steamer. The last thing I need is a chronically sick man on my hands.' He looked up at the sky where an egret was idly circling. 'Mind you, you've got to watch out for the Nile perch. It's a tasty enough fish if eaten fresh but leave it out in the sun for a bit, and it can play havoc with the stomach.'

'Like Ready Rations, no doubt,' Béranger observed.

Caspasian shrugged. 'I really couldn't say.'

That evening at dinner, the key members of the two expeditions gathered as usual in the dining room. The legionnaires and Gurkhas had eaten earlier and could now be heard gambling with dice and cards on the lower deck outside, closely supervised by Sergeant Kraus and Ganga who watched like hawks to ensure there were no disputes.

With Sir Hubert still out of action and Captain Yassos occupied on the bridge, Caspasian expected the gathering to be limited to himself, Béranger, the Professor and the Simonins. However, when Michelle Simonin appeared by herself, explaining that her husband was feeling a bit under the weather and would be taking a light supper in their cabin, Caspasian could not help noticing how his spirits lifted at the anticipation of a pleasant evening engagement in good company, conveniently pruned of all its disagreeable elements.

The Professor steadied the back of Michelle's chair as she sat down. She thanked him quietly and he occupied the seat next to her. Béranger and Caspasian sat on the opposite side, Caspasian discreetly ensuring that he ended up facing Michelle. As they settled for the meal, she glanced up at the same time as Caspasian. Their eyes met and she flashed a brief smile before turning to the Professor who had enquired after her own health.

'I am fine, thank you,' she replied. As she spoke, she reached up and brushed her hair back from her face. Caspasian noticed the slender wrist and the delicate bone structure of her hand. Her profile was exquisite and her hair shone.

'In fact,' she continued, 'I have found the whole of this voyage entrancing. It is amazing to think that life alongside the river has changed little since ancient times. And the wildlife is spectacular.'

'You have not been frightened by Captain Yassos' tales of crocodiles?' Béranger teased.

Michelle laughed. '*Pas du tout.*'

Caspasian was aware that he was probably staring at her but was unable to wrench his eyes away. He loved the way her lips pouted as she answered Béranger. Separated from her husband she became an altogether different woman. Suddenly she turned towards him and discovered his intimate attention. Instead of being embarrassed or affronted, she smiled and addressed him.

'So who do you think will discover the lost city first, Captain Caspasian? The French or the British?' There was a twinkle in her eye but the question was in no way mocking.

Extraordinarily, Caspasian was overwhelmed by the feeling that she was somehow the older and more experienced of the two of them. There was something in her tone and in her manner that was far beyond her years. He could attribute some of this to the hard lessons that life married to a monster like Simonin must have taught her. He well knew that there was nothing like disillusionment to age the spirit. But it was more than this, for shining through the disillusionment was another quality, surprising in a girl of Michelle's unfortunate marital circumstances. It was strength of character and, combined with it, was a mature humour. There was a resilience in her, a refusal to be broken. To this Caspasian warmed.

'The Professor has yet to convince me that there is anything to be discovered, Madame.'

'Please,' she interceded, 'call me Michelle.'

A waiter had arrived and was busy serving them with brown Windsor soup. Béranger frowned at the unpromising liquid, nudging his bowl and noting the sluggish motion of the contents.

The Professor wagged a finger at his fellow diners. 'I have been disappointed to discover that Captain Caspasian is a cynic, Michelle. He does not believe in the vision of glory I see before us all.'

'Before the French, you mean,' Béranger corrected.

'As you will,' the Professor conceded. 'My point is, you have first to believe if you are to achieve anything.'

'Well, you see Professor,' Caspasian said. 'That's where we part company, you and I. I am just a simple soldier with a job to do. If I can get you, Sir Hubert and the rest of the party into and out of the desert safely, then I will have achieved the only thing I need to. I will leave the visions to you.'

Caspasian noticed that Michelle's handbag lay in her lap and that she kept one arm looped through the shoulder strap. It was the same one that had been snatched by the thief in the Cairo market and that she had risked her life to retain. Suddenly she looked up and caught the direction of his gaze. Her smile stiffened slightly and she shifted the bag so that it was out of sight.

For the main course the cook had prepared roast pigeon. They were easy to come by as most of the Nile villages bred them. Arrayed on a giant platter, they were brought in with great ceremony, dishes of ladies' fingers, stuffed courgettes, egg plant, lentils and mountains of saffron rice accompanying them. To one side the cook placed a ta'miya dip and, to eat with it, a wonderfully coarse bread pungent with fenugreek. Béranger produced two bottles of red wine which he directed one of the waiters to serve.

The Professor held up his glass for a toast. 'To the success of our expeditions. May the mystery of King Menes be solved once and for all.'

'And may we all return alive to celebrate it,' Béranger added.

'I'll drink to that,' Caspasian agreed, raising his glass to Michelle. She smiled at him and reached across the table to chink glasses.

After the meal, while the Professor and Béranger settled themselves with cognac and cigars, Michelle made her excuses, thanked the gentlemen for their company over dinner and left the room. Caspasian remained for only a couple of minutes more himself and then left too. As expected, he found Michelle outside on the deck. She was standing by the rail with arms folded, the small bag clasped in her hands, staring out across the moonlit Nile at the passing landscape. A stand of tall date palms was silhouetted against the darkening sky which was fighting off stars without success. A swarm of white ibis homed in on a cluster of trees and off to one side the iridescent flash of a passing kingfisher shot through the dusk like miniature lightning.

Caspasian moved towards her, coughing quietly to announce his presence. She half turned, registered his proximity, and returned to her contemplation of the night. The giant paddles at the stern of the vessel slapped the water's surface rhythmically, the noise of the engines muffled almost into silence deep in the bowels of the steamer.

Before Caspasian could speak, Michelle said, 'It's a peaceful sound, isn't it? I could stand here all night listening to it.'

Caspasian agreed. He could also imagine that a night long vigil at the rail must surely be preferable to whatever might be awaiting the young woman back in her cabin where Émile Simonin would be biding his time, nursing his appetites in anticipation of his wife's return. He fumbled around for something fitting to say but, finding nothing, simply placed himself by her side as if such a gesture might be interpreted as a demonstration of understanding and sympathy. It was.

Michelle hugged herself and shivered. 'Isn't it extraordinary how the temperature drops after nightfall?'

'Just wait until you get into the desert,' Caspasian said.

'Yes. I am looking forward to it but I am also a bit frightened,' she confided.

'Béranger will look after you,' Caspasian said, instantly regretting sounding so glib and cheery.

'I know he will. You knew each other in the war?' Michelle asked.

'Briefly.'

She paused and Caspasian suspected that she was weighing her next statement carefully before entrusting it to him.

'Verdun,' she said at last, exhaling a deep breath like a confession. The single word seemed to drain her, for a long moment leaving only a husk.

Caspasian glanced down at her arms where the small hand-bag was invisible. A faint glimmer of understanding entered his mind. 'It almost broke the French Army,' he said.

Still with eyes fixed on the fading riverbank Michelle said, 'It did break my family. It broke me.'

'And yet you are here.'

Michelle laughed, a hard heavy sound that Caspasian felt should not have come from a woman like her. 'As you say, Captain. I am here.' She said it with finality as if announcing a death sentence, or like a doctor informing a patient that the illness is terminal.

'Who did you lose at Verdun?' Caspasian ventured to ask.

'My father and all three of my brothers.'

For a moment Caspasian wondered if she was about to break down, but with a mounting sense of outrage he realised that she had long ago moved beyond such collapses. He realised that he was seeing a woman who had endured her fill of hurt. And she had lived on.

Lost for words he resorted to a mumbled, 'I'm so sorry.' Although it sounded hollow to him, Michelle dipped her head in grateful acknowledgement.

'I was not the only one to suffer,' she said.

'Indeed,' Caspasian admitted. 'But all suffering comes down to things like this, doesn't it? Lots and lots of individual losses. Individual tragedies.'

Michelle shrugged agreement, completely dry-eyed.

'Do you have a photograph?' Caspasian asked, indicating the handbag.

'Yes,' she replied, but made no move to share it with him.

'And Monsieur Simonin?' Caspasian persevered, aware that he might be chancing his arm too far, but desperate to know more about Michelle.

She heaved a deep sigh. 'Monsieur Simonin is my husband,' she said bitterly. She turned to look Caspasian full in the face. And he understood. He was desperate to know how such a woman as Michelle had ended up married to a creature like Simonin but, after all, did it really matter? The fact was that they were married. In the tragedy of their situation it was almost an irrelevance how it had come about. Numerous women had been forced to save themselves from a life of poverty through convenient marriages after the war had robbed them of their loved ones. The reasons for a tragedy did nothing to resolve it, just as the reasons for a thunderstorm did nothing to stop the lightning from cracking open the sky.

'Once again, Madame,' Caspasian said, 'I am so sorry.'

Again she laughed, this time less bitter. She even reached out and placed a hand on Caspasian's shoulder as if consoling him. As if it had been him who had suffered the hurt.

'Do not be, Captain. The world continues to turn and the river runs on,' she said gesturing at the Nile below them. 'I used to be unable to see how it could. But it does. The experience of every individual day teaches me that. That, if little else.'

'Indeed, Michelle.' Then, as an afterthought, he added, 'If there is anything I can do . . . ever . . . you have only to ask.'

Uncertain himself what he had exactly meant by that, and of the extent of his self-imposed commitment, he was grateful when Michelle accepted the offer with a grateful bow of her head. For although both of them knew that the statement could lead nowhere, both also knew where it had come from. From a past of hurts and loss that had been, in spirit, common to both of them. And in such a recognition they established contact. In the silence there was a momentary communion between them, a recognised understanding, that lasted only until Michelle turned abruptly on her heel and walked resolutely away along the deck in the direction of her cabin and of her husband.

9

By the time the steamer docked at Abu el Said the following morning, Béranger had his men already paraded on deck with their packs on and stores assembled for offloading. Over their khaki drill uniforms they wore the loose linen sand-coloured gandourah that had become popular for desert campaigns, a lightweight baggy overcoat with ample pockets. Round their necks each man had wound his chèche, the pale khaki desert scarf. Each regiment of the Legion had its own way of wearing it. For some it went round the neck, for others it was worn crossed over the chest, the two ends tucked into the waist belt. Still others looped it round the head in the manner of a Tuareg warrior. In combat it doubled as field dressing, bandage or sling.

Every képi sported a pale khaki cover and neck flap, and both Kraus and Béranger had managed to get hold of motoring goggles for use in a strong wind.

Slung over every man's shoulder was the thick sausage-shaped barda, the bed roll that had replaced the knapsack, the '*boudin*' of the Legion marching song. Each one was a tent section which could be buttoned together with others to form a shelter. In it, blanket and greatcoat were rolled, together with spare clothing and mess tin. The whole effect was cumbersome, uncomfortable and swelteringly hot on a desert march, all of which contributed to the irony of '*Le Boudin*'.

Béranger had ensured that all his men were armed with carbines instead of the older Lebel and Berthier rifles, and for heavier fire support they had Chauchat light machine guns and the Hotchkiss MMG. Simonin had scoffed at this as excessive but Béranger had ignored him.

A wire had been sent ahead so that a score of porters and camels was awaiting the vessel in readiness for the start of the land journey.

The Simonins were the last to appear. Michelle was dressed in a pair of jodhpurs, ankle-length brown leather riding boots, cream-coloured cotton blouse and dark brown sun hat. She had tied her hair in a bun, fixing it in place beneath the hat's brim. Over her arm she carried a light jacket and around her neck she wore a loose patterned scarf that she could pull up to cover her mouth and nose when the ride became dusty. Watching her, Caspasian noticed that the handbag had been replaced by a small brown leather pouch fastened to her belt.

Monsieur Simonin was fussing over their personal luggage which now consisted of numerous cow-hide Gladstone bags and several rucksacks into all of which the contents of the portmanteaus had been laboriously decanted. Caspasian could not imagine that Monsieur Simonin had any intention of actually carrying any of them himself.

As the gangplanks were swung across and secured, the legionnaires swarmed ashore, eager to be getting on with the expedition. The long river journey had been constraining for them and they reminded Caspasian of hounds being unleashed.

'Go steady with those bags!' Monsieur Simonin shrieked as four of the newly hired porters clambered over the piles of baggage, seeking out the easiest carries and jogging back ashore with them. In his haste, one of the porters overbalanced and watched in horror as his load slipped from his grasp and splashed into the foaming water swilling between the sides of the steamer and the shore.

'Idiot!' Simonin called, hands clasped to the sides of his face as if suffering from acute toothache. 'Béranger, sort him out.'

Béranger, already on dry land, stared hard at Simonin and then waded into the water up to his knees until he was able to reach out and retrieve the bobbing package.

The Professor stood with Caspasian and Ganga to bid their French competitors farewell. Caspasian heard a door slam behind him and turned round to see Sir Hubert wobbling into the daylight, shielding his eyes against the glare. His cheeks were hollow and his complexion ashen, but life had returned to his tongue at least.

'Are those buggers off at last?'

'Our French friends are departing, if that's what you mean,' the Professor chided good-naturedly.

Sir Hubert grunted. 'Taking that Kraut Kraus with them I hope. Too bad about the filly, though,' he said, leering at Michelle. 'I rather fancied a piece of that myself.' He rubbed his unshaven chin, the finger nails rasping like crickets. 'That lucky bastard, Simonin. How does a fat slob like him end up . . .'

'I think there's some kedgeree left on the breakfast table, Sir Hubert,' Caspasian said sharply. 'It's a bit cold and the fish oil's congealed but I can have some brought to you if you want.'

Sir Hubert wavered on his uncertain feet and blew out his cheeks. 'Don't . . . I . . .'

'The chef's even sliced some hard-boiled eggs into it. One of them was a bit runny, but I find it so much more complete with egg, don't you?'

Waving him quiet, Sir Hubert spun away and fled, unable to speak. Caspasian looked at the Professor and shrugged. 'Was it something I said?'

The Professor shook his head dismally. 'I can see I'm going to have fun with you two. Please can you just try and get along together, at least until the expedition's over? That's all I ask. It isn't much, is it?'

'With a man like Sir Hubert it's asking a very great deal,' Caspasian answered solemnly. 'But I'll try.'

'Good.'

Caspasian turned his attention to Ganga. 'How are the men?'

'All fine, saheb.'

'Really?'

Ganga grinned. 'Well, you know what Gurkhas are like on the water. Everyone will be glad to get ashore.'

'Just another two days. We'll be going for the city from a different angle than the French. Our two different routes will be like the two sides of a triangle, converging on pretty much the same point. Monsieur Simonin and the Professor disagree over the exact location but personally I think they're all wasting their time.'

'Just point us in the direction and we'll march, you know us, saheb.'

He saluted and left. Caspasian looked out over the quayside watching the French expedition get under way. Béranger and Sergeant Kraus had imposed order on the chaos that had greeted them when they had arrived, and Monsieur Simonin was now being manhandled onto a kneeling camel. Four legionnaires were at work on the project which was taxing their ingenuity as well as their muscles. Caspasian searched the crowd that was standing around the spectacle, everyone offering advice at the top of their voice, and suddenly found Michelle. She was standing to one side, ignoring her husband, and instead was watching Caspasian. He was instantly relieved that he had not been grinning at Monsieur Simonin's predicament. However, as he returned Michelle's gaze levelly, he saw the corner of her mouth twitch. The next moment she was smiling. As if in concert, there was a roar of outrage from the camel as it was goaded to its feet by a variety of sticks wielded by the handler and a lively group of children gathered around him. The legionnaires stood back, perspiring, to observe their handiwork, and like the erection of a giant marquee, Monsieur Simonin rose shakily atop the protesting camel.

Caspasian returned the smile warmly. Michelle's eyes held his a moment longer and then she turned away, gathering her things and walking across to where Béranger was readying her own beast and handler. Within half an hour the French expedition had gone, disappearing out through the houses of the settlement in the direction of the desert. On Béranger's orders, Sergeant Kraus bellowed the opening lines of '*Le Boudin*' and as the legionnaires stepped out at their unique slow marching pace, arms and open hands swinging at their sides, they sang, the words pounding the hot air like the beats of a drum.

With the French expedition departed, the attention of those left on the quayside switched back to the paddle steamer as Captain Yassos ordered the gangplanks to be withdrawn and the ropes to be cast off. The giant wheel at the stern ground into action, churning the water, and with a blast on the whistle the vessel put out into the middle of the river and set off again, heading south up the Nile. A great cheer went up from the villagers and along the deck the Gurkhas waved back.

The following two days passed painfully slowly for Caspasian. He was anxious to get going and was surprised to find himself subjected to nagging fears that the French expedition really might find something out in the desert, and before the British team. While he was careful to keep such thoughts to himself, he could tell that both the Professor and Sir Hubert were worrying along similar lines. Meal times became silent affairs, conversation reduced to the polite. Eventually Caspasian excused himself from them altogether, electing to take his meals with Sergeant Ganga and the men where livelier chatter prevailed. It was reminiscent of life on operations on the North-West Frontier, sitting cross-legged in a circle over mess tins of steaming rice and lentils, talking about everything and nothing. Hearing the gossip from the men's villages. Whose wife had given birth, whose farm had suffered a landslide, whose father was pressing his son to send money to buy land to add to the family plot. It was all part of the communication between an officer and his men that Caspasian so loved, in contrast to his less fluent communications with his brother officers in the mess. Somehow that had never achieved the same levels of ease.

Finally the day came when, with a blast on the whistle, the steamer announced its approach to Al-Balis. As had happened with the arrival of the French expedition, the village emptied its occupants onto the quayside to greet the vessel. Caspasian, Ganga and the Gurkhas had been up since first light preparing the stores so that, on docking, they would be able to set out promptly. For the soldiers' breakfast, Ganga ordered a brew of tea and a large basket of chapatis. Caspasian stood on the deck, a mug in one hand and a rolled chapati in the other. He had ambushed the ship's cook on his way to the main dining room bearing a large dish of kedgeree and had spooned a generous helping into a mess tin. Now, with some of it scooped and rolled into his chapati, he ate happily, hugely relieved to be on the verge of activity once again.

It was distressing therefore when Sir Hubert failed to make an appearance, even after the stores had been transported ashore and loaded onto the waiting camels, and everyone else, the Professor included, was ready for departure.

'Where the devil is the man?' Caspasian asked angrily as he paced the quayside. A few yards off, the camels roared and belched, sleepy eyelids drooping deceptively. Venturing close to one of them out of curiosity, Bharat peered at the scruffy hump. With surprising speed the affronted animal swung its head round and bit him. With a yelp, Rifleman Bharat jumped away.

Out of patience, Caspasian strode back up the nearest of the gangplanks and thundered down the deck in the direction of Sir Hubert's cabin. He banged on the door and went straight in. There was no one there. Sir Hubert's personal baggage had already been conveyed ashore and loaded onto the camels and the cabin offered no clue as to his whereabouts.

Captain Yassos leaned over the rail from the bridge above and asked what the matter was. He was anxious to get under way on the return journey to Cairo where he had a new cargo awaiting. He was unable to help Caspasian but pointedly inspected his watch and scowled impatiently.

Shinning down the steps to the lower deck, Caspasian made his way to the dining room and burst through the door. Sir Hubert sat calmly at the breakfast table, legs crossed, his chair pushed back and an old paper lying open on his uppermost knee. He looked up irritably as Caspasian tumbled into the room.

'Caspasian! Whatever are you playing at?'

Caspasian stared at him. 'Everyone's waiting for you. The camels are loaded. We're waiting to go.'

'Jolly good. I'm delighted to hear it. However, it may have escaped your notice, but I have been ill these last few days. Now, for the first time, my appetite has returned and I'm damned if I'm about to say goodbye to civilisation without first enjoying a hearty breakfast.' He craned round in his chair to survey the sideboard where an array of silver dishes steamed pleasantly. 'There are some damned fine devilled kidneys left and I fully intend to finish them and have another cup of coffee before joining you.'

Caspasian blinked, lost for words. He felt his gorge rise and fought to keep his temper under control. Outside in the full glare of the sun, the Professor, Ganga and the rest of the Gurkhas were waiting as the heat started its inexorable rise towards the crescendo it would reach around the middle of the day.

For several seconds Sir Hubert returned Caspasian's stare. Then, with calculated disdain, he said, 'Run along now. There's a good chap,' and returned to his paper, humming merrily to himself.

Caspasian contemplated the dish of devilled kidneys and imagined it upturned on Sir Hubert's neatly trimmed head. He pictured the coffee cascading down Sir Hubert's crisp white shirt front, and finally he toyed with the image of Sir Hubert gliding magnificently over the side of the paddle steamer into the gilded water swilling around the outlet to the village's archaic sewage system.

'Are you still here?' Sir Hubert said without taking his eyes off his paper.

With a heavy sigh of regret, Caspasian surrendered his visions and withdrew from the dining room, closing the door calmly behind him before his instincts got the better of him. In the village square adjoining the quayside, the Professor looked at him quizzically when he returned.

'Still at breakfast?' he asked.

Caspasian nodded. The Professor smiled pleasantly and patted Caspasian on the shoulder. 'I'm afraid this won't be the first time you will have to remind yourself that working alongside civilians is a very different kettle of fish to operating in a purely military environment. Things simply don't always happen when you expect them to. Certainly not when dealing with an aristocrat who is bankrolling the expedition. To an extent we are all in his hands.'

'For now perhaps,' Caspasian said solemnly. 'For now.'

In the desert village excitement had reigned ever since Mahmud's return. All the men of fighting age had occupied themselves with preparations. The vast array of firearms had been cleaned and cleaned again. While rust was not much of a problem in the dryness of the desert, sand was. It seeped into every part of a rifle, insinuating itself into the breech, the magazine, into the barrel. Unless a weapon was regularly checked, stoppages would occur. And if the moving parts of a weapon jammed at the crucial moment, it could mean the difference between life and death.

To ensure that everyone in the tribe was ready for the encounter with the intruders, Mahmud had planned a modest training exercise. They were to mount a raid on an opposing tribe more than a hundred miles to the south of their own village. They were people with whom Mahmud had been in savage conflict before, contesting rights of access to wells that fell ambiguously where their two territories marched. Disputes had erupted into violent confrontation every two years or so. Now however, Mahmud decided it was timely to initiate a small containable tribal war. It would serve to harden the men and sift out any who might not have stomach enough for a serious fight.

Yakub had recovered since his previous bout of fever and, as was usual when he was well, the young men had insisted on taking him along with them. He was viewed as talisman rather than mascot, and for him to witness their prowess in battle was considered the height of good fortune. It was as if it sanctified it, all of which served Mahmud's wider purpose admirably.

For the raid, Mahmud assembled some five hundred warriors, calling them in from outlying villages and establishing rendezvous points with them where the force would gather, swelling in size at each muster. As they grew in number, the warriors' aggression mounted. Spirits soared. They were free of village life, free of their wives and children who remained securely behind. Free of the cares of everyday humdrum existence. Life accelerated as the mission brought a welcome intensity to their daily routines. It was as if they were being focused under a magnifying glass, concentrating into a fine laser's point. When they came into contact with the selected enemy, fire would burst forth as a result, and in the conflagration they would be purified. Or killed, Mahmud recognised. But then perhaps it was all the same thing.

As they approached the territory of the opposing tribe, they reversed their march routine, travelling by night and lying up during the day. Night-time riding was the easiest. A clear sky specked with stars was like a route map laid out above them, with directional arrows to follow. Furthermore, the chill of the night kept them alert. There was little chance of dozing off when the teeth were chattering and the cloak was clenched tight about the shoulders.

When the first signs of the rising sun were detected, Mahmud would send scouts hurrying ahead to locate a lying-up place where the force might rest throughout the scorching daylight hours. Usually mountainous jebel offered plenty of shelter. A steep-sided ravine might be secured with sentries placed on the highest vantage points. Then a meal could be prepared, followed by a welcome sleep. When they were close to the enemy, cooking fires were prohibited and the men fed on cold rice, salted goat meat, unleavened bread, dates and figs.

As evening approached and the sky darkened, preparations would be made for the coming night's ride. Camels would be saddled, weapons checked and cleared of sand, baggage packed and stowed. Once the dark had completely fallen and the stars were all in place, the journey would recommence, only this time made even more intense by the closer proximity to the enemy and to action.

Finally the day came when they had crossed the tribal border and closed to within a mile of the enemy village. Scouts had already pinpointed the location and reported that many of the menfolk appeared to be absent, possibly on a raid of their own elsewhere in the vast desert. Mahmud gathered his commanders and issued his orders for the attack. The aim was to seize cattle, to kill anyone offering resistance, and to withdraw before the main body of the enemy could be summoned home.

It was decided to attack shortly before last light. That way they could complete the raid in daylight and then take advantage of darkness to make good their escape. It would be difficult for anyone to follow them and by dawn they would be well away, their booty secure in their possession.

The long day's wait was the hardest of all, lying quietly in a ravine within striking distance of the enemy's village. Shortly after midday an old shepherd stumbled into the mouth of the ravine, preceded by his herd of goats. He stared dumbstruck at the assault force mustered in the shade, but was seized before he could run and raise the alarm.

'What shall we do with him?' one of the older men questioned.

Mahmud singled out one of the boldest of the young fighters, a youth who had been bragging of the men he would kill. 'You,' he said, 'kill him.'

The youth stared back at him, horrified. He did not move.

'What's the matter? Kill him, I said.'

'But he's only an old man. And unarmed. A prisoner.'

Mahmud closed upon him, shoving his face inches from the youth's. 'We have had to listen to your boasts. It's time you learnt what killing's really like. Now do it.'

He drew his own knife and handed it, hilt first, to the youth who stared at it as if it was a writhing viper he was being offered.

'I will not order you again,' Mahmud said quietly, his voice brimming with menace.

Slowly, the youth reached out and accepted the knife into his own palm. His fingers closed about the hilt. He clenched it in his fist and made it his. Going up to the old shepherd, he looked briefly in the man's eyes, but only briefly, and quickly thrust the knife in deep. It was a messy blow. The old man staggered back, injured, but not fatally.

In a second Mahmud was on the youth, kicking him and slapping him hard with his open hands, cursing and swearing at him. The youth backed away and then, when Mahmud gave him a pause, closed upon the old shepherd to complete his task. This time he gripped the man from behind and drew the knife across his throat as if slaughtering a sheep. In his death throes, with strength drawn from desperation, the shepherd spun round in the youth's grasp and sprayed him with bright scarlet fountains of blood. The youth dropped the knife and staggered backwards, tripping and falling as the old man grovelled and scrabbled in the sand, finally dying.

'My knife,' Mahmud prompted.

The youth stared in horror at the implement, blood-drenched sand matting its handle and blade. Slowly he ventured towards it and picked it up.

'Clean it,' Mahmud said as the youth approached him. The youth wiped it clean on his own garments, then handed it to Mahmud.

'You will now bury the body and sit by the grave until we are ready to move off. Think about what you have done. Think about the life you have just ended. And before you brag next time, remember all of this. Remember it well. Death is not a game.'

Shaking, the youth went across to the corpse and heaved it away. One of the commanders came up beside Mahmud, concerned. 'How will he fight, after this?'

'With a care, I hope. Bravely, but with a care.'

When Mahmud judged the moment had come, he signalled the men to prepare themselves. Everyone mounted their camels and goaded them to rise. Rifles were drawn from their holders and couched in laps, cocked and ready.

With a final glance around the assembled force, Mahmud turned to Yakub. The old man sat very erect, legs crossed, bare feet in the crook of the camel's leathery neck. He stared straight ahead, piercing eyes locked on something only he could see, a beatific smile lighting his whole face. Suddenly, he put back his head and cried out, a long unintelligible wailing sound that made even the hardiest warrior shiver.

'It is time!' Mahmud shouted. 'Yakub has given us the signal. We attack!'

With shrieks and yells, the entire force set their sticks to the camels' hides and charged from the ravine. In the village everyone was resting at the end of the day. Cooking fires had been lit, menfolk were gathered around in small groups discussing the day's events and exchanging gossip, while their women prepared the evening meals.

As the sound of the approaching force grew louder, people stopped what they were doing. They stood up, curious and alert, wondering. Then, as understanding dawned, panic broke like a torrent sweeping throughout the settlement. Men ran for their rifles, women gathered up their children and herded them into their houses, dogs barked maniacally and goats, sheep and camels scattered.

By the time the leading elements of the raiding party broke into the outskirts of the village, the first of the defenders had retrieved their weapons and were already firing the opening rounds of the battle. Beside Mahmud one man fell, struck in the centre of the chest. Then another toppled from his saddle to be trampled under the hooves of the following beasts. Mahmud's men aimed and fired as they rode, most shots going wide of their marks, but one or two finding their target.

Beside Mahmud, old Yakub rose in his saddle and whooped, whirling his riding crop around his head as if at a celebration. Only Mahmud could recognise the old man's battle cries. To the young men they were unintelligible mantras. Among them was the war cry of the Hadendowahs, the most feared warriors of the Mahdi that had struck terror into the redcoats all those years ago when Yakub had been a young man. But here there was no steel-tipped infantry square to be broken. Here there were not Gatlings or Martini-Henrys volley firing with the iron discipline of the hated British soldiers. Here there were only tribesmen, and it was not long before the shock of the surprise attack had turned the tide, routing the makeshift defence and reducing it to a slaughter.

'Secure the livestock,' Mahmud ordered. 'We have not come here solely to prepare ourselves for the real fight that is to come. We will return home brimful with gifts.'

'What of the women and children?' one of his commanders asked him.

'Leave them,' Mahmud ordered. 'And leave whichever of the men throw down their rifles and surrender. We will take their guns and ammunition with us, but we will not inflict a massacre.'

The commander looked at Mahmud doubtfully but one fiery glance from Mahmud was sufficient to send him on his way, disseminating the order down through the ranks.

Settling his camel beside that of Yakub, Mahmud regarded the old man warmly. Yakub was smiling at the fighting before him, the blazing dwellings, the prone bodies, encompassing everything with the same peaceful contemplation. Mahmud understood that Yakub was barely there. His tortured mind was raking through the embers of its own past ruin and had for the moment produced something of harmony with which it could toy. The savagery now present on all sides was not even a distraction. With a sigh, Mahmud returned to the battle, now drawing to its natural conclusion, wondering at the regret he detected in a part of his own mind that, unlike Yakub, he was not able sometimes similarly to escape. Madness was a refuge as well as a curse. And after all, it was the search for a refuge that had brought old Yakub to the tribe all those years before. But that was a long time ago. For now there were cattle to be gathered and arrangements to be made for the return home, before the main fighting force of the enemy came back to find their village laid waste.

10

The desert was not as Michelle had expected it. Riding some way behind her husband, she had finally got used to the strange motions of the camel, and was now looking around her with interest, shielding her eyes with one hand, while guiding the ungainly beast with the other. Fortunately, Béranger had insisted that a handler should walk beside the camel's head to ensure that Michelle was not caught off guard by the creature's wayward nature. From time to time the man would look up at her, grinning wickedly, his eyes straying unashamedly to the outline of her breasts and to her slim waist. Michelle had scowled at him at first but as it seemed to encourage the man, she was now doing her best to ignore him.

Being her first real excursion into a desert, she had imagined golden rolling sand dunes, clusters of waving date palms grouped around the neatly circular pool of an oasis, colourful Arab tents leaning on poles and guy ropes. All the trappings, in fact, of Rudolph Valentino's *The Sheikh*. Instead they had entered an ugly wilderness of rock and sand, where sheer walls reared up, culminating in jaggedly flat summits. The cliffs rose straight out of the desert floor and were more of a reddish colour than gold. There was not a palm tree in sight, and certainly no limpid pools of water or Arab tents, as in her mind's eye.

Nevertheless, though ugly it was exciting. She was on an adventure and ever since girlhood she had dreamed of such things. Somehow it seemed unreal to be involved in one at last. She felt as if she kept wanting to pinch herself to understand that it was actually happening. She really was here in Egypt, on a camel in the desert, riding in the company of legionnaires in search of a lost city and the undiscovered tomb of a legendary king.

She smiled to herself at the thought of it, and then, noticing the handler walking below grinning at her anew, she drew her scarf haughtily over her nose and mouth, fixing them in place to achieve a modicum of privacy. Unconsciously she reached down and touched the pouch at her belt, wondering whether they would be proud of her if they could see her at that moment.

The nights were the most splendid she had ever experienced however. Being far removed from civilisation, the night sky was the clearest she had ever seen. Without the corrupting influence of a city's lights, the sky was a rim to rim profusion of stars, sharp and crystal clear. The camp fires countered some of the effect, but as Michelle discovered, one had only to move a small distance away from them in order to view the sky in all its beauty. There was something extraordinarily primitive about it. Sitting by herself away from the others, arms locked about her knees, she felt there was almost no separation in time between herself and those unknown people who had first constructed the Nile civilisation all those millennia ago. Indeed, it was as if she and they were living concurrently, all of them staring out into the same muddled pinpricks of light.

Her contemplation was interrupted one night as she sat quietly by herself after supper. The fires were being allowed to die down, and behind her she could hear the laughter and chat of the legionnaires and the Arab porters and guides. Her husband was holding forth about something or other, and Béranger was disputing with him in his own inimitable way, resisting robustly, yet with a tact and discretion that Michelle had found surprising in a soldier.

A pebble suddenly rolled to the ground in front of her, coming from the top of a sand dune that disappeared into the darkness. It was followed by a small cascade of sand like a miniature landslide. Michelle started and sat up, alert. She stared hard into the darkness but could see nothing beyond the vague shapes of the dune before her.

'Is anyone there?' she called out tentatively, but then realised the stupidity of the enquiry as anyone who might be hiding in the darkness would not only be unlikely to answer her, but in all probability would speak neither French nor English.

Slowly she got to her feet. She took a few steps forward before realising the pointless risk she was taking. There were a score of armed men at the camp fires behind her. She walked briskly back to the encampment. Sergeant Kraus was the first to see her approaching.

'Is everything all right, Madame?' he asked.

Michelle smiled, a little embarrassed. 'I thought I heard something. There was a stone, it . . .' her explanation petered out as she heard herself speak to the gathering, all suddenly silent and expectant. She understood how she must resemble a frightened little girl. True to the impression, her husband clucked indulgently.

'*Ma chérie*, I am sure there is nothing to be afraid of. You are safe amongst the men,' he said, including himself generously as one of the group.

Béranger retrieved his pistol from the holster lying beside his bed roll. 'Kraus, bring two men with you. Let's take a look.'

Monsieur Simonin started to object, but Béranger was adamant. 'I would rather be certain. I will sleep easier.' He smiled at Michelle and guided her along with him. 'Show me the place.'

Michelle led them back to where she had been sitting and pointed out the small sand slide. 'It is probably just a desert fox or something,' she said dismissively.

Béranger and the legionnaires left her where she was, her husband hovering in the background, reluctant all of a sudden to continue as one of the group. With Kraus leading the way, the legionnaires made their way out into the darkness. 'Spread out,' Kraus called.

While Michelle waited, she heard their footfalls and further pebbles rolled down into the light cast by the distant camp fires behind her.

'Over here,' Kraus's voice called.

'What have you got?' Michelle heard Béranger respond.

'Come and see.'

It was several minutes before the search party returned and when they did, they came from an altogether different direction. Monsieur Simonin looked round in surprise. 'Whatever is it, Béranger? You've quite frightened Michelle.'

Michelle glanced at her husband indignantly, but Béranger's thoughts were elsewhere, a look of deep concern furrowing his brow. 'I'm afraid it was no desert fox, Michelle. Kraus has found footprints and, further away in a gully, hoof prints. It seems someone's been reconnoitring our encampment. They didn't expect anyone to be this far out and you surprised them,' he said, patting Michelle on the arm. 'Well done.'

Monsieur Simonin's face fell. 'Who ever would want to creep up on us?' He scowled. 'You don't think it's that wretched Professor and his British team, do you? Spying on us?'

Béranger did not even bother to reply. Instead he spoke urgently to Kraus. 'I want the sentries doubled tonight, and each post is to have a machine gun fully deployed and ready to fire. Site them to cover all the main approaches. Everyone else is to have their weapons at hand. Tell the men to dig shell scrapes, and prepare some for Madame and Monsieur Simonin too. Is that clear?'

'Yes, *mon Capitaine*.' Sergeant Kraus saluted and jogged away to brief his men.

To Michelle's relief the rest of the night passed without incident. However, at first light, when Béranger sent out a small clearing patrol to circuit the camp's perimeter, they came back with even more alarming news. It appeared that not only had the camp been thoroughly reconnoitred during the night, but intruders had crept right in amongst the tethered camels and stores and helped themselves to some of the rations. Strangely this seemed to cheer Béranger.

'It shows they were probably just harmless thieves.'

'Harmless thieves!' Monsieur Simonin said, outraged. 'It is obvious you are not financing this expedition out of your own pocket, Capitaine.'

'Nor are you, Monsieur,' Béranger said with surprising lack of concern.

Monsieur Simonin started to object but Béranger was already engaged elsewhere, overseeing the dismantling of the camp and the preparations for the day's journey.

As the day wore on, Michelle noticed how Béranger and Kraus had adjusted the order of march to bring her, her husband and the pack animals to the centre of the column. Legionnaires had been placed round the outside in a loose cordon, pushing out quite some distance on the flanks. Whenever the terrain opened out, Béranger would send the flank guards even further afield to scout any position from which an observer might take pot shots at the column. When the landscape closed in, men were put out to act as pickets, occupying the high ground as the main body passed by below.

As the heat intensified, Monsieur Simonin forgot his earlier concern and instead concentrated on his own physical discomfort and misery. Michelle was seldom without his moaning and complaints at her side, until, making some excuse or other, she goaded her camel into a trot and, leaving both her handler and husband behind, moved forward to join Béranger at the head of the column. Monsieur Simonin protested and attempted to follow, but without success.

Béranger looked round as Michelle rode up beside him and, with great skill, managed to slow her camel to a walk. She settled back with a broad proud smile.

'You are getting the hang of this admirably, Madame,' Béranger said.

'I am doing my best. This must all be very routine for you.'

'The desert is never routine. Anyone who treats it as such is sure to die young,' Béranger said.

'Do you know how lucky you are, Capitaine?' Michelle said.

'Yes, Madame. I do. Which is why I chose this life. I may never end my days a rich man, but I will have lived well. I will have seen things ordinary occupations never put in the way of other men.'

'But do you not miss the company of a wife?'

Béranger laughed. 'How do you know I am not married?'

Michelle pondered. 'Call it a woman's intuition.'

'And you are exactly correct, Madame. Marriage and the Legion have always been uncomfortable bedfellows.'

'Is it the same for all soldiers?'

Béranger glanced at Michelle but she was studiously gazing out across the sand. 'I can't say, Madame. The Legion is probably the most unfriendly towards marriage. But soldiering, in whatever army, is an odd quixotic sort of occupation.' He grinned at her. 'To a large extent we are all misfits. Not criminals exactly, but there has to be something of the brigand in a man to make him want to wander the earth with a gun in his fist, do you not agree?'

She nodded.

'Take Caspasian for example. An odd sort of bird in ordinary society, but out here in a wild place like this, he fits like a hand in a glove.'

He glanced at her again and could see that she was thinking. As if in response she said, 'What do you know about Caspasian?' Then, lest her interest be misinterpreted she added quickly, 'As you say, he seems an odd sort of bird.'

Béranger played along and told her what he knew, of Caspasian's youth in Yokohama and of his wartime experiences. 'But I will tell you one thing, Madame,' he concluded some time later. 'There is not another man I would rather have alongside me on an expedition like this.'

Michelle smiled. 'Then it is rather a shame that he is running the competition, isn't it?'

Béranger laughed. 'We are not in competition. Not Caspasian and me. We professional soldiers leave that sort of thing to the administrators.'

'Like my husband, you mean?'

Béranger blanched. 'I did not mean any offence, Madame.'

'And I took none,' she reassured him quickly.

She was attempting to turn her camel about to return to her place at her husband's side when Béranger reached across and seized hold of her reins. She glanced up at him, startled, but his eyes were narrowed at the horizon. 'A moment, Madame. Stay where you are.'

'What is it?'

'I don't know. There was something . . .'

And then Michelle herself saw it too. Sunlight glinting off metal or glass. 'Who is it?'

Béranger remained like a tracker dog, focused on the distant point of light that flashed again and again. Suddenly he spun in the saddle. 'It's a signal. And it's not ours.' He hunted out Kraus but the German sergeant had already spotted it himself and was hurrying forward.

'Kraus, how far are we from cover?'

'The scouts reported in half an hour ago. The open country gives way to jebel a mile from here. There'll be good rock cover there.'

'Good. Get the column to speed up.'

Kraus was in the act of turning his camel when he caught sight of something. He opened his mouth to shout, reaching out towards Béranger at the same time to yank at his reins. Sniped from nearly six hundred yards the shot missed its mark and instead slammed into the neck of Béranger's camel. In shock and agony the stricken beast reared up and bellowed. Blood spouted from the livid wound, spattering the front of Béranger's linen gandourah as he tumbled from the saddle.

'Ambush!' Kraus screamed, checking quickly to ensure his captain was unhurt. Béranger lay dazed on the ground, shaking his head to clear it. Free of his directions, the camel chased off across the sand, tossing its neck wildly as if to free itself of the pain and the blood that trailed behind.

A fusillade of shots rang out, each stemming from individual firers carefully located well out of sight. Fortunately for the legionnaires, the snipers were inexpert marksmen. Firing at their maximum range, their fire was more nuisance than lethal to the legionnaires. Harassing fire. Béranger's screen flank guards had accomplished their task. They had kept the enemy at arm's length. They had bought the time that was now saving them more serious casualties. Nevertheless, it was only a while before the attackers adjusted to the circumstances and then the first rounds began to find their marks. First one man and then another was struck.

While the legionnaires returned fire under the direction of Kraus, Béranger ordered the remainder of the column forward at best speed. Riders goaded their camels into ungainly trots and set off towards the jebel that reared up some distance before them. The ambushers had chosen their ground well for there was no cover to be had in the immediate vicinity. As the column sped away, it left behind half a dozen dead littering the sand. Bullets spurred the survivors on their way, pocking the soft ground like giant rain drops. More of the camels were hit and their riders fought to control the frantic animals.

'Why don't you counter-attack?' Monsieur Simonin shouted at Sergeant Kraus.

'It's too far and all across open ground, Monsieur,' Kraus answered abruptly. 'They'd cut us down before we got even halfway.'

'You're scared! You damned coward.'

'Monsieur!'

Simonin looked round sharply at the sound of Béranger.

'If you have nothing constructive to say, keep your mouth shut.'

Simonin scowled but said nothing, spurring his camel after the others. Béranger glanced at Kraus but the German had returned to his task of co-ordinating the rearguard. For him, Simonin's opinion was of as little importance as the belch of a camel.

As the mounted part of the column drew clear of the ambush site, Kraus established a firing line of legionnaires who withdrew using fire and movement. One group would lay down suppressive fire while their partners ran after the column. Then, they too would go to ground and lay down fire on the located enemy positions while their comrades gathered up their belongings and dashed after them, the two groups leapfrogging backwards.

At one point some of the attackers, seeing their quarry escape, rose from their fire positions and dashed after them. The moment Kraus and his men saw a clean target they brought down a withering fire upon them. From where he stood, Kraus could see the sand suddenly dancing around the enemy snipers. One after the other, they flinched and fell until no more followed. They had learnt their lesson and would treat the legionnaires with greater caution from now on.

Leading the fleeing column, Béranger had remounted on one of the pack animals whose load he had cut loose. He could now see the approaching rock formations of the jebel clearly. There was not much further to go. They were nearly there. Michelle was close behind him and, further back, her husband clung to his camel, hands clutching the reins out at his sides as he tried to steer the confused animal. The dismounted handlers streamed along in the rear, fleeing after the column as best they could. One or two of them had disappeared into the desert, deciding to take their chance either with the attackers or else on their own, seeking out their own escape route.

By the time Béranger reached the first outcrop of rocks, his camel's hooves ringing at last on solid ground, more than half the handlers and porters had fled. Kraus and the remainder of the legionnaires were close behind, having achieved their task of keeping the attackers at bay.

'Up there!' Béranger bellowed at his entire party, pointing towards a circular plateau ringed with boulders. 'We'll make a stand there.'

Kraus looked up, breathing hard after the chase. In a second his mind had evaluated the scene and judged it secure. As ever, Captain Béranger had made an instant but sound tactical assessment. The plateau would offer them clear fields of fire back in the direction of their attackers. Anyone trying to storm the position with a frontal assault would be mown down, particularly when the legionnaires had managed to unpack the Hotchkiss machine guns from the pack animals, assemble them and bring them into action. The only question mark in Kraus's mind, as he made his way up through the steepening rocks towards the plateau, concerned the higher ground he could just glimpse to its rear. Anyone up there could well have dominance over the plateau. He had to concede that it was unlikely. The position looked unscaleable, but then he could not see what the approaches behind it were like. But that was the nature of combat. Snap decisions based upon incomplete information. You just had to do the best you could, given your experience and the knowledge available at the time. No commander ever knew all there was to know. Information was always at a premium.

As Kraus bounded up the last of the rocks, his legionnaires struggling hard to keep up with him, he glanced up and saw Béranger and the Simonins waiting for him together with the handful of porters and handlers that had not fled. While some of the men took up fire positions to cover the rear in case their attackers were still pursuing them, the rest laid hands on the camels and tore apart the loads to get at the machine guns.

'This'll teach them to ambush us,' Simonin said triumphantly as he observed the activity from the rock where he had collapsed, panting heavily, sweat pouring off him. Michelle had taken herself off to one side and was giving assistance to one of the porters who had been winged by a bullet. Although it was only a flesh wound, it was bleeding profusely. Béranger had shown her what to do and she was fastening a tourniquet around the arm, tightening it until the flow of blood stopped.

At last Kraus set hands on the first of the Hotchkiss and felt the comforting touch of the lightly-oiled gun metal. 'Now we'll show those bastards,' he muttered as he slid a gun onto its mounting, locking it home with a reassuring clunk.

They were safe at last. Barring surprises, they had made it through the ambush.

From his vantage point to the rear of the plateau, Mahmud watched with quiet satisfaction. The plan had worked to perfection. The column he had been instructed to destroy had done exactly as he had intended, making their way directly to the plateau which was to be the killing ground. In the process, just as Mahmud had hoped, they had given him a fine demonstration of their capabilities. Having watched the entire engagement, he now knew their strengths and weaknesses. He had witnessed the fire discipline and deployment drills of the legionnaires, seen their marksmanship skills, and now, as events unfolded below him, he was taking careful note of the machine guns being hurriedly assembled and brought into action. Had he committed his entire force to battle from the outset, the Hotchkiss guns would have taken a heavy toll. Now, however, he would be able to counter their effect by other means. His experience of such weapons was limited. His paymasters had taught him as much as they thought he needed to know in order to carry out his mission, but he regretted being so out of touch. Restricted to small desert operations and raids, he had had little chance to put their teaching into practice, and they had seen no reason to equip his men with modern weaponry. Rifles were all they thought he needed. Grudgingly Mahmud reckoned they were probably right. Nevertheless, as he watched the legionnaires below him deploying their weaponry, he felt a slight apprehension. It was always the same whenever encountering the unknown.

He raised his binoculars and tightened the focus onto the small group of figures. He could see the officer busily giving orders. Mahmud smiled wryly. How the officers loved to give orders. He would see this one dead first of all. Mahmud turned to one of his commanders at his side and asked for a man by name, the best marksman in his force.

'Him,' he said simply, pointing out Béranger when the marksman arrived at the trot. The man slithered down onto his belly and crawled forward, eyes following the direction of Mahmud's pointing finger. When he had acquired his target he nodded grimly.

'Make sure you get him with your first shot,' Mahmud whispered. 'Without direction they will fall apart.'

'It will be done.'

Then Mahmud turned his attention to the other members of the foreign expedition. He had identified the woman early on, noting her by the way she moved. It would be an added bonus if he could lay hands upon her before she died in the next phase of the attack. Of course he had not been able to see her face at this distance, but she looked slim and young. His instructions had been simply to destroy the expedition and kill everyone in it. How and when he did it was entirely up to him. If he chose to keep the woman alive for a while and enjoy some sport with her, that was his affair. Goodness knows, he had been without the company of such a woman for long enough. He could barely remember the last time. The women of the village were all well and good, but down below he suspected there was a woman of real quality.

He dismissed the sergeant as an irrelevance. Like any subordinate he would undoubtedly lack any real initiative. Used to obeying orders, the man would most likely fold once his officer had been killed.

Mahmud had heard of the fat man and had been especially briefed about him. Him Mahmud would slaughter like a sheep, with a knife blade drawn deeply across the throat. He would probably bleat like a sheep too, and bleed like one. An example would have to be made, however, to dissuade others from similarly venturing onto Mahmud's land.

When he was content that he had evaluated the situation, Mahmud nodded to his commanders, indicating that they were to continue as planned.

'This is it, my friends.' He looked about him. 'Where is Yakub?'

'We left him with the camels,' one of the commanders replied. 'He seemed little interested in the ambush and indicated that he wished to be left alone.'

Mahmud nodded. Poor old Yakub. At least he would be safely out of the way.

Turning again to the plateau below him, Mahmud raised his hand. All along the ridgeline men watched him eagerly, their rifles at the ready. Until now they had lain out of sight, hidden below the skyline for fear that one of the hated enemy might detect them. Now they prepared to move forward and open fire. Only seconds remained. Every man gripped the stock of his rifle and gathered his legs beneath him ready for the signal.

And then it came.

Everything had gone reasonably well, Béranger was thinking. The ambushers had attempted to follow up their initial attack, but had been held at bay by the legionnaires' accurate fire. Now, with the machine guns ready to go into action, it appeared that the enemy had gone to ground. Confining themselves to a desultory sniping, they had taken cover amongst the sand dunes and rocks some distance beyond the rocky outcrops that ascended towards the plateau. They had obviously noted the strength of the legionnaires' defensive position and had deemed it unassailable without reinforcements.

And that was what troubled Béranger most. He was perturbed to find his mind agitated. They had broken clean, made good their escape, achieved high ground, and were now regrouping. At their backs stood an unscaleable rock face which, while it severed any line of further withdrawal, nevertheless restricted the enemy's options as well. Attack from that quarter was impossible. So why was he feeling troubled?

Sergeant Kraus, acting in accordance with standard battle procedure, had strung out the legionnaires to establish a perimeter, ensuring that every approach was covered by fire. Now he was busy siting the machine guns, checking that the arcs of each Hotchkiss and Chauchat overlapped with those of its neighbour. As Béranger watched him he decided that they would probably remain where they were for the night and take stock in the morning. His own inclination was to cancel the whole expedition and return as speedily as possible to the Nile, wiring for a steamer to take them back to Cairo or else commandeering a felucca or two.

On the other hand, he had been given a mission. To find the lost city of King Menes. Why should they be distracted by bandits? Such raids were to be expected in any desert enterprise once one got some distance from the Nile valley. The desert interior was awash with such warring tribes. Of course he would have to consult Simonin. Béranger found it hard to anticipate his response. Which would get the upper hand – Simonin's cowardice or his greed? It would be a fine decision and Béranger found himself looking forward to the agony it would cause Simonin.

He went across to Michelle. The man she had been assisting was now resting as comfortably as might be expected. A legionnaire medic had attended to him, the wound had been dressed and Michelle was once again looking for something to do. Béranger noticed how she left her husband quite alone. Nor had Simonin summoned her. For now he was content to take cover behind the largest rock on the plateau, sharing it with no one.

'Are you all right, Madame?' Béranger asked.

'Quite all right, under the circumstances,' Michelle replied, smiling. Béranger was astounded to note that she seemed virtually radiant. Far from having been frightened by the attack, Michelle Simonin had come into her own. At no time had Béranger seen her panic. On the contrary, she had rallied some of the fleeing porters and handlers, persuading them to remain with the expedition. It was an admirable feat. In his experience, calmness under fire more often signified stupidity rather than courage, and he was convinced that Michelle Simonin was anything but stupid.

He reached down for his water flask, unscrewed the stopper and held it out to her. She accepted it gratefully and drank, stopping herself after several mouthfuls.

'I am sorry,' she said wiping her mouth. 'Do you have enough to spare?'

Béranger looked around doubtfully. 'We're fine for now. Kraus managed to save most of the pack animals. If we're lucky we might find water in the hills behind us. We'll have to see.'

He smiled at her, put the flask to his mouth and tipped his head back. As he did so he staggered. Michelle reached out to steady him.

'Careful,' she said, smiling.

Then the sound of the shot reached them, and the next second Sergeant Kraus was charging at her. Beside Michelle, Béranger sank to the ground, a look of surprise on his face. Kraus reached them and in one huge bear hug, gathered up both Michelle and the fallen body of Béranger and bundled them into cover.

As Michelle lay there stunned, Kraus's hands moved rapidly

over Béranger's tunic, searching expertly for both entry and exit wounds.

Béranger grasped his hand and thrust it away. 'Organise the defence,' he whispered. 'Bring the machine guns to bear.'

His eyes injected the orders with the urgency his voice was unable to manage, but Michelle could see his consciousness fading. His fingers scrabbled at his holster and she helped him unfasten it. He withdrew the Ruby semi-automatic pistol and tumbled it into her waiting hands.

'Take this, Madame.' He tried to focus on her eyes. 'Use it,' he said.

Kraus hesitated, but the shot that had struck Béranger was now followed by numerous others as, from all along the ridgeline overlooking their position, a hail of rifle fire began to pour down onto the exposed plateau where the legionnaires were sheltering. Béranger grabbed at Kraus's lapels. 'Take charge. Get them out of here.'

Kraus needed no other order. One of the porters screamed and fell, struck in the back. Two of the legionnaires lay still in the dirt, while their comrades struggled to manhandle the machine guns around. But the ridgeline to their rear stood on top of a sheer cliff face and from their mountings none of the Hotchkiss gun barrels could be elevated high enough to achieve the necessary trajectory. They were useless.

Caspasian arched his back and stretched. Sitting cross-legged on his camel, he could feel his body going to sleep. His feet tingled inside his leather boots from the poor blood circulation and he wiggled his toes as best he could. Straightening his neck, he tucked his riding crop down one riding boot and flexed his fingers, interlocking them and stretching his arms out. He felt the joints crack pleasurably and with a deep sigh of contentment allowed himself to collapse back into the lolloping heap that every camel rider became on a long journey. The rhythmic pulse of the camel's methodical plod had been lulling Caspasian into a half-sleep. Working against the beast's own trudge was the swish of the bundles of forage and firewood that hung from the saddle and knocked against the camel's bulbous flanks. It was mind-numbing, especially when combined with an endless vista of featureless terrain and a temperature soaring ever higher.

He turned in the saddle to check on Sergeant Ganga and the rest of the Gurkhas. Only two of them had ridden camels before, but in the last few days all had become accustomed to the unfamiliar beasts with remarkable determination. Only Bharat continued to distrust them, perching behind his mount's neck as if sitting on a land mine, rarely taking his eyes off the back of the animal's unconcerned head.

Ganga caught Caspasian's eye and winced, shifting in his seat and rubbing his backside. 'I am starting to miss my cool dark armoury, saheb,' he said, encouraging his camel to close up with Caspasian's. When he had managed to pull up alongside, he took out his water bottle and drank. Caspasian noticed that he did it sparingly, exercising the caution of an old soldier, uncertain when and where he would next be able to refill it. Water had been one of the biggest problems when planning the loads for the pack animals. Each man needed at least 8 litres a day, and half as much again if involved in any form of strenuous activity. Even sitting still the body could use up to half a litre an hour in high temperatures. Consequently there was an entire string of camels carrying nothing but water in huge bladders. Naturally Caspasian was hoping that they would be able to replenish their supply at waterholes along the way, but there was a strong chance that it might prove to be too saline or otherwise unfit to drink. He had had to plan for the worst.

Salt was another vital requirement. Each man carried his own supply as part of his personal equipment and it was Ganga's job to ensure that no one forgot to take his daily ration.

Apart from water and their own fodder, the camels carried food for the expedition. Coffee and tea, powdered milk, sugar, dates and figs, jerked mutton, rice, flour, onions, lentils, and a variety of spices to make it all edible. Should they encounter nomadic tribesmen, it was Caspasian's intention to buy fresh meat, and to do this he had brought an assortment of useful articles to use for barter. Cutting implements, mirrors, bolts of cloth, rope and several yard high pillars of salt which were always at a premium in the desert. Ganga had suggested bringing a few extra guns and boxes of ammunition to trade but Caspasian had decided against it lest they be turned upon the expedition itself.

As luxuries, he had included some bottles of brandy and whisky which he excused as being for medicinal purposes. However, when checking the baggage he had taken a look at Sir Hubert's personal cargo and discovered that it included Madeira, port and several bottles of claret, as well as a large box of Havana cigars.

Apart from this there was the tentage, bedding, a wealth of digging and other implements associated with the archaeological work, pots and pans and cooking utensils, fuel for cooking fires and lamps, and an array of guns, ammunition and explosives that Sir Hubert had exclaimed was highly excessive, but that Caspasian had insisted upon including. The Professor had said that the explosives could not possibly be used for archaeological work, but Caspasian had placated him by saying that they might come in handy for some other task. The Professor had eventually relented.

Glancing behind him, he saw the long train of camels snaking back. It was an impressive sight.

'How is Harkabahadur?' Caspasian asked. 'Caused any trouble yet?'

'Not a bit. He keeps himself to himself, does what he's told and nothing more.'

Caspasian nodded. He knew that Ganga was keeping a close eye on the battalion troublemaker and was comfortable to leave it at that. 'How far do you reckon we've travelled today?'

Ganga considered. 'About ten miles so far.'

Caspasian nodded. 'My estimate too.' He took out his map case and opened it on his lap, steadying it against the motions of the camel that rocked it to and fro like a boat in a heavy wash. To navigate he was using dead reckoning, working off a combination of compass bearing and distance travelled. With some difficulty he placed his protractor on the surface of the map and drew in the line of march, measuring out the miles travelled and marking the spot where he now estimated the column to be. At their present position there were pitifully few features on the map but the situation was due to change in a day when, so the map showed, they would enter the rugged mountainous jebel.

'There's a well marked here,' Caspasian said studying the map closely. 'At least I think it's supposed to be a well. Worth taking a look at though. It's only a slight detour off our line of march.'

Ganga leaned across and peered at the spot where Caspasian's finger rested. 'Might be, saheb. If it is, we could recharge the water bladders before entering the jebel.'

'Exactly. Let's give it a shot.'

Caspasian made the necessary calculations, took a bearing off the map, using his protractor, set it on the dial of his prismatic compass and then, squinting through the compass eyepiece, located the direction on the ground. 'Over there. We should make it by last light.'

'Do you want me to send out scouts?'

Caspasian glanced up at the sun. 'In a couple of hours. No point just yet. We're still too far away.'

'I'll send Anand and Birbahadur as one team and Dhanprasad and Akalbahadur as another. They can zigzag across the bearing until one of them finds the well.'

'Fine.'

Caspasian was not surprised when Sir Hubert objected, unable to see the point of a detour, however slight. 'It could mean the damned Frenchies get to the city before we do. If that happens, I'll have your guts for garters, Caspasian.' He shifted the position of his cork helmet so that the brim angled low over his eyes. The green puggaree pleated round the base was dark with sweat.

'Sir Hubert,' Caspasian replied patiently, 'if our water runs out we won't reach the city at all.' He had contemplated keeping news of the detour to himself but eventually felt it his duty to inform the Professor and Sir Hubert.

Sir Hubert swore under his breath. 'All right then,' he said at last. 'But I want us back on course immediately thereafter.'

Several hours later, when the scouts had been sent out and the day was wearing into evening, Ganga suddenly sat up in his saddle and shaded his eyes towards the horizon. Caspasian pulled out his binoculars and followed Ganga's line of sight. Beneath the eyepieces his mouth creased into a smile.

'How the devil did you spot them?' he asked, incredulous.

Ganga shrugged modestly. 'A sniper's eye, saheb.'

Through the binoculars Caspasian could just make out a small disturbance on the horizon which he took to be the tiny dust cloud thrown up by riders. Normally it would have been difficult to judge the exact distance as the shimmering effect of the heat haze corrupted the clarity of vision. During the hottest part of the day, a man standing only two hundred yards away might be rendered invisible behind a wavering curtain of light, but now, towards the last part of the day, the sun worked in Caspasian's favour. Lowering itself at his back, it served to highlight the approaching riders in the distance.

Sure enough, a short time later a triumphant Anand and Birbahadur closed with the column and announced that they had found the well and that they had rendezvoused with Dhanprasad and Akalbahadur who they had left there. Should the column not make it by last light they would light a fire to guide them in.

'Did you test the water?' Ganga asked.

'No.'

Ganga and Caspasian swapped glances, bracing themselves. 'Why not?' Caspasian asked slowly, dreading the answer.

'Because the well was dry,' Birbahadur announced merrily.

Ganga looked at Caspasian and sighed. 'Do you want to tell Sir Hubert or shall I?' Much as he would have loved to shirk the task, Caspasian shook his head. Sir Hubert was furious, but chilled his anger to a white-faced sullenness. When they eventually arrived they found that Dhanprasad and Akalbahadur had used their initiative and, while waiting, had started to dig. The well was little more than a deep depression in the otherwise unbroken sandy surface of the desert. Round about lay several clumps of bone dry scrub, long since devoid of life. The two riflemen had dug to about five feet by the time the column arrived, but the earth and rock at the bottom of the hole was as dry as the surrounding sand.

To Caspasian's surprise, Sir Hubert suddenly produced a suggestion.

'The men can construct a desert still. I read about them in a travel book. Gertrude Bell, I think.'

Caspasian sighed but forced himself to look attentive as Sir Hubert continued, warming to his topic. 'You dig out a shallow depression, place a container in the bottom of it and then stretch a tarpaulin across the top, weighting the centre with a stone so that it sags down, the lowest point being exactly above the container underneath. The heat of the sun raises the temperature of the air and soil under the sheet until the water vapourises. When the air under the sheet becomes saturated, the vapour condenses on the underside of the sheet and runs down into the collecting container.'

'That's correct,' Caspasian began carefully, reluctant to strangle Sir Hubert's constructiveness at birth. 'The problem is that it takes two square yards of tarpaulin for one still, and each still produces only half a litre of water in a twenty-four hour period.'

Sir Hubert's face started to fall.

'So, as each of us needs, say, a minimum of ten litres a day, you'd need twenty such stills per man. But, even if we had enough material and containers for all of them, the effort we'd expend in digging that many holes would push our daily water requirement through the roof, to at least twenty litres a day, so then you'd need forty stills per man, and so on. Like the rainbow's end, attainment of the aim recedes as the task progresses. It's a great idea, but only in a survival situation when it might, just might keep a man alive. And we're not that far gone yet.'

Sir Hubert bridled. 'But I thought you said we needed to replenish the water bladders. If it wasn't that necessary after all, why the devil have you brought us all out of our way?'

'Sir Hubert does have a bit of a point,' the Professor chided good-naturedly, removing his Palmerston Panama and rubbing his forehead wearily. He was tired and Caspasian could see that the exertions of the desert journey were taking a toll. 'Perhaps it would have been better to send the scouts here in the first place before diverting the entire expedition.'

'That would have split the party for too long,' Caspasian said. He was reluctant to admit to them that he had no confidence in his men's ability to navigate their way back to rejoin the column, given the quality of the soldiers he had been allocated by the Colonel.

'So what do you intend to do now?' Sir Hubert said, gleeful to have set the Professor against Caspasian.

'Establish camp for the night. Over there,' Caspasian replied, pointing some distance away. He turned to Ganga. 'Get a fire going and hot water on the boil. We could all do with a cup of tea.'

'Amen to that,' the Professor said with immense relief.

'But what about the well?' Sir Hubert persisted, unwilling to let Caspasian off the hook so easily.

Caspasian dismounted and retrieved a bulky satchel from the heavily laden flank of one of the pack camels. 'Leave that to me.'

While Ganga sorted out the porters and handlers, setting them about their usual duties for a night halt, Caspasian went across to the two Gurkhas leaning on their long handled shovels, and inspected their handiwork. 'I want that another two feet deep.'

They sighed, wiped their brows and set to work. As they did so, Caspasian knelt down beside his satchel, unfastened the flap and took out several sticks of explosives, a primer, detonator, a length of fuse wire and a roll of sticky tape. Dhanprasad and Akalbahadur exchanged stares of alarm and quickened their digging.

Taping the sticks of explosive together, Caspasian forced the primer into the top of the bundle, inserted the detonator into it and then fitted one end of the fuse wire into the slim open neck of the detonator. Using his teeth, he gingerly crimped shut the thin metal, clamping it onto the wire. Measuring as he went, he unfurled more wire from his roll, calculating the burning time as he went to give himself long enough to get clear.

By the time the two Gurkhas had completed their task, Caspasian could see that, less than a hundred yards away, the camp had been set up and a couple of welcoming fires had been lit. Water had been boiled and around one of the fires tea was being served to Sir Hubert and the Professor.

Caspasian peered down into the hole. 'OK, you two, off you go. Well done.'

The Gurkhas gathered up their jackets, shovels and rifles and scampered away towards their friends. When they were clear Caspasian lowered his bundle into the bottom of the hole and placed a number of large rocks on top of it, wedging them firmly in place to direct the force of the blast downwards. Then, once he had unravelled the length of fuse wire away from the hole, he took out a lighter, flicked open the lid, spun the flint with his thumb and watched as a fat yellow flame sprang into life. He touched it to the end of the fuse wire and held it steady until a deep red glow showed that the flame had taken and the fuse was burning. Flipping his lighter shut, he laid the smoking end of the lighted wire on the ground, retrieved his satchel and walked away, heading for the camp fire, careful to resist the urge to run like hell. The last thing he needed was to stumble in the dark, strike his head on a stone and end up sprawling dazed beside the explosive-filled hole when the flame burned all the way into the heart of the heat-sensitive detonator.

At the camp fire the Professor's spirits were lifting in direct proportion to the amount of hot sweet tea being swallowed. Ganga handed a large enamel mug to Caspasian as he gently lowered the satchel to the ground and sat down beside the Professor.

'Khana in thirty minutes, saheb,' Ganga said. Seeing Sir Hubert's raised eyebrow he translated. 'That's food, saheb.'

'Better go easy on the water,' Sir Hubert cautioned.

Ganga shook his head. 'No need, saheb. We'll have plenty for cooking and washing too.'

'You sound very sure.'

Ganga shrugged. 'Caspasian saheb's taken care of it.'

Sir Hubert frowned sceptically. 'Oh? And how has he done that?'

Caspasian pulled back his sleeve and checked his watch. 'Professor, if I may,' he said calmly, putting an arm round him and drawing his head down. Across the fire from them Ganga squatted down on his haunches and hugged his head in his hands. Sir Hubert looked thoroughly mystified.

The boom of the explosion shattered the quiet desert night. The ground trembled with the shock waves and a moment later a rain of dust, dirt and debris showered down upon the gathering. One or two substantial pieces of rock thudded to earth and Sir Hubert went flying backwards, tea everywhere.

'What the . . . !'

As the last of the falling projectiles pattered softly onto the surrounding sand, Caspasian sat up and dusted himself off. 'One stick too many, eh Ganga?'

Ganga pushed himself upright, similarly brushing the fine coating of dust off his clothes and pondered thoughtfully. 'Maybe half a stick, saheb. We'll see.'

'We will indeed.' Caspasian rubbed his hands gleefully. 'But first tea.' He held his cup up to his nose and sniffed the scent. 'I've been dreaming about this all day.'

Ignoring the film of dust on the surface he sipped the tea with closed eyes. 'Wonderful. All I need now is some hot food, a space to lay my bed roll and I'll be a happy man.'

Spluttering and spitting out debris from between his teeth, Sir Hubert gathered himself. 'Next time you're going to blow us all to kingdom come, give us a damned warning, all right?'

Caspasian nodded happily. Some time later the food was brought and, after eating, Caspasian and Ganga each picked up a paraffin lamp and led the way back towards the water hole. In place of the neat round excavation that the two Gurkhas had created, there was now a huge jagged crater and, in the middle of it, a rapidly spreading pool of brackish looking liquid was bubbling up from the ruptured ground.

'You don't expect us to drink that?' Sir Hubert said, his face contorted with disgust.

'Not like that,' Caspasian reassured him. 'We'll filter it first and then either boil it or, to save fuel and time, purify it with chlorine tablets. It should be all right to drink, but even if it isn't we can use it for washing and cooking.'

'And I doubt the camels are fussy,' the Professor observed dryly.

It was on the following day that Ganga noticed the column was being shadowed.

'They are very good,' he said with a mixture of admiration and concern.

Caspasian was not surprised that he himself could see nothing at all, not even with the binoculars. He did not bother to ask whether Ganga thought they were just inquisitive nomads passing by, or trouble. Standard drills dictated only one course of action. Assume the worst until it proved otherwise. Trouble.

Without halting the column, Caspasian and Ganga extracted two light machine guns and their associated ammunition from the pack animals and issued hand grenades to the two NCOs. Lance Naik Ramprasad was the only one Caspasian really trusted with such a device, but face dictated that Naik Indrabahadur receive a couple as well. It would not be proper for his subordinate to be armed with grenades and not him. Having spent years in the officers' mess, Indrabahadur stared with alarm as Caspasian planted a grenade in each of his hands.

'Don't worry. They don't explode until you pull out the pin,'

Caspasian said smiling. 'And when you do, make sure you remember to throw it. The grenade, that is. Not the pin.'

All the riflemen withdrew their Lee-Enfields from the canvas carrying cases strapped to their camel saddles and laid the rifles across their laps. Magazines were fully charged, a round in the breach and the safety catch applied.

Ganga deployed the men in pairs, one pair at the front of the column, one at the rear and one on either flank. Together with Caspasian, he himself rode at the front of the column, keeping the two light machine guns with them so that they could deploy wherever the need arose.

Noticing their preparations, the Professor asked what was wrong. Caspasian passed on Ganga's warning.

'Nothing to be alarmed about. I'm just taking precautions, that's all. If anyone's watching us, it doesn't do any harm for them to see that we won't be a push over. Might make them think twice before attacking.'

By nightfall the column found itself approaching the start of the jebel. In the distance everyone could see the skyline disrupted by jagged rock formations rising up out of the desert. Red in colour, they towered up into the darkening sky as the travellers approached, only to fade from view and melt into the night as the sun disappeared below the horizon and the temperature began to drop.

Caspasian shivered and sank his hands deep in his pockets. 'It's going to be cold tonight.'

The Professor had joined him. Together they looked up into the night sky. The first of the stars were hardening into quivering icy points, a huge rich depth of blackness between them that dwarfed the two men gazing upwards. The camels were being coaxed into a leaguer, muzzles roped loosely together, legs hobbled. Caspasian had considered only allowing cooking fires before dark to make it harder for an intruder to pinpoint the camp's position, but he had relented. There was no point in frightening everyone. Any self-respecting desert nomad would have no problem locating the camp, fire or no fire, and even if their intentions were hostile, Caspasian could hardly expect the expedition to move onto an operational footing for the rest of the duration unless there was some more persuasive evidence of impending danger. He did not doubt Ganga's caution for a second, but it would need to be corroborated before he instituted more severe defensive measures.

Corroboration came in the early hours of the morning. One moment Caspasian was sleeping soundly, the next he was wide awake, surrounded by gunshots and shouting.

As usual he had posted two sentries. The only difference was that after detecting a tail the day before, he had armed them with the Lewis light machine guns instead of simply their rifles. When the enemy struck, Caspasian's precaution proved to have been a lifesaver.

The sentries were sited together as a pair so each could ensure the other stayed awake. Ganga had prepared a rota so that each man did a two hour stint, shift changes being staggered so that one man swapped over every hour, on the hour. This meant that there was always one man totally fresh and rested, and the other, who had already completed one hour of sentry duty, had eyes and ears accustomed to the night, familiar with his arcs of observation and able to brief the newcomer. The two light machine guns lay side by side, and together they managed a wide arc of fire covering the approach that Caspasian had judged the most likely. Before siting the sentries, he had made a complete circuit of the camp perimeter, approaching it himself from some distance away. Years of frontier operations against the Pathans proved him right.

The hostile tribesmen had attempted to rush the camp, intending to sweep right into it on foot, hacking, slashing and shooting their way through the members of the expedition. What they had not counted on was the sharp hearing of Rifleman Harkabahadur Limbu, the ex-guard room prisoner, and the rate of fire that a brace of Lewis machine guns was capable of producing.

Caspasian rolled out of his bedding and snatched up his holster that lay beside his wooden camel saddle. Strapping it on, he pulled out the Webley revolver and slithered across to the Professor and Sir Hubert. 'Stay where you are. Whatever you do, don't stand up.' Before either of them could say a word he had gone.

He and Ganga had arranged the layout of the camp in the manner of a clock face. The sentry post was at twelve o'clock, but it had been pushed forward of the perimeter some thirty yards to take advantage of a rise in the ground that gave an improved field of fire out into the desert beyond. At each of the three o'clock, six o'clock and nine o'clock positions, further pairs of riflemen had been sleeping and, next to each of them, a shell scrape. At the first sound of alarm, every man rolled out from under his blanket and into the depression, taking his rifle with him, charged and ready. Camels, stores, handlers, porters, the Professor, Sir Hubert, Sergeant Ganga and Caspasian all occupied the centre of the clock face. The shooting had terrified the camels and their handlers alike, but with nowhere to run, the handlers stayed rooted to the ground, holding tight to the tethering ropes of their animals.

Crouching as low as he could, Caspasian ran forward to the sentry position. Ganga appeared behind him, rifle clutched in one hand, drawn kukri in the other. They tumbled into the large shell scrape together, bumping into Harkabahadur and his comrade, Bharat, who had only been on duty a few minutes.

Harkabahadur swore as Caspasian fell against his legs, spoiling his aim. The butt of the Lewis was pulled hard into Harkabahadur's cheek and he was firing short controlled bursts into the darkness. A short way in front of the position Caspasian could just make out three motionless bodies.

'Good work.'

Harkabahadur ignored the compliment and let rip with

another savage burst of fire. 'Tell that woman to stop wetting herself and get some fire down,' he spat, jerking his head at Bharat who lay wide-eyed behind a smoking but silent Lewis gun. After the initial engagement when he had fired out of sheer terror, he had exhausted his magazine and appeared to have forgotten his loading drills.

Ganga lurched forward and whacked Bharat across the shoulders with the blunt edge of his kukri. Bharat squealed but got the message. He fumbled with the release catch, removed the empty drum magazine from the top of the weapon, and with trembling fingers replaced it with a full one. He cranked back the cocking handle, grimacing at the effort required, and nuzzled down behind the gun sight in search of a new target.

'Flares?' Ganga asked.

Caspasian considered. Flares were two-edged, revealing your own positions as well as the enemy's.

'Yes. But put them as far away as you can.' The enemy was unlikely to be familiar with the effect and would probably be thrown off balance. By the time they had realised the light could help them too, the flares would have burnt out.

Ganga popped open the verey pistol, slid in a cartridge and aimed at a low angle to project the round well away from their own position. He fired. The gun jumped in his fist and the flare shot away, bursting a couple of seconds later.

'Eyes,' Caspasian cautioned just before it burst. Everyone in the shell scrape closed one eye to maintain at least some night vision. Everyone except Bharat who flinched and rubbed his eyes, dazzled by the sudden glare. Ganga popped off a second flare, angling it away from the first one to give a wider arc of light. This done, he cursed at Bharat and lifted him bodily from behind the gun. Tossing him aside like a sack of rice, he dropped down behind the Lewis gun himself.

The desert in front of them was suddenly bathed in a pale green light and there, crouching uncertainly and wondering whether or not to rush the camp again, a score of tribesmen stared upwards, momentarily blinded by the flare. Rabbits in headlights.

Instantly Harkabahadur and Ganga were onto them, Harkabahadur starting from the left and working inwards, Ganga from the right. There was no need for Caspasian to co-ordinate their fire. Both were professionals and did it automatically.

Bullets snapped and thudded into the gathered tribesmen, ripping into them. Others danced in the livid sand, small bursts erupting upwards around the tumbling and fleeing bodies. The next moment the flares died and night returned, only this time it was riven with the screams of the enemy dying and wounded.

In an effort to redeem himself and be helpful Bharat had picked up Ganga's discarded flare gun. 'More flares?'

Caspasian shook his head. The combination of flare and machine gun had achieved the shock effect he had intended. Better to leave it as a short sharp example of what the Gurkhas could do, rather than dilute it with more of the same. Further flares and fire would not have the same effect now that the enemy had withdrawn from the immediate vicinity of the camp.

'What about the enemy wounded?' Bharat asked, peering over the low parapet in the direction of the pitiful moans.

Harkabahadur sneered. 'Leave the bastards.'

'Saheb?' Bharat persisted doubtfully.

'Harka's right,' Caspasian said reluctantly. 'If we can hear them, so can their own side. It'll act as a deterrent. Besides, I want to give the survivors the chance of retrieving them. If we go out now and bring them in, we'll prevent their own men from doing so later. We'll be lumbered with them.'

'Clearing patrol at first light?' Ganga said.

'Yes. And everyone to remain stood-to until then.' Caspasian peered towards the east. He could just see the faintest evidence of the night starting to weaken. They would not have long to wait.

Sure enough, by the time Sergeant Ganga led a four-man patrol forward of the perimeter to check on the enemy's whereabouts, the tribesmen had silently returned to gather up their dead and wounded before withdrawing from the field of battle. From the blood trails Ganga estimated up to eight dead and as many wounded, some badly.

Sir Hubert and the Professor were ashen-faced when they came to the morning's fire to receive their mugs of tea. The civilian handlers and porters were terrified and gabbling to one another about the stupidity of continuing further. Caspasian and Ganga noticed that although most of the Gurkhas were calm and philosophical about the engagement, only Harkabahadur stood out from the crowd. He was positively glowing. There was a new spring in his step that neither of them had seen in him for months, certainly not back in barracks in Cairo when confined to a life of drill parades and peacetime duties. Harkabahadur had thoroughly enjoyed himself.

12

Although he was reluctant to admit it, the absence of his Quartermaster was actually turning out to be not nearly as serious as Colonel Humphreys had anticipated. In fact, knowing that he had been so shabbily deserted, the rest of the regimental officers were rallying round as never before to help out with preparations for the High Commissioner's birthday parade. The end result was that the barracks had become a hive of frenetic activity as everyone sought to outshine everyone else in their efforts to assist above and beyond the call of duty.

Nevertheless, Colonel Humphreys minded. He minded considerably. It was not so much because Caspasian had been selected for the expedition. The Colonel well knew of the man's capabilities and had no doubt that he was the best person for a job like that. No. He minded because once again Caspasian had slipped through the net of duty, as Colonel Humphreys saw it. Responsibility. Loyalty to his brother officers even. He had shown himself to be not one of the team. He was separate. Apart. Damn him.

Oh, Caspasian was devoted to the Gurkhas all right. To the men themselves. Imbued with their martial spirit and so on. Look how he had thoroughly corrupted that Sergeant Gangabahadur Limbu. The two of them were like peas in a pod. Brothers in crime.

The Colonel sat at his desk, musing deeply. He liked to use his office for rumination. Less so for work. A glass-panelled door separated him from the Adjutant, Captain Tremain, who laboured feverishly in the adjoining office which, while smaller, was stamped with the marks of far greater industry. Whereas the Colonel's office was light, spacious and tastefully bedecked with select trophies, presentations and regimental memorabilia, the walls of the Adjutant's office bore only a plethora of charts, timetables, nominal rolls, forecasts, calendars, notice boards, maps, plans, memos and orders of the day. Even a casual observer could tell that he had entered the hub of the regiment. This was where things happened. It was the engine room. If the Colonel's office was where decisions were made, the Adjutant's was where those decisions shed their noumenal quality and acquired flesh and bone, exiting steely-eyed into the wider world of the regiment.

Colonel Humphreys pushed back his chair and sighed, forcibly thrusting Caspasian from his mind. It would not do. There was too much else pending. He resisted for only a second the urge to place his feet on the desk, then dropped them heavily on the near right-hand corner, crossed at the ankle. Leaning back, he folded his hands behind his head and settled more comfortably. He was a big man and he had a big man's relationship to the things around him. There was no redundancy in his movements. He moved in direct lines like a Roman road.

'Tremain!'

The bellow trembled the glass pane in the office door through which the Adjutant exploded.

'Colonel?' he gasped, still on the move. There was a clatter behind him as the furniture in the outer office resumed its pre-detonation stasis.

'Parade.'

Captain Tremain waited for more, his mind scrolling through the possibilities as his mouth opened and shut and his eyes searched the Colonel's impassive face for clues.

'Recce,' the Colonel continued, studying his toecaps which were only just below his eye level. 'What time did we say?'

'The reconnaissance is at ten hundred hours, usual attendance. Rehearsals begin the day after tomorrow.'

The Colonel pondered this. 'Fine. We'll do the recce and then have lunch at the Cavalry Club afterwards. Book a table, there's a good chap.'

Captain Tremain ran some numbers in his head. 'That'll be for ten of us.'

'Eleven. I've asked Harry Ghazali to join us. He'll be on the recce to advise on the police angle, so we can hardly all push off to the Cavalry Club afterwards and leave him standing. Besides, the fellow's not a bad chap. For a local.'

'No,' Tremain said, unconvinced.

When the allotted hour arrived, Colonel Humphreys rendezvoused with his company commanders and the rest of the reconnaissance team outside Battalion Headquarters, they climbed into the waiting cars and set off for the site where the parade was to take place later that month. For security as well as political reasons, it had been decided to stage the High Commissioner's birthday parade in the grounds of the Gezira Sporting Club. It was to be a low key affair, the whole thing designed not to antagonise or become embroiled with a demonstration planned by the Wafd party for the same day. The demonstration, which all the organisers assured the authorities would be peaceful, was due to take place around Ezbekieh, some way across the city. There should therefore be no risk of the two events coming into any sort of proximity to one another.

The British well knew that the Wafd had only planned the demonstration for the same day as a provocation, and although neither side was prepared to back down and alter the planned and advertised date of their own event, neither side wanted confrontation. This way, with the Nile safely flowing between the British and the Egyptian gatherings, it was hoped that both might pass off peacefully. Face would have been saved on both sides, and the British administration in Egypt could continue uninterrupted until the next flashpoint, whenever that might arise. It was a delicate balancing act that the High Commissioner was determined to carry off.

The parade, which was to involve two battalions of infantry and a selection of minor units, was to take the form of an inspection followed by a march past. In between the two, the High Commissioner would present long service and good conduct medals to certain nominated individuals. The Gurkha Pipes and Drums would participate with the brass band of the British regiment on parade, but to circumvent the problems of the different speeds of march between a Gurkha rifle regiment and a British line regiment, both units and their associated bands would march past separately, the Gurkha rifle regiment and its Pipes and Drums coming second and only setting off once the British regiment and its band had completed its circuit.

When Colonel Humphreys drove through the gates into the Gezira Club, the other members of his recce group hot on his heels, he was disgruntled to see the British regiment's commanding officer and his entourage just completing their own recce and preparing to set off. Colonel Withers of the Sussex Fusiliers paused as he was about to get into his car.

'Gordon. Good of you to bother, old boy,' he said chuckling.

Colonel Humphreys shot a furious look at the Adjutant. Tremain blanched sickly. 'The Brigade Major told me the recce was ten hundred hours, Colonel. I'm certain.'

Pinkerton, the Brigade Major strode angrily across. 'Didn't you get my message, Tremain? We had to advance the timings to zero eight hundred hours. Apparently there's some blasted polo match starting in thirty minutes.'

Colonel Humphreys stepped in. 'Thirty minutes is all a Gurkha regiment needs, Bob.'

Major Pinkerton blinked at him painfully, struggling to be polite. 'That's just as well, Colonel. We'd better get a move on. This way.'

Colonel Withers hauled himself up into his staff car and waved generously. 'Have fun, Gordon. Better make sure you're not late on the day. Bit of luck the Fusiliers are on first. That'll give you some leeway in case you sleep in again.'

There was a collective rumble of giggles and cheers from the Fusilier officers to which Colonel Humphreys bowed his head in gracious acknowledgement. 'Just you worry about keeping your men in step, Horace. Mind you, once the Gurkhas step out, no one will be watching your shower anyway.'

Colonel Withers wagged his finger playfully at his adversary and signalled his driver to depart.

'I'll speak to you later about this,' Colonel Humphreys mouthed savagely at the Adjutant. 'I want chapter and verse, got it?'

'Yes, Colonel,' Tremain said miserably, swearing he would scalp the clerk who had failed to pass on the BM's message.

As Colonel Humphreys and his men were talked through the format of the parade by the Brigade Major, they walked the course, the Regimental Havildar Major and Captain Tremain both making copious notes.

'You've already had the instructions on paper, so this should simply be confirmation. We'll crack any problems at rehearsals,' Pinkerton said curtly, unable completely to mask his irritation. Nevertheless, knowing the Colonel's own phlegmatic reputation he forced a smile and tried to be pleasant.

Harry Ghazali, who had been talking with the club's security officer, joined the group as they were concluding the parade details. Pinkerton greeted him and made the introductions which Colonel Humphreys allowed him to conclude before announcing that he and Ghazali were old acquaintances.

'As you know, Colonel,' Pinkerton continued, refusing to be riled, 'you are to detail one rifle company for guard duties. Chief Superintendent Ghazali will be the company commander's point of contact for liaison with the police. Intelligence doesn't think the Wafd is going to disrupt the parade in any way. Rather, their demonstration is seen as cocking a snook. They want it to go peacefully as much as we do. After the terrible events of '24, the fallout for them was catastrophic. The last thing they want is a repeat. Nevertheless, we have to be on our guard. Which is where Chief Superintendent Ghazali comes in.'

He deferred to the Chief Superintendent who smiled genially. 'I am having to devote maximum resources to policing the demonstration of course,' Ghazali began. 'Although there will be military units on standby, it is the intention to keep them well out of sight so as not to antagonise the Wafd supporters and provoke a violent reaction. Even so, I want to allocate at least a hundred constables to the High Commissioner's parade so we will be using auxiliaries elsewhere whenever possible. Bearing in mind the relatively secluded nature of the club and the ease with which it can be isolated by the installation of roadblocks on the bridges connecting it with the main part of the city, I do not foresee major problems.'

Colonel Humphreys nodded. 'Well done, Harry. This is Major Marcus Dobbs. He's OC B Company which will be assisting you.' Dobbs stepped forward and shook hands. 'The two of you probably need to get your heads together but I'll leave that up to you.'

When the tour of the club grounds was complete, Major Pinkerton said his farewells and prepared to leave, waiting for Ghazali to accompany him. As he made to leave however, Ghazali found himself held back by Colonel Humphreys.

'I just need a few words with the Chief Superintendent, if you don't mind, Bob,' the Colonel said. When he saw that the BM intended to wait he added, 'It might take a while. I shouldn't bother hanging on if I were you.'

When Pinkerton had left the Colonel extended his invitation to Ghazali to join them for lunch. Ghazali accepted gratefully.

'Capital,' the Colonel declared, and led the way to his staff car.

The Cavalry Club in fact had absolutely nothing whatsoever to do with cavalry of any sort. Located near the Opera House, it was an Indian restaurant that had been established by three brothers just a couple of years after the end of the Great War.

In particular, it was noted for its curry lunch buffets and the Colonel, a keen lover of Indian food, had made it the unofficial mess of the Twelfth Gurkhas for so long as they remained in Cairo.

The welcome at the door was profuse. 'Your usual table is waiting, General Humphreys,' the proprietor announced cheerily.

The Colonel beamed at Ghazali. 'I gave up trying to correct him months ago. In any case, it's probably the only time I'll be called General.'

Ghazali laughed. 'Nonsense, nonsense,' he chided politely, wondering how on earth such a seemingly obtuse man had ever made it beyond Captain. He could not resist a certain affection for Colonel Humphreys, but as far as Ghazali was concerned the man was still too much like the vast majority of his countrymen. Imbued with the unexamined certainty that, in the English, evolution had attained its highest form of self-expression. Caspasian, Ghazali's other recent contact in the Twelfth Gurkhas, was a different kettle of fish however. But then he was only peripherally English.

The thought of Caspasian set the Chief Superintendent wondering, so that once all members of the Colonel's entourage had helped themselves to an initial plateful of delicacies and were seated with cold beers in front of them, he could not resist asking whether any news of the expedition had yet been received.

The Colonel was chewing happily. Instantly his carefree demeanour altered. 'Caspasian?' he said heavily as if he had bitten on something suspicious. 'I wish the expedition all the best of good fortune, but Caspasian himself can stay in the bloody desert for all I care.' He snorted. 'In fact he might as well stay there, because his career will be a desert after this.'

Ghazali nodded, his suspicions confirmed. 'A bit of a renegade, is he?'

'Renegade?' the Colonel stormed. 'A blasted pain in the

backside, that's what he is. His last posting handed him an extraordinary opportunity on a plate and he completely muffed it.'

Ghazali looked confused. 'That's odd. He didn't strike me as the incompetent type.'

Reluctantly the Colonel had to concede. 'He wasn't incompetent at all. That's part of the problem. He thinks too much. He's a moral being too,' he said, blinking with surprise at his own insight.

'Ah,' Ghazali said, understanding.

'Anyway,' the Colonel continued with a hurried swig of beer, 'I allow him back into the regiment, let him take on a responsible position, give him a second chance, and look what he does!'

'You can hardly blame the young for their impetuosity. After all, it's the sense of adventure of men like Caspasian that built the British Empire in the first place.'

While his face remained directed at his plate, the Colonel's eyes swivelled onto Ghazali. 'I see he's got you fooled.'

'I assure you I don't fool easily,' Ghazali countered.

'No.' The Colonel finished his mouthful, scrubbed his lips on his napkin and sighed deeply. 'I suppose you're right. He's not that bad, though I hate admitting it. Which is why I don't like seeing him . . .' he sought the words helplessly.

'Unwilling to play the game?' Ghazali offered.

The Colonel scowled. 'Damn you, Harry.'

Ghazali laughed and raised his glass to the Colonel. 'You see, I can be a bit of a renegade too.'

'So I hear. You've been stirring up quite a hornet's nest with your investigation into the Turkish murders, I believe?'

'The Turkish community needs stirring up,' Ghazali said. 'They are burying their heads in the sand.' He pondered. A rueful smile came to his lips. 'Quite literally in fact.'

The Colonel guffawed. 'Ha! Very good, very good. Burying their heads in the sand. I like it.'

Ghazali shrugged. 'Of course we shouldn't really treat it so lightly. The leaders of their community are being assassinated one by one.'

'And you still don't know why?'

'Not a clue. But I'm jolly well going to find out.'

The Colonel reached across and poured Ghazali some more beer. Glancing up at the serving tables he saw that Tremain and the others had already moved on to the next stage, helping themselves to some of the hotter curries. He slapped Ghazali on the back. 'Come on. Let's forget the Turkish community, the Wafd demonstration and the High Commissioner's parade and get stuck in.'

'And Caspasian?' Ghazali asked mischievously.

'Him too. In any case, he's probably having the time of his life.'

A galloping camel was a sight to behold. A long line of galloping camels was even more so. But a long line of galloping camels, each with a frantic Gurkha clinging to its saddle was truly spectacular, Caspasian thought. From his position at the rear of the fleeing column he found it hard to suppress a smile, despite their straitened circumstances which had deteriorated rapidly following the night attack on their camp.

The Professor was bearing up surprisingly well, riding like an expert. Sir Hubert had withdrawn into a silence that was only broken when he chose to complain about something. Sergeant Ganga was riding close to Caspasian, the two of them bringing up the rear and the handlers and porters had diminished drastically in number through desertions. The loss of the men themselves was bad enough, but far worse was the theft of camels and stores that they took with them, most serious of all, the water bladders. Sufficient remained for now but Caspasian was becoming concerned. They would have to find water soon or their problems would multiply.

Following the night raid, the tribesmen had returned within

hours and in greatly reinforced numbers so that it became clear to Caspasian that these were far more than just bandits who had chanced upon the column with an eye to booty. They had also learnt from the mauling they had received at the hands of the Gurkhas during the night raid. Showing greater respect for their opponents, they had kept their distance, preferring to snipe from maximum range, withdrawing when pursued, but returning the moment the Gurkhas had reformed and continued their march. Overall it gave Caspasian the unpleasant impression of a pack of jackals stalking a wounded but still dangerous buffalo. They were patiently biding their time for the meal they knew would eventually be theirs. At the same time, they were constantly reassessing the state of the wounded animal, weighing their chances for a further assault.

Caspasian was at a loss to know who they were. He had discussed it with the Professor and Sir Hubert, but neither of them had come up with any ideas. They could only assume that they had unwittingly strayed into the territory of a particularly aggressive tribe who were set on the wholesale slaughter of the expedition and the theft of all its assets.

In the midst of all the chaos and the running fight into which the expedition had deteriorated, Caspasian had also been thinking of Michelle and wondering whether the French expedition had encountered the same hostile reception. There was nothing he could do about it, but the thought of her becoming the captive of such men left him feeling sick.

They had entered a dramatic landscape of broken jebel, huge towering rock features rising sheer out of the sandy plain. In between them, the broad open stretches of desert were gradually narrowing, channelling the fleeing column into ever narrower confines where the lack of space for manoeuvre began to worry Caspasian. He had considered attempting to retrace his steps, leading the column in a fighting withdrawal back the way they had come, towards the Nile, but it seemed that whenever they tried they found the tribesmen waiting for them in strength, as if they were consciously herding the expedition forwards, ever deeper into the inhospitable world of sand and rock.

Navigation had become extremely difficult. Not only were the maps so vague as to be almost useless, but in the flight and the frequent skirmishes, Caspasian had found it impossible to take accurate bearings and estimates of distance, so that now he could hardly be sure where they were. He reckoned that his estimate of their position could be as much as a hundred miles adrift. All thoughts of the lost city had vanished from their minds which were now focused solely on escape and survival.

'I think we can slow down now, saheb,' Ganga shouted. His face wore a pained expression, not from fear but from the discomfort of the ride. The moment he saw Caspasian give serious consideration to his proposal he quickly reinforced it. 'I haven't seen anyone for several miles.'

'All right then.'

With immense relief Ganga signalled the front of the column which began the process of slowing the camels to a trot and then a walk. Far from being straightforward, it entailed supreme efforts on the part of the Gurkhas, two of whom became unseated, falling heavily into the sand. Akalbahadur was quickly on his feet, clambering back aboard his mount, while Bharat lay moaning on the ground, his bewildered animal circling him inquisitively. Harkabahadur rode up beside him and lowered the muzzle of his rifle until it was aiming straight at Bharat's head. Bharat stared back in horror.

'Do you want me to shoot him?' Harkabahadur asked nonchalantly.

Sergeant Ganga glared at him, suppressing a smile. 'Stop mucking around, both of you. Bharat, get on that camel now or I'll let Harka do it.'

Bharat looked from one to the other and muttered angrily. With a great show of pain he staggered to his feet and attempted to remount.

For the next few hours the column made its way deeper into the rough jebel. The ground became a pitted mess of strewn rocks through which the camels picked their way. A low jagged ridgeline cut across their line of march and behind it others loomed menacingly, each higher than the last.

'There'll be a way through,' Caspasian said, studying the rock formations through his binoculars.

'You sound very sure of yourself,' Sir Hubert commented sourly.

'There's always a pass. You just have to find it.'

Ganga rode up beside him. 'I don't like it, saheb. It looks good country for an ambush.'

'I was thinking that too. No point alarming the others though. Besides, there's not much we can do about it just now.'

As they approached the first of the ridgelines intersecting their path, a sliver of shadow grew and spread until Caspasian could see that it broadened into a narrow defile disappearing into the mountainside. He halted the column short of it and called everyone together.

'We've got to get through and this seems to be the only way. Obviously we're not simply going to ride straight in lest it's a trap. I'll go in first, taking one man with me.'

'Only one man?' the Professor said, amazed. 'If it's a trap you'll be killed.'

'If it's a trap we'll be killed however many of us go in. I'm gambling on it being clear. The rest of you will take up a defensive position here under Sergeant Ganga. If you hear firing you are to make your way back to the Nile as best you can. By only taking one man with me I'm not depleting the force more than is absolutely necessary.'

'If it's as simple as that,' Sir Hubert said loftily, 'why take anyone with you at all? Why not go alone?'

Caspasian kept his temper in check. 'Because when I'm satisfied it's clear I can send him back to bring you forward while staying in place myself to make sure the situation doesn't alter in the meantime.'

All eyes turned on Sir Hubert who remained silent, his self-satisfied smile suddenly robbed of smugness.

For the column's leaguer position Caspasian chose a piece of high ground with good fields of fire on all sides. Placing the remaining camels and stores in the centre, he left Ganga to deploy the men.

'I'll take Harka with me,' he said.

Ganga glanced at him doubtfully but Caspasian was already preparing to move off. Harkabahadur stared in astonishment, a slow smile of pride lighting his face.

Riding away from the rest of the column and the reassuring sound of the machine guns being assembled and sited, Caspasian felt suddenly very exposed. He smiled bravely at Harkabahadur and was impressed to see not the slightest concern on the Gurkha's face. He knew little about the man except his reputation as a trouble-causer, but what he had seen of him on the expedition so far made Caspasian question it. Clearly the man had no time for pretence, less still for kow-towing. Diplomacy played no part in his life and it had been to his detriment. Caspasian felt he, of all people, could sympathise.

The rock faces of the defile closed about them and as they entered the shadows the air became pleasantly cooler.

'They might just let us ride through undisturbed and then hit the column when we return with it,' Harkabahadur said. He did not seem particularly interested to hear Caspasian's own opinion but rather was thinking aloud. Caspasian smiled to himself, wondering if Harkabahadur was testing him, seeing how far he could push him, whether he would allow himself to take offence. Caspasian made no comment.

'The only way to know for sure whether the pass is unguarded is to scale the highest peak and have a look.'

Caspasian rode on in silence, liking the direction of the man's thinking. He was not prepared simply to take orders but wanted to use his brain. No wonder he had fallen foul of the system, Caspasian reflected.

'Well?' Harkabahadur asked at last.

'Well what?'

'Aren't we going to scale the sides?'

'Not here. It's too steep. We'll ride round.'

Harkabahadur snorted. 'Do you think we've got time? This could go on for miles. One of us has then got to ride all the way back to fetch the column.'

Caspasian regarded him with interest. 'You're very free-spoken for a rifleman,' he observed, softening his words with a friendly smile.

Harkabahadur shrugged gruffly, embarrassed. 'It doesn't suit everyone.'

'Hence the guard room.'

'Sometimes,' Harkabahadur replied.

'What about NCO selection? Didn't you pass the cadre?'

'Yes,' Harkabahadur said starkly. 'But there was no vacancy. And by the time there was, I was too old. Younger lads had come up behind me.'

What he did not say was that some of the younger lads were probably better connected in the invisible network of tribal influence and family and village relationships that existed in every Gurkha regiment and, indeed, throughout much of the Indian Army. For a man wholly on his own it was often a harsh environment in which to prosper. It made the tensions within the officers' mess look as tame as a welfare scheme. Nevertheless, Harkabahadur had mentioned none of this, declining to hide behind a screen of excuses. He had learnt to accept his fate, however unfair. Caspasian admired him for it.

Caspasian looked up at the towering rock faces on both sides and selected the highest peak. 'Could you make it up that one?'

Barely checking, Harkabahadur fired back, 'Yes, saheb.'

Caspasian dismounted and took hold of Harkabahadur's reins. 'Off you go then. While you're away I'll move further down the defile to see where it goes. We'll RV back here in, what . . . ?' he consulted his watch, '. . . say, two hours. Does that give you enough time?'

'That's fine,' Harkabahadur said sternly, slinging his rifle across his shoulders and tightening his webbing straps in readiness for the scramble up the rock face.

When he had gone, Caspasian followed the course of the defile, leading both camels with him. He had barely gone half a mile when he heard footsteps behind him and looked round to see Harkabahadur. He had unslung his rifle and as he drew near he gave the hand signal for enemy.

'I heard voices,' he hissed, clearly relishing the excitement. 'Once I had climbed just a short way I saw there was another defile running parallel to this one. There is someone in it. If we go another hundred yards further on, the two meet. We can surprise them there and kill them.'

Caspasian's mind raced. The enemy numbers were unknown but, if he and Harkabahadur withdrew, they might be running away from only a couple of tribesmen. A goatherd even. At the very least they should hide and observe.

'Come on,' he said, leading the way in search of a hiding place. They found one just in time and forced the camels as far back into the shadows as they could. With weapons ready, they slid forward to watch.

A large open area the size of a rugby pitch spread across the junction point of the two defiles. So long as the tribesmen continued in their present direction they would emerge into view but then move away from Caspasian's position. On the other hand, if they turned to head out to the open desert where the column was waiting, they would walk straight past Caspasian and Harkabahadur who would then be discovered and forced to open fire.

They did not have long to wait. The figures appeared but, being some distance away, it was impossible to see them distinctly, just the loose billowing garments they were wearing.

To Caspasian's relief they turned away from him. He heaved a sigh and swapped smiles with Harkabahadur.

Just then, wind gusted down the defile, bringing with it a cloud of hot dust and something else. A sound. Caspasian listened, frowning to identify it. Then it came again, and the next moment he was smiling broadly, stepping out into the open and waving exaggeratedly at the retreating figures. Harkabahadur stared at him in amazement but Caspasian ignored him, for he was still listening to the faint strains of '*Le Boudin*'.

13

The moment Caspasian stepped out into the open he was spotted by the legionnaires. A cry of alarm went up and they darted for cover until he called out, holding his arms wide, hands open and empty. Harkabahadur stared at him in astonishment until he too realised who the figures were and followed Caspasian's example, moving out of cover.

One by one the legionnaires rose from the ground. Sergeant Kraus barked orders and Caspasian could see the legionnaires starting in his direction. There were far fewer in the party than previously. To his relief, as they drew closer, he saw Michelle, walking beside her husband who was leaning on a stick for support.

'Where's Béranger?' Caspasian called as they approached him.

Sergeant Kraus gestured to a makeshift stretcher that was being carried by two of his men. Caspasian went quickly across to it and saw Béranger lying there, unconscious. His chèche had been converted into an improvised bandage and fastened around his middle. It was caked with sand and dried blood.

'How serious is it?' Caspasian asked.

Sergeant Kraus shrugged. 'Our medic was killed in the attack, but I don't think the Capitaine's life is in immediate danger.' He wiped a grimy hand across his stubbled cheeks. 'No more than the rest of our lives, that is. As far as I can tell the bullet exited cleanly through the small of the back without puncturing any vital organs. It missed the spine, thank God. He's lost a lot of blood though. My biggest worry's infection. It's impossible to keep the wound clean.'

'One of my men's trained as a medic. He can have a look at him.'

'Where is he?' Kraus asked, glancing back at Harkabahadur who stood, rifle in hand, watching suspiciously.

Caspasian explained that he had left them behind and had been scouting ahead.

'The pass is clear,' Kraus said. 'We've been hiding here for two days. The enemy force has pushed off for the moment but they'll be watching us. I know it.' He scanned the ridgelines overhead and briefly recounted what had happened to the French expedition since leaving the paddle steamer.

'How on earth did you manage to get away when Béranger was hit? Surely they had you at their mercy?' Caspasian asked.

Kraus gave an evil smile. 'We took a hostage. It was incredible. One minute we were fighting for our lives, the enemy closing in. I thought that was it. We were dead. Then, Madame Simonin notices this old fool stumbling about in the open. Just wandering along as if he was on holiday. I took a bead on him and was about to pull the trigger when I noticed his mates were desperately trying to get to him and pull him down. He wasn't just some old idiot, but someone they valued.'

'So how did you get him?'

Kraus chuckled. 'Didn't have to. He wandered straight over. Seemed to be singing to himself. The moment I grabbed him the firing stopped. The enemy withdrew. Didn't seem to know what to do about it. And that's the way it's been ever since.'

Caspasian looked once more at Béranger and laid a hand lightly on his shoulder before turning away and asking to see the old man.

'He's over here. Don't expect to get any sense out of him though. The man's as mad as they come.'

They found the old man sitting on a rock guarded by two legionnaires. He looked up as Caspasian and Kraus approached and smiled pleasantly at them. Caspasian tried to speak to him in Arabic but the old man kept on smiling as if he had not heard.

'See?' Kraus said. 'His brain's as useless as a priest's dick . . . begging Madame's pardon,' Kraus added quickly, noticing that Michelle had joined them.

'Sergeant Kraus, my husband would like to know what we're going to do now.'

Kraus glared across to where Émile Simonin sat slumped on the ground. 'Of course, Madame. Tell Monsieur that dinner will be served at eight.'

Michelle sighed. She looked exhausted. Kraus instantly apologised, adding, 'I will speak to Monsieur myself, Madame,' and sauntered across to Simonin.

Left together, Michelle and Caspasian looked at each other.

'Not quite how we expected things to turn out,' Caspasian remarked.

Michelle tried a smile. Her skin was coated with a fine layer of dust that gave it a reddish hue. 'In my experience, Captain, things rarely do turn out as we expect. So, what do we do now?'

'We join forces and fight our way out.'

'Just like that?'

'Have you a better idea?'

Michelle smiled and looked down at the old man who was taking an interest in their conversation. 'Perhaps our friend here might assist us in our escape.'

Caspasian considered the ragged figure perched beside them. 'I'd guess he must be the leader's father. A close relative or something. Whoever he is, it was a piece of luck that Kraus got him.'

'If he hadn't, we would all be dead by now.'

'Indeed,' Caspasian said, keeping to himself his thoughts that Michelle might be the only one not to have been killed, although she would probably soon have wished herself dead along with the rest of them.

Kraus returned a moment later, suppressing his anger.

'What's up?' Caspasian asked.

'Monsieur wants a camel,' Kraus said, exasperated.

Caspasian smiled. 'Don't worry. He can have one of ours.' He turned to look for Harkabahadur. 'Harka, ride back and fetch the column. We'll wait here.'

As Harkabahadur left, Kraus looked doubtful. 'Shouldn't we move to join your column? Why press on? Surely it makes more sense to retrace our steps?'

'I'm not sure I could. Since we've been pursued it's been impossible to keep an accurate fix on our location. If I'm right, however, beyond this range of hills we should be able to head due north and strike the Nile further down river.'

'Are you sure?' Kraus asked, unconvinced.

'Frankly, no, but at least we have some cover here in the jebel. The open desert we've just come through is a killing ground. Nowhere to run or hide.'

'That's true enough,' Kraus agreed. 'All right then. We join up and press on.'

There was a shuffling noise behind them. 'What's all that about joining up?'

They turned to see that Monsieur Simonin had entered the discussion. 'I'm not joining forces with the British if that's the last thing I do.'

'In that case, Monsieur,' Kraus said, 'it will be.'

'Don't talk nonsense. They haven't dared touch us since we took the hostage, have they? We don't need the British,' Simonin said proudly. 'In fact, it's the British who need us. Our hostage will protect them as well, don't you see?'

'Monsieur,' Kraus persevered with a patience that Caspasian could tell did not come easily to him. 'Yes, we have one raddled old lunatic, but the British have water, food, ammunition, soldiers and,' he said, pausing for effect, 'camels.'

He left a space for his message to sink in. Simonin considered it all carefully, but the notion of a ride on a camel had won Kraus's argument for him, as he knew it would.

'All right,' Simonin said at last, grudgingly. 'But I want it noted that I only conceded under the most extreme duress.'

'Whatever you say, Monsieur,' Kraus said boredly, already walking away to muster his men.

Simonin looked loftily from Caspasian to Michelle. 'Well, shall we go and sit in the shade, my dear?' he said at last to his wife. She stared at him, her face expressionless. 'No. You go.'

He shifted his weight from foot to foot. 'Michelle?'

'Go!'

He glared at her. 'Damn you, woman.' With a dismissive wave of the hand he stormed away.

Caspasian arched a hand over his eyes and peered up into the blazing sky. 'Actually the shade's not a bad idea.'

Michelle smiled. 'It must be his first. Let's go over there,' she said, pointing in the opposite direction. They found some shade at the foot of the rock face near the place where Caspasian and Harkabahadur had been hiding. Caspasian kicked aside a few stones to clear a space and they settled side by side on the ground, backs against the stone wall which was surprisingly cool. Caspasian took out his water bottle, popped out the cork and handed it to Michelle. She accepted it gratefully and drank. When she had quenched her thirst, she handed the bottle back to him and wiped her mouth with her scarf.

As he tipped back his head to drink, Caspasian noticed that Michelle still wore the pouch on her belt. He refastened the bottle back in its holder and pointed to the pouch. 'Your family?'

Michelle nodded.

'I would very much like to see them,' Caspasian said. 'If you wouldn't mind.'

She thought about it for a while, staring away across the pass, and then, just as Caspasian was beginning to think she had decided against it, she unfastened the leather flap and withdrew a soiled white envelope. The edges were brown and creased with age and wear. Opening it, she carefully slipped out an even more battered photograph. Just one. Looking at it tenderly herself for a moment, she passed it across. With great care, Caspasian received it with both hands.

He had been expecting to see four men in military uniform, like tens of thousands of similar photos that had been taken and then treasured since the terrible conflict that had torn the heart out of countless families. To his surprise, instead he found himself looking at a family group which must have been taken some time before the war. A man smiled broadly from the centre of the group. He was sitting on a tree stump in a meadow beside a stream. A woman stood at his side, one hand resting on his shoulder. Around them three young boys stood immobile with the greatest of difficulty. One had just moved his hand to knock his brother's head. The hand was slightly blurred, still moving all these years later. The father was dressed in shirt-sleeves, a baggy pair of old trousers and, around his calves, the leather gaiters of a farmer.

Most of all, Caspasian's eyes were drawn to the figure of a small child on the man's lap, a girl. Even though she was very young he could tell that it was Michelle. There was a quizzical expression on her face as she studied the camera, and one corner of her mouth was lifted as a smile hovered there, uncertainly.

The whole scene was cast in sunshine, except where the overhanging bough of a tree dappled the ground at their feet with shade that, like the hand, was blurred. It had been a day in high summer, a breeze coming across the meadow and finding the family group.

Caspasian sighed, running one hand through his hair. An almost unbearable sadness overwhelmed him as he considered the figures. He had seen Verdun. The thought of those young boys and that smiling father embroiled some years later in that charnel house of slaughter was appalling. Even he, who had seen so much, could barely imagine the agony they must have felt as, one by one, their number was depleted by tragedy, after tragedy, after tragedy, after tragedy. Who had succumbed first? The father or one of his sons? And what of the two women waiting at home?

'Your mother?' Caspasian asked.

'Dead,' Michelle answered. 'She died of a broken heart. It was too much for her to bear. She . . .' Michelle turned her head away, but when Caspasian stole a glance at her he saw that her eyes were red-rimmed but dry.

So only the little girl had lived on, Caspasian reflected, looking now more closely at the small figure on the man's lap. How could that be, he wondered? How could such a thing happen? Was it a triumph that such a life should continue, or merely a cruel failing of the whole system that life should so torture one of its own by obliging them to exist after all the others had perished?

'I am so sorry,' he said, painfully aware of how inadequate his words must sound, ringing as hollow and empty as the dust-filled breezes that were sweeping through the lifeless jebel all around them.

Michelle accepted back the photograph and without another glance at it, replaced it in its envelope. She inserted the envelope back in the leather pouch and fastened the flap and buckle.

'I understand now why you would not surrender your handbag to the thief.'

She laughed. 'This thing,' she said tapping the pouch, 'has got me into all kinds of trouble over the years. You can't imagine.' She looked him full in the eyes. 'But it has never left me. Not once.' She glanced away as if embarrassed. 'It is all I am. One photograph.'

'No, Michelle,' Caspasian said, placing his hand on her forearm.

'Oh, he thinks I'm more,' she flashed back vehemently,

thrusting her chin in the direction of her husband, invisible through the heat haze clinging to the desert floor. 'But only like some accoutrement for him. A plaything.'

Caspasian ventured the question that had been nagging at him ever since he had seen Michelle in the garden of the Residency in Cairo. 'How did it happen? The marriage, I mean?'

Michelle pulled her arm out of Caspasian's light grasp and hugged her knees. Noticing what she had done and regretting the loss of his touch, she glanced quickly at him and smiled, checking. 'The Simonin family owned the land that my father farmed. Émile was the only son. His mother was a hard old woman. Bitter and savage. To everyone except her son on whom she doted. She had connections and made sure that her precious Émile escaped the war and conscription. He was sent away to Paris to indulge his passion for archaeology. Not to mention his other passions,' she added heavily.

'When my family was dead, my mother barely cold in her grave, the farm was repossessed but old Madame Simonin was merciful enough to give me a job in the big house,' she continued bitterly. 'And that was where Émile found me. What else could I do? I was a child. I was alone and I was terrified.' She laid her head back against the bare rock. 'His mother was furious when she discovered that we were to be married. It was one thing for her son to make use of the servants for his amusement, but quite another for him to propose to one of them.'

'And why did he?'

'He said that he loved me and I believed him. Later I realised what he meant by love.'

'And now?'

Michelle chuckled. 'Right now he would exchange me for a camel, a glass of claret and a wedge of cheese.'

Caspasian smiled. 'Well I don't know about the claret or the cheese, but I'm sure I can manage the camel.'

She turned her face towards him and smiled too. Before he knew he was doing it, Caspasian cupped her chin in one hand, leaned forward and kissed her on the lips. Michelle remained motionless, neither pulling back nor returning the kiss. Considering.

When Caspasian let her go they regarded each other carefully. 'I expect you have been to some of the places I have been, John Caspasian,' she said at last. She placed her hand over her heart. 'These terrible places.'

'I expect I have.'

She nodded to herself, weighing the import of his answer. 'I'm not sure that people like us should be together.'

'Survivors, you mean?'

She tilted her head, thinking. 'Ghosts,' she said.

Caspasian smiled. 'Do you think we are as insubstantial as that, you and I?'

'I know we are,' she said, her expression serious but compassionate.

'There were times in the war when I felt like that. Insubstantial. Usually after a battle. It took a while to decide whether I really had survived or not. Funnily enough, it got harder the longer the war went on. Sometimes I really used to doubt I was alive. In some ways it gave me a sort of comfort. Thinking I was already dead.'

'So what happened to change it?' Michelle asked, settling to hear his answer.

'Life happened. It was as if I myself was just a lung and that life was the stuff breathing through me. I'm not sure which was which though. Perhaps it was life that was breathing me. I was being breathed by life. Either way, it was a dynamic relationship. We were mutually dependent. Like fish and water, air and lung. Each flows through the other, interwoven. I move through life. Life moves through me.' He chuckled, remembering.

'Are you going to tell me that the dead live on?' Michelle asked, her voice suddenly hard and unyielding.

Caspasian weighed his words carefully before replying. 'I think it's more a question of do we live on?'

'That's avoiding the issue. Of course we live on. Look at you and me. We're here, aren't we?'

'Yes. So it seems. But how do we live on? Like ghosts or like human beings?'

'Ah,' she said.

'Yes. Ah,' Caspasian echoed. 'I believe we have a choice. To live on as ghosts or as survivors.'

'Survivors robbed and stripped of all essence, all reason to live,' she said, her voice rising, desperate.

'There is no real choice, Michelle,' Caspasian said calmly. 'Remember what the ghost of Achilles said to Faustus. Something about it being better to be the lowliest beggar amongst the living than king of all the dead in the underworld.'

'I have been a beggar, Caspasian. And frankly I would rather join my father and brothers in the underworld.'

'We all will eventually. That's one wish that will definitely come true, Michelle. All too soon, if these tribesmen come at us again. But while we're alive, why not see where life can lead? See what else it just might have to offer. You never know, you just might be in for a surprise.'

'With him at my side?'

'That's up to you,' Caspasian said.

She shook her head angrily. 'Oh, how easy for a man to talk. What? I should return to cleaning as an occupation, should I?'

'Michelle,' Caspasian said gently. 'There are a thousand things you could do. A person with your intelligence and character. Your determination. For God's sake, look what you've been through! A person doesn't come through that without determination and strength of will. Use that. Use it to change from ghost to survivor. And then, maybe, from survivor into something else, something better.'

She looked away, but Caspasian could see that she was thinking over what he had said.

'And what about you?' she said at last. 'Why are you still locked in as a survivor? Why haven't you moved beyond that on to something else, something better?'

Caspasian smiled. 'Perhaps I'm still trying.'

Michelle laughed, but now it was a gentle sound. Peaceful and tender, not harsh like before. 'All right, John Caspasian. You win. I'll concede the point but not the argument. The jury's still deliberating on that.'

'I hope they make the right choice, Michelle. I really do.'

She reached across and took his hand and together they waited for Harkabahadur's return with the column.

The Professor, when he arrived, was delighted to see the Simonins safe. When he had greeted them, he looked at Béranger and shook his head. 'It is absurd. That an archaeological expedition should result in the loss of so many lives and such injury. If only we could communicate with them I'm sure we could come to some arrangement. Pay some sort of tribute, perhaps, for safe passage.'

Sir Hubert laughed. 'Really, Miles, don't be an ass. How could we trust them? They'd take whatever we offered and then kill us all the same.'

To his extreme discomfort, Caspasian found himself agreeing with Sir Hubert. 'However, the French seem to have stumbled upon something with this old man. While a tribute might not be workable, hanging onto this hostage just might,' he said.

With the remnants of the two expeditions now united, Caspasian oversaw the reallocation of supplies amongst them, much to Sir Hubert's annoyance. He was livid to see their own water supplies being shared with the French team but Caspasian ignored him. When they were ready to move again, Caspasian detailed the order of march and they set off. A camel had been provided for Michelle and another for her husband, less out of compassion than practicality. Caspasian realised that if Simonin had to walk he would hold back the entire party.

After a further two hours' travel, the defile began to widen and ascend, until they found themselves labouring up an ever-broadening incline, strewn with boulders. The landscape on all sides was as desolate as any Caspasian had seen and he secretly began to have serious worries about finding any sort of water supply. Just by looking at the water bladders he could see that they were almost empty. He estimated that they had supplies for perhaps one more day. Three if they cut the rations still further, but he was loath to do it as he could see that everyone was already suffering. The last thing he needed was for men to start dropping from heat exhaustion.

The tribesmen had reappeared but were keeping their distance, while making no secret of their presence. At times they approached almost to within rifle range and, whenever they did, Sergeant Kraus asked Caspasian whether he could open fire. He fancied taking a pot shot at them, and Caspasian could see that Ganga was also wondering whether he could drop one or two of them. Caspasian ordered them to keep their rifles slung. So long as the tribesmen were not posing a threat he could see no point in antagonising them. He had enough problems as it was.

The steep incline finally began to level out. The highest of the jebel peaks fell away on the flanks and they found themselves emerging onto a plateau. It stretched away in front of them, strangely shaped rock formations looming in the distance.

'Extraordinary,' the Professor mused, riding alongside Caspasian. 'I've never seen anything like it. We could be on another planet.'

Michelle had remained close to Caspasian's side since the two expeditions had joined forces, much to the annoyance of her husband, but Émile Simonin was more concerned with maintaining a makeshift awning he had rigged over his head to keep the sun off.

Michelle shaded her eyes and looked hard at the horizon, but it was obscured by a thick haze. Beside her, Caspasian consulted his compass. His map was now all but useless, showing only the barest features. The Nile showed as a distant ribbon of blue, but, peering across at the map, Michelle could see how he was gradually leading them on a route that took them back towards it.

Ganga goaded his camel forward with difficulty. He called out.

Caspasian turned, irritated to have been distracted from his route-planning. 'What is it?'

'The tribesmen,' Ganga said, looking worried. 'They have gone.'

'Well? That's excellent. Why are you looking so miserable about it?'

Ganga shook his head, clearly puzzled. 'I don't know. But something doesn't feel right.'

Caspasian had known the Gurkha sergeant long enough to have respect for his intuitions. He took out his binoculars and scoured the surrounding landscape. There was no sign of the tribesmen. They had vanished.

'Wonderful!' Sir Hubert and Monsieur Simonin remarked together. 'We are free.'

Caspasian laughed and waved a hand at the immensity of the desert. 'Sure, if you call this free.'

He suddenly became aware of a commotion some way back and turned to see Sergeant Kraus and two legionnaires remonstrating with the old man they had taken hostage. Caspasian halted the column and went back to see what was the matter. The old man seemed very distracted by something, and kept repeating the same unintelligible sentence over and over again.

'Perhaps he wants to rejoin his friends,' the Professor ventured.

Caspasian shook his head. 'I don't think so. He keeps pointing at the sky.'

They looked up but above them the blue sky was empty save for the blazing sun pouring down its unbearable heat upon them. Then Sergeant Kraus noticed something in the distance and went pale. He pointed into the horizon and, when Caspasian looked, he noticed how the heat haze had diminished. In its place the horizon had blurred with a thin band of dirty brown.

'What is it?' the Professor asked.

Experienced in the desert, Kraus knew the answer. 'Sandstorm.'

'Of course,' Caspasian said. 'That's why the tribesmen have left. They're running for cover.' He scanned around but all he could see was a jumble of rocky features some miles distant.

Kraus saw where he was looking. 'We'll have to make it to there.'

'We'll try at least. It's too far to retrace our steps back to the defile.'

'Don't you think it might pass us by?' Sir Hubert asked, the edge in his voice betraying his rising panic.

No one bothered to answer him. Kraus and Caspasian were too busy gathering their men and preparing to move on.

'You'll be needing these,' Kraus said, handing Caspasian Béranger's goggles.

'Thank you.' Caspasian turned to the others. 'We ride as hard as we can,' he shouted so that everyone could hear him. 'If we can make it to that feature we should find shelter of some sort. If not, then God help us.'

As they set off, kicking their camels into a trot, he glanced back at the approaching storm. Already the band had thickened and was growing still as the livid clouds of swirling sand came ever nearer, whipped into a frenzy by savage howling winds.

Those without camels ran alongside, keeping pace as best they could. The old man, still under close guard, had forgotten his earlier alarm and was singing, a high warbling sound that clung eerily to the stiffening air, sending a shiver down Caspasian's spine. It was an eerie tune, but one that was somehow familiar. Pushing it from his mind, Caspasian pressed on.

It was not long before he felt the first light flurry of breeze on the back of his neck, deceptively gentle. It was hot and it carried fine grains of sand that filtered down the back of his shirt. To be caught in the open by the full force of the storm, he knew, could mean anything from burial alive to having the skin flayed from the bones. Yet however fast they moved, the rocks in front never seemed to get any closer. They were always agonisingly just out of reach like a mirage.

The gentle breeze became a stiff wind. As the wind started to grow into a howling gale, Caspasian gathered everyone together and bellowed out his instructions, fighting the noise of the mounting storm in order to be heard.

'Everyone dismount,' he yelled. 'I'll lead the way from here on a bearing.' The distant rock features had been abruptly snatched from view, but not before he had managed to take a fix on them with his prismatic compass.

'Tie the camels together in a string. For God's sake make sure the fastenings are secure. Everyone hold on to something. Visibility's going to get so bad you won't be able to see your hand in front of your face. Now do as I say!'

When he was sure that his orders had been carried out, he moved to the front of the column, alarmed to see that in the space of only minutes visibility had clamped right down to within a few yards. Already the rear of the column had been swallowed up by the swirling sand and, as he watched, the cloud swept the length of the column towards him until he was only able to see two camels' distance. Using a length of rope he quickly fastened one end to his belt and the other to Michelle's. She in turn secured herself to the Professor who was tied on to the first camel's saddle. Cloths had been tied around the animals heads to cover their eyes and shield their noses and mouths to prevent them panicking. Ganga clung steadfastly to the reins of the first camel in the string, ensuring it kept moving.

Sergeant Kraus had taken up station at the rear of the column but his shouted commands had been snatched away by the manic wind. In the centre of the column, Monsieur Simonin, Sir Hubert and the old hostage with his guards, clung terrified to the labouring beasts that stumbled on through the mounting maelstrom, while Captain Béranger mumbled delirious in his unconscious state, cocooned in a hammock.

By the time Caspasian judged that the nearest of the rock formations was little more than five hundred yards away, the storm had taken possession of them. It encased them as if in liquid stone. The sand tore through every opening in their clothing, howling in the ears and nose, forcing its way between lips and clenched teeth. Nearly everyone staggered on with eyes firmly shut, except Caspasian who, at the head of the column, squinted into the wall of sand through his goggles, checking his compass needle every few paces to ensure they maintained the correct course. Tugging against his belt he could feel the rope that fastened him to Michelle and, through her, to the rest of the column behind them. He glanced round and was horrified to discover that he could barely see her although he knew that they were less than a yard apart. She appeared to him in glimpses like a wraith, hair flying wildly, one hand over her face, the other outstretched towards him. With his free hand, Caspasian reached out for her. He felt his fingers fasten on hers. They clasped each other and held tight, edging forward, step by laboured step.

14

Mahmud flung himself up the rocks, leaving his camel down below in the care of one of his men. Others of his commanders followed him, all of them apprehensive about his dark mood.

'This should never have happened,' he called back over his shoulder, continuing all the while to climb, higher and higher. 'We should have slaughtered all of them by now.'

Already the wind was whipping in between the rock faces, scouring them smooth with sand as they had been doing for thousands of years, sculpting them into weird unearthly formations. On detecting the storm's approach, Mahmud had reluctantly broken off the pursuit of the enemy force and retreated to one of several known refuges where they would be able to wait out the storm safely. His men were gathered in the narrow defile below, stripping their camels of packs and saddles, goading them to their knees, hobbling and blindfolding them. The men themselves would then crawl into the rock crevasses and cover themselves tightly with blankets and rugs, there to wait secure and safe until the worst of the sandstorm had blown over.

Mahmud's concern was not for his men however. He knew they would be safe now that they had managed to reach the defile. Nor was he concerned for the enemy. In other circumstances the storm would have been a godsend. It would have done Mahmud's work for him, splitting the enemy column into a dozen pieces, each one becoming utterly lost and eventually perishing. Unprepared for such a thing, the enemy would be blinded, their equipment literally plucked from their hands, the clothes from their backs by the force of the wind. Any that might survive would be completely at Mahmud's mercy when the storm eventually passed.

But instead of glee Mahmud felt only anger. Anger and desolation. He was livid and frantic at the same time. Livid with his men for having allowed old Yakub to stray unattended right into the enemy's hands, and frantic because he knew that Yakub's chances of survival were now greatly reduced. The enemy would not know how to survive. They would perish, and Yakub, being in their care, would perish along with them.

Even if any amongst the enemy knew how to survive such a sandstorm, Mahmud thought he had seen them caught in the open. He had been forced to break contact with them in order to reach cover himself. His commanders had pleaded with him and he had left it until the very last moment. Now, as he bounded up the last of the rocks and flung himself flat on the topmost, he desperately scanned the desert below for signs of the enemy. The entire landscape from horizon to horizon was melting into one enormous swirling cloud of sand. It was like the annual flooding of the Nile where fields and farms were similarly covered. But here the flood was airborne and it was happening within minutes. Even as he watched.

'There!' one of the commanders shouted, his outstretched hand pointing hard. 'I see them!'

Mahmud narrowed his eyes, shielding them with both hands, and squinted to see. Sure enough he could just make out a thin line of camels and men. They appeared to be keeping their formation, possibly secured together by ropes, and this gave him hope that whoever was in charge knew what he was doing. But as he watched he saw the enormous bank of sand roll over them like a tidal wave, dwarfing the column as it crashed in from the sky. One moment they were visible, the next they had vanished utterly, consumed by the desert's fury.

Mahmud sank back, his face set in stone. The storm had seized them. Moments later the sky itself was obliterated as the storm's outermost fingers reached out towards Mahmud's position, safe though it was in the cover of the rocks.

'Come!' his commanders shouted, dragging themselves from the exposed plateau, scurrying back down into the safety of the defile. 'Come, before we are blown off!'

Mahmud knew that they were right. He had to get into cover. When the storm had passed they could go out and search for Yakub, although he knew that they would be searching for dead bodies, not living beings.

Why had the old man wandered off? Mahmud felt tears prick at his eyes as he recalled the moment the legionnaires had seized old Yakub. A gun had been held to his head and he had been dragged in front of them, threatened with execution unless the tribesmen broke off the attack. They had had no alternative. The young men had been the hardest to convince. Some amongst them, Mahmud knew, were all for ignoring the hostage and continuing with the slaughter. They had no respect for the aged. No respect for visions.

The only small consolation was that Mahmud's mission would now be accomplished. Both columns would be destroyed. Mahmud's paymasters would never know the personal cost to him however. They would never know the cost to him. The cost of an old friend.

It was hard to tell whether he was moving forward or merely shuffling his feet on the spot. For all he knew he might have been making good progress, but without any points of reference whatsoever, Caspasian could only continue leaning into his direction of travel and push steadily forwards, ensuring all the while that he maintained contact with Michelle behind him and, through her, with the column strung out to the rear.

Everyone was locked into their own chaotic terrifying world. A world private to them, of noise, heat, pain and fear. Speech was useless because ears were deaf to any sound but the howling of the wind. Eyes could scarcely see a hand held in front of them. Terms like front and back, left and right, up and down had lost all meaning. Each person thrashed around as if tied in a sack, like a rat being drowned.

The only link was the rope fastened to their belt, securing them to the people next in the human chain. It was an umbilical cord every bit as life-giving as if they had each been a helpless foetus.

Caspasian crouched down and lifted his prismatic compass to his face, cupping the palm of one hand over it to glimpse the direction of the needle. He was maintaining his course, but without visibility he was having to check his direction every few steps. It slowed his progress dramatically but there was no alternative.

Suddenly Michelle stumbled into him. He stood up and gripped her shoulders, peering through the swirling sand at her face. He placed his mouth beside her ear.

'We can't be far from the rocks. Can you make it?'

He knew it was a pointless question as death was the only alternative to reaching cover. Nevertheless when he drew back and looked at her she was nodding her head.

'Good girl,' he mouthed. She cocked her head to one side and waved a hand in the air to show she had not heard him. He gripped her arm tightly and squeezed it before turning to move on, drawing her carefully after him. He fingered the rope securing her to him to check it was holding fast. His fingers moved round to the back of her belt and he could feel the rope disappearing tautly into the moving wall of sand indicating that the others were close behind.

As he stumbled on, clutching tight to Michelle's hand, Caspasian was assaulted by nagging doubts. What if he missed the rocks and was leading the entire column deeper into the open desert? They could not keep going under these conditions for long. Eventually people's strength would give out, individuals would fall by the wayside, the column would fragment and then death would pick them off one by one. They would be buried alive in the sand and suffocate.

Then he began to fear that even if they made it to the rocks, what if shelter still eluded them? They would be little better off than they were now.

Feeling panic start to rise, Caspasian fought for control. He steadied his breathing as best he could, in spite of the extreme physical exertion of the march. He moved his legs into a sanchin stance, the knees flexed, directing strength into the hips and thigh muscles, and as the wind hit him head on he slid his feet forward into it. His stomach became a wall of steel which the wind pummelled. It tore through his shirt and scoured his skin. It blasted against his face and raged at him, but still he pushed on. His breathing was steady now, imperturbable. He felt calm, all panic had vanished and confidence swept in to replace it. Sanchin. The so-called hourglass stance. A stance of immense strength. An hourglass – full of sand. Very appropriate.

Tugging against his hand he could feel Michelle being knocked off her feet. She was struggling heroically somehow remaining upright.

Caspasian's feet gripped the ground even as it moved beneath them. He focused his mind down through the abdomen, the tanden, seat of strength, projecting his energy down through his thighs and legs, down through the shifting sand to the firmer ground he pictured beneath it. He concentrated on that and drove relentlessly onwards.

He picked up such a momentum that when his face hit rock he was momentarily stunned. Instinctively he put out his free hand. The touch of solid rock against the palm, immovable and firm, was more comforting at that moment than a drink of iced water. He pulled Michelle to him. Taking her wrists in his hands, he placed her palms against the rock face. He saw her face nodding at him and knew that beneath the mask she was smiling.

But a wall of rock was not shelter. Not yet. The question now was which way should he turn, to the left or the right? He had only glimpsed it at a distance before the storm had closed about him and robbed him of vision, and it had not been possible to note any details of the rock formation. He was sure that at some point it would crack, providing a fissure or other opening into which they could squeeze for shelter.

Without thinking, Caspasian moved to the left, drawing Michelle after him. With his left hand holding tightly to her, he moved along the rock face, feeling his way with his right hand. The wind seemed to be slamming itself against the wall like a maniac in a cell, as if it wanted to tear it from the earth and hurl it out into space. Caspasian leaned against the rock as he went, intent on maintaining his contact with it, fearful lest the desert reclaim him and, with him, his comrades who were depending on him.

Suddenly the wall gave way and he tumbled to the ground, Michelle falling after him.

'An opening!' he shouted to her as they picked themselves up. Keeping a hand in contact with the rock, Caspasian worked his way around the corner. Sure enough, he discovered that the further he went the more the storm weakened, unable to follow him inside with its full force. It raged and howled at the outer edges, but as Caspasian continued on, visibility returned, inches at a time. He glanced above him and saw the sand swirling overhead. Then even this lessened and he found himself staring up at rock high overhead.

'It's a cave!' he shouted triumphantly.

Michelle was beside him and, next in line, Sergeant Ganga stumbled into view, emerging from the wall of sand like a swimmer rising up out of the sea. A camel blundered into them, coughing and roaring in outrage and terror. Only the blindfold kept it from rampaging. Ganga struggled to calm the beast. But more of the expedition were now appearing, each man and animal coughing and spitting like hags to clear the sand from their throats and noses.

Caspasian pulled Ganga to him and placed his mouth beside his ear. 'Go and see how far back it goes,' he shouted.

Ganga nodded, drew his kukri to cut himself free of the rope, and made his way deeper into the gloom. The Professor and Sir Hubert staggered in, collapsing onto hands and knees on the ground.

'Keep going,' Caspasian commanded, grasping each of them in turn by the scruff of neck and the belt and propelling them forward like sheep being hurled into a pen. Even Sir Hubert was too exhausted to protest but just shuffled away.

One by one the Gurkhas appeared, Bharat fumbling into Caspasian with outstretched arms like a blind man. Caspasian swiped away his hands and rubbed the man's eyes clear of sand. Bharat opened first one and then the other, blinking in surprise to find himself still alive. Everyone's skin and clothing was caked with a thick coating of sand until they resembled walking statues conjured into life.

With a fit of coughing, Monsieur Simonin staggered into the growing crowd of people and animals.

'*Mon Dieu*, what a hellish place. I have never seen anything like it before.'

Caspasian stared at him in horror. There was no one behind him and hanging from his belt the end of the piece of rope dangled uselessly.

'Where's the next man?' Caspasian shouted across to him.

'What are you talking about?' Simonin answered angrily. He was in no mood for the remonstrations of the British Captain. He had suffered enough already and considered himself lucky to be alive. The next second he found himself shoved up against the stone wall, Caspasian's face inches from his own.

'I said, where's the next man in the line? It was your job to make sure they were following. We were each responsible for the next man in the line.'

Simonin shook himself free like a large dog that had just

emerged from a river. His coat shuddered and a cloud of sand flew from it. 'Get your hands off me!' he ordered haughtily.

Caspasian swore and dashed to the mouth of the cave where sand swirled in violent eddies. It met him face on, forcing him back into the shelter.

He began to refasten the scarf around his mouth and nose. Ganga rushed to his side. 'Saheb, you can't go out in this. It would be madness.'

'Someone's got to find them and bring them in. If I don't they'll die. All of them.'

'But you'll never find your way back.'

Caspasian scanned the muddle of men, animals and equipment littering the cave. 'Quick, get me a length of rope. The longest you can find.'

Reading his intention, Ganga located some rope on one of the baggage animals and unfurled it. Caspasian secured one end tightly around his waist and gave the other end to Ganga. 'Reel it out as I go, just as if I was rock climbing. When you feel it run out and go taut, hang on for dear life and whatever you do don't let go.'

'What are you going to do, saheb? It'll be like looking for a needle in a haystack.'

'Just leave that to me.' And with that, Caspasian plunged out into the storm. The last sound he heard was Michelle calling his name, but then the storm closed about him and once again he was all but blinded by sand and wind.

Making his way back along the rock face, he edged away from the cave. Now that he did not have to bother about constantly checking his direction on the compass he made reasonably good time, one hand trailing lightly along the rock face. Suddenly the rope on his belt snapped taut as he reached the extremity of its range. Back at the far other end, secure in the cave, Ganga braced himself, looping the end of the rope around his own waist, tying it off securely, and then holding tightly with both hands. Michelle stood at his side, staring intently into the storm outside the cave's mouth, her eyes searching after Caspasian.

Ganga noticed how the rope angled sharply around the side of the rock, rubbing against it. He smiled as he realised what Caspasian was up to. Out in the storm, Caspasian took a deep breath, turned away from the wall and stepped out into nothingness. Keeping the rope taut all the time, he intended to swing outwards in a gigantic arc, with Ganga and the cave mouth as the fulcrum. Should the rope snap he knew that he would be lost. He had taken a rough fix on the compass before leaving the relative security of the rock face but as his direction was changing with every step, it was next to useless. The slightest error and he might end up staggering out into the empty desert to die. All he could do would be to curl up into a tiny ball and hope not to be buried alive.

Pushing away from the rock face was like leaving behind a lifeboat in the middle of a raging storm-tossed ocean. His one consolation was that he knew, on the other end of the rope, Sergeant Gangabahadur Limbu would be hanging on for dear life. Ganga would die himself before he released his hold on the rope.

Sweeping outwards into the desert, his stumbling footsteps describing an enormous half circle, Caspasian advanced with arms outstretched. For all he knew he might at that very moment be passing within an inch of one of the legionnaires. He would do so without ever knowing it.

He shouted out every few steps, directing his voice outwards into the storm. It was almost useless but he had to try everything. It was impossible to tell how far he had gone. The whole process was physically exhausting and, although it seemed that he had been out for hours, he knew that in reality he might only have been going for a few minutes. Nor was it any use looking in the direction of the taut rope. It simply disappeared into the storm a foot from his body.

He was thinking about this when he fell headlong into the

sand. Something had obstructed his feet and he cursed as he went over. However, in falling he had landed on something that was harder than sand but softer than packed earth. He scrabbled in the dirt at his feet and his fingers touched cloth, rough hessian. Instantly he was digging furiously. Suddenly a figure rose out of the ground gasping for air like a corpse on resurrection day. It seized him by both shoulders, a drowning man struggling with his rescuer. Caspasian recognised it as one of the legionnaires who had been guarding the old hostage.

The man's eyes were wide with terror but Caspasian shook him until he registered Caspasian's presence. 'We are not far from safety,' he shouted into the man's ear. 'Where are the others?'

Only half aware of the question, the man hunted around him, studying the ground in bewilderment. Caspasian understood and started to dig furiously. A second legionnaire emerged, followed by the old hostage. He sat up and rubbed his eyes, then wailed with fright and snatched at Caspasian like a small frightened child.

Locating the rope at the legionnaire's belt, Caspasian traced it to the next man in the string, and then the next. The camels that had been with them had all disappeared but luckily the men had been able to cling together. Caspasian found Béranger, mercifully still unconscious and swathed in the blankets covering his stretcher. He brushed the thickest of the sand off them and lifted the edge to check he was still breathing. He thought for a moment that he saw one eye open briefly but he was distracted by someone stumbling into him. There was a sudden thrashing of arms and legs and a flurry of cursing that could even be heard above the storm. With a flood of relief Caspasian knew that Sergeant Kraus had arrived.

Kraus dropped to his knees and gripped Caspasian. He gave the thumbs up.

'Is everyone accounted for?' Caspasian yelled.

Kraus nodded exaggeratedly. Caspasian located the end of

the rope securing the legionnaires together, tied himself onto it, and then felt for his own rope that would lead him back to the cave. He found it. All they would have to do now would be to hold on tight to each other and follow the rope back to the safety of the cave. He stood up and collected in the slack, waiting for the rope to go taut whereupon he could start to lead the way home. The slack continued to come in. As more and more came in, gathering in a pool at his feet, Caspasian felt his heartbeat speeding. His gut began to feel like a lead weight was dragging it down. The next moment his fears were confirmed. He was standing there, the far end of his rope in his hands, hopelessly frayed. Examining it he realised that as he had edged sharply round the mouth of the cave and along the rock face, part of the rope must have snagged on a sharp piece of rock. His walking motion would have agitated it, causing it eventually to saw itself clean in two.

He turned round and saw Kraus standing close beside him, staring at the frayed end dumbstruck. Tossing the useless rope aside, Caspasian retrieved his compass from its pouch, lifted the lid and studied the sand-encrusted face. He tried to appear more confident than he actually felt but one glance at the expression on Kraus's face and he knew that his show of bravado was misplaced.

'We're fucked!' Kraus shouted. 'You should have stayed where you were, Captain!'

There was a commotion behind them and they turned to see the old hostage dancing maniacally in the storm. His hair flew wildly about his head as he whirled and spun, singing at the top of his lungs. Once again his terror had sought refuge in madness.

Caspasian returned to his compass. 'This way,' he shouted, indicating the direction of march with his hand.

At that moment both Caspasian and Kraus heard a rifle shot resounding in the distance. They looked at each other expectantly. Strangely, it was in the opposite direction to the one

Caspasian imagined the cave to be, opposite to the direction of his compass bearing, but it was unmistakably the report of a Lee-Enfield. Caspasian had always been taught to trust the compass over intuition, but that trust presupposed that the bearing had been set correctly. And it was not intuition that was set against it now, but the rifle fire from a British weapon.

Then a second shot was fired and Caspasian was able to get a better fix on the direction. He smiled. Ganga had found a solution. Something so obvious and yet Caspasian himself had not thought of it. Like a foghorn, Ganga was using his rifle fire to indicate his direction to the men lost out in the storm. To reinforce the fix, Caspasian prepared his compass and waited for the next rifle shot. Exactly on the minute it came and Caspasian hurriedly took a bearing as back-up. Then, with the line of legionnaires re-established and Kraus bringing up the rear, he set off anew, heading back towards the cave where Ganga waited, his rifle pointing skywards as Michelle waited at his side with watch in hand, calling out each time the minute hand hit twelve. Each time she did so, Ganga fired.

An age later, Caspasian stumbled exhausted into the cave mouth. Michelle rushed forward to seize him as his knees gave way and he sank to the ground. The Professor and the Gurkhas gathered around the incoming legionnaires, helping them into the safety of the cave, severing the ropes that tied them together and setting them one by one onto the ground. Water bottles, albeit depleted, were shared and the legionnaires gulped greedily as life returned to their limbs.

Only Sergeant Kraus stood apart, scanning the press of people and animals. Suddenly he found what he was after and strode through the middle, shoving people roughly aside. Sergeant Ganga looked up from Caspasian as Kraus rounded on the seated Simonin, hauled the astounded man to his feet, drew back his clenched fist and punched him full in the face. Simonin squealed, the sound muffled by the hands he threw up in front of himself to ward off the following blows that rained down upon him. His legs buckled and he dropped to the floor, blood gushing from his nose and lips.

'Help me! The man's gone mad. He's going to kill me!'

Ganga rushed across and tried to restrain the enraged German, but it was not until a further four Gurkhas had joined in the struggle that Kraus was successfully dragged from his prey and calmed down. Caspasian got tiredly to his feet and walked over but before he could ask why Kraus had punched the man, Kraus held up a loose end of rope hanging from his belt.

'The bastard cut it,' he said in explanation.

Caspasian lifted the end and examined it. Sure enough it had been cut. The severed end was clean and straight. He turned his eyes upon Simonin.

'Oh, don't be ridiculous,' Simonin stammered, starting to feel he was losing the argument and becoming severely frightened at the prospect. 'Of course I did no such thing. Why ever would I want to cut the rope?'

'Why indeed?' Caspasian asked.

'Because it was all too difficult for the bastard,' Kraus offered, his voice low and dangerous. 'He couldn't take the weight any longer of the rest of us dragging him down, pulling on him. He became tired, he knew he'd be all right if he remained on the end of your line and he didn't give a damn about us. So he cut the rope.'

Simonin opened his mouth to protest but instead of doing so he stood back, defiant, knowing that Caspasian, the Professor and Sir Hubert would not allow the German sergeant to harm him. 'You are all talking nonsense and I refuse any longer to be cross-questioned like this. You have no right. I am the head of the French expedition and that is all there is to it.' With that he folded his arms across his chest and took a step backwards, out of harm's way.

The Professor spoke up. 'Really, Monsieur Simonin, your behaviour is outrageous.'

'Most ungentlemanly,' Sir Hubert contributed, secretly rejoicing that he had not succumbed to the same temptation.

But Simonin was beyond caring. He straightened his collar and tie, took out his handkerchief and dabbed at the blood still running from his nostrils.

Before anyone could intervene, Michelle stepped swiftly forward and slammed the open palm of her right hand sharply across her husband's face. There was a resounding crack as it met flesh and Simonin staggered, almost losing balance. Swaying upright again he focused on his wife with a look of absolute shock registering on his face.

'My pretty . . .' he began, but Michelle's hand had already been drawn back for a second swing. As it came forward, Caspasian caught it firmly by the wrist and held it there. Michelle resisted for a moment and then calmed.

'You have shamed me for the last time,' she said, her voice pure loathing. 'For the last time.'

With that she turned abruptly and walked back to the mouth of the cave, standing there with folded arms, staring out into the raging storm.

Kraus stared at Caspasian. 'Let me finish him. He deserves to die. Throw him back out into the storm where he belongs. See how he likes it out there!'

For a moment Simonin looked worried, eyeing Caspasian timidly to see how he would decide. The reply did not come from Caspasian.

'Kraus, leave Monsieur Simonin alone.'

Everyone turned to seek out the speaker and to their amazement, Béranger was leaning up on his stretcher, supporting his weight on one elbow. With Simonin forgotten, they rushed across to Béranger's side. Caspasian cushioned the wounded man's head in his hand and eased him back onto his stretcher. He could see that the effort of speech had taken its toll on him.

'It is all right,' Béranger reassured him. 'I can feel the strength returning.'

'Nonsense. Lie still,' Caspasian ordered.

Without protesting, Béranger looked at Kraus. 'Your men

are now under the command of Captain Caspasian, is that clear?'

There was a mutter of protest from Simonin but it was ignored and he judged it politic not to press the point. Kraus glanced at Caspasian and then at his men. He nodded. 'Yes, *mon Capitaine.*'

Béranger knew that Kraus respected Caspasian and that he would obey orders, as he had always done. To the letter. Content, he closed his eyes. 'Let me rest for a while longer,' he said quietly. He smiled weakly at Caspasian. '*Nos anciens ont su mourir,*' he crooned, picking his way painfully through '*Le Boudin*'. '*Pour La Gloire de la Legion. Nous saurons bien tous périr, suivant la tradition.*'

Caspasian nodded in admiration. 'Your predecessors might well have known how to die, but no one's dying here today. Neither in the tradition of the Legion nor in any other way.'

He straightened the blankets covering Béranger's body and stood up. 'Mind you, I can't speak for tomorrow. But that's another day.' Béranger chuckled and turned away to sleep.

It was time for Caspasian to take stock. Every member of the party was exhausted and they had barely two days' water left. There was plenty of food but little ammunition after the engagements with the tribesmen. They were most likely lost in a vast region of unexplored desert and jebel, and there was an enemy force of unknown size waiting somewhere, ready to renew their attacks upon them.

For now, however, the storm was working to their advantage, shielding them from the enemy. Although they were unable to navigate in it or even to see where they were, neither could the enemy. Even when it passed, there would be a short breathing space in which the enemy would have to find them again. For now they were safe. There was therefore little they could do except rest, eat, drink sparingly, and redistribute the remaining weapons and equipment in preparation for the next stage of the journey. The temptation to sink to the ground and sleep was almost overpowering, but Caspasian knew that when the storm lifted, they would have to move quickly in order to take full advantage of the clean break from the enemy that it had afforded them. They had to steal a march and try to make good their escape before the tribesmen themselves recovered and pursued them to the cave. There might not be any tracks to follow by the time the storm had blown itself out, but in all likelihood the location of the cave would be known to them. It would certainly be one of the first places they would look.

Caspasian issued orders to the two sergeants and then located the Professor and Sir Hubert. Whereas he and his men had things to do, there was no point in the civilian members of the team losing valuable rest time. The Professor and Michelle protested. As expected, Sir Hubert was asleep in minutes, closely followed by a resonant snoring from Monsieur Simonin, the noise aggravated by the blocked air passage in his swollen nose.

Finally, when he was content that everything had been done that could be done, Caspasian ensured that Ganga had organised a sentry roster whereby two men would be posted by the cave mouth, and then went in search of Michelle. He found her lying by herself in a fold between two rocks. She had drawn a blanket over her but when she saw him approaching, she pulled back one corner, holding it open for him. Too tired to care about propriety, Caspasian crawled in beside her. Settling down, they lay on their sides, face to face. Michelle reached out and touched his cheek. On impulse, Caspasian kissed her. He tasted sand on his lips and wiped it away. Michelle smiled at him, wiping more sand from her own mouth. When Caspasian looked at her again she was fast asleep. He gathered her into his arms and shifted onto his back, staring up towards the roof of the cave, obscured in the overhead gloom. Listening to the storm raging beyond the cave mouth, darkness closed about him and then he too was sleeping.

15

He was awoken by the silence. Opening his eyes was a slow painful process. The lids felt as if they were cemented together. Caspasian shifted his position and tried to lick his lips. They were cracked and dry, coated with fine grains of sand. With difficulty he worked up some saliva and moistened them. He licked the tip of one finger and used it to rub his eyes, gently. Slowly they opened. He could feel a weight bearing against his side, pressing him into the rock against which he lay. He looked down and with his first blurred vision saw that it was Michelle. Her face was hidden, obscured by her hair which was no longer dark and lustrous but the colour of sand. He stroked it, disturbing the sand which tumbled in a soft cloud as if he was awaking Sleeping Beauty who had been slumbering beneath the accumulated dust of centuries.

She stirred, raising her face to him like some subterranean spectre emerging from the earth. It was light, Caspasian noticed. Murky shards penetrated into the gloom of the cave, their beams crammed full of dust. He sat up and looked around. The bodies of his companions lay all around, each one similarly covered in sand. For now, colour had ceased to exist, all save the light reddish brown of the sand. Of the few remaining camels, only one had bothered to shake itself and stand. It stood incongruously in the centre of the large cave looking about with an air of lofty detachment, as if the whole escapade was really too shambolic and that it no longer wished to be associated with any of it. From its flanks hung the last remaining water bladder. Even from that distance Caspasian could see that it was virtually empty. It was a mercy that everyone was still asleep. Once awake they would be consumed by a raging thirst and there was little with which to satisfy it. Let them sleep on, he thought. Mercy was short-lived enough as it was.

He got to his feet, every muscle and sinew aching terribly, screaming out for a bed with clean white sheets. Straightening up delicately like an old man, he shuffled towards the cave mouth, making his way around any sleeping bodies he encountered. The two sentries looked up as he approached and nodded a greeting. Ganga and Kraus had chosen to divided the duty fairly by posting one Gurkha with one legionnaire. Naik Indrabahadur looked wearily up at him. On the rock opposite, a gaunt looking legionnaire sat slumped but awake. Just. Caspasian smiled but suspected that, masked by sand, it came out more as a miniature facial landslide.

'Anything?' he asked. His voice rasped oddly. He coughed to clear his throat.

Indrabahadur shook his head. Caspasian could see his lips moving, denoting an answer, but no sound came out. His throat was clogged like Caspasian's.

Caspasian squinted into the daylight outside the cave. The storm had passed and now the early morning sunlight was strengthening with a vengeance. It blazed down as if trying to make up lost time. He could feel the heat from where he stood. He took a step forward and it was like approaching a furnace. A sense of desperation struck him. What point in surviving the storm simply to die of thirst now that the sun had risen? Quickly he got a grip of himself. There might well be explosives left in the packs on one of the remaining camels. He would have to find a likely spot and blast for water. It had worked once. It might work again. He had to try.

His eyes were drawn to a slim line of footprints leading from the cave out into the desert. They were fresh, the sides clean and unscuffed. He looked questioningly at Indrabahadur. This time

Indrabahadur coughed harshly to clear his throat before attempting to speak.

'The Professor saheb,' he said croakily. And with a jerk of his chin he indicated the direction in which the Professor had ventured out for a walk.

'God almighty,' Caspasian muttered to himself. This was hardly the place or the time for a morning constitutional. He went quickly back to his sleeping place and picked up his holster and revolver, shook the gun free of sand, checked the cylinder to make sure it was full, and buckled it on as he returned to the mouth of the cave.

The moment he stepped out into the full light of day he winced and covered his clenched eyes. It was so dazzling he was blinded. Slowly his sight returned bit by bit. First a bright yellow blur, then a sliver of desert sand, and finally the full enormous vista. The rock face rose at his back but in front there was nothing as far as the eye could see. It was early and the heat haze had not yet completely stolen the horizon from view. Staring out into the desert, Caspasian felt utterly dwarfed. He located the Professor easily, not just from the uncomplicated line of footprints leading straight to him, but because he was the only object in sight. As Caspasian walked towards him he felt the sun beating down on his head and shoulders with almost physical force. Water. They had to find water.

He was about to say as much to the Professor as he drew near, when he heard that he was chuckling to himself. He was shaking his head and clicking his tongue like someone upon whom the secret of a puzzle has just dawned, a puzzle seemingly intractable yet with an answer that has turned out to be all too obvious.

'Ah, Caspasian, dear fellow,' he said when the two of them were side by side, 'I'm glad it's you.'

'Oh?'

'Yes, and I want to see your face. Too bad I don't have my camera on me. I hope to God it's safe in my pack.'

Mystified, Caspasian smiled, brushing back his hair which felt like wire wool. 'What's up?'

'The game, Caspasian. The game is up,' the Professor said with unabashed delight. 'Captain, allow me to give you a military command.' With that, the Professor adopted an unlikely imitation of standing to attention and said, 'About turn!'

Caspasian smiled and turned slowly, starting to wonder if the sun had made the otherwise rational Professor lightheaded. The next moment his mouth dropped open. Looking back towards the cave he found himself facing not a bare rock face, but the vast legs of a seated figure. It was carved in the rock, although from the waist up the detail was missing, either toppled or worn away through the centuries and millennia. When complete, Caspasian judged it must have towered as high as the dome of St Paul's. On either side of it, two majestic beasts sat stiffly. They too were badly worn but he thought they resembled griffins. The figure was resting one hand on the shoulders of each of them.

The Professor pointed excitedly. 'Look at the ring, Caspasian. Do you see it?'

Caspasian shaded his eyes and studied the ring on one of the fingers of the figure's left hand. The sun was shining full upon it. It bore a series of markings which he took to be hieroglyphs. He looked back to the Professor who nodded enthusiastically. 'That's it,' he said, confirming the suspicion that had only just started to dawn in Caspasian's mind. 'It says Menes. Great King.'

Caspasian stared in renewed wonder. He looked to either side of the figure and now saw that the rock face extended to both left and right for possibly a mile in each direction, slowly curving away. Behind it, he could just make out other ridges signifying range upon range of steadily rising jebel mountain. He reached up and scratched his head, astounded. 'But, where's the rest?' he said. 'Surely this can't be all? I mean, why build a statue out here in the middle of nowhere?'

The Professor laughed, all signs of tiredness gone. 'But don't you see? Five, six, seven thousand years ago this wasn't the middle of nowhere. Look at this!' He bent down and scooped up a handful of sand and held it out for Caspasian to inspect. He stirred it gently with his finger sending some of it cascading into the air in a gossamer stream. And Caspasian saw it then clearly. Lying in the palm of the Professor's hand, mixed in with the sand, were several tiny shells.

The Professor saw the light dawn on Caspasian's face. 'Exactly. This spot, right here where we are standing now, was once a mighty river, a tributary of the Nile perhaps. The statue would have stood beside a busy waterway, an inland trade route, announcing to all who passed that they were now in the Kingdom of King Menes.' He paused, his eyes glittering. 'They were now at the city of King Menes, the first ever pharaoh. The founder of all the many dynasties that came after.' He beamed, slapping Caspasian on the shoulder. 'We've found it. We've found the city of King Menes!'

Caspasian stared back at the rock face, the two enormous legs rising out of the desert floor. The cave in which they had sheltered was just to one side of them. 'But where? A statue's one thing, but a city?'

'Oh, it'll be here all right,' the Professor chided confidently. 'There'll be a pass nearby, or a route over the top. I'll wager it's on the other side of the ridge.' He broke away and started back towards the cave. 'Come on. We must tell the others. We've work to do.'

Caspasian was so swept up with the Professor's enthusiasm that it was only when they were almost back at the cave that he remembered. 'Just a minute. We're out of water and the tribesmen are going to be looking for us today. It won't be long before they find us.'

'Oh, don't worry about them,' the Professor said, waving aside the warning as if Caspasian had merely cautioned him against mosquitos. 'Where there was once water, there might still be water. And as for the tribesmen, I wouldn't be surprised if they're afraid of this place. They're bound to have known about it. It's probably got some sort of taboo connected to it.'

'And if it hasn't?' Caspasian asked, hurrying after the Professor.

'Then you and your merry men will have to persuade them to leave us alone. I've spent a lifetime dreaming of a find like this. I'm not going to give it up now, not without a fight.'

Caspasian hefted his revolver holster. 'I've no doubt the tribesmen will be only too happy to oblige.'

When the others had been roused and presented with the news, Monsieur Simonin was the first to respond, reacting with surprising speed. He dashed out of the cave and into the desert until he was able to look back and make out the carved figure, as if by his speed alone he might reclaim the discovery from the British Professor. His face was a strange mixture of rage and wonder. Sir Hubert made his way outside at a more leisurely pace, congratulating the Professor on his discovery and similarly trying to take charge of the unfolding events. Only the Professor seemed excited by the discovery for its own sake, as opposed to the effect it would have upon his future career.

Caspasian left them to it and instead went in search of the last of the water which he gave to Michelle and Béranger. He found them together. Béranger was now fully conscious though unable to rise from his stretcher. Michelle was helping Sergeant Kraus and one of the legionnaires to see to his bandages.

As expected, it took some persuading to get Béranger to accept the offer of a drink and he only did so after Michelle herself had drunk her fill. However, Caspasian noticed how mostly she simply made a show of drinking, convincing though it was. He could not help marvelling at her.

Now that the figure in the mountainside had been discovered, it begged the question of where the rest of the city might lie, particularly the tomb of King Menes. Reluctantly, Monsieur Simonin put his head together with the Professor and Sir

Hubert and the three decided that a search of the immediate area was the best course of action if they were to locate the actual tomb itself and the lost city, if one existed at all. When this was proposed to Caspasian he stared at them all in amazement.

'What about the tribesmen? More particularly, what about the water supply?'

'What better place to search for water than right here?' countered the Professor. Caspasian had to agree that he did have a point. On the subject of the hostile tribesmen however, the Professor was less resolute.

'We still have the hostage,' Sir Hubert offered. 'He seems to act like a protective charm. All we have to do is dangle him in front of them, a gun to his head, and they'll continue to keep their distance.' He paused, looking around for support. 'Won't they?'

Caspasian was in two minds. His first inclination was for them all to get out of there as fast as they could, before the tribesmen could locate them. However, before the expedition could do that they had to secure a new supply of water. Food stocks were sufficient for the moment but without water they would be dead within two days and unable to operate efficiently well before that. The search for water was his first imperative and as this would involve covering the immediate area, it dovetailed nicely, though unintentionally on Caspasian's part, with the designs of the archaeologists. The two searches could become one and the same.

Of almost equal concern were the tribesmen. Caspasian estimated that they could expect to see them at any time, possibly as early as later that day. That said, now that the expedition had lost its handlers, porters and most of its camels, it was unlikely that, even if they were to leave the area immediately, they would be able to outrun the tribesmen.

The more he thought about it, the more Caspasian found himself considering an altogether new course of action. If they were not able to outrun the tribesmen, and if the use of the hostage was too uncertain a guarantee of safe passage, then the only other recourse would be to take them on. The members of the expedition, legionnaires and Gurkhas, would have to turn the tables on them by means of an ambush. If they could inflict a sufficiently bloody nose, then perhaps the tribesmen would withdraw and leave them alone. In order to achieve this, a thorough reconnaissance of the area would be needed to select the ground for the ambush. So, to his surprise, Caspasian found all three strands coming together, the search for water, for the city and tomb, and the search for a killing ground. All of them boiled down to the same thing. They could not simply leave. They had to explore the neighbourhood. With luck it would reveal the answers to all three questions.

While Sergeant Kraus prepared everyone for the move, Caspasian and Sergeant Ganga left the cave and conducted a small search of their own to establish the best route for them to take. Sure enough, just as the Professor had predicted, they located the start of a rough track that led away from the flat desert plain, up into the rising jebel. The sandstorm had scoured it, exposing a rocky path that ascended, gradually at first, but becoming steeper the further it climbed. As Caspasian studied the rocks he noticed how several of them appeared to have been fashioned by tools. Returning to the cave to fetch the others, he led them back to the spot and showed the rocks to the Professor. The Professor stooped over them, examining them closely.

'But this is wonderful!' he exclaimed. Monsieur Simonin agreed, starting to forget his rivalry, swept up in the mounting enthusiasm of the find.

As the day wore on, so the path grew steeper and steeper. Whenever they halted and looked back the way they had come, they could see the desert plain receding. From their new vantage point they could see for miles. Sand and rock stretched behind them, an inhospitable world in which Caspasian knew the tribesmen would be searching. So far there was no sign of any pursuit but it could not be long in coming.

In order to negotiate the increasingly steep and narrow track, Caspasian had ordered the column to move in single file. Every water bottle was virtually empty. The scarce resources had been husbanded with the tenderest care for as long as possible until now, wherever Caspasian looked, he could see someone or other testing the depths of their bottle, tipping it and shaking the empty vessel to coax from it the last few drops. They did not have long to live.

Sure enough, an hour later, with the sun approaching its zenith, the first man keeled over. Caspasian knelt beside the fallen legionnaire and saw that his skin had the telltale blue tinge. He knew that unless the man was given water very soon, his exhaustion would deteriorate into full heat stroke. The skin would become hot and dry, all sweat gone from his body. His temperature would soar and convulsions would quickly be followed by death. They had to find water. They had to find it now.

He called the party leaders together so that they could consult. His recommendation was that while the column should continue to make its way slowly up the track, exerting themselves as little as possible, he and Ganga should go on ahead with the satchel of explosives and try to find a likely water source. He was painfully aware that the sound of the blast would be like a beacon signalling their presence to the tribesmen, but there was no alternative. They were about to start dying from lack of water anyway.

Without exception the other team members agreed to his proposed course of action. So, slinging the satchel over his shoulder, Caspasian and Ganga set off up the track, quickly leaving the main body behind to nurse itself steadily forwards, following in their wake.

The first hundred yards were the hardest, stepping out at a fast pace, pushing themselves up the track. Muscles ached, denied water, even though Caspasian had ensured that all the men took salt tablets to avoid cramps. Then, as they settled into their pace, the going got easier. He knew that to an extent it was illusory. Dangerous even. He had known the fittest men collapse suddenly from lack of water. There was no way the body could be prepared to go without it for any substantial length of time. Physical fitness helped but eventually the lack would catch up with you. When reserves had been expended the bill would be presented. It could come at any time.

In front of him Ganga was going strong. The Gurkha's head was down and he was marching at a steady pace, powerful thigh and calf muscles propelling him up the rocky track. He was cradling his Lee-Enfield in the crook of his arms and had tightened the straps of his pack to shift the weight high on his shoulders where it was more easily carried. Caspasian knew he would have blanked out his mind, focusing on his breathing. Though marching quickly, he was placing his feet carefully with each rapid step to minimise the effort. A slip or tumble would only expend energy unnecessarily.

Caspasian looked around, his mind starting to wander. He thought of Michelle. She was an extraordinary girl. He had to get them out of this if only for her sake. She was young, her life ahead of her. This was no place or manner for a girl like her to die.

He looked up and was surprised to see how far Ganga had drawn ahead. As always, the Gurkha sergeant's superior fitness was telling. Caspasian reached up a hand to wipe his brow. He looked at his palm. It was bone dry.

'Oh, shit,' he murmured. In the same instant he noticed how the ground around him was wavering. Shimmering gently as if his feet were surrounded by a miniature heat haze all of his own. He could feel his head spinning and the exertions of the climb were becoming harder and harder to endure. He thought he would sit down and rest. Just for a moment. Somewhere, deep in his mind, he could hear a voice. It was telling him not to. It was saying that this was how a man dies. Crawls into a spot of shade, falls asleep and slips from sleep to unconsciousness within minutes and then to death a short while later. But surely it would not hurt for just a minute? What could be the harm? He was not intending to stay there for any length of time, after all.

Seeking out a low rock caught in the shade of its larger neighbour, Caspasian stumbled across and slumped down onto it. His legs felt like jelly but once he sat down he relaxed. It felt wonderful. He felt so tired, exhausted to his very bones. He leaned back against the larger rock and shut his eyes.

A voice inside him was screaming, yelling abuse at him. Cursing him with all the obscenities he had ever heard in the barrack rooms of his military career. With all the vileness he had heard on the ships and in the ports of Asia as a boy. All of it was directed towards the transmission of one simple message. To open his eyes. Yet, try as he may, he could not. For Caspasian was already asleep.

The shock of the water on his face was harsher than a slap. It struck him with full force and blew him awake. He opened his eyes as a second jet hit him and he blinked. His head reeled and he felt nauseous, but he knew that to vomit would be to lose what tiny bit of water remained in his system.

Through the water and the delirium he could just make out a face. It was planted directly in front of him. A dark frown creased the brow, a frown of concern. Ganga. Caspasian could see the lips moving but hearing only came with a supreme effort.

'Saheb! Wake up!'

Ganga's hand was lightly slapping Caspasian's cheek. Not so lightly in fact. Caspasian could feel his whole head jarring with each blow.

'The water . . .' he mumbled.

In response Ganga nodded and poured more over him, being careful only to wet his lips and tongue and not allow him yet to drink his fill.

'No,' Caspasian gasped, irritated that his meaning had been misconstrued. 'The water . . . where did you get it?'

Ganga's face was lit by an instant smile. 'Come,' he said, placing one hand under Caspasian's arm and hoisting him to his feet.

Shakily, Caspasian followed the Gurkha up the track and over the brow of the crest. The path dipped into a hollow before disappearing over the next crest and ducking out of sight beyond. Towards the other side of the hollow Caspasian heard the most wonderful sound. Running water. Amazed, he staggered forward, supported by his friend.

'Here,' Ganga said eagerly. 'Just a bit further.'

Caspasian could hardly believe his eyes. A deep but narrow cleft opened in the ground and the sweet noise emanated from it. Caspasian peered down and saw the glimmer of water, clear and fast-moving. He fell onto his stomach and wriggled closer, reaching one arm down into the cleft until his whole hand was immersed in the slender stream. He scooped some up in his palm and put it to his lips. It was the best taste in the world.

'That's not all,' Ganga said, steering Caspasian away when he judged that he had drunk enough. 'Come and look at this.'

Reluctantly Caspasian left the stream and followed Ganga. They walked across towards the further crest where the track ran over the edge. It was only at the last minute, as he closed up to the brink, that Caspasian saw what Ganga had discovered. The ridge came to an abrupt end, the path winding sharply downwards and entering a far-reaching valley ringed with barren jebel. But in the valley itself, dusky green palm trees clustered thickly, and on every side, stretching from the foot of the ridge back across the valley floor, lay acre upon acre of tumbled dwellings. The ruined city of King Menes.

Caspasian stared at it speechless, even his thirst receding, overwhelmed by the splendour of the ruins. Toppled columns and statues, avenues of pillars, the jagged walls of stunted buildings and huge, uprising figures of beasts and men. It was a spectacle the like of which he had never seen before.

'Dear heavens,' he exclaimed quietly.

Ganga stood at his side. He shifted his felt hat to the back of his head and scratched the bristles of his shaven scalp. 'A pity if we don't live to tell anyone about it,' he observed.

Caspasian laughed. 'I'm not sure the Professor will care.'

When Ganga arrived back at the slow-moving column with news of the water supply and of the city, the effect was electric. Fresh reserves of energy appeared in everyone, bearing them swiftly up the steep slope. When they reached the top, the Professor was the only one to ignore the stream. Instead, he hurried across to join Caspasian on the crest.

'Oh, my. Oh, my,' he said quietly, his eyes sparkling as they roved across the landscape below. 'This is more than I could ever have hoped for.'

In spite of the dangers surrounding them, Caspasian was happy for him. He had grown fond of the small Professor. He thought he deserved this triumph.

To keep watch on the track up which they had just come, Caspasian detailed a four-man team under the command of Lance Naik Ramprasad. With him he left Riflemen Harkabahadur Limbu, Anand Sherpa and Birbahadur Rai. As they were going to be close to the only confirmed water supply, none of them objected. In addition to their own rifles, he ordered Ganga to give them two Lewis light machine guns, a stack of spare drum magazines and a satchel of hand grenades. The track they had to guard appeared, so far, to be the only entrance into the valley. As it was narrow and steep, Caspasian judged that the four men should be able to hold off a greatly superior enemy force for a considerable time. They had weapons and ammunition, food and, more importantly, they now had water. Things were looking up, he reflected, as he set off down the hill to catch up with the column. Under the leadership of the eager Professor it was now proceeding down to the valley

floor at breakneck speed. Against all his expectations they had
found water as well as the city. What was more, they were in a
good position to hold off the enemy when they eventually
caught up with them, as he knew they soon would.

The scramble down to the valley floor took over half an hour
but when they reached the bottom of the path, the end came
suddenly. One moment they were winding their way down the
rocky precipitous track, and the next they piled headlong into
dense head-high scrub. It was a thick tangle of gorse and thorn
and Caspasian, together with Sergeant Ganga and the remaining four Gurkhas, had to move to the front of the stalled
column, draw their kukris and hack their way through. After
about fifty yards they suddenly burst free and emerged at the
edge of the plain.

Bounded by a ring of high jebel mountains, it extended for
several square miles, a sunken world as if inside the cone of an
extinct volcano. The Professor drew alongside Caspasian and
whistled softly. 'Where the devil do we start?' he asked gleefully.

'The water supply,' Caspasian replied. 'We'll try to locate
one down here and set up camp beside it. The stream on the
ridge runs underground but it must come down here somewhere.'

There was a sudden commotion behind them and the old
hostage broke away from his guards and rushed forward. The
legionnaires ran after him, catching him with ease, but as they
were leading him away Caspasian had an idea. Somehow the
old man seemed familiar with the valley. He seemed to be
trying to make his way to somewhere.

'Let him go,' Caspasian ordered. The legionnaires looked at
Kraus. He nodded, giving his consent. The moment they
released their hold on his arms, the old man gambolled away
merrily. Caspasian looked around at his companions and
shrugged. 'Let's see where he's off to.'

As they followed the old man their eyes were everywhere.

His route was taking them into the very heart of the ruins and on all sides partially buried buildings and statues begged them to stop and examine them more closely. Several times Caspasian, Ganga and Kraus had to encourage the Professor away from some inscription or other, coaxing him forward.

Then, at last, they found where the old man had been heading. He ran up an avenue of rearing sphinxes, rounded the corner of a toppled dwelling, and there it was in front of them, a broad and shining pool of water, ringed with palm trees that stared down at their own reflections in the calm surface. Everyone stopped and stared in thirsty wonder. Caspasian was just about to urge caution, suggesting they test the water first to ensure it was safe to drink, when the old man ran straight in. When he was waist deep, he threw the water all over himself with his hands, laughing and grinning at those left on the bank. He cupped handfuls into his mouth and swallowed it.

'I suppose it's all right then,' Sir Hubert said.

'Maybe it was the water that turned his head,' Kraus suggested sarcastically.

'Well I'm going to try it,' Monsieur Simonin countered, and strode boldly in up to his ankles.

Caspasian stepped forward and hauled him out. 'Just a minute. If we're going to drink this water, I'd rather you kept you feet out of it please, not to mention the rest of your body.'

There was a chorus of agreement and Simonin sullenly withdrew. With much coaxing the old man was lured from the water. He wandered back towards the outstretched hands waiting for him and submitted himself without a struggle. His clothes were sodden but would soon dry in the intense sunshine.

As he trudged away, wet feet slapping on the rocks bordering the pool, his clothes pulled half off him by the weight of water, Caspasian watched him closely. There was something strange about the man quite apart from his madness, but he could not identify what it was. And there had been the tune that had struck a distant chord in Caspasian's mind. As he watched him go, Caspasian considered the worn battered frame. For the first time, now that the old man's wet clothes hung loosely from his shoulders, Caspasian noticed faint markings, though whether battle scars or tribal tattoos, it was impossible to say. The man's skin was so wrinkled and weathered by sun, sand and time, that he resembled a piece of driftwood cast up on a shore and left to warp and dry in the sun, salt-soaked and drained of the once vibrant identity that had previously marked it as a living thing.

'Just a moment,' Caspasian called after him.

The old man carried on walking.

'Company . . . Halt!'

At the sound of Caspasian's command, the old man shuddered to a halt, heels together, spindly legs and bent back as rigid as he could manage. Slowly he turned, a confused expression on his weather-beaten face. Caspasian went towards him smiling kindly and put a hand out to his gnarled shoulder where one of the marks had become visible. He leaned closer and studied it. Slowly his smile broadened. Then he turned to the other shoulder, gently easing off the rags. What he saw there made him stare in utter amazement. He had been right. They were indeed tribal tattoos. British regimental tattoos. From the army of Queen Victoria.

16

'A British soldier? That? Don't be absurd.' Sir Hubert turned away in disgust.

The Professor went quietly to the old man and inspected the tattoos. He chuckled. 'I'm afraid Caspasian's right, Hugh. What's more, there's a name here. Jacob.'

'Let me see.' Sir Hubert marched sullenly across. The old man shrank away from him but the Professor calmed him down.

'See?'

Sir Hubert peered closely and with extreme distaste. 'That means absolutely nothing. He could have been some native skivvy in the old days. You can't tell me he's anything but another miserable wog.'

'A wog, as you put it, doesn't brace to attention or hum old music hall songs,' Caspasian said.

'Course he does. He might have been a water-carrier or something. Gunga-bloody-Din. A camp-follower.' Sir Hubert suddenly thought of something else. 'If he was an old soldier, why would the tribesmen hold their fire when they saw he was in danger? Aha! There! Answer that!'

Caspasian and the Professor looked at each other. Neither of them could.

'Maybe he changed sides,' Michelle offered.

'Great! That's all we need. A bloody deserter,' Sir Hubert stormed. 'In that case, let's shoot the old bugger and have done with it.'

'No one's going to shoot anyone,' the Professor said hurriedly when he saw a spark of understanding and terror flit across the old man's face.

'Well as far as I'm concerned his name's Jacob,' Caspasian said, smiling at the old man who responded with a broad toothless grin.

'Yakub,' he said giggling.

'There you are, you see!' Michelle put an arm round his shoulder. 'I'm going to give you something to eat,' she said kindly, leading him away. 'Come with me. Jacob.'

'Go on then. Waste our meagre rations on the old ragbag.' Sir Hubert shook his head in disgust. 'In any case, none of this gets us anywhere. We've still got a job to do.'

'That's true enough,' the Professor said.

With the immediate excitement over, the group split up and went about their various tasks. For Caspasian there was a considerable amount of preparation to be done.

As the pool provided water for drinking, cooking and washing, as well as shade and a coolness that was welcome after the harshness of the desert and jebel, the decision was taken to establish a camp as close to it as possible. With the arrival of the tribesmen an ever-present threat, defence was the other key consideration. So, pulling the two factors together, Caspasian selected a ruined building some thirty yards distant from the pool. The Professor thought the building might once have been a caravanserai owing to its location close to water, but particularly to its layout. Although none of the walls was now taller than shoulder-height, the pattern on the ground was of a dwelling of numerous smaller rooms grouped around a large central courtyard. One substantial corner had been consumed by sand drifts, but there were still ample rooms left to accommodate the surviving members of the expedition.

Michelle had made her intention clear to have nothing further to do with her husband. She therefore selected a room for herself as far away from him as possible. Caspasian was encouraged to note that her choice was only yards from his own. He helped her rig a canvas sheet across one corner of it to form a comfortable shelter from the elements. How long they would be left in peace to enjoy it, however, was a question he thought it best not to raise.

The Professor showed no interest in settling down at all but was anxious to get on with an exploration of the ruined city, seeing as the tribesmen might interrupt them at any moment.

'Caspasian,' he remonstrated desperately, 'there's not a moment to lose. I've waited for this all my life. Now I'm here, the last thing I'm going to do is dig a foxhole and prepare for an attack. I'm standing in the middle of a city that has been lost to the civilised world for several millennia. You must understand.'

Caspasian sympathised with him. 'I'll do what I can, Professor. If you want to explore the city then go ahead, but keep well away from the track that we came down.' He smiled. 'I'm going to prepare a little welcome for the tribesmen.'

'Why not take Jacob?' Sir Hubert offered sarcastically. 'You can hold a gun to his head and threaten to blow his brains out.'

'And if they let me?'

'Do it then.'

Caspasian turned to leave. 'Any more bright ideas?'

'No, I'm serious. It worked for Kraus.'

'The tribesmen were probably confused. Caught off guard. I doubt they'll be prepared to hold back a second time. I don't want to push our luck.'

'It's Jacob's luck you're pushing. Not ours,' Sir Hubert chortled.

'Sir Hubert,' Caspasian said walking away, 'shut up.'

'I say!' Sir Hubert stood looking after him. He turned to the Professor. 'Did you hear what he said to me?'

The Professor smiled. 'Come on, Hugh. Let's get started.'

With only a couple of hours of daylight left, Caspasian knew he had to act quickly. Taking Ganga and Sergeant Kraus with him, as well as all the remaining explosives and hand grenades, he went back to the foot of the track where it descended the hillside and entered the valley. He selected a vantage point, jogged across to it and sat on a rock to survey the lie of the land.

As he studied the features of the terrain he began to feel a calm descending upon him. He had his weapons and now he had the ground. All he had to do was match the one to the other, catch the enemy where he wanted them, and engineer their destruction. It sounded simple. In theory it was. The trick, as he well knew, was to carry out the plan in practice. That was where the true skill lay. In achieving it, all manner of imponderables would come into play. No plan survives first contact with the enemy, he had been told. How true that was. The best laid plans got you only so far as the opening shots of the engagement. Thereafter it was free play. That was when factors like training and professionalism came into their own, but with his present scratch force these were unknown quantities. To what extent could he rely on Kraus and his legionnaires? Kraus appeared to be a good man, but what about those under him?

Similarly with his own Gurkhas. Sergeant Ganga was second to none when it came to a battle, but the dismal little force the Adjutant had allowed them to take on the expedition was hardly going to make regimental history.

When he had considered all the factors and devised a plan, he summoned Ganga and Kraus beside him and crouched in the dirt. With his hand he swept a clear space and began to mark in the key features. There was the track entering the plain, the thick belt of gorse through which it passed, the open plain in front of it before the first of the ruined buildings, and then the mass of fallen statues and rubble that extended all the way to the waterhole and their present encampment. He focused their attention on the open plain.

'This is where we'll engage the enemy.' To one side there was a shallow wadi where a watercourse had once run, many years ago. Now it was bone dry but provided excellent cover for firers. On the opposite side, the plain ascended gradually towards a sheer rock face.

'The enemy is channelled at this point. Once they break out of here they get into the city and we'll be swamped by their greater numbers.' He stabbed a finger in the dust where his rough map indicated the plain. 'This is where we'll fix them. Pin them down and knock the stuffing out of them.'

Kraus sucked his teeth making an unpleasant whistling sound. 'I agree it's probably the best we can do, Captain, but it would be nice to have some artillery.'

'Which is where the explosives and the grenades come in,' Caspasian said. 'Not exactly the artillery you had in mind, but if we bury charges throughout the area where the enemy is likely to take cover from our small-arms fire, laying cables so we can detonate them remotely, it's the next best thing.'

He turned to Ganga. 'Have we got any white phosphorous grenades left or were those lost along with all the other stuff?'

Ganga hefted a sack in his hand. 'We've got about half a dozen, saheb. That's all.'

'That should be enough,' Caspasian replied.

'What are those for?' Kraus asked, intrigued.

Caspasian pointed across the plain to the gorse bordering the foot of the hillside and obscuring the base of the track from view. 'Once we've got the enemy pinned down on the plain I intend to detonate the white phosphorous grenades in the gorse. It's tinder dry and the incendiaries will set it ablaze in seconds. It'll create a wall of fire at their backs, severing their line of withdrawal. With luck it'll cause them to panic.'

An evil smile lit Kraus's face and he regarded Caspasian in a new light. 'Where do you want my men, Captain?'

'I want you to establish a fire line in the sunken river bed. From there you can rake them from the flank.'

'Defilade fire,' Kraus nodded approvingly. 'I like it. Too bad the Hotchkiss have gone. The last of them was lost in the storm.'

'LMGs?' Caspasian asked hopefully.

'A couple of Chauchats with a few mags each. That's all.'

'It'll have to do.'

'And me?' Ganga said.

'You and I, together with the rest of the lads, will form a second fire line here,' Caspasian said, sketching in the line in the dirt where his map denoted the start of the ruins. 'In effect we'll be creating an L-shaped ambush, legionnaires on the left flank forming the upright part of the L, Gurkhas here in the ruins forming its horizontal base. The right flank is guarded by the slope and rock face, and at their backs the tribesmen will have a wall of flame. They'll be caught in the open, and the ground beneath them will be mined with explosive charges and grenades.'

'We'll only just have enough cable to lay to all the charges on the plain. It won't possibly reach the line of gorse. How are you going to detonate the phosphorous grenades?' Ganga asked.

'I'm not. You are,' Caspasian replied. 'I estimate the range to be . . . what? . . . five hundred yards. Do you reckon you can hit a satchel of grenades at that range?'

Ganga scoffed in disgust. 'You can take one of my stripes if I can't.'

'If the grenades don't do the job we can always try using tracer rounds,' Kraus suggested. 'They'll get a nice blaze going as well. Not as fast maybe.'

'No, it has to be the grenades. I need to create the instant shock effect. One moment their withdrawal route will be there, the next moment . . .' Caspasian snapped his fingers, '. . . it's gone.'

When Kraus and Ganga were satisfied with the plan and clear about their own part in it, they brought their men forward and briefed them. Then, with the sun descending rapidly, they set off to bury the charges and cable in the places Caspasian had indicated. He had concentrated upon all areas of potential cover where the tribesmen were likely to congregate once they came under small-arms fire. Any depression, however shallow, was mined. Ganga himself positioned the satchel of white phosphorous grenades, securing it to a high branch away from the enemy's line of advance so it would go unnoticed, hanging it so it was in clear view of his own fire position in the ruins. When he had tied it to its branch, he jogged back to the ruins, snuggled down behind cover, adjusted the backsight on his Lee-Enfield, and checked that he had unobstructed line of sight. It was perfect. One round should do the job.

Content that everything was in hand, Caspasian started up the track towards the four-man group he had left on the top of the ridgeline guarding the approach to the valley. They had to be well briefed as their withdrawal would be crucial to the success of the plan. They not only had to lure the tribesmen into the trap, but they also had to make good their escape under fire, rejoining Caspasian, Ganga and the rest of the Gurkhas at the fire line. The added weight of their firepower was going to be badly needed. First they would have to cross the plain themselves and they would hardly be able to achieve this if the tribesmen were going to be hot on their heels. Somehow they would have to engineer a delay on the enemy so as to allow themselves to break clean and make good their escape. As Caspasian trudged up the steep track his mind worked furiously, worrying at the problem until, by the time he emerged over the crest of the ridgeline and waved across at Harkabahadur, an idea had formed, a solution that just might work.

It was well after dark by the time he got back to the ruined caravanserai near the pool. He was reassured when, as he drew near, a sentry challenged him from the shadows, the ominous sound of a rifle bolt halting him in his tracks. He stopped dead and gave the password that Ganga had circulated earlier that evening.

'Pass,' came the response from a grinning Dhanprasad of the catering platoon, finding it hard to take his role seriously as a proper rifleman at last.

The camp was busy with preparations for the coming fight. Kraus and his legionnaires were readying themselves, while Ganga had gathered the remaining Gurkhas all of whom were cleaning their rifles and the light machine guns. While the Lee-

Enfield had an excellent reputation for not jamming in even the worst conditions, the sand managed to work its way between every moving part of the rifle's mechanism. Ganga was not going to take any more chances than he absolutely had to.

'Any luck, Professor?' Caspasian asked wearily as he slumped down beside the fire where the three archaeologists were conferring. He noticed that Michelle had made herself scarce.

The Professor looked up. 'Ah, Caspasian. That depends,' he said mysteriously. His previous enthusiasm seemed diminished.

Caspasian helped himself to some food from a pot suspended over the flames. Much to Sir Hubert's disgust it was a Gurkha curry prepared by Dhanprasad and Akalbahadur, the two cooks. Pools of reddish-coloured oil floated on the surface and finely sliced chilies lay in ambush amongst the pieces of meat, gristle and bone, the onions and lentils. It was a rough cookhouse curry where nothing was wasted, however unpalatable to western tastes, a far cry from the version which would appear on the tables of the officers' mess.

'You sound less than inspired,' Caspasian said, tucking in to his plateful with relish.

The archaeologists swapped glances before Sir Hubert said caustically, 'It seems we might not be the first ones to discover the site after all.'

'That's hardly surprising,' Caspasian answered, wiping some oil from his chin and scooping up a second helping in his chapati. 'The tribesmen undoubtedly know of it. They probably come here from time to time, if only to use the water source.'

The Professor sighed. 'It's more than that,' he said. He picked up something from the ground beside him, holding it out so that Caspasian could see it in the firelight.

'A shovel,' Monsieur Simonin said unnecessarily. 'Rusted and old, but not . . .'

'Not five thousand years old,' Sir Hubert cut in. He skimmed a small stone angrily at the fire.

Caspasian shrugged, nonplussed. 'Tribesmen have shovels. Maybe they were in for a spot of tomb-robbing. It doesn't mean you're not the first proper expedition to find the city. In fact you must be or else we'd all have heard of it before.' Caspasian bit on a chili and sucked in air to cool his burning mouth. 'Or maybe a previous expedition did find it, but they all perished before they could get out with the news. The tribesmen probably killed them the same way they're trying to kill us.'

Once again the three archaeologists exchanged glances before continuing. 'There's more,' the Professor said uncomfortably.

'Oh?'

'Just before we turned back in order to get here for last light, we reached the far side of the city ruins.' He pointed into the darkness in the rough direction of the place.

'And?'

'And we found something else.'

'Which is?' Caspasian prompted irritably, anxious to get on with his meal and then to catch some sleep before the coming fight. Archaeology was hardly his prime concern at the moment.

'A landing strip.'

Caspasian's hand stopped halfway to his mouth.

'And it looks as though it's been used recently,' Sir Hubert contributed, skimming another stone into the heart of the fire which crackled in protest, spitting a cinder onto Caspasian's boot where it fizzled to death on the leather.

Monsieur Simonin shrugged hugely. 'What I can't understand is why anyone discovering the site would keep it quiet.'

'It could be that they didn't know the value of what they'd found?' Sir Hubert offered, preparing to skim yet another stone but dissuaded from doing so by one look from Caspasian.

Béranger came balancing precariously into the outer edges of the firelight. 'Or perhaps they don't want anyone to know what they're up to, whatever that may be,' he said from the shadows. Everyone looked round in surprise. Caspasian put down his plate and went quickly to his assistance. Béranger waved aside his helping hand. 'I am feeling much recovered, thank you. But I am perturbed to hear of the Professor's discovery. I feel that we might be in greater danger than we imagine.'

'That's great enough as it is,' Caspasian said.

Béranger selected a spot beside Caspasian's and lowered himself to the ground. Caspasian offered him some food which he accepted gratefully.

'Sir Hubert, you said the airstrip looked as though it had been used recently. What gave you that impression?' Béranger asked.

'A runway's been marked out with stones and there are tyre marks which don't look particularly old,' Sir Hubert replied confidently.

Béranger and Caspasian looked at each other. 'I think we are thinking the same thing,' Béranger said.

Caspasian nodded. 'The tribesmen aren't just attacking us for fun. They're protecting something.'

'Something to do with this site,' Béranger said.

'Something that's hidden here perhaps,' Caspasian added.

The Professor, Sir Hubert and Monsieur Simonin stared at the two soldiers. 'Whatever could that be?' the Professor said. His eyes brightened all of a sudden. 'The tomb of King Menes perhaps?'

Caspasian shrugged. 'Perhaps. It might be considered worth killing for, particularly if we're talking about big sums of money. But then why keep it a secret? It's only worth anything once it enters the public domain. Until then it's worthless junk. A full water bottle's considerably more valuable out here.'

'Why not try asking Jacob?' the Professor suggested.

Caspasian shook his head. 'I think the poor old fellow's had enough shocks for one day. Leave him in peace.'

'Well, whatever the case, nothing can be done about it until first light,' Béranger said. 'As soon as the sun comes up, I suggest the Professor, Sir Hubert and Monsieur Simonin conduct a search as best you can for the source of the secret, while I join Caspasian in the defence of the valley.'

Caspasian started to object but Béranger cut him short. 'Please, John. My wound is not as serious as it was. My place is beside my legionnaires. That is where I will be when the enemy comes.'

'*La gloire de la Légion?*' Caspasian said.

Béranger smiled. '*Pour la Légion.*'

Caspasian took one look at the Captain and knew there was nothing he could say to dissuade him. Béranger put a hand on Caspasian's shoulder. 'Kraus has told me about the old man. Jacob. I bet you never expected to find your Ancient Mariner here in person, eh?'

Caspasian laughed. 'That's true enough. Unfortunately, Jacob's not quite as lucid as the Ancient Mariner. Not yet, at least. As in the Rime, his "soul hath been alone on a wide wide sea, so lonely 'twas that God himself scarce seemèd there to be."'

Béranger nodded. '*Bien sûr.*'

'In Jacob's case the years of solitude have completely turned his head. No man can survive unmarked complete immersion in an alien culture, whatever Jacob's status with the tribesmen, be it captive or friend. Perhaps, over time, he was both.'

When Caspasian had finished eating he took his leave and made his way to the open-air room he had selected as his quarters. The night sky was as clear as crystal, and as cold, the temperature having plummeted soon after the sun had disappeared. Nevertheless he was glad that the room was exposed to the elements. There were few things as enjoyable as going to sleep under the stars, particularly when you knew you would not be woken in the night by the unpleasantness of rain drops and a sleepy-eyed scurry for shelter. Here in the desert the sky was unfamiliar with clouds for the majority of the year.

He lay down and settled for the night. A moment later Michelle appeared at his side. She had her own bedding with her and, unrolling it next to Caspasian's, slipped beneath the blanket, pulling it up to her chin and shivering. He put an arm round her and held her to him.

'I can't get used to the desert being so cold at night,' she said. Caspasian could hear her teeth chattering softly and feel her shoulders gently shuddering.

Together they lay back and stared out into the night sky until thoroughly disoriented, feeling as if the heavens and themselves had been turned upside down. It felt as though they were suspended above the stars and were looking down into the glittering abyss. Michelle clutched at Caspasian to calm the vertigo. With him as her fixed reference point she felt anchored to earth once again.

He realised what she was doing and smiled. 'It's no use,' he said turning away from the stars himself. 'When we look at each other and at the stones around us, our minds have been tricked. They believe they're grounded once again. In fact they've always been suspended in a vacuum. That's what the earth is. Both comfort and illusion. An illusion of stability. I think it's one reason I love being out in the open like this. You see things as they really are.'

'No more illusions,' she said quietly. 'Illusions are usually kinder than the truth. Me, I'd give anything to have mine restored to me.'

He stroked her hair, remembering her photograph. 'I can understand that,' he said.

'Look at it,' she said, her voice calm yet defeated. 'Don't you find the stars frightening? All that emptiness? So cold and futile? It belittles us into nothingness. Against its timescale our silly little lives are too brief even to be like fireflies.'

'I used to think that. Sometimes I still do. But I remember something my grandfather said to me. That life is more about intensity than longevity.' Caspasian extended one arm and swept a hand across the heavens, encompassing everything that lay beyond them. 'What is it all? A muddle of fire and stone. Blindly spinning around. What's remarkable about that?

'Then consider us, the human consciousness.' He tapped her lightly on the head, forcing a smile from her. 'We might only be around for the blink of an eye, but in the space of that blink just look what we accomplish! We contemplate the entire universe. We seek to understand it and to grasp our place in it. When you set that against a jumble of stone lumps whirling about, which is of greater significance? I don't care how long the planets and stars have been at it, I'd set a single kind human thought against the lot of it.'

Michelle regarded him carefully, reaching up to brush back a strand of his hair. 'So you and I are more significant than all the stars, is that it?'

'You're damned right we are,' he said smiling. 'Why else do you think they've been labouring away all these aeons, if not to give rise to creatures like us? Minds that can fill all that empty space, contemplation binding the whole thing together into one magnificent whole.'

Michelle smiled at him and whistled softly. She traced the line of his chin with her finger tip. 'Well who would have imagined that? You're not the hardened cynic you pretend to be. The Professor will be pleased.'

Caspasian chuckled. 'Oh, I am when it comes to human affairs. Life in abstract is so much easier than the real thing.'

'You cheat.'

'No,' he corrected. 'Survivor.'

He shifted onto his side and ran his fingers through her hair, clean and lustrous again from the pool. His face was so close to hers that he could feel her breath move softly on his skin. Beneath the blanket, his hands found her, unfastening her blouse. She warmed to his touch and as they kissed they slipped clumsily from only their essential clothing. Blankets obstructed their limbs, entangling them, but the night was too severe for either Caspasian or Michelle to want to cast them aside. Instead they felt their way across each other's bodies, exploring with touch. Fingers and lips criss-crossed time and again until, with a barely audible moan, Michelle clutched at the earth as if to prevent herself from being plucked out into space. Caspasian buried his face in her breast, breathing in her scent, leavened with the sharp tang of the fine red soil beneath her. His whole body trembled, locked into hers, slowly steadying into stillness once more as they rolled apart, only their hands in contact, clasped. Above them the stars blinked and quivered like small animals awaking, startled to find themselves observed.

Harkabahadur was the first to spot the movement on the track. The night on top of the ridgeline had been bitter. He sat with his back to a boulder, woollen pullover over his flannel shirt, blanket around his shoulders and canvas cape over that, yet still he was shivering violently. The chip of a stone out in the darkness came as a relief. While he knew instantly that it heralded trouble, he was grateful that in a few moments he would be excused the strictures of sentry duty. Action would release his limbs. If he could get them to move again.

He reached out with his boot and nudged Lance Naik Ramprasad Lama. He did not rate the NCO from the signals platoon but he had little choice other than to accept his command. Caspasian had turned out to be a good officer, unlike many others that Harkabahadur had run across in his troubled career. Harkabahadur did not want to let him down. The man had trusted him. Such a move deserved to be repaid.

Ramprasad grunted, reluctant to wake up. Harkabahadur delightedly levelled a harder kick at his ribs. When he shot up in response, glaring angrily at the rifleman, Harkabahadur simply pointed into the gloom and gave the hand signal for enemy. He rejoiced when he saw the expression of cold fear on Ramprasad's face.

The other two were shaken awake and together all four couched themselves behind their rifles and the light machine guns, ready for the coming engagement. A further stone fall beyond their vision over the top of the crest announced the arrival of other men. Harkabahadur felt the exultation mounting inside him. A fight. It was what he lived for. Unconsciously he reached down and fingered the hilt of his kukri, loosening it in its leather-bound wooden scabbard. Secreted inside, the blade was honed to as fine an edge as was possible. Soon it would be wet with blood. Soon it would achieve its reason for existence, like Harkabahadur himself.

Anand, the youngest of the four, stared round-eyed down the track. Next to him, Birbahadur nestled down behind one of the Lewis guns. A veteran of numerous engagements on India's North-West Frontier, he was wholly unimpressed by the thought of what was to come, largely because he had few thoughts at all. When he did, they related to his farm in the foothills of the Himalayas, to his wife who was waiting there for him and to his six children, the youngest four of whom had only the slightest recollection of their father who had been away so long with the paltan, the regiment. He tested the drum magazine on top of the gun and flicked the safety catch silently onto the fire setting, stifling a bored yawn as he did so. Harkabahadur glanced at him. Their eyes met and they smiled. Harkabahadur knew that neither he nor Birbahadur were ever going to set the world alight. That was not their role. They were not even big enough to be cogs in the machine of empire. But he knew that they were the oil. Without them, and without thousands of others like them the length and breadth of the empire, no cogs would turn and nothing would happen. They were not going to set the world alight, but they were the tinder without which there would be no fire.

It was only when the figure of a man appeared in front of

them that the four Gurkhas realised how the dawn had crept up on them. He rose out of the ground, head and shoulders, then chest and abdomen, growing in size and outline as he walked stealthily towards their position. He was testing the approach, rifle held ready in his hands. Harkabahadur looked at Ramprasad and raised his eyebrows, impatient for the signal to open fire. Ramprasad had frozen.

'*Guruji!*' Harkabahadur hissed contemptuously.

Ramprasad stared at him stupidly. 'What?'

Harkabahadur cursed under his breath. '*Janta*,' he muttered. Birbahadur giggled into the butt of his light machine gun, enjoying the likening of his NCO to a pubic hair.

For a moment Harkabahadur considered using his kukri to deal with the tribesman silently but a second head showing above the skyline betrayed the presence of the man's comrades. Instead, Harkabahadur brought his rifle into the aim, sighted on his target's sternum, and squeezed off a single round. The second he had done so, his hand automatically worked the bolt, whipping out the smoking empty brass cartridge case and slamming another round into the hot breech. As he did so, he looked over his rifle sights and saw the first man blown backwards out of sight, arms flung out to his sides, weapon clattering to the ground.

There was a growl of rage from the gloom and half a dozen of the dead man's companions rose up and came forward in an attempt to rush the Gurkha position. Birbahadur was waiting for them. This is easy, he thought as he tightened into his gun and pulled the trigger, squirting out short bursts of fire into the oncoming bodies. Not a patch on the Pathans. They would never have been so stupid.

The thought had hardly emptied his brain when there was a massed cry and a score of tribesmen came over the crest from the Gurkhas' right flank less than fifty yards distant.

Harkabahadur cursed. The enemy had been working their way around them. Quickly he swung his rifle onto them and cracked off two rounds. Two men fell. Belatedly, young Rifle-man Anand Sherpa brought his Lewis gun into action, joining Birbahadur in putting down a ferocious weight of fire onto the enemy force. Bodies twisted and tumbled, but on the extremity of the group, two men closed to within a few paces of the Gurkhas. Not trusting his aim under such pressure, Harkaba-hadur stood up, grasped his rifle by the stock and swung the brass-plated butt at the first of them. It took the man on the side of the face. Harkabahadur saw the whole jaw jump sideways out of its sockets and a startled look fix in the man's eyes before he went down.

But his comrades were right behind him. One of them swung at Harkabahadur with a long-bladed sword. Instinctively Harkabahadur brought his rifle up to block the cut. The blade bit deeply into the wood and lodged, the momentum of the swing jarring the rifle from Harkabahadur's grasp. Without hesitating, he drew his kukri from its scabbard, the blade rasping as it swung into the growing light. He struck at the side of the tribesman's neck. With his wrist Harkabahadur turned the cut into a slice, using the heavily weighted tip of the blade to pull itself clean through flesh, cartilage and bone. Without waiting to see the result, he drew the blade clear of the wound and swung to meet the next man. With a backhand stroke, Harkabahadur cut upwards and outwards, the blade describing a huge arc. The oncoming tribesman tried to stop himself short but his own momentum carried him on, straight into the vicious blade swing which caught him in the throat. His head lolled back, blood spouting upwards in a bright jet.

Before he could recover his rifle, Harkabahadur caught sight of the next wave of tribesmen. They were everywhere now, swarming over the crest and tearing towards the hard pressed Gurkhas.

'Pull back!' he screamed at his comrades. He glanced at Ramprasad, but the lance naik was frantically working the bolt of his rifle. Without a second thought Harkabahadur took command. He kicked out at Anand and Birbahadur. 'Back, I said. Leapfrog in pairs.'

Neither of them even thought to consider Ramprasad. Harkabahadur was the natural leader of the group. He seemed to know what to do. He was the only one giving any orders. Instinctively they trusted his judgement. Their lives now depended on it.

17

With the sound of the first rifle shot Caspasian was awake. He knew instantly where it had come from. Distant, faint, but for him a clarion call to arms. Ganga and Kraus too were on their feet within a second. Béranger eased himself carefully upright, anxious not to reopen his wound.

Michelle sat up and rubbed her eyes. She watched Caspasian buckling on his revolver. 'What do you want me to do?'

'Stay with the others,' he said. 'I don't want you anywhere near the fighting. If the plan works, they won't reach the city ruins.'

'And if it doesn't?'

'Then we're lost.'

She smiled, frightened but trying to hide it from him. As he prepared to leave, she got up quickly and ran to him, kissing him deeply and holding on to him. Tenderly he released her fingers, looking hard into her eyes. 'Have you still got the pistol Béranger gave you?'

'No, I returned it to him.'

He pressed a small .32 Ruby automatic pistol into her hands. 'Use this if you have to.'

She stared at it.

'Do you know how to fire it?'

She nodded. With one final kiss he was gone, jogging out of the ruined caravanserai, collecting Béranger, Ganga and Kraus on the way. With them gone, the Professor gathered the others together. 'So much for old Jacob. It seems the tribesmen have decided they can do without him after all.'

Jacob looked up at the mention of his name and giggled. The

Professor regarded him sadly. 'Right, well we might as well make best use of our time.'

'Excellent,' said Monsieur Simonin. 'We can look for the tomb.'

'No, actually we're going to check the airstrip. If we're not able to fight, I think we should at least do something that might help Caspasian.'

Sir Hubert sneered. 'And how on earth do you think the airstrip's going to help?'

The Professor shrugged. 'I don't know. But we might find something there that may be of use.'

Monsieur Simonin protested. '*Mon Dieu*, when will we get another chance to look for the tomb of Menes?'

'If we don't help Caspasian you'll be in a tomb of your own, Monsieur Simonin,' the Professor rebuked sharply.

'And what about that?' Sir Hubert said pointing to Jacob whom the legionnaires had deposited with the archaeologists before leaving to take up their positions.

The Professor smiled and went towards the old man, holding out his hand to help him to his feet. 'We will take our friend with us,' he said kindly.

Michelle appeared and went straight across to help him, pointedly ignoring her husband. 'Caspasian wants me to come with you,' she said.

Monsieur Simonin could not resist. 'Oh, I see, it's Caspasian now, is it? How quickly you switch your affections, my dear.'

Michelle rounded on him. 'How can I switch my affections when I have never had any for you, you bastard!'

The Professor tried to calm her. 'Please, both of you. We've got enough on our plates without the two of you fighting as well.'

Chastened but sulking, Monsieur Simonin withdrew, leaving the Professor and Michelle to bring Jacob along with them and together they all headed for the site of the airstrip to see what they could find there.

As they went, Michelle felt a hand on her hair and spun round in alarm. Old Jacob stood smiling at her. He stroked her head as if she was a stray dog.

'There there,' he said, as surprised at the words coming out of his mouth as Michelle was to hear them.

By the time he reached the site that had been prepared for defence, Caspasian could see in the far distance the small detachment of Gurkhas fighting their way back off the ridge-line. The whole hillside behind and above them was alive with the darting figures of tribesmen.

'They'll be lucky to get back here,' Ganga observed.

'They've got to. We need their firepower,' Caspasian said.

While Béranger and Kraus took the legionnaires away to the dry river bed, Caspasian sited his small handful of men. The cables to the explosive charges had been laid so that all of them led back to a single firing point where Caspasian intended to put himself. He had selected a clump of tumbled stone, strengthening it into a makeshift strongpoint by the use of sandbags and whole branches of thick gorse cut from the belt astride the track down which Harkabahadur and his men were now retreating.

Close beside him, Sergeant Ganga readied his weapons, checking his rifle and setting the sights, blowing some particles of sand from the top of the breech. He laid out several spare clips of ammunition on a stone at his right-hand side and squinted between two rocks to check he was still able to see the satchel of phosphorous grenades across the open ground in front of them.

On the left of the strongpoint, Naik Indrabahadur and Rifleman Bharat jumped down into the foxhole they had dug the previous evening. Fifty yards to Caspasian's right the two cooks, Dhanprasad and Akalbahadur, similarly pre-pared themselves for the coming fight. All were apprehensive but only Bharat was making it known.

'I really shouldn't be here,' he mumbled to Indrabahadur. 'I should have been in the clerks platoon, manning the head-quarters orderly room. I'm not an infantryman.'

'That's true enough,' Indrabahadur said scowling as he hefted a sandbag into place in front of him. He punched it into shape. He would rest his left wrist on it when holding the stock of the rifle. It would help eliminate movement, steadying his aim.

Caspasian took out his binoculars and scanned the sunken river bed on the left flank. He spotted Béranger's head and shoulders and saw him placing his legionnaires. Kraus was everywhere, checking each man's arc of fire with typical German thoroughness. Caspasian smiled. It was a tragedy that they had been on opposing sides in the war. The man was a professional. No wonder it had taken the Allied armies so long to engineer the defeat of him and his kind.

When he checked on the distant track again, he was shocked to see that the withdrawal had deteriorated into a running fight. They were close enough now for him to be able to make out individual identities. At first Ramprasad was nowhere to be seen, but then he caught sight of him. He had fallen behind and as Caspasian watched, he saw the enemy closing upon him. He glanced down at Ganga who was also transfixed on the flight. Reading Caspasian's mind Ganga sadly shook his head.

'No chance, saheb. Even I can't help him at this range. I'd be as likely to hit him as the enemy.'

Caspasian put his binoculars to his eyes again and saw the enemy close upon Ramprasad. One of them took a swipe at the fleeing Gurkha with a sword. The man was halted in mid-air and knocked sideways. Harkabahadur had sniped him with a shot fired while on the run. But there were others, and now Harkabahadur had to look out for himself if he too was not to be caught. Left to his own devices, Ramprasad drew his kukri, but in the next instant he was overwhelmed. Caspasian saw a frenzied hacking as the lance naik disappeared beneath the press of bodies.

'Time to help the three survivors,' Caspasian said resolutely. Ganga nodded, selecting two of the slender firing cables that snaked out across the sand. He looked to left and right, checking on the other Gurkhas until they nodded acknowledgement that they were ready.

Eventually the three fleeing Gurkhas disappeared from view, dropping down to the valley floor and entering the belt of dense gorse and scrub. Hot on their heels the tribesmen tumbled after them. Shots rang out as the Gurkhas fired and reloaded on the move. When they finally emerged from the scrub there were only two of them left, Harkabahadur and Birbahadur. Anand, the young Sherpa from the highest of the Himalayan foothills, had vanished, cut down as he ran.

Caspasian waited until they were twenty yards out in the open, sprinting furiously across the open ground towards the strongpoint where they could see him standing, and then gave the signal. Ganga tugged on the two cables and behind the running Gurkhas, where the track emerged from the gorse, two clumps of smoke grenades burst asunder, belching thick white smoke that billowed rapidly to form a spreading cloud, concealing the Gurkhas from the tribesmen. Instinctively, the pursuing tribesmen stopped dead in their tracks. They had never seen a smoke screen before and panicked at the sight of it. Caspasian knew that their caution would only last for a few seconds but hoped that would be sufficient to see the Gurkhas safely into cover.

They were more than halfway across when the smoke screen started to dissipate, drifting lazily away across the plain, fading back into nothingness.

'Now,' Caspasian said, chopping his hand sharply downwards. At his signal the Gurkhas to left and right of him opened fire, Ganga joining them. Rifle bolts rattled back and forth and .303 bullets snapped across the open ground in search of targets. On the left, the legionnaires waited in silence, ducking out of sight below the deep dry river banks. The sudden shock effect of the concentrated rifle fire from the Gurkhas was enough to halt the advance of the tribesmen. Caspasian knew it would not last. A handful of rifles would never do the job alone.

A few moments later Harkabahadur and Birbahadur closed the final yards and toppled panting over the parapet and into the firing pit. Both were gasping, sweat soaking their shirts. Birbahadur had taken a bullet in the thigh but it had passed through cleanly without hitting either vein or artery. His face was pale, registering shock. Adrenaline had carried him through the flight but now he slumped to catch his pounding breath, the shock caught up with him and he started to black out. Ganga emptied some water over his face and thrust the bottle into his hands, urging him to drink.

'Come on, *daju*,' he said. 'No time to rest now.'

Harkabahadur had seized Anand's Lewis gun when the Sherpa had gone down, his own rifle discarded on the ridgeline, the enemy's sword still lodged in the stock.

He hunted frantically. 'Magazines?'

Ganga pointed to a satchel on the ground. Harkabahadur dived at it, tore open the flap and pulled out a fresh one. Clipping it on top of the weapon, he grabbed a couple of spares and sought out a good fire position.

'Here they come,' Caspasian said calmly, kneeling down behind the parapet and bringing a Lee-Enfield into the aim. He adjusted the sights. 'Whatever you do, don't get shot until you've detonated the grenades on my orders, is that clear?' he said to Ganga.

Ganga grinned as he stared one-eyed through his sights, selecting a fresh target. 'I'll try, saheb.'

Across the plain the tribesmen were fanning out, spreading like a pool of water inexorably claiming ownership of the flat ground, flooding into the empty space. Bodies fell but there were always more to take their place. Caspasian noticed that as they spread, they were being drawn to the left by the natural flow of the land, towards the waiting legionnaires. Someone in authority had obviously noticed the sunken river and was intending to use it to outflank the Gurkha position.

All the while he was firing, Caspasian kept an intermittent watch on their progress. He trusted Béranger and Kraus but it did not stop the anxious fluttering he could feel in his stomach.

When the tribesmen were halfway across the plain and almost at the edge of the sunken river the legionnaires sprang into action. As one man, they popped their rifles over the bank and opened rapid fire. The unprepared tribesmen whose attention had been wholly fixed upon Caspasian's strongpoint were caught completely unawares.

Caspasian could feel the shock effect on them. He could sense the battle now. He could feel it. Its mood, its course. He ceased firing and looked up, considering.

'Now,' he said simply.

Ganga gingerly laid his rifle aside and sat up behind the parapet to take hold of the numerous cables that led away from the position. 'Any particular order, saheb.'

Caspasian shook his head. 'Keep it random. No pattern.'

One by one Ganga tugged on the cables. Out across the middle of the plain, the explosive charges began to detonate. When they had buried them, the Gurkhas had packed pieces of rock tightly on top of the charges. Now, as they exploded, they burst upwards, shattering the rocks into jagged shards which fired outwards at all angles and in all directions with the devastating effect of shrapnel or shell splinters.

Instantly the assault faltered. Hit from two sides by intense rifle and light machine gun fire, and with the explosions now detonating throughout their ranks, the tribesmen instinctively threw themselves to the ground. But wherever they took cover, in depressions, ditches or hollows, it seemed that the enemy artillery sought them out. Not realising that the charges had been sited to achieve exactly this end, they succumbed to Caspasian's plan and suffered accordingly.

Groups of them began to turn and run. At the rear, Caspasian could see the commanders urging them to stand fast, but they were fighting a losing struggle. Fear had begun to set in. Surveying them through his binoculars, Caspasian knew the thoughts that were coursing through their panic-stricken minds. Flight was starting to appear their only option for the valley floor had proved to be too terrible a place to advance.

Caspasian moved across to Ganga and relieved him of the cables. There were only a few left untriggered. 'OK,' he said. 'Let's cut off their retreat.'

Ganga nodded and settled down behind his rifle. As he had anticipated, his visibility across the battlefield was now partially obscured by drifting smoke and sand thrown up by the explosions and the reports from the enemy's own weapons. Nevertheless, he sighted on the point where he knew the satchel of white phosphorous grenades was secured. He waited. In between the drifting smoke he caught a glimpse of it, though only for a second. He could feel Caspasian's eyes anxiously upon him. This was the moment in the battle when the tide was to be turned. It was up to him, Ganga, to bring it about. Without a clear shot it would not happen. The last of the explosive charges had now been detonated. It would only take moments for the enemy to realise there were no more to follow. Confidence would return, the initiative would change hands again, shifting back to the enemy. The day would be lost, and a lot more besides.

For a second only, a break appeared in the smoke. The satchel loomed briefly. Ganga swung his aim onto it, inhaled, exhaled and held it, empty. He steadied himself and gently squeezed the trigger, following through the shot before opening his left eye and checking the result. The smoke had closed again, cutting his line of sight. But through the smoke there was a brilliant orange flash and the dull thud of the exploding grenades. They detonated in succession, each one bursting through the smoke and sending incendiary showers of burning phosphorous in all directions. Where they fell on the tinder dry gorse and scrub, fires started immediately. The same breeze that had caused the smoke and cordite to drift across the battlefield now blew the flames, fanning them and lighting a broad swathe of gorse. The fire leapt and crackled, rising into the smudged sky in great black streamers. Soon, a wild conflagration stretched right across the rear of the surviving tribesmen.

'OK, let them have it,' Caspasian said, and both Gurkhas and legionnaires poured a torrent of bullets into the enemy. Lewis guns chattered as their drum magazines juddered in tight circles on top of their breeches, Lee-Enfields cracked savagely, bolts worked with professional speed, and from the river bed, carbines and Chauchat light machine guns tore into the flanks of the enemy. Some of the tribesmen tried to flee up the rising ground on the right but the few who made it to the top of the slope found their way barred by an unscalable rock face. They were trapped. As the realisation sank in, panic became rife. Men began to throw down their weapons. Some, terror-stricken, hurled themselves into the fiery gorse in an attempt to break through to freedom on the other side. Those who survived to re-emerge did so as human torches, their arms flailing in a futile effort to extinguish their burning robes.

At last it was over. A handful of the tribesmen located a small breach in the gorse and all those who were still able to run converged on it and fled, leaving the valley behind them, the blood-stained sand strewn with their dead, dying and wounded. Slowly the firing ceased. Ganga signalled for the Gurkhas to stop, and from the sunken river bed, Kraus's powerful voice boomed out with the same order directed at his surviving legionnaires. They had taken casualties and Caspasian was shocked to see how few rose uncertainly into the open. Clambering over the bank, Béranger came into view. He raised his arm high above his head and waved his pistol at Caspasian.

'We've done it!' he shouted.

Caspasian smiled and waved back. It was not a moment too soon. He was not sure about the legionnaires, but the Gurkhas were almost out of ammunition, down to the last handful of rounds per man. The explosives and grenades had been completely expended. Nevertheless, the enemy was defeated. The day had been won.

One by one, the Gurkhas and legionnaires emerged from their firing positions, standing up and shaking their limbs loose. On directions from Kraus and Ganga they fanned out across the open plain checking on the dead and attending to the wounded who they gathered together beside Caspasian's strongpoint. It was not much of an aid post, but it would have to do. In all some two dozen prisoners were taken, their weapons confiscated and arranged in a pile under the watchful eye of two guards. On the far side of the plain the gorse was burning itself out, plumes of thinning smoke rising high into the sky in long straight lines. Those who had fled the battlefield had long since vanished.

When Caspasian was content that everyone still living had been gathered together, he ordered the move back to the waterhole. They were all parched with thirst and the injured needed to have their wounds dressed. What he was going to do with them was another matter, but for now water was, once again, the prime consideration.

They set off back towards the pool, the legionnaires bringing up the rear with Béranger and Kraus. Caspasian, Ganga and the Gurkhas led the way, the prisoners shuffling miserably in the centre. Though not far, they trudged slowly, exhausted, hot and thirsty. Fatigue had set in. The exhilaration of the battle had receded, leaving them tired and lacklustre. The intense heat of the day worked on their exhausted minds, lulling them into a state of half-wakefulness. As they drew near to the pool they saw the Professor, Sir Hubert, Monsieur Simonin and Michelle seated in a circle.

'Find anything?' Caspasian called out when they were within earshot.

There was a light breeze and it whisked his words away. No one answered him. He walked closer. 'Where's Jacob?' he called out when only thirty yards distant.

Still no one answered him. Then, Michelle looked up. She opened her mouth, and at that moment Caspasian froze. He stopped dead in his tracks. Walking behind him, Ganga stumbled into his back, mumbling an apology. Caspasian started to turn, his eyes scouring the surrounding stones and statues, walls and ruins. They had entered the avenue that led to the pool. As he turned, his hand went to his holster. That was when the firing began.

From all sides a fusillade of rifle fire rang out, ferocious and from close range. The bullets tore into their ranks, striking down Gurkha, legionnaire and prisoner, all as one. Caspasian had just had time to throw himself against Ganga, toppling the two of them over backwards and as they fell, they rolled, scrabbling into a ditch beside the upended stone figure of a seated man. Bullets smacked into it, bursting the stone into chips that ricocheted within inches of the two hiding men.

Indrabahadur and Birbahadur went down in the first flurry of shots. Then the two cooks, Dhanprasad and Akalbahadur. Harkabahadur leapt sideways, diving into Bharat and together they scrabbled behind cover, hugging the earth as bullets attempted to seek them out. The prisoners were running and falling in equal measure. Behind them, the legionnaires had grouped instinctively around Béranger. As Caspasian watched he saw the front of Béranger's jacket burst into a swathe of red patches. He staggered, his knees buckled and he went down, firing all the way. His eyes met Caspasian's and it seemed as though he was smiling. It was recognition, one soldier to another. A salute. A farewell.

Kraus was screaming out orders, but all those to whom he could give them had fallen. He knelt, furious and enraged, blazing away his final rounds until the firing pin was slamming uselessly into an empty chamber. Miraculously he remained unhit, shielded by the bodies of his fallen comrades.

'Enough!' a powerful voice commanded. The rifle fire died away. 'Stand up!' the voice ordered. Caspasian held Ganga down firmly. He had his revolver in his hand and thoughts were racing through his head. Options. Courses of action. From his position it was impossible to see who had ambushed them or where an avenue of flight may lie. He longed for a smoke grenade, cursing himself for not having kept some phosphorous to hand.

'Unless you come out in the next ten seconds I will order the woman and the others to be shot.' There was a pause and then the voice came again. 'Watch.'

There was a scream which Caspasian recognised as Sir Hubert. Craning round the statue that shielded himself and Ganga, Caspasian saw Sir Hubert being hauled to his feet and prodded away from the seated group. 'Caspasian, do as he tells you!' he shouted, his voice losing all pretence of self-control. 'Get up, damn you man!'

Ganga looked at Caspasian, questioning. Caspasian shook his head.

'Caspasian, you bastard! Get up!' Sir Hubert shrieked in terror.

'Why should I trust you?' Caspasian shouted, ignoring Sir Hubert's plea and addressing himself to whoever was now in charge.

'Because you have no choice,' came the reasonable response.

Ganga shrugged in sympathetic agreement.

'Why not just shoot us now and have done with it?' Caspasian shouted back. 'You've got us at your mercy as it is. Why not finish it?'

'Don't question my motives. Either get up now or this prick gets shot. And then the rest of them. One by one, while you watch.'

From the man's voice, Caspasian knew that he would do it. Ruthless. Matter-of-fact. He had encountered the sort before. What struck Caspasian most was the man's accent. It was from somewhere in the Levant, but he could not place it.

Reluctantly, Caspasian stood up, expecting to feel lead slamming into his body as he moved away from the cover of the fallen statue. Across from him, Sir Hubert heaved an enormous sigh, his expression first relieved and then quickly angry.

'Why the devil didn't you stand up when the man told you to? You'd have seen me killed without batting an eyelid, wouldn't you? You're nothing but a cheap little . . .'

The gunshot from behind him sent Sir Hubert staggering forward into Caspasian's arms like the blow from a hammer. He slumped against Caspasian's chest, Caspasian catching him under the armpits. Sir Hubert stared bewildered into Caspasian's eyes as if searching for guilt, wondering how Caspasian had managed to strike him down without a gun. Before it dawned on him that the shot had been fired by his captor, Sir Hubert was dead. His head fell forwards and Caspasian lowered him to the ground.

The speaker stepped into the open. A wisp of smoke rose from the muzzle of the pistol in his fist as harmless as a cigar. 'What a worthless human being,' he said with contempt, glancing down at Sir Hubert's lifeless body. The man smiled pleasantly at Caspasian. 'Don't you, of all people, tell me I shouldn't have done that. He was clearly no friend of yours.'

Caspasian studied the man before him. Of medium height, he was neatly dressed in a stone-coloured lightweight suit. Incongruously for their surroundings, he wore a collar and tie and, beneath the brim of a panama, his eyes stared calmly back. From his attire it was clear he had not just crossed the desert on foot. He reached up and brushed a trim moustache as he contemplated his captive.

'My name is Kalkan,' he said. From around the avenue of

statues, other figures emerged, all well armed with sub-machine guns and carbines. They herded the survivors together into a tight little group. Kraus glared back at them, tossing aside his rifle only after several muzzles had been levelled at him. Ganga, Harkabahadur and Bharat joined him, all of them similarly disarmed.

The tribesmen who had been prisoners until a moment ago returned, sulking. Some of them spat at the new prisoners and kicked them, rejoicing that the tables had so unexpectedly turned. Only one of them remained aloof, nursing a slight wound in his right upper arm. As Caspasian watched, he moved towards the man called Kalkan who observed him icily.

'You incompetent idiot,' Kalkan said to the tribesman. 'You are given the simplest of tasks and you muck it up wonderfully. You really are a waste of the money we've been paying you.'

Caspasian saw the tribesman's hand go to his belt, but the dagger he had worn there until recently had been removed when he had been taken prisoner. Kalkan smiled but otherwise chose to ignore the gesture. Instead he took a step forward and patted the man on the shoulder. 'Forgive me. I spoke hastily. Go and round up your men and bring them here. We have work to do.' He glanced up at the sky. 'I want to be on my way before last light. I'm going to need all the hands you can gather. And this time keep that old fool out of the way. I don't want him mucking things up again.' He turned to Caspasian. 'My friend Mahmud has a soft spot for the old cretin. I believe you know him as Jacob?'

The tribesman stepped forward and to Caspasian's surprise spoke in English. 'It is a debt of honour. Do not discredit it. Yakub spared the life of my father in battle. He taught me their tongue. I have honoured my father's debt to him, and I will always do so.'

Kalkan nodded boredly. 'Just keep him out of the way.'

When Mahmud had gone, Caspasian and the others were herded together with the Professor and Monsieur Simonin.

Michelle came and stood next to Caspasian. The Professor edged closer.

'I'm sorry to let you down, Caspasian. They surprised us,' he said under his breath.

'Where the devil did they come from?' Caspasian replied.

'They were here all along. They've got . . .'

'No talking!' Kalkan commanded, jabbing his pistol in their direction. 'Seeing as how my good friend Mahmud has managed to get almost his entire force wiped out – a considerable feat for which I commend you, Captain – I am going to need the assistance of everyone here. Now move!'

At his signal, his men gathered round the perimeter of the grouped prisoners and herded them away, heading past the water pool which lay tantalisingly close, and on through the ruined city. They walked for the best part of half an hour until eventually they emerged at the far side and Caspasian was able to see for himself the airstrip that the Professor had described. Sure enough, stones had been placed to mark out the area where the ground was firm enough to take the weight of an aircraft without the wheels sinking into it. What was more, beside each marker stone was a large tin, half-buried in the sand. From the smell Caspasian could tell that they had only recently been filled with kerosene to enable the strip to be used for night landings.

To his surprise the group was shepherded on past the airstrip and towards a thick belt of palm trees that rose some five hundred yards on the other side. As they approached, Caspasian was able to distinguish the outline of a tall structure. The ground suddenly began to descend and, just on the far side of the treeline, he found himself looking at a vast mastaba, an ancient tomb built in the huge rectangular design that was used before the development of the pyramid. He glanced at the Professor who nodded at him sadly.

'The tomb,' he said resignedly. 'We found it. But they were waiting for us.'

'No talking!' Kalkan shouted. 'If I have to tell you again you will be shot.'

Caspasian had little doubt that eventually it was Kalkan's intention to shoot them in any case, just as soon as they had served whatever purpose their captor had for them.

The entrance was on the far side of the huge rectangular structure and consisted of a low portal in the stone side, disappearing down into the black depths of the earth. Kalkan halted, waiting until the prisoners were assembled. The tribesman Mahmud returned with a dozen of his followers. Kalkan sighed irritably. 'How the devil am I supposed to manage with no more men than this? It's ridiculous. At this rate I'll be lucky to get away before tomorrow morning.' He checked his watch. 'If I'm not back in Cairo by . . .' he shook his head angrily, leaving his words hanging ominously in the air.

'Well, gentlemen,' Kalkan said, taking a deep breath in an effort to cheer himself. 'I expect you would like to see the treasure for which you have braved desert, jebel, sandstorm and savage onslaught?' He surveyed the group before him. Monsieur Simonin, in spite of the sweat pouring off him, wore an expression of pure avarice at the prospect of what he was about to see. Fear had been replaced by an emotion that, for him, was even more powerful.

'After you,' Kalkan said, gesturing to the Professor at the head of the group.

The Professor was nudged forward towards the entrance by the gun of his closest guard. He glanced at Caspasian but Caspasian was looking away from the tomb's entrance. For beyond the ruined outbuildings gathered around the mastaba, he had seen something. In amongst the tall date palms, some of the guards were tearing down huge camouflage nets revealing underneath them, first an enormous wheel, then the undercarriage, then a wing and finally the full body of a Breguet 14 aircraft and, beyond it, another. He had also heard the calls and commands they exchanged as they laboured and had recognised the language they were speaking. A small part of the confusion raging through his head was dispelled, for when their captor had identified himself as Kalkan, both his name and the language of his followers had marked them out as Turks.

18

Inside, the tunnel was dark and claustrophobic. The Professor was just able to walk upright. Behind him, Caspasian was forced to stoop which made the whole process far more uncomfortable the further they penetrated into the vast tomb. The Professor felt his way, outstretched hands running down the walls on either side. Eventually, frustrated at the slow pace, a guard clutching a pistol in one hand and a kerosene lantern in the other, pushed roughly to the front and took the lead.

After some distance the tunnel angled sharply downwards. It turned, first to the left and then to the right, until Caspasian lost track of their direction altogether. The air became damp and stale and suddenly something slithered from under their feet.

'Snake!' the Professor cried. Behind Caspasian, Michelle pressed into him, clutching at his shoulders.

'Keep moving!' Kalkan shouted from further down the line.

The snake had vanished from sight, disappearing down a crack between the stone slabs lining the tunnel. Strange drawings decorated the walls, but though the Professor was desperate to stop and examine them more closely he was forced onwards as fast as he could manage.

Before they realised it the tunnel ended. The guard stepped over a raised threshold and jumped down into a sunken room, the Professor stumbling after him. Caspasian caught him by the scruff of the neck and saved him from sprawling on all fours. One by one the others followed until the entire group and their guards had entered. Kalkan moved to the front and smiled. The light from the few lamps cast an eerie glow and revealed that they had entered a small antechamber. The walls were covered with a profusion of paintings. Caspasian heard the Professor's intake of breath as he marvelled at their exquisite beauty.

Kalkan noticed it too and smiled. 'Time to see the tomb room itself, Professor. The moment you've been waiting for.'

He led the way towards the far side of the room and for the first time Caspasian became aware of another doorway, larger than the one through which they had just come. Kalkan's guards gathered around their prisoners in a tight circle, lanterns held high.

'Gentlemen, follow me,' Kalkan announced, turning quickly to add, 'Not forgetting the lady too, of course.'

They entered the main burial chamber. The guards fanned out and held their lanterns aloft. The Professor stared speechless at the spectacle before them. The room was large, rectangular and high-ceilinged. A stone sarcophagus stood in the centre and around the walls, wooden boxes and crates were piled high in a haphazard fashion. While Kalkan looked on, enjoying the entertainment, the Professor moved from crate to crate and inspected them. He walked across to the sarcophagus and leaned over the edge standing on tiptoes to examine the inside. He turned back to Kalkan, his expression puzzled.

'But . . . I don't understand.'

Kalkan chuckled. 'How wonderful. Oh, I am enjoying this. What don't you understand, Professor?'

'The contents of the burial chamber and sarcophagus . . .'

Kalkan shook his head, beaming. Caspasian bent down to examine one of the crates and understood, his heart sinking. He could barely start to imagine the Professor's disappointment.

'The pharaonic treasure?' the Professor asked.

Monsieur Simonin leapt forward and started to hunt around the room as if expecting to unearth something of value.

'There never was any,' Kalkan said, holding his arms out at his sides.

Monsieur Simonin stared at him, eyes frantic. 'But if grave-robbers stripped the tomb in antiquity, why has nothing ever emerged on the black market? Nothing, not even a whisper until the papyrus scroll fragment.'

Again Kalkan shook his head. 'Grave-robbers never stole anything from here because there was never anything here to steal. The tomb was prepared during the lifetime of King Menes, but long before he died the river changed course, leaving the city high and dry. The city died of natural causes. Trade and people moved away. The King and his court along with them.'

'To?' the Professor asked expectantly.

Kalkan shrugged. 'Who knows? You see, the real tomb of King Menes is still undiscovered. His treasure, if there really is any, is still somewhere out in the desert. Or, should I say, beneath the desert.'

'How do you know all this?' Monsieur Simonin said.

'From the Turkish expedition which discovered and excavated this city and tomb.'

The Professor looked at him suspiciously. 'I've never heard of any such expedition.'

'Nor I,' said Monsieur Simonin, folding his arms defiantly across his chest. 'Nothing is known of it in academic circles.'

Kalkan nodded, smiling contentedly.

'And the crates?' the Professor said. 'What's in . . .'

'Guns,' answered Caspasian. He stood up, brushing the dirt from his hands after his examination of one of the crates.

'Guns,' Kalkan said, confirming.

The Professor and Monsieur Simonin stared at one another, puzzled. 'No treasure . . .' Monsieur Simonin said, deflating visibly. He sank down onto the nearest crate, mopping his brow.

'Not quite true,' Kalkan said mysteriously. He walked across to the sarcophagus and, leaning in, hefted out a wooden box with difficulty, depositing it on the ground. He unfastened the catch at the front and raised the lid, allowing it to drop open. Monsieur Simonin leaned forward and stared mesmerised at

275

the contents. The box was heaped to the brim with gold coins. He reached and picked one up, holding it towards the light of the nearest lantern. He frowned.

'This is Turkish,' he said. 'Ottoman.'

'Yes. Hardly pharaonic but together with the other boxes in there,' Kalkan said indicating the sarcophagus, 'worth a considerable fortune.'

The Professor sank down beside Monsieur Simonin. 'Guns and gold,' he said to himself aloud. He laughed bitterly, shaking his head. 'All this way for guns and gold.'

'Oh, you shouldn't be so dismissive,' Kalkan said. 'Pharaonic treasure would merely sit rotting in some museum. Beyond price perhaps, but in real terms quite worthless.' He gestured at the surrounding crates of weaponry and at the gold coins, gleaming in the pale yellow light cast by the lanterns. 'This, on the other hand, is going to change the course of history.' He pointed at his prisoners. 'And all of you are going to help do it.'

'But . . .' the Professor began.

Kalkan cut him short. 'Enough of talking. Seeing as Mahmud is now somewhat short-handed, I am going to need the help of all of you. Everything has got to be loaded onto the planes and it's got to be done immediately. So get moving!'

The guards placed their lanterns around the room to provide sufficient light to work, and then goaded the prisoners into action. Kalkan closed and refastened the box of coins and directed Mahmud and his men to take care of the money. The prisoners were to haul the crates of guns and ammunition back into the daylight and load them onto the planes. Monsieur Simonin stared in horror at the size of their task.

'It cannot be done! Not in this heat, and through that tunnel. It will kill me,' he protested generously.

Kalkan pointed the muzzle of his pistol at him. 'Unless you do what I say, I will kill you myself.'

The Professor got wearily to his feet. 'I think we had better do as this gentleman orders.'

'Well done,' Kalkan crooned. 'Every inch the perfect English gentleman. Just as I would have expected.'

'What about the girl?' Caspasian asked.

'She can work too. I'm sure she is as robust as our Turkish women. However, if she is not, I am sure my guards can think of some other use for her.'

Caspasian started to protest but Michelle placed a hand on his shoulder, stopping him. 'Don't worry about me. I can do it.'

They set to work, Monsieur Simonin and the Professor picking up the first crate that the guards indicated. They seized the rope handles that were fastened to either end and half-carried and half-dragged the crate back across the antechamber and into the tunnel. Harkabahadur and Bharat laid hold of another, while Kraus and Ganga picked up one each, slinging it over their shoulders. Bent double, they made their way agonisingly back towards the daylight.

Caspasian selected a smaller crate and together with Michelle, began to carry it out. Mahmud and his men took hold of the cases of gold coins, closely watched by Kalkan and his Turkish guards. Caspasian noted their suspicion of the tribesmen. His mind was working furiously.

When they eventually stumbled into daylight outside the tomb's entrance, the Professor and Monsieur Simonin dropped their crate to the ground and sat on it, gasping for air and wiping away the sweat that was pouring down their faces.

'This is no good,' Monsieur Simonin panted. 'I am going to die. I will have a heart attack, I assure you.'

The Professor smiled good-naturedly. 'My friend, you will probably prove to be the strongest of us all.'

Monsieur Simonin shook his head and muttered. Harkabahadur and Bharat, Kraus and Ganga, staggered past them on their way towards the two waiting aircraft, now freed of their camouflage nets and standing proudly in the full glare of the sun. The two pilots chatted idly in the shade of the date palms, watching the working party with bored detachment. They had opened the cargo hatches and left a single guard beside each one to oversee the loading of the wooden cases on board. Caspasian shaded his eyes and blinked in the glare of the sudden light. He took in the situation, watching and waiting, biding his time as he evaluated his options. Stripped of his weapons when he had surrendered to Kalkan, it was frustrating to be so close to the firearms in the crates without being able to lay hands on them.

On his way back to the tunnel entrance, Caspasian saw one of Mahmud's men approaching, labouring under the weight of a case of coins. Caspasian waited until the man had drawn alongside and then tripped and collided into him. The man overbalanced and only managed to stop himself falling by letting go of the case. It hit the ground and the lid sprung open. Gold coins spilled into the sand. The man cursed and took a swipe at Caspasian. Caspasian allowed the blow to land, wincing and dropping to the floor, profuse apologies bubbling from him. He scrabbled for the coins, stuffing them back into the box. The man bent down to help him and together they cleared up the mess. One of the Turkish guards came running over and went to strike Caspasian with the butt of his pistol. Caspasian scuttled away, shielding his face from the blow and crying out for leniency. Contemptuously the guard waved him away and watched as he made his way back to the tunnel entrance to join Michelle who was waiting for him.

'What was all that about?' she asked.

Caspasian ushered her into the tunnel quickly. 'You'll see.'

The guards had secured lanterns the length of the tunnel to aid the carrying of the arms and the gold to the outside world, but it was still gloomy inside and as Caspasian and Michelle passed more of Mahmud's men in the semi-darkness, it was difficult to avoid jostling them as they edged past. Caspasian received more curses and kicks, but held his temper firmly in check, bowing his head apologetically and continuing on down into the bowels of the tomb towards the central burial chamber and the next load.

They worked relentlessly until the sun began to dip low in the sky and the shadows of the date palms stretched across the sand and crept up the walls of the giant mastaba. Slowly, the crates of guns, the cases of ammunition and the boxes of gold coins had been transferred from the burial chamber to the holds of the two aircraft. The chamber itself finally stood empty, as did the sarcophagus that had never been used for the mummified body of King Menes. The Professor, at the start of his last trip to the daylight outside, looked at it sadly, dreaming privately of what might have been. He thought about it all the way back up the long difficult tunnel until he and Monsieur Simonin staggered out of the entrance. The aircraft looked a long way away, the crate hanging between the two men seemed heavier than all those that had gone before.

Monsieur Simonin suddenly let go of his rope handle and sank to the ground. 'I have had enough,' he moaned. From his knees, he toppled forwards and lay face down in the sand. 'I can do no more.'

Kalkan was there in a second, his pistol levelled at Simonin's head. Caspasian and Michelle, their own progress halted by the pair who were now blocking the tunnel exit, dropped their own load and edged round the side of the Professor to see what was the matter. Michelle stood looking down at her husband. There was an expression of pity on her face. In spite of everything she had suffered at Simonin's hands, Caspasian was relieved to see that she was still able to feel compassion for the man.

Simonin rolled onto his back, pushing himself upright into a sitting position, resting his weight on his hands. His clothes were soaked with sweat and matted with sand and dirt. His hair was dishevelled, his tie cranked halfway round the side of his neck, his top button wrenched from its thread and hanging open. He looked up at her beseechingly as Kalkan clicked back the small neat hammer of his pistol.

'It doesn't matter,' Kalkan said. 'You've done almost every-thing that needs to be done.'

Simonin kept his eyes on Michelle, hearing Kalkan's words and sensing the pistol's threatening presence, but ignoring them.

'I am sorry,' he said to her quietly. 'Forgive me, my dear. Do you think I chose to be like this?' he said, his eyes sweeping over his slack crumpled body before returning to her face. 'Do you not think I would have liked to be a hero? The hero of your dreams? I tried. Believe me I did.' He attempted a smile but was too close to breaking point for it to be anything but lost in his despair. Caspasian could see that Simonin was fighting hard not to collapse into a flood of tears. Instead he took a deep breath. 'None of us choose the role fate casts for us, the person we are born to be. I came out as Émile Simonin,' he said, his mouth twisting with self-disgust as he pronounced his own name. 'A joke, no? Well someone has to play the fool, the bastard. And that was me.' He fixed his eyes on her, searching deeply. 'How I wish it could have been other than this. That I could have been other than this . . . this . . . this heap of . . .'

'Émile!' Michelle said sharply, halting him in mid-sentence. She started towards his side but Kalkan switched his gun from Simonin to her.

'Stand aside, Madame. I am touched by this wonderful speech from this heap of shit.' He smiled sweetly. 'I think that was the word he was after.'

Michelle strode forward and raised her hand to strike him but Kalkan stepped easily beyond reach. He pointed the gun back at Simonin and Caspasian saw that he was pulling the trigger.

'Kalkan!' he said quickly. 'Before you murder another of our party, don't you think you should let us finish the task you set? You said you've got to be on your way and it'll take every man of us to complete the loading of your planes.'

'I don't need you any more. The task is as good as done. Mahmud's men can finish it off now.'

Half a dozen tribesmen had gathered on the edges of the confrontation to watch the execution, Mahmud and Jacob with them. Jacob looked sadly at the figure of Simonin crumpled on the ground, pity clouding his eyes. Kalkan hailed the nearest of his guards. Two of them answered his call, the rest being occupied near the planes. But two would suffice, he judged. Both were armed with sub-machine guns. Behind Caspasian, Ganga, Kraus, Harkabahadur and Bharat had appeared out of the tunnel and stood in a huddle, staring hard at the Turks and Mahmud's men.

'Mahmud,' Kalkan said without taking his eyes off the prisoners. 'It is time to finish this.'

Mahmud grinned and ordered his men to ready their weapons. Ganga glanced at Caspasian, waiting for instructions. Caspasian caught his eye but shook his head. Not yet.

'As we're going to die, Kalkan, at least satisfy our curiosity. Tell me about the Turkish expedition. What happened to it?'

Kalkan smiled. 'They all died too.'

'Died? Or were murdered?' Caspasian said.

Kalkan acknowledged that Caspasian had guessed correctly. 'It was during the Great War. The expedition had located the city in secret. It was to have been a great boost to Ottoman morale. But it came too late. The war was lost. We knew that. There were other priorities to be considered. Who cared about rubbish like this?' He waved a hand dismissively at the ruins and the tomb. 'The Ottoman Empire had been betrayed, and it has been betrayed ever since by those who would turn our face to the west. But not any more.' He pointed to the two aircraft with their cargos of arms and money. 'Not once we put all of this to use.'

Caspasian nodded, light dawning. 'The murders in Cairo?'

'All our work. And not just in Cairo but throughout the Levant and Turkey, and all financed with gold taken from here. A few pieces at a time. Hidden here since the end of the war. We needed a hiding place that was totally secure, you see. Somewhere no one even knew existed. What better than a legendary city, undiscovered? Oh, there was a handful of troublesome archaeologists to deal with but that was no problem. We have been removing all those who have betrayed us to the west. Now it is time to recover the empire that was lost. That has been our task. Our mission.'

'Our?' the Professor said.

'The Mamluks,' Caspasian said, the pieces falling into place. 'Chief Superintendent Ghazali mentioned them to me. It's a theory he has pieced together. An Ottoman secret society. They were formed in the last days of the war. They took their name from the caste of warrior slaves that once ruled Egypt. Some people have maintained the secret society doesn't exist. That they're just a convenient rumour used by the police to cover their own incompetence at solving random and unconnected murders.' He regarded Kalkan. 'And I suppose you are the Bey?'

'Mamluks? The Bey? What the devil are you talking about, Caspasian?' Monsieur Simonin said, getting awkwardly to his feet with the help of Michelle.

'The Bey is head of the Mamluks,' Caspasian said without taking his eyes off Kalkan.

Kalkan shook his head. 'You are correct in most of what you say, but I am not the Bey. The Bey was the divisional commander of a secret mission towards the end of the war,' he said. 'He was given charge of a shipment of gold that was to bribe the Arabs to give up their support of the British and abandon their revolt in the desert. But he was a man of far greater vision than that. He could see the mission was futile. We had already been defeated. Why throw good money after bad? With an eye to the future, he disappeared, the gold along with him. He used the gold to set up the Mamluks. He became the Bey. The gold bought weapons and influence. We used this valley not just as a hiding place but as a training ground. We have paid Mahmud well to guard its secret from the rest of the world.'

'So when a real fragment of papyrus emerged that would expose the location, you had to try and get hold of it!' the Professor said, astounded. 'To keep the valley and the ruins a secret because your gold and weapons were stored here!'

Kalkan nodded. 'Of course. But all that is now in the past. It is no longer relevant because our time has come. But me? The Bey?' Kalkan cocked his head. 'No. I am not the Bey, I hate to disappoint you. I only serve him. You are about to be executed by a mere underling. I hope that does not disappoint you?'

'More murders, Kalkan? When will it all stop?' Caspasian asked.

'It won't. Not yet, at least. Not until we've toppled Ataturk himself and seized power in Istanbul. But one thing at a time. First we start here in Cairo. And we start tomorrow.'

Caspasian stared blankly, wondering. 'What's special about tomorrow?'

Kalkan chuckled. 'How quickly you have forgotten. Forgotten your own High Commissioner's birthday parade.'

Caspasian felt himself go cold as the full impact of Kalkan's words sank in.

'And after his assassination, the British troops will be trigger-happy, don't you think? Sufficiently to open fire on the peaceful demonstrators of the Wafd party as they march innocently through the city centre. Of course we will help them a little. Fire a few shots ourselves just to get things going. Then, when the Wafd finds weapons readily at hand,' he continued, pointing to the planes, 'how do you think they'll react? Turn the other cheek? I don't think so. It will be the start of the uprising that will drive the British out of Egypt. It will sever the Suez Canal and your link with the east. It will be the signal for the Mamluks to rise and seize power in Istanbul and to topple both British and French empires throughout the Levant. The Ottoman Empire will be re-established. We will have had our revenge.'

Caspasian shrugged. 'And where does humble old Mahmud fit in with this great plan of yours?'

Kalkan frowned. His speech had run away with him. He had forgotten Mahmud standing quietly at his side.

'He and his men have served us loyally, guarding the cache all these years. He will be rewarded,' Kalkan said quietly, noting Mahmud's satisfied grin.

Caspasian nodded. 'He'll be very pleased. More rewards on top of the gold and arms he and his men have been stealing from under your noses.'

Kalkan smiled. Mahmud glared at Caspasian, enraged.

'If you don't believe me search them,' Caspasian said.

'How dare you,' Mahmud shouted furiously. 'I am a man of honour. I would never allow such a thing.'

'No? Then search him,' Caspasian said pointing at the man he had tripped in the dirt and whose box had been split open.

Kalkan waved aside the suggestion. 'Nice try, Caspasian, but it won't work.'

Mahmud held up his hand. 'No. He has cast doubts on the reliability of my men. We will see.' He called the man over and began to search him. His hands suddenly froze, emerging a second later from a fold in the man's robes bearing four gold coins. The man stared down at them in horror.

'He put them there!' he shouted, pointing at Caspasian.

'Oh, of course I did,' Caspasian said. 'And I suppose I planted the coins on all your other men, Mahmud, didn't I?'

Mahmud rushed to another of his men and after a brief search produced another coin, and then more from yet another man. Caspasian noticed that Kalkan's smile had faded and he was staring at Mahmud stoney-eyed.

'Mahmud,' he said calmly. 'Is this how you repay me? Have I ever been anything but fair to you? Did the Bey himself not promise you a role in our future triumph when he established the secret cache here, entrusting you with its protection?'

Mahmud glared at him. 'Do you believe I have betrayed you?'

'What am I supposed to think? You yourself have found the gold on your own men.'

As the two men spoke, Mahmud's men had moved apart from the two Turkish guards until the two groups confronted each other, the prisoners disregarded on the sidelines. Alongside Caspasian, Ganga and Kraus prepared themselves. Harkabahadur caught Bharat's eye, indicating the nearest of the Turkish guards. Bharat stared back at him, terrified, but Harkabahadur had set his heart on the sub-machine gun in the man's fists. He was going to have it.

'I will prove my innocence,' Mahmud announced. He seized the man who Caspasian had tripped and on whom the first coins had been found. 'I will punish this man in front of you.'

The man shrank from Mahmud. There was a howl of protest from the rest of the tribesmen, wondering which of them might be next. One of them moved his hand towards the knife in his belt. A Turkish guard cranked back the cocking handle of his sub-machine gun, and then everything happened at once. One of the tribesman's comrades went for him. The guard fired.

Gunfire erupted between the two groups. Kalkan screamed for calm but his voice was drowned out. Two of Mahmud's men went down in the burst of fire from the Turks. From beside the two Breguets, more of the Turkish guards came running, guns at the ready. Seeing them approach, the rest of Mahmud's men dived for cover.

Caspasian leapt for Michelle and knocked her to the ground out of harm's way before darting at the closest of the tribesmen. With clenched first he fired a snap punch at the man's jaw. It smacked into flesh and as the man went down, Caspasian stripped the revolver from his grasp. He glanced across and saw Harkabahadur and Bharat grappling with a Turkish guard, trying to wrest the sub-machine gun from his hands. There was a burst of fire, sickeningly muffled as the muzzle dug into Harkabahadur's stomach. The next instant, the Gurkha was being hurled backwards by the force of the shots, mortally wounded. In a livid rage, Bharat leapt at the Turk and clubbed him to the ground. His boot swung and struck the fallen man in the face. He reached down and snatched up the sub-machine gun, firing a burst into the guard, killing him stone dead. Caspasian had never seen such an expression of rage on Bharat's face. He was a different man. In an instant the malingerer had gone.

Kraus and Ganga had gone straight for two of the tribesmen, knocking them down and seizing their weapons, two Lee-Enfield rifles that had been stolen earlier from the Gurkhas. With punches and kicks they subdued their opponents, turning the rifles on the approaching Turkish guards and stopping them in their tracks with a blizzard of rapid fire.

Seeing the sudden turn of events, Kalkan swung his aim onto the closest of the prisoners, Michelle. He pulled the trigger but the bullet found Émile Simonin in its path. With one hand Simonin thrust Michelle safely aside, with the other he attempted to fend off the bullet. It smashed through his hand, taking Simonin's middle finger with it. He winced, too shocked even to scream. Kalkan fired again, and then again, pumping bullets into Simonin's shuddering body.

Kalkan's guards shouted for him to run, firing a hail of covering fire from their positions where they were pinned by Ganga and Kraus. Mahmud's men were fleeing, dropping their weapons as they ran. They had seen enough of what the Gurkhas and legionnaires could do. It was time to leave the field of battle to others. Mahmud made one attempt to rally them and then rounded on Caspasian. Howling with rage he rushed upon him. Caspasian raised his revolver and pulled the trigger. The gun misfired. In the split second it took him to recock the hammer, Mahmud was upon him. Caspasian dropped the revolver to free his hands and, as Mahmud closed, he grabbed him by both shoulders, brought his right foot up and into the pit of Mahmud's stomach, and sat down. Mahmud's forward momentum thrust Caspasian backwards, but instead of allowing the two of them to collapse in a heap, Caspasian rocked back using his foot as a pivot and swung Mahmud clear over the top of him.

The force of Mahmud's landing knocked the air from his lungs, but he was too experienced a fighter to allow his opponent to reap the benefit and rolled out of the way as Caspasian rushed upon him to finish it. Instead of a winded man Caspasian found himself facing a long-bladed knife. The blade lunged at his gut and he only just managed to palm it aside, contacting Mahmud's wrist and turning the weapon upon him. Mahmud yelped as the tendons strained and tore. It was too late to react. With one sharp thrust, Caspasian drove Mahmud's own blade hard into him, deep into the solar plexus. Mahmud's eyes bulged and he dropped to the floor, dead. There was a howl and Jacob rushed upon the lifeless body.

Caspasian looked up and saw Kalkan now clear of the fighting. He was withdrawing with his guards towards the planes. Ganga and Kraus were putting down accurate fire now, sniping with deadly effect. Three of the Turks lay unmoving in the sand, and Kalkan had decided he did not want to jeopardise the wider mission by staying around to see the prisoners killed. It was time to leave. The desert would take care of the troublesome Gurkhas and the lone remaining legionnaire. He had other business in Cairo. The planes were loaded, the pilots ready, Caspasian and his men would be unable to stop him once he was airborne.

While his guards put down fire with their sub-machine guns on Caspasian and his party who were hugging tight into cover around the entrance to the tomb, Kalkan ordered his pilots to start the engines. Caspasian tried to edge forward but bullets threaded the sand in front of his face, forcing him back. He looked across to Ganga, appealing for help but Ganga signalled that he was almost out of ammunition, as was Kraus.

To their frustration, the first Breguet with Kalkan on board taxied away from the date palms towards the airstrip where two parallel lines of stones marked out the firm ground.

'Bring it down,' Caspasian shouted. 'You've got to!'

Ganga checked his magazine. There were two rounds left. He looked across at Kraus but his magazine was completely empty. There were no other weapons within range. Although the last two Turkish guards had withdrawn to the second plane which was starting to taxi away from the palm grove, their fire was accurate and there was no way Ganga could move forward.

He steadied himself and took aim at the first plane, but as it turned onto the airstrip and the engine surged, it blew up a gust of sand that obscured it from view. He looked desperately at Caspasian, knowing any shot would simply be wasted on the giant aircraft. He had no idea where the fuel tanks were, and the pilot in the cockpit was at the far end of the Breguet, out of view. Caspasian read his thoughts and cursed.

The second aircraft was already approaching the airstrip as the first one accelerated down the lane marked out between the stones and slowly lifted into the pale blue sky, climbing clear of the valley, banking away from the ruins and turning in the direction of Cairo.

The moment the second aircraft reached the airstrip and accelerated ahead, the two guards slammed the door shut, safe inside and on their way. The second their fire stopped Ganga was up and running forward.

'Where's he going?' Kraus called across to Caspasian.

Caspasian looked and to his consternation saw the squat Gurkha sergeant running not towards the retreating aircraft, but angling away from it, heading back towards the city ruins. It was only when Ganga was halfway towards his destination that Caspasian realised what he was up to. The tall statue of a sphinx rose out of the sand between two tumbled columns. Ganga was heading straight for it, ignoring the plane, though only for the moment.

Reaching the foot of the sphinx, he slung his rifle across his shoulders and started to climb, hauling himself up, scrambling as fast as he could, yet breathing steadily all the while to preserve his aim. At last he reached the shoulders and settled himself cross-legged, his back against the beast's majestic head. He unslung his rifle, slightly loosened the sling, and threaded his left forearm through it. Grasping the stock, he braced his left elbow against the strap until it was taut, creating a rock-steady support for the rifle. He put the butt in his shoulder and nestled his cheek against the warm wood, settling into a perfect firing position.

Caspasian, Kraus, Bharat, the Professor and Michelle all watched with held breath, willing him to succeed. Cross-legged on the shoulders of the sphinx, like some calmly malevolent imp, Ganga breathed in, the barrel of his rifle rising in line with the plane that lifted gently from the valley floor.

'He's misjudged it,' Kraus said aloud, more to himself than the others, casting a professional eye over Ganga's coming shot.

'Not Ganga,' Caspasian said.

The plane cleared the ground and started to bank. As it did so, it brought the cockpit round and into Ganga's line of fire.

'He'll never do it. It's much too far,' the Professor said.

On the shoulders of the sphinx, Ganga exhaled, emptying himself and bringing the muzzle of his rifle down and onto a perfect line with the cockpit. Judging the speed of the plane, he shifted his point of aim to compensate, steadied and fired. Instantly, before waiting to see the result, he reloaded with his final round and took aim again. From the plane there was no sign of a result. The Breguet started to swing away from him, following the previous aircraft. Ganga fired again. All rounds expended, he lowered his rifle and watched, calm and expectant.

The first thing Caspasian and the others saw was the slightest dip of one wing. Then the whole aircraft suddenly dipped, banking savagely back towards the valley, coming down in a steep angle. The engines revved but it was too late. Just at the last moment before impact, the nose lifted and the plane bellied into the sand. The force of the landing tore one side of the undercarriage clean off. The tip of the starboard wing ploughed into the sand carving a great swathe in the ground. The pitch of the engine soared and the propellers raged impotently. Then, as quickly as it had come down, everything died. Clouds of sand engulfed the plane as it ground to a halt and finally was silent.

A cheer went up from the party standing around Caspasian and from his position on the statue, Ganga swept off his hat and threw it high into the air. Only Caspasian stared hard-eyed after the rapidly diminishing outline of the first Breguet. Kalkan had escaped from them and Cairo was only a matter of hours away. A short night flight and he would be there, his plans intact, his lethal cargo still sufficient to achieve his ends.

19

'Honestly, Harry, I really do think you're overreacting. There is absolutely no way I am going to divert any more men away from the High Commissioner's birthday parade. It's bad enough as it is, confining it to the grounds of the Gezira Sporting Club. I've already had one rifle company taken away from me for policing duties. If this goes on there'll be no one left for the parade at all. The whole thing will be a disaster. A complete fiasco.'

Colonel Humphreys stood staring out of his office window in Battalion Headquarters, hands clasped behind his back, his broad shoulders presenting the exasperated Harry Ghazali with a suitable representation of the obstacle he had been trying to overcome for the last half hour.

'Colonel, all my intelligence points to coming trouble.'

'All the more reason to have my men close to the High Commissioner ready to protect his person.'

'The security arrangements for the parade are quite satisfactory as it is,' Ghazali explained yet again. 'The island will be cordoned off from the rest of the city and on top of that every entrance to the club grounds will be closed. All guests will be directed to the main entrance where my own men will work alongside the military police to screen every individual and ensure they are fully accredited and on the guest list drawn up by the Residency staff themselves. It is the march in the city I am most concerned about.'

'Then you need to speak to GHQ, not some poor underling like me.' The Colonel turned and smiled kindly at the Chief Superintendent. 'They're the ones you need to convince.'

Ghazali sighed. He walked across to the armchair he had just got out of and slumped back into it. 'Exactly. GHQ.' He looked at the Colonel, appealing. 'If anyone can talk sense into them, you can. You know they won't listen to a mere wog,' he said distastefully. 'Copt or not, I'm still an Egyptian and therefore suspect in British eyes.'

'Come now,' the Colonel said, chastened. He came and perched on the arm of the neighbouring chair. 'No one regards you with anything but respect, Harry.'

Ghazali leaned forward, sensing the opportunity. 'Then speak to them. Get them to allocate more resources to the march. There's going to be trouble, I know it. I've never seen the city like this. It's not just the murders in the Turkish community. The Wafd are up to something. There are agitators at work and I fear for public order.'

'Do you really believe that stuff about some secret society at work? What are they called?'

'The Mamluks.'

'That's the fellows.'

'Actually, yes I do.'

Colonel Humphreys regarded him with amusement. 'Good Lord.'

There was a knock on the door and Captain Tremain looked in. 'Sorry to interrupt, Colonel, but the men are ready for inspection.'

The Colonel nodded, dismissing Tremain. Ghazali stood up and the Colonel escorted him to the door. 'OK, Harry. Leave it to me. I'll give the BM a ring. I doubt he'll listen but I'll pass on your concern, all right?'

Ghazali smiled, knowing that nothing would really happen. He had done his bit. He could do no more. 'Thank you. And good luck with the parade tomorrow,' he said.

'Don't need luck,' the Colonel said gamely. 'It's all in the preparation.'

'Exactly.'

When Ghazali had gone, the Colonel and the Adjutant made their way down the stairs and out onto the parade ground. Colonel Humphreys heaved a huge sigh of utter contentment as he surveyed the ranks of Gurkhas drawn up before him. As he appeared, the Regimental Havildar Major called the assembled companies to attention and then himself marched briskly forward towards his commanding officer. When he was within several paces of him he halted, thrust his pace stick under his left arm, the brass-tipped end of it clinched in the web between the thumb and forefinger of his left hand, while with his right arm he saluted with rigid perfection. His face was set in lightly perspiring stone. His eyes, darkly ferocious, drilled holes in the air an inch above the Colonel's head.

'Battalion ready for your inspection, saheb.'

Colonel Humphreys saluted. 'Thank you, Havildar Major. Carry on.'

The Regimental Havildar Major saluted and whipped about, the heels of his dazzlingly polished boots grinding mercilessly into the parade ground in search of the foundations. Returning his pace stick to the right hand he fired himself across the parade ground, arms swinging like a metronome gone berserk, a wind-up toy possessed. Colonel Humphreys and the Adjutant followed at a more sedate pace, the two of them casting expert eyes over the companies, evaluating the effect of the whole before immersing themselves in a meticulous examination of the minutiae.

'Front rank, stand fast. Remainder, stand at . . . ease!'

As the Regimental Havildar Major's words of command ricocheted off the surrounding buildings, echoing throughout the camp like the trumpets of Jericho, Colonel Humphreys and Captain Tremain commenced their inspection. In the face of such magnificence, Harry Ghazali's cautionary words melted from the Colonel's mind.

*   *   *

'Get some more light over here,' Caspasian shouted. Crouched beside the crashed Breguet, he examined the crumpled under-carriage in the thickening darkness. In the cockpit window overhead, two neat holes had been punched in the glass in front of the pilot who sat slumped over the controls, dead from bullet wounds to the head and chest. In the cargo compartment in the rear, the two Turkish guards, crushed to death by the cases of weapons, were being removed by Ganga, Kraus and Bharat.

'What do you hope to do?' the Professor asked.

Caspasian shook his head. 'I don't know. I just think that if we can get this infernal machine into the air somehow, then we might be able to navigate back to Cairo and then . . .'

'Crash land and kill ourselves?' the Professor offered. 'It's madness.'

'What else do you suggest?' Caspasian said desperately. 'Even if we made it out of here alive and got through the desert to the river, at best speed we couldn't be back in Cairo for a month. Here we've got a plane that hasn't been totally destroyed. It is our only option. If we don't make it back to Cairo in time to stop Kalkan, then goodness knows what will happen. We know what he's planning to do. Countless num-bers will die. It will be the spark for war throughout the Levant. Perhaps even wider.'

'You don't have to tell me that,' the Professor said, examin-ing the buckled wheel. 'I just don't see how we can reasonably expect to get this thing off the ground.'

Kraus squatted down beside them, wiping blood from his hands. He studied the undercarriage. 'I don't know anything about repairs, but if you can manage to make this crate airworthy, then I can fly it.'

Caspasian and the Professor stared at him in disbelief. Kraus smiled sheepishly. 'I always wanted to be a flyer. In the war I went for selection but was turned down. Not a gentleman, you see.'

'Then how can you say you'll fly it?' Caspasian asked.

Kraus shrugged. 'As the war went on they became less fussy. Once all the gents had been shot out of the sky they had to resort to the bottom of the barrel.' He grinned. 'That's where they found me.'

Caspasian and the Professor grinned.

'You old dog,' the Professor said playfully.

'Mind you, I lost more aircraft through crash landings than through enemy action,' Kraus added.

'Just you get us on the ground at Cairo and I'll get out alive,' Caspasian said.

'Yes, but first we have to get this contraption into the air,' the Professor said, studying the problem with renewed interest.

'The first thing we can do is to lighten the load,' Caspasian suggested. 'We can offload all the crates.'

'Good idea,' the Professor said. 'And while you're doing it, see if you can find anything that can be used to replace this metal strut. It'll have to be strong enough to take the full weight of the aircraft.'

'What about wood?' Caspasian asked.

The Professor shook his head. 'Not strong enough. The date palms would be all right but it would take too long to fell one and then trim it down to size.'

Kraus stood up. 'I'll see what I can find.'

While he went off to search the contents of the hold, the Professor summoned Ganga and Bharat and directed them to start digging a hole around the buckled wheel. Supports were to be erected to take the weight of the wing while the undercarriage was being fixed. Once that was done, if it could be done at all, the Professor estimated that the plane should be able to pull itself upright under the power of its own engine so long as the repaired wheel had a gentle slope in front of it for it to climb up. Ganga and Bharat went away to look for any sort of digging implements.

'Remember the old shovels we found when we first got here,' the Professor shouted after them.

Back beside the entrance to the tomb, Caspasian found Michelle. She had used stones to fashion a burial mound over her dead husband. Caspasian went to her side. She looked at him and tried a weary smile.

'Isn't it strange how things turn out?' she said. 'Émile, of all people. Dying a hero's death. Against all expectations.'

'He must have loved you after all, Michelle.'

She considered this. 'In his own way perhaps. In any case, it's over now.' She took a deep breath and hugged herself against the mounting cold. 'It's strange, but I don't feel the great liberation that I always thought I would feel when I was freed from him.'

'I'm not surprised,' Caspasian said. 'Freedom can be pretty daunting at the best of times. But here, coming the way it did and in our present circumstances . . . well.' He left it at that.

She allowed him to lead her away from the grave. They were halfway across the airstrip and heading for the plane when there was a shuffling noise out in the darkness. Caspasian drew his revolver and cocked the hammer. A shape separated itself from the black background and came towards them. It was old Jacob. He was whistling softly to himself, and now Caspasian recognised it, an old marching tune from the army of the Queen Empress herself, though somewhat corrupted and disguised by strains of local Arab additions. When he saw Caspasian and Michelle he broke into a little jig like an organ grinder's monkey. Michelle reached out her hand towards him and instantly he quietened. He studied it carefully, a thing of great interest and then, understanding her intention, took gentle hold of it and fell in alongside the walking couple.

By the time they got there the Professor and his team were hard at work. He looked up excitedly as Caspasian approached. 'Look what Kraus found!' He stood aside to reveal a mortar barrel propped against a stone. 'It's perfect. As strong as they come and about the right size. A little short perhaps but Kraus is confident he can manage the take off.'

Caspasian looked questioningly at Kraus.

'I said the take off,' Kraus said, excusing his bravado. 'The landing's another matter.'

They worked throughout the night and as the first signs of day glimmered sleepily in the east, pushing away the darkness and dimming the stars, the Professor and Kraus examined their handiwork and pronounced themselves satisfied.

While the group stood clear of the lopsided Breguet, Kraus climbed into the vacated pilot seat and strapped himself in. The engine coughed and spluttered but eventually fired. The pro-peller burst into life, roaring defiantly as clouds of black exhaust fumes belched into the clean morning air. Slowly Kraus pushed the throttle forward. The wheels bit and the repaired undercarriage creaked and groaned. Caspasian could see the bonds straining.

'It's not going to hold,' the Professor shouted above the noise, his earlier confidence dissipating. He tried to signal for Kraus to cut the power but Caspasian stopped him.

'It's got to hold. As it is we'll be lucky to make it back to Cairo in time.'

With a sudden lurch the plane shuddered free of the depres-sion it was in. In response, Kraus opened the throttle and power surged to the propeller which dragged the Breguet out onto the airstrip. Ganga and Bharat cheered.

'Right, everyone,' Caspasian shouted above the din, snatch-ing up the sub-machine gun he had taken from one of the dead Turks, 'let's climb aboard.'

They grabbed their belongings and jogged out towards the roaring aircraft that Kraus was swinging round in a danger-ously tight circle, lining up on the airstrip. It was only when he was almost at the door that Caspasian noticed they were missing someone. He looked back and saw old Jacob staring wild-eyed at the plane.

Caspasian handed his sub-machine gun to Michelle and helped her in through the door. The aircraft had slowed but

Kraus was reluctant to halt altogether lest he be unable to get it started again. Ganga, Bharat and the Professor piled in after her, while Caspasian dashed back for Jacob.

Understanding his intent, Jacob suddenly turned and started to sprint in the opposite direction. Caspasian cursed and dived at him, laying hold of the old man's tattered robe and dragging him to a halt.

'Come on,' he shouted above the noise of the engine. Jacob shook his head furiously. In response, Caspasian bent and put his shoulder into Jacob's stomach, coming upright and hoisting the old man onto his shoulder as he did so. Jacob screamed all the way to the door of the Breguet, fists drumming on Caspasian's back, whereupon Caspasian tossed him inside the plane.

'Tie him up!' he shouted to Ganga, pulling himself in just as Kraus, believing everyone to be safely on board, unleashed the engine and set the Breguet surging at breakneck speed down the runway. Barely inside the door, Caspasian was hurled to the back of the cargo hold, snatching at the Professor for support as he shot past him.

Together they tugged the door closed and fastened it. There were two small portholes in either side of the fuselage which gave a limited view of the outside world. They could see the date palms screaming past, then the mastaba, the graves of Émile Simonin and the others, the ruins of the city, the sphinx from which Ganga had brought the plane down, and finally the rock face and the track down which they had first made their way into the lost city of King Menes. Jacob screamed all the way into the air, shaking his head from side to side, willing himself to be somewhere else, anywhere but in this boiling tumbling cauldron of infernal noise.

The nose lifted, everything inside the plane vibrated and shook, wrenching at the securing nuts, bolts and straps as if the entire machine wanted to burst itself asunder, reducing itself to its constituent parts. Then the wheels left the ground and the plane was up. The wings wobbled from side to side and the whole machine juddered and creaked like a galleon in a storm. From the cockpit came a triumphant whoop as Kraus pulled back on the stick and grinned proudly back over his shoulder.

When he was content that everyone was safe and sound in the cargo compartment, Caspasian made his way forward and crawled in beside Kraus. He looked out of the cockpit window, the draught from Ganga's bullet holes threatening to rip out the entire glass screen. He checked the compass for direction and leaned close to shout into Kraus's ear.

'We can head north-west until we hit the line of the Nile and then follow it north all the way to Cairo.'

Kraus considered this for a moment. 'Yes but I can knock an hour or two off the flight time by taking a more direct route across the desert, hitting the Nile further north. Like the third side of a triangle. Why go straight and then up, when we can cut across?'

'Because we don't know exactly where we are,' Caspasian shouted back.

Kraus shrugged, unperturbed. 'The Nile stretches all the way. We've got to cross it at some point. Even if we miss it we'll see the Red Sea or the canal even. At least we'll know where we are.'

'And the weather?' Caspasian said.

'If we hit any kind of cloud or storm we're lost,' Kraus answered with a cheerful smile.

'OK then,' Caspasian said at last. 'Try it. If we can save a couple of hours it could make all the difference.'

He looked at his watch. The sun was now well up in the sky. In Cairo he could imagine the last minute preparations. He knew the parade was to take place at the Gezira Sporting Club on the island bisecting the Nile. The bunting would have been strung from the trees, at the Residency the garden would be being prepared for the tea party later that day. In the regiment's lines the soldiers would be completing the polishing of their equipment before the companies fell in on the parade square prior to the move to the club grounds across the city. He could hear the words of command being barked out by havildars and havildar majors, by the jemadars and subedars.

The Subedar Major would doubtless be with the Colonel and Adjutant, running through the detail of the parade. Everyone would be worrying and hoping that it would all go to plan.

In the streets of Cairo the police would be marking off holding areas for the troops who were to be on standby in case of trouble when the demonstration march got underway. They would be cordoning off the bridges across the Nile and setting up road blocks. The organisers of the demonstration would be remonstrating with them, uttering assurances that the march was merely a peaceful demonstration of their opposition to the British presence in the country. As all of this was happening, ordinary people would be going about their daily business. Shops and market stalls would already be open, stall-keepers shouting to advertise their wares. Just another day as far as they were concerned. Politics was of less concern to them, so long as the status quo left them to get on with their lives.

Of course they would like their country to be fully independent, but if the British kept out of their way, what was the big problem? They would leave eventually. Conquerors and occupiers like them always had, back down through the centuries and the millennia. Conquerors came and went. Empires rose and fell like the tide. It just took a bit longer, that was all. The principle was the same though. Rise and fall. Nations were like breath. So long as all was quiet and peaceful, then the really important things could continue and the ordinary people would be prepared to turn a blind eye and leave politics to those more driven, while they got on with the ordinary things of life like raising one's children, earning a living, making do.

Elsewhere in the city, concealed like a dormant virus, Kalkan was waiting. Biding his time. Caspasian stared out of the cockpit's window at the desert rolling past below and thought of Kalkan. He would be in Cairo by now with his lethal cargo of arms, ammunition and gold. His men would be preparing themselves, taking the arms to holding points throughout the city ready to distribute to the angry mob once hatred and the desire for revenge had been stirred like a hornet's nest.

Caspasian was jerked back from his reverie by Michelle tugging at his sleeve. She waved for him to come back into the cargo compartment. With a final check on the compass needle, Caspasian worked his way back below, easing himself down through the tight space and into the middle of the others. They were grouped around old Jacob.

'Listen to him,' the Professor said. 'He's started speaking.'

Jacob looked from one to the other. He had calmed and was now looking very pleased with himself. 'Under 'is frone,' he suddenly blurted out in an accent that was an outrageous mix of Cockney and Arabic. 'Boom!' He accompanied it with a flowering gesture of his hands, imaginary mushroom clouds blossoming upwards into the sky. He burst out in a peal of cackling laughter, his toothless gums pink and smooth as a baby's. 'The Viceroy goes boom! Talk about a funder box, eh?' And a stream of cackles and sputum erupted from his mouth.

Caspasian grinned and slapped him on the back. 'Thank you, Jacob. Thank you very much. When did you overhear this?'

Jacob grinned back, seeing Caspasian as if for the first time. 'Boom!' he said suddenly. He turned to Michelle. 'Boom!' Then to the Professor. 'Boom!'

'I think we get the picture,' the Professor said kindly, patting him on the arm.

Ganga looked at him doubtfully. 'How can we trust him, saheb? The man is a dumba. Completely lato.'

'Have you got any better ideas? If they're going to assassinate the High Commissioner, how do they do it? Bomb or sniper. If it's a sniper he could be anywhere. At least with this we can narrow our search a little. The main thing is to get there in time and stop the parade.'

'And how do you intend to do that, saheb?' Bharat asked, starting to look terrified again, his earlier ferocity having dimmed.

'Exactly,' Ganga said. Then, with an embarrassed smile he added, 'You're hardly someone they're going to listen to, are you? Cancel the whole parade because you say so?' He shook his head.

'I don't know how I'll do it but I'll think of something,' Caspasian answered.

Some time later, a package came whistling back to land in the middle of them. Kraus peered back from his seat in the cockpit. 'Lunch is served,' he shouted. 'The pilot had some grub hidden away.'

Hungrily they tore open the package and found a whole salami, a block of cheese, half a loaf of bread and a flask of brandy. 'Not bad, not bad at all,' the Professor said as he hunted around for a knife. Bharat's eyes were popping out of his head as he stared at the food. He tore his kukri from its scabbard and handed it over. The Professor eyed it doubtfully. 'I think you'd better do it,' he said, handing over the salami.

Ganga quickly relieved Bharat of it. 'I'll do it. If Bharat measures out the portions we'll be left chewing the skin.'

He deftly sliced the salami and then set to work on the cheese, dividing everything into seven equal portions, before handing them round. Kraus reached back and took his, handling the plane with one hand while he fashioned a crude sandwich with the other, cramming it into his mouth unceremoniously. The plane gave a lurch in protest and he cursed through a bulging mouth as he whipped both hands back to the stick to steady the aircraft.

In the cargo hold, Jacob was examining his food suspiciously, testing each piece with his tongue.

'What will happen to him?' Michelle asked.

'I don't know. The modern world will come as quite a shock,' Caspasian answered, looking at Jacob sympathetically. 'It's hard to imagine the impact it'll have on him. With luck he'll get a place in a home for old soldiers. If not, he'll end up begging on the streets. I'm not going to let that happen to him.'

Finding the food edible after all, Jacob was gnawing happily with his gums, gazing out of the window at the desert below like a seasoned flyer.

After she had eaten, Michelle snuggled down, leaning against Caspasian's shoulder to get some rest. The noise of the engine and the motion of the Breguet soon lulled her asleep. Caspasian put his arm round her and began to doze himself.

It only seemed a moment later that Ganga was prodding him awake, but a quick check of his watch showed that he had been sleeping for some time.

'Where are we?' he asked urgently, scrabbling to his knees and waking Michelle in the process. He edged his way forward to join Kraus.

Kraus smiled and pointed confidently beyond the nose of the aircraft. 'Cairo,' he said. Caspasian peered ahead but could see nothing except desert, flat and featureless. The panic showed on his face because Kraus raised his eyes heavenwards and stabbed a finger sharply down to the port side of the aircraft. He banked the Breguet so that Caspasian could get a better view and there beneath them was the thin meandering streak of the Nile.

'How much longer?' Caspasian shouted.

Kraus shrugged. 'It can't be long.'

'It had better not be.'

Caspasian settled himself beside Kraus and, to his relief, several minutes later he was able to distinguish three pin pricks on the horizon.

'Giza. The pyramids!' shouted Kraus.

Caspasian grabbed his hand and shook it vigorously. 'Good flying!'

'We're not down yet. You can congratulate me when we're on the ground at the aerodrome.'

'We're not going to the aerodrome,' Caspasian said. Kraus looked at him. He noted the set of his jaw and the light in his eyes and was not happy. Not happy at all.

'We're going to land on Gezira.'

'Where?' Kraus asked, not wanting to hear the answer he knew was coming.

'On the polo pitch where the . . .'

'Where the parade's being held,' Kraus concluded, nodding his head as if accepting a death sentence. 'Do you realise I can't actually fly this thing?'

'You seem to be doing a fine job to me,' Caspasian said.

'Yes, but I've no idea how it's going to like the landing. With the mortar barrel propping up one side of the undercarriage we'd be lucky to make it down safely even on a proper runway. And you want me to land on a polo pitch. Do you have any idea how long that is?'

'Do I look like the polo-playing type to you?'

'Frankly, yes.'

'In the light of your good service over the last few days I'm prepared to disregard that,' Caspasian said smiling. 'Ganga said they'd never listen to me. He asked me how I was going to stop the parade. Well I've decided. I'm going to land on top of it.'

'No, I'm going to do the landing. I'll probably end up in a British prison for this.'

'Nonsense. They'll give you a medal.'

'A fat lot of good that'll do me if I'm dead.'

'In which case they'll give you a hero's funeral.'

'Not much consolation,' Kraus said. He tightened the leather shoulder harness straps, riveting himself into the bucket seat. 'You'd better get the rest of them to tie themselves down.'

Caspasian nodded agreement and squeezed back to join them. When he had explained their course of action he was met with resigned stares. They knew him too well to try and object, apart from which they knew that it was the only way to guarantee putting an end to the parade. They just hoped they would be in time.

'Saheb,' Bharat ventured as diplomatically as he could, 'what if we go to the aerodrome first and then . . . ?'

Before he could finish he felt the coldness of steel against his lips and looked down to see Ganga's kukri stopping his words. The blade winked at him with reflected light, spotless save for a thin shred of salami skin. Behind the blade, Ganga's smiling face was shaking almost imperceptibly.

Bharat smiled back sheepishly. 'I've never been to the Sporting Club.'

From points on the horizon the pyramids grew to dominate the landscape, their geometrical precision contrasting starkly with the irregularities of everything else, both natural and manmade. The outskirts of the city were now beneath the Breguet. Looking down, Caspasian could see the plane's tiny shadow winging its way over the sprawling suburbs like the silhouette of a rather ungainly bird.

He checked on Michelle, ensuring she was securely fastened to the sides of the cargo hold. The Professor was checking on Jacob who was dozing, blissfully unaware of what was about to come. Bharat sat with tightly shut eyes, mumbling a prayer. Ganga was sitting back calmly, hands running over the pouches of his webbing to check all were fastened, a standard procedure that for him was completely unconscious. Second nature. His Lee-Enfield lay across his lap, his kukri, cleaned of the salami skin and other fragments, safely in its scabbard awaiting its next task.

When Caspasian was happy he had done everything he could, he clambered back to take his seat beside Kraus, but Kraus shook his head firmly. 'Get back there with the others. Quick! Gezira's coming up on the nose.'

Reluctantly, Caspasian did as he was told. He knew that the

moment the plane came to a halt he would have to be out and running. The assassination could take place at any moment.

Before he left Kraus alone in the cockpit, he peered ahead. There was Gezira Island drawing towards them rapidly. He waited until the last moment before crawling back into the hold and joining Michelle, hugging her to him in an effort to shield her. He waited until he could see the outline of the polo pitch. He waited until he could see the shapes of the massed ranks of infantry and the sunlight shining on the instruments of the brass band. He waited until he could make out the formation of the Gurkha Pipes and Drums standing in the rear of the ranks of his own regiment. He waited until he could see the array of hats and topis bedecking the spectators' stands. He waited until he could see the sudden upturning of a myriad of faces, squinting up questioningly into the heavens, in the direction of the banking and rapidly descending Breguet, that limped out of the sun and lurched and ducked and dived towards the earth and the neat and manicured grounds and playing fields of the Gezira Sporting Club, where the High Commissioner had just arrived and taken his seat at the start of his birthday parade.

20

There were few things the Colonel loved so much as a parade. For him, there was nothing to compare. It was an opportunity for the regiment to show off in all its finery. His regiment. The regiment to which he had devoted his working life, his army career. At the conclusion of his present command tour he would leave it for good. His regimental soldiering days would be over and the remainder of his years before retirement would be spent in the wider arenas of the army. A succession of staff appointments would tie him increasingly to a desk, punctuated, if he was fortunate, with one or perhaps two further command appointments at brigade and divisional level. Beyond that he knew his abilities would be unable to propel him.

But even these two further appointments would hardly be anything like as enjoyable as the command of his own regiment that he was presently honoured to hold. For the regiment had been his home virtually since he stepped out of the gates of Sandhurst all those many years ago. He knew every man within its ranks, the villages they came from and, in many cases, their fathers and uncles who had served in the regiment before them. A brigade on the other hand was a conglomeration, a random mix of units with whom he might not have been involved before. There would be service units as well and, for Colonel Humphreys the worst of all, artillery units. He had a particularly and wholly irrational dislike of gunners. A division would be even more of a mix, the loyalties and bonds of the regiment watered down still further until altogether unpalatable.

He looked about him as he sat two rows behind the High Commissioner's dais, the raised platform where the salute would shortly be taken during the march past by all the troops on parade. It was a wonderful day. He breathed in the warm air and for once exulted in the smells of the city. Sitting with hands on knees he flexed his fists and stiffened his back, pushing his chest out like a billowing sail, filled with the same sense of power. He was halfway through his tour. Just over one year to go. By God he was going to enjoy it!

His spine tingled, the hair on the nape of his neck bristled and tears pricked at the corners of his eyes as he heard the skirl of the bagpipes. Marching on at the rifle regiment pace, the Pipes and Drums flooded the arena with their presence, out of all proportion to their relatively few numbers. He bit back the emotion and braced his nerves, jaw set firm and eyes narrowing as he surveyed the massed ranks of Gurkhas sweeping past, the rifle companies marching on. The battalion second-in-command was leading them, Colonel Humphreys' presence being required among the spectators. In truth, while he loved to watch drill, he did not much enjoy taking part himself. It was sufficient to know that those wonderful men down on the parade ground were his. At least for two years. He turned to nudge his wife, her face shaded under the brim of a spectacular hat.

'What d'ye think of that then, Daphne, eh?'

Reluctantly she dragged her eyes from their study of Doris Edginton's dress and glanced boredly at the soldiers.

'Yes, dear.'

When the companies reached their places on the improvised parade ground cum polo pitch, they halted and turned to face the dais and spectator stands. The Regimental Havildar Major checked and amended the dressing of the ranks in conjunction with the Adjutant and the company havildar majors, and then the entire parade was stood at ease to await the arrival of the High Commissioner. Because of the heat, the High Commissioner was in fact already there, waiting discreetly out of sight. Too long a delay was likely to result in some of the British troops fainting if made to stand still in the full glare of the sun for any length of time.

At a signal from his ADC, the High Commissioner came forward and took his place. The spectators all stood, the parade was called to attention, and the band struck up for a general salute. Colonel Humphreys stood as rigid as an oak and as majestic, the left side of his chest bedecked with his many campaign medals. Out in front, he could see Captain Tremain, the Adjutant, holding his sword in the salute, hilt to his lips, while the band played and the entire field stood frozen in a moment of pure perfection. Colonel Humphreys felt as if he could ascend into heaven there and then. What could be more glorious than this?

'Gordon?'

His wife's voice cut through his reverie like a flush of cold water. He shushed her irritably.

Then he received a gentle dig with her elbow. 'Gordon, what's that?'

'Quiet, woman!' he hissed without opening his mouth more than was anatomically necessary. He was appalled that she should have broken the spell.

The moment the band stopped at the end of the general salute, Colonel Humphreys heard it, a low strange noise that had separated itself from the other more distant noises of the city beyond the club grounds. It was the grumbling growling noise of an engine some distance away, but growing steadily louder and more persistent like a mosquito that had found a way through the net and was intent on ruining one's peace.

Reluctantly he glanced upwards. The sky had been smudged by the city's haze from its earlier pure blue into a pasty grey. At first he could see nothing, just the irritating hum of an approaching aircraft. But as it grew ever louder he at last managed to distinguish it, slowly separating itself from its background and adopting the form of a mail plane, he thought.

'Disgraceful,' he muttered to his wife. 'The bugger's going to

overfly the parade! You'd have thought they'd have been told
to keep away. Someone's head's going to roll for this!'

More heads were turning among the spectators, although on
the polo pitch itself the officers and soldiers remained with eyes
rigidly to the front. Captain Tremain was puzzled as he stared
straight ahead at the stands and saw everyone looking not at
him and the men behind him, but off to his right and up into the
sky. He could hear the sound of an aircraft engine now and
would have loved to look but, as Adjutant, it was unthinkable.
The entire regiment would see him. As Adjutant he was
guardian and protector of discipline, the epitome of perfectly
correct example. An Adjutant was the very incarnation of
regimental rectitude, the drill manual in human form. Avatar
of the scarlet-bound King's Regulations.

There was a raised voice from the stands. A cry, no less.
Captain Tremain heard it.

'Oh, my goodness!' it said loudly. An extraordinary excla-
mation to resound at a birthday parade for the High Commissioner. Tremain was alarmed. The preparations had been
painstaking. Nothing was to be allowed to go wrong. Yet,
from just outside the right-hand periphery of his vision he
could hear the noise becoming a roar and his willpower vied
with every muscle in his neck to keep from glancing round. To
do so would bring about the end of empire. His career would
be in tatters. He would never command. He would be shunned
in the street. Women would smirk at him from behind their
hands as they passed quickly on the other side of the road.

'Tremain, get out of the bloody way!'

Colonel Humphreys' voice cut through the growing din like
a bugle through a battle. In the stands before him, Tremain
could see people starting to jostle and jump for cover. The High
Commissioner himself stood his ground, staring bemusedly off
to the flank from which the noise was coming. Slowly, and
against every sternly reproving voice in his conscience, Tremain
turned his head. His mouth went dry and his eyes widened as

he found himself inspecting the frontal aspect of a large and very dishevelled Breguet that appeared to be limping down at a very unusual angle on the final approach to a landing. A landing on the polo pitch where he and the assembled ranks of soldiers were currently on parade.

Thought slowly linked itself to thought in his mind and he spun on his heel turning to face the regiment, rummaging for a relevant word of command that would remove his men speedily from out of harm's way. To his shock and horror he saw that the polo pitch was already emptying, Gurkhas and British troops flying in all directions. There was a sickening crunch as the plane touched ground and the makeshift undercarriage buckled and was torn free. As Tremain started to run he wondered whether the piece of undercarriage cart wheeling after him could really be the mortar barrel that it so closely resembled.

One wing of the plane bit into the dirt, screamed and was split raggedly in two. The whole fuselage bellied into the trim grass of the pitch, gouging a great and ever-deepening trough in its wake. Finally, as the engine pitch soared to a scream, the propeller tore itself free from its mounting and hurtled away over the top of the spectator stand, the High Commissioner charting its progress with interest from his dais.

Having pushed his wife clear of the panicking crowds, Colonel Humphreys vaulted over the railings fronting the stands and ran towards Tremain, meeting him halfway. Together they stood and stared horror-struck at the dismantled Breguet, its engine dying as its power was cut by the pilot they could see strapped into the cockpit. Colonel Humphreys felt his rage building and without any thought for his own safety, started to walk determinedly towards the aircraft, murder in the forefront of his mind. As he did so, the door in the fuselage slammed open and Caspasian jumped down onto the ground. The Colonel froze solid. Their eyes met and Caspasian saluted.

'Colonel.'

Rage could take many forms, adopt many colours, create many sounds. In Colonel Humphreys, standing rigidly on the polo pitch amidst the ruins of the High Commissioner's birthday parade, it manifested itself in complete silence and immobility. But it was only the silence and immobility of the apparently slumbering volcano. Beneath the mantle turbulent forces were at work, rivers of molten rock were stirring, hot beyond heat, obliging their way towards the surface through layers of stone-like self-control that they shouldered aside, pushing ever closer towards the fragile cone. An ever-so-slight trembling of the utmost peak was the first sign of the mammoth turmoil within, but just at the moment preceding eruption a hand clapped down on the Colonel's shoulder and the High Commissioner was at his side.

'Gordon, whatever's going on?' He looked from the Colonel to Caspasian, the struggle to recall the vaguely familiar face evident in his narrowed eyes. 'You're that fellow who went with the expedition, aren't you? What's the meaning of this? It had better be good.'

Caspasian cast a quick glance across to the dais. The parade had been stopped and the High Commissioner was still very much alive. Disaster had been averted. So far.

'Sir, you must get under cover right away. I don't have time to explain now.'

'Oh, yes you bloody well do!' exploded the Colonel. 'In fact you'll have plenty of time to explain as you prepare the defence for your court-fucking-martial.'

From the plane behind him, Caspasian could hear the rest of the expedition's survivors tumbling out of the cargo hold. They hurried across to join him. The Professor was first at his side, closely followed by Michelle. Sergeant Ganga and Rifleman Bharat were trying their hardest not to be seen by their commanding officer, discovering that the one remaining wing was an excellent place to achieve this, even though it exposed them to the quizzical stares of the massed companies jumbled on the sidelines of the polo pitch. They could hear the whispered questions turning to sniggers and were starting to wish the plane had crashed rather than managing to land.

The High Commissioner restrained the Colonel with a tired sigh. A diplomat by nature as well as profession, it had been a guiding principle of his life that everyone should have their say, and the more extreme the circumstances, the more rigidly the principle should be applied.

'Captain . . . ?'

'Caspasian, sir,' Caspasian replied crisply.

'Caspasian, please explain what's going on and why . . . ?' he waved his hand helplessly in the direction of the wrecked aircraft from which Kraus was only just struggling free.

'Your life's in danger. There's a plot to assassinate you. Here. Today. And after that, the Wafd demonstrators in the march are going to be fired upon as if by our own troops.'

The High Commissioner looked almost sorry for the dishevelled Captain before him.

'What blithering drivel is this?' the Colonel shouted.

'Please, Gordon,' the High Commissioner said, starting to become irritated with the Colonel's temper. He had always found something extremely vulgar in anger, one reason he had never joined the army where it was generally accepted as a virtue. 'Caspasian, what are your grounds for all of this? Who told you?'

Caspasian sought out Ganga. 'Sergeant Ganga! Bring Jacob over here, please!'

'Ganga,' the Colonel muttered under his breath. 'I might have bloody known.'

A few seconds later Jacob was prised from the plane where he had been cowering. The sight of so many people, most of them in uniform, terrified him and he struggled and squirmed in Ganga's iron grip all the way to Caspasian's side.

'Sir,' Caspasian said. 'This man is an old soldier. He was taken by the Mahdi's forces when Khartoum fell and has been a prisoner ever since.'

'Good heavens!' The High Commissioner examined Jacob warily, uncertain whether he was the victim of some grotesque practical joke. The old man was ragged and wretched beyond belief and all signs of Queen Victoria's army had long since vanished from his person.

'Tell him, Jacob,' Caspasian said hopefully. 'Tell him what you told me.'

Jacob looked from one to the other of them, then beheld the Colonel's stark contempt and burst into tears.

'Oh that's wonderful,' the Colonel said sarcastically.

'Please, Colonel,' the Professor cut in. 'Give him a chance.' He turned to Jacob and calmed him. 'Come on, Jacob, speak to us.'

'The Mamluks,' Jacob said at last.

The High Commissioner stared. 'Who?'

'The Mamluks, sir,' Caspasian said. 'It's the name of the people behind the murders. They took their name from . . .'

'I know who the Mamluks were, thank you,' the High Commissioner said heavily. 'And I've also been briefed on the secret society theories. But what was all that about my life being in danger?'

'It's absolute rubbish, I'd say,' the Colonel interrupted.

At that moment, there was an ear-shattering explosion and the dais was burst asunder, splinters of wood firing out in all directions as a bright orange ball of flame engulfed the flimsy structure and set light to the spectator stand. Women shrieked and screamed. Someone was hit by a flying fragment and the sight of blood sent the crowd running helter-skelter. Caspasian grabbed the High Commissioner and dragged him to the ground.

As the sound of the blast subsided and the crackle of the spreading fire mingled with the screams of the panicked and fleeing spectators, the High Commissioner looked up, his face pale. He brushed the dust from his clothes. Though shaken, he was quickly in control of himself once again.

'Colonel,' he said briskly, 'check to see if anyone's injured.'

Colonel Humphreys stared at the empty space where the dais had stood only moments before, struggling to comprehend what was happening. His rage and frustration were being dowsed with a soldier's instinct for an emergency. Actions needed to be taken, procedures set in motion, precautions taken, culprits apprehended, inquiries held.

'Tremain!'

Leaving the Colonel to carry on as he saw fit, the High Commissioner allowed Caspasian to help him to his feet. 'I owe you an apology,' he said, regarding Caspasian in an altogether new light. 'By God, sir, I do.'

'I'm afraid the trouble's not over yet, sir,' Caspasian said quickly, embarrassed by the gratitude. He recounted everything that Kalkan had said regarding the demonstration, the provocation that he and his men were going to engineer, and the distribution of weapons which would enflame the situation into a full scale uprising.

'But it could start anywhere,' the High Commissioner said. 'How can we possibly know?'

'What about the route of the march? The Wafd must have liaised with the police about it. Harry Ghazali! He'll know. If we can look at the route we might be able to work out the Mamluks' firing point.'

'Excellent idea!'

By now the police and troops were starting to get the panic under control. Harry Ghazali was located in the main club house where he had established an incident room. When he saw the High Commissioner his face was flooded with relief.

'Thank God you're safe,' he said. He smiled at Caspasian and clapped him on the arm. 'I saw the plane from the window. I should have known who it would be.'

The High Commissioner quickly relayed what he had heard from Caspasian. Ghazali stared gloomily at the floor as he listened intently.

'Yes, of course we know the route of the march, but it's already well underway. The Mamluks could strike at any moment.'

'A map. Have you got a map with the route marked on it?' Caspasian asked.

'Yes, but not here,' Ghazali said. 'It's at police headquarters. We can be there in a few minutes though.'

'Right, let's go,' Caspasian said. He rushed to the door. Ghazali hesitated a moment. 'Sir,' he said to the High Commissioner, 'I'd like you to remain here if you don't mind. Just until I'm confident the trouble's under control.'

'That's fine by me, Ghazali. You and Caspasian get a move on and see what you can do. I'll alert GHQ to warn the troops that are policing the march.'

Ghazali led the way quickly to his car. The police driver, seeing them approach, opened the back door and saw them in. He started the car and with Ghazali barking out instructions, sped off towards the exit from the Gezira Sporting Club. Out of the car window Caspasian could see smoke billowing from the stands where the fire had now taken firm hold. Beyond that, the wrecked Breguet lay in a sad and broken heap like a beached whale, grotesquely out of context in the centre of the polo pitch. He saw Colonel Humphreys standing fast in the middle of the chaos, yelling out commands at Tremain who appeared unsure in which direction to scurry first. The Colonel was like some grand Victorian hero in the centre of an infantry square that was on the point of breaking, holding firm, single-handedly preventing a rout. Caspasian briefly glimpsed the Professor, a protective arm around Michelle, leading her towards the security of the club house. And lastly he saw Kraus, Ganga and Bharat, all three of them wrestling with a maniacal Jacob, spooked beyond recall by the explosion and the maelstrom of running and uniformed figures. His long years of desert life had come to the most abrupt of ends and as he vanished from view,

tugging against the restraining hands, Caspasian felt a pro-
found sympathy for him.

Once out of the club, the car swung round the corner, tyres
skidding, and sped towards Khedive Ismail bridge and the city
beyond. Harry Ghazali rolled across the rear seat and collided
into Caspasian but speed was of the essence now. Every minute
and every second counted.

'You've done really well, Caspasian,' he said, peering out of
the window to check on their progress. 'If it hadn't been for you
the High Commissioner would now be dead.'

'Thank God we got there in time.'

'Indeed.'

The road block on the bridge was quickly passed, Ghazali
flashing his identity at the armed police guards. 'Not far now,'
he said as they hurtled round another corner and onto Kasr el
Nil. The police headquarters building stood behind formidable
walls. Topped with barbed wire, they sported loop holes and
lookout towers, but the guards were few in number, most of the
force being deployed on duty out on the streets. Indeed, the
streets themselves were quiet. Caspasian realised he had been
wrong to imagine life continuing uninterrupted. The demonstration was some way off, but people had taken the government warnings to heart and were keeping away lest trouble
erupt.

Screeching to a halt, the car came to rest in a cloud of settling
dust. Before the driver could get out to open the rear door,
Ghazali was out and sprinting for the main entrance. 'Keep the
engine running,' he shouted back to the driver.

Caspasian bolted after him, in through the door and up the
stairs that led to Ghazali's office, taking the steps three at a
time. He burst in through the door but the office was empty.

'Ghazali!'

'In here,' came the reply. 'In the map room.'

The voice came from a side door and Caspasian went
through to find himself in a spacious well lit room with one

wall occupied by floor to ceiling windows and the opposite one covered with a large scale map of the city.

'Your own private ops room. Very nice.'

Ghazali was busy studying the map on which a meandering line marked in red crayon denoted the route to be taken by the marchers. Pins had been placed to indicate the positions of security forces, blue for police and green for military.

'We're looking for some sort of vantage point close to one of the green pins,' Caspasian said.

'How can you be sure?'

'The Mamluks have to make it seem as though it's the British troops doing the shooting. To get away with it they'll need to be able to snipe from behind the troops without being detected themselves.'

He stepped forward to the map and joined Ghazali in scrutinising the detail of the route. 'It's like looking for a needle in a haystack. It could be absolutely anywhere.'

'Don't you think they might have chosen more than one location to shoot from?' Ghazali said. 'It would probably be best if we divide our efforts. You study the west side of the map and I'll look at the east.'

Caspasian shook his head, eyes riveted to the web of streets at the city centre. 'No. They only need one initiation point. It only takes one flash point to start a fire. It would be too suspicious if there was more than one. That would point to a conspiracy. It would be too scientific.'

Ghazali stood back from the map and smiled. 'You really are very good, you know.'

Caspasian dismissed the compliment. 'My Colonel doesn't think so.' But his attention was on the map. He was beginning to home in on the key green pins clustered around the George Hotel on Shari Ibrahim Pasha. He took a red crayon and circled the area. A moment later he tapped the map triumphantly, marking the spot with a cross and then circling it. 'There! I'd put money on it.'

'And why?' Ghazali asked.

'Because it would be the perfect stage for what Kalkan and the Mamluks intend. The march is forced by the terrain to narrow and concentrate as they go past the hotel. British troops are in the closest proximity to them at that point, closer than anywhere else on the march, there's a park on the other side of the fence providing an escape route for the marchers after they've been fired upon so they can spread throughout the city taking the news with them and,' he pointed to several features on the map, 'there's a wealth of vantage points from which a sniper or a machine gun could fire without being easily seen.'

Satisfied, Caspasian turned to go. Ghazali was speaking urgently into the phone. He cupped his hand over the mouthpiece. 'I'm calling for reinforcements.'

'We can use the troops who are there.'

'No. This is a police matter. The military's there as back-up only.'

Caspasian checked his watch. Time was passing. As far as he was concerned the imperative was to get out on the ground. Reinforcements be hanged. Nevertheless, Ghazali was in charge. The demonstration was indeed a police concern. For the moment.

Ghazali listened to the answer coming over the handset, nodded and hung up. 'Right, let's go.'

They tore down the stairs and out past the bewildered desk officers on duty. The driver was behind the wheel of the car, engine revving. They piled into the back and set off with a screech of tyres out into the main street. At the junction with Shari Madabegh, they swung south and hurtled along at top speed. Ghazali reached inside his jacket and took out a French Lebel 8mm pistol, checking the load and safety catch. Caspasian spun the cylinder of his Webley revolver, replacing the empty cases with fresh rounds.

Suddenly they came to the end of road where it joined Shari Gami Sharkas and there, in front of them, file upon file of Wafd demonstrators chanted in unison. The noise rose up from the crowd like a great storm as tens of thousands of voices sang out their protest, clapping and shouting with all the power of their lungs.

'Back up!' Caspasian shouted, leaning forward and grabbing the driver's shoulder. The driver skidded to a halt and rammed the car into reverse.

'We're going to have to walk from here,' Ghazali said, opening his door and jumping down. He spoke quickly to the driver, ordering him to get clear of the marchers and return to the police headquarters.

On foot, Ghazali and Caspasian made their way down to the junction of the two roads. As the crowd flowed past with the irresistible force of flood water, they caught sight of the two men. Some of them jeered at Caspasian, others urged restraint. Caspasian could feel the mood. It was on a knife-edge. The slightest spark would ignite a conflagration that could engulf the country. If Kalkan had managed to issue his weapons to distribution points around the city, then Caspasian did not like to think where the shock waves of such a blood bath might end.

'I think we'd better take a back route,' Ghazali said, ushering Caspasian from the crowd.

They walked briskly away from the fringes of the marching crowd, heading back up Shari Gami Sharkas and taking a right turn down a side road. Ghazali led the way down a series of narrow streets until they came at last to Shari Ibrahim Pasha.

'It's just up ahead,' Ghazali said, breathing hard with the effort. Caspasian was impressed with how the older man was coping. Reaching the main road, they paused a moment. The way appeared clear, the road being eerily deserted. Warned of the demonstration, the shopkeepers had closed for the day, boarding themselves shut for protection against trouble.

'The George Hotel is left from here. About a hundred yards and on the right,' Ghazali panted, stepping out from the side road. Here and there they could see policemen waiting nervously for the head of the march to reach them. They wielded their long batons and took practice swipes at the sultry air.

The George Hotel stood back from the road, set in its own grounds behind a wall. Across from it, iron railings bordered the road and would channel the marchers as if through the waist of an hour glass. Beyond the railings, the dusty brown grass of the park stretched away, its few trees offering scant shade in the afternoon blaze. A further hundred yards up the road, Caspasian could just glimpse the bonnets of the army trucks protruding from a side road. One of the soldiers poked his head round the corner to peer down the road. He was wearing the broad-brimmed felt hat of the Gurkhas. Caspasian made a mental note and went on after Ghazali.

'Right, where the hell do we go from here?' Ghazali said. They had reached a crossroads outside the hotel. 'We've got a bank with a clock tower over there, the hotel behind us, the Kingston Bar and Grill, the park with little or no cover for a sniper, and the Clarence Theatre.' He appealed to Caspasian. 'What's your choice?'

Caspasian did a quick study of the ground. 'If I were a sniper I'd choose the theatre. Possibly on the roof.'

'Why not the hotel or the clock tower on the bank?'

'The hotel's too busy and the bank's too secure.' He shook his head. 'No, it's the theatre for me.'

'OK then, let's go,' Ghazali said, starting towards it.

'What about the reinforcements you called for?'

'They'll be here any minute. I don't think we've got the time to wait.'

To reinforce his point, at that moment they heard the distant chanting of the crowd and looked down the long avenue to see the head of the demonstration march rounding the far corner, turning inexorably in their direction. Banners were held aloft where the demonstrators marched twenty abreast.

'I can get a platoon of Gurkhas,' Caspasian called after him.

'They're best kept out of sight. One glimpse of them could

antagonise the crowd. Believe me, the police will be here any second.'

As expected, the theatre was closed, the doors locked and the windows shuttered.

'We'll try the stage entrance,' Ghazali said, veering off round the side of the building.

An alley led between the theatre and an office block that stood next to it. Several storeys high, the two buildings robbed the passage of daylight, casting it in deep gloom, the air hot and stagnant. Rubbish and rotting vegetables were piled along the sides, their fetid smells cloying the air.

'Here we are,' Ghazali said, arriving at the stage door. He tried the handle. It was locked.

'Allow me,' Caspasian said, moving Ghazali safely to one side. Ghazali drew his pistol in readiness. Caspasian brought the ball of his right foot up, the sokuto, and tested the door with two light mae geri front kicks accurately placed to the side of the lock and handle. The door moved easily on its loose hinges. He smiled, drew back, and delivered the third kick with full power and speed. The lock was propelled clean through the door which was left shuddering in place, casually swinging open on the dark interior.

'Come on!' Ghazali said, and ran inside, pistol at the ready. Caspasian followed him. He found himself in a long narrow corridor. A small glass-fronted booth stood to the left-hand side. Empty. Ghazali had disappeared up the steps at the far end and Caspasian could hear his footsteps pounding up stairs and running deeper into the theatre.

'Ghazali!' he shouted. 'Slow down!' They were on dangerous ground. For all he knew there might be a reception committee waiting for them. Ghazali's disembodied voice fired back at him. 'No time. What if we're wrong? The march is almost here. We might have to search the bank next.'

He was right. This was no time for caution. Caspasian went after him, up the stairs and down another corridor.

'Where are you?' he called as softly as he could. He hoped the sniper, if he was there at all, would be on the roof and out of earshot. If not, he was bound to have heard them coming.

'Over here,' came the reply.

The corridor came to an end at the edge of the stage where pitch darkness took over from the gloom.

'Where?'

'Here,' came Ghazali's voice. 'I'm trying to find the blasted light switch.'

Caspasian moved forward. Beneath his feet the wooden planks of the stage creaked. He reached out in front of him, arms outstretched to feel his way. His fingers met material. The curtains, vast and billowing, disappearing high overhead. He moved back, angling away from them to where he estimated the centre of the stage to be.

'Got it!' said Ghazali.

The lights came on with a clunk, harsh and dazzling. But in the instant of glare, Caspasian saw that he and Ghazali were not alone. Standing in a circle around them, half a dozen large suited men levelled guns at Caspasian. Beyond them, appearing from behind a stack of scenery close to Ghazali, a seventh man stepped forward. Kalkan.

'Ghazali, shoot!' Caspasian shouted. He knew that his hand would never make it to his own revolver in time, but Ghazali's pistol was drawn, the muzzle even pointing in Kalkan's direction.

Ghazali looked down at his gun and laughed. 'Do pardon me,' he said, addressing Kalkan. He moved his pistol away.

Caspasian felt as if he had been kicked in the gut. He stood rooted to the spot, staring unbelieving at Ghazali.

'You're one of them.'

Ghazali smiled at him. 'I'm afraid so, John. You really shouldn't have been so good. Too good for your own good, you might say.' He shook his head with admiration and then turned to Kalkan. 'He came straight here. Just like that.' He clicked his fingers and then positioned his pince-nez on the bridge of his nose to view Caspasian all the better.

Kalkan eyed Caspasian dangerously. 'Perhaps, but he's not that good. After all, who's holding the guns?' He gestured for one of his men to remove Caspasian's revolver.

'Harry, I don't believe you can let this happen,' Caspasian tried desperately, feeling horribly vulnerable once he had been disarmed. 'You. A Copt. This will spell disaster for your people.'

Ghazali's smile froze. 'Don't call me that. A Copt? The Copts are lackeys of the British Empire. I am Turkish.'

Caspasian suddenly felt as though his limbs were weighed down with lumps of iron. 'Of course. You, a Turk. I should have known. The cigarettes, if nothing else. One of the things you just couldn't give up. I suppose you're another one of the so-called Mamluks.'

Kalkan smiled coldly. 'He's more than just that, Captain Caspasian.' Respectfully, he moved to introduce Harry Ghazali. 'Allow me to present the Bey.'

21

'Can't you drive any faster?' Michelle urged, leaning over his shoulder.

Kraus muttered a curse as he fought with the gear stick of the unfamiliar vehicle. 'The Breguet was nothing compared to this piece of junk.'

'I do hope we're not being hasty,' the Professor said.

'How can you say that?' Michelle answered, rounding on him. 'Jacob was right about the bomb, wasn't he?'

'Yes, but if we're about to accuse a Chief Superintendent of Police of being the Bey, the leader of the Mamluks, and all because a half-crazed septuagenarian claims to recognise him, well . . .'

Seated in the front beside Kraus, Ganga turned his head. 'If Caspasian saheb is in trouble, then we owe it to him to go and help.'

'Yes, but is he in trouble?' the Professor said.

Ganga stared through the front windscreen again. 'Caspasian saheb is always in trouble.'

'Then we'll help him out of it,' Kraus said, finding the right gear and shoving the stick hard in with a sickening crunch.

The car shot across Khedive Ismail bridge, slowing for the road block but then accelerating away as the police guards came forward to inspect their passes. They heard shouts behind them and ducked low, but no one fired. The policemen had seen the uniforms, albeit tatty, and without the presence of an officer to direct them, decided it was safest to ignore the car load of foreigners.

'Which way is the police headquarters?' Kraus said to everyone in general.

'Right,' Ganga replied, not quite as sure as he would like to have been. He had only had cause to visit it on one previous occasion when helping the Adjutant retrieve a soldier from police custody after the man had enjoyed a rowdy evening on the town without a leave pass.

Luckily, a few moments later he recognised the building up ahead. 'There!' he said with relief.

Kraus swung the car into the compound. 'Come on.' He switched off the engine and they all leapt out.

'We can't just wander in,' the Professor said.

'Just watch.' Kraus strode forward, the others following in his wake. The duty desk officer met them inside the front entrance, his questioning stare matching the coolness radiating from the flagstones paving the vestibule.

'Can I help you?' He cast his eyes rapidly over the ramshackle group in front of him, a squat Gurkha sergeant, a square-headed man wearing the insignia of a sergeant, but not in any army with which the police officer was familiar, an elderly man looking decidedly world-weary, and an extremely attractive, if dishevelled, young woman upon whom the police officer allowed his eyes to dwell far longer than was either necessary or polite.

Kraus stepped forward. 'We're here to see Chief Superintendent Ghazali.'

Reluctantly the duty officer withdrew his eyes from Michelle, redirecting them at Kraus with distaste. 'The Chief Superintendent is not in.'

'Then can you tell me where he is? It is essential that we see him.'

The duty officer allowed himself a supercilious smile. 'I'm really not at liberty to say. His movements are confidential, particularly at a time like this.'

'All right then,' Kraus said, feeling the sweat prickle under his collar indicating a rise in his temperature which had nothing to do with the heat outside. 'Can you show us to his office? We will wait for him there.'

Again the policeman smiled the same smile, cranking up Kraus's temperature another degree. 'I'm really not at liberty to do that.' He pointed to a row of hard wooden benches. 'Feel free to wait there if you wish, although it might be some time before the Chief Superintendent returns.'

Kraus turned to the Professor and said in a loud voice, 'I'm sorry, Assistant Commissioner. There seems to have been some mix-up by the Chief Superintendent's staff.'

The Professor stared back round-eyed but swallowed his reply, nodding thoughtfully instead, his brow furrowed with displeasure. Doubt flickered across the duty officer's face.

'Did you say Assistant Commissioner?'

'Yes,' Kraus said in a matter-of-fact tone, turning to go. 'Assistant Commissioner of Police, Palestine. Liaison visit.'

'I'm monitoring your crowd control techniques,' the Professor added, settling into the role. 'It really is too bad the Chief Superintendent's not here. We had an appointment. Still, if he's forgotten or if someone failed to pass the message . . .'

The Professor attempted to sound irritated, difficult for him. The duty officer was round the desk in a single heartbeat.

'Just a minute,' he said, catching hold of the Professor's sleeve to prevent his departure. 'I'm not sure where the Chief Superintendent has gone but I'm sure he wouldn't mind if you waited in his office. In the meantime I'll see if I can contact him.'

The Professor checked with Kraus who took over. 'All right,' Kraus said gruffly. 'But do hurry up. We did have an appointment after all. It really is too bad.'

The duty officer called for a constable to show them up to Ghazali's office and once they were through the door, Kraus dismissed the man, peering out into the corridor a few moments later to check that he had gone.

'Right, what now?' the Professor said.

'We search,' Michelle replied, already leafing through the papers strewn across Ghazali's desk. 'If Jacob's right and Ghazali is the Bey, there must be something here to lead us to him.'

'Here!' Kraus shouted from the map room he had discovered. 'Look at this,' he said, pointing to the wall map detailing the city streets. 'It looks like it's marked out the route of the march.'

'And this crayon marking is in Caspasian's hand,' Ganga added triumphantly, pointing to the small, boldly-drawn circle and cross around the George Hotel and the theatre. 'I'd know it anywhere.'

'That must be where they decided the sniper was most likely to strike,' the Professor said.

'And if he went there with Ghazali, not knowing . . .' Michelle stopped short, the realisation of the danger to Caspasian sinking in.

'Then let's go,' Kraus said, leading the way out of the door and down the stairs again. At the foot of the steps, the duty officer looked round at them in surprise. 'Is anything the matter?'

'Everything,' Kraus stormed. 'It's disgraceful. Being kept waiting like this.'

'But you've only just . . .'

'Disgraceful!' Kraus exploded as they all rushed past, heading for the exit. 'The Assistant Commissioner is most displeased.'

'Most!' the Professor called back over his shoulder.

There was the splutter of the car engine starting and a moment later they screeched out of the compound and onto the main road in a cloud of dust, heading for the George Hotel where, at that moment, the front ranks of Wafd marchers were starting to converge.

*   *   *

In the circle of guns, Caspasian knew he had only seconds to act. In the distance he could hear the chanting of the approaching crowd. If left to pass by in peace they would continue with their march, their protest registered by the authorities, and tomorrow would find the government and British administration of Egypt intact. The Suez route to India and the east would remain open and unhindered, and the empire would live to fight another day. But if Ghazali and Kalkan had their way, in the space of the next few moments all of that would change. With the lead marchers massacred, supposedly by British troops, an uprising would start that would enflame the country and, most likely, the entire Levant. The only person who stood between the two alternative outcomes was Caspasian.

'So Ghazali,' he said, desperately trying to buy time. 'Who's going to do it? Who's going to pull the trigger?'

'Which trigger?' Ghazali replied pleasantly. 'On the marchers or on you?'

'On the marchers. In the wider scheme of things my fate is of little consequence.'

'Correction, Caspasian. Your fate is of absolutely no consequence whatsoever.'

Caspasian smiled. 'Fair enough. My Colonel always did say I had an inflated opinion of myself.'

'That was probably the only thing he has ever said that was correct,' Ghazali said.

'You take a pretty dim view of him.'

'Colonel Humphreys? Dim is exactly the right word.' Ghazali gave a dismissive wave of his pistol. 'Fodder for the empire. Nothing more. Just like all those other unimaginative, red-faced lobsters which Britain manages to produce with such tiresome proficiency.'

'The same unimaginative red-faced lobsters that kicked the Ottoman Empire into touch,' Caspasian said. 'Unimaginative men like Allenby I suppose.'

'Allenby was an exception.'

'And Lawrence?'

Ghazali smiled. 'Lawrence was imaginative, I grant you, but he was also a fool.'

'How so?'

'He was unable to succeed in his own society so he ran to a more primitive one where he could compete.'

'Maybe, but the Arab revolt which he helped to lead ran rings around you. And what was your response? Having failed to beat him on the field of battle, you were going to try to bribe the Arabs. To pay them off. Was that your own idea, Ghazali, or were you just the functionary? The fodder, as you put it? And you dare talk to me about unimaginative!'

He could see that Ghazali was becoming riled. His face had gone pale and he was rising to the bait. Caspasian judged it was time to push the message home.

'When you were given charge of all that gold, it must have been a huge temptation to take the lot and run. I can understand that,' Caspasian said reasonably, sympathetically. 'Your empire was in ruins, your army defeated. Who would ever know? No one would be left to pursue you.'

'That's not the way it was!' Ghazali shouted back. 'If I had wanted to run I would hardly have stayed in Cairo. Yes, I saw the way things were going, how others were all too ready to betray the old empire instead of refashioning it.' He tapped his temples. 'I had the vision to see into the future. Into an alternative future where the Ottoman Empire would not be defeated, merely dormant. I established the Mamluks, and through them I have been working tirelessly to move my people step by painful step into positions of power, through assassination, bribery, blackmail and through sheer will power. Don't you dare call my motives into question!'

He was seething, his voice rising ever louder. 'Who the devil are you to speak to me like this? You are a nobody. An underling. The lickspittle of underlings.'

Kalkan coughed lightly to get his attention. 'Bey, the march-ers,' he prompted quietly.

'They can wait,' Ghazali snapped, furious now. 'I want this dog butchered. Here, now, in front of me. I want . . .'

Caspasian's moment had come. With each sentence that he and Ghazali had exchanged, Caspasian had been moving, a step at a time, closer to the edge of the stage. As he had done so, he had brought himself into perfect line between two of the Turkish guards, the one next to Kalkan at the rear, the other one opposite him at the edge of the stage. In doing so he had obstructed their fire. Were they to shoot they would risk hitting each other.

As Ghazali ranted, Caspasian burst into action. Ducking as he ran, he hurled himself at the small opening of the prompter's box several yards away, the hood at stage floor level barely two feet high. Just before he heard the first gunshot ring out, he went into a forward roll, finishing smack in front of the hood and slithering head first down into the darkness within.

'Stop him!' Ghazali screamed. Bullets smacked in pursuit, but the two men closest to him had hesitated as Caspasian had intended, neither wishing to hit his comrade by mistake. The split second this bought Caspasian had been all he needed. He was underground, and the balance of power had shifted just enough to give him a chance. The slightest chance.

Tumbling into the darkness of the tiny cramped box, Cas-pasian found the door had been bolted from the outside. But the wood was old and poor quality and it split asunder with a single empi elbow strike, the only blow Caspasian could employ in the confined space. He fell out and found himself in a dark cavernous space beneath the stage. Looking up he could see the light above from the stage penetrating the cracks in the floorboards. Bullets punched their way through, trying to seek him out, each one stabbing a slender shaft of light down below. Behind Caspasian, one of the Turks was trying to work himself into the prompter's box after him, but he was doing so feet first, lacking Caspasian's dexterity. Caspasian waited until the man's back was in full view, wriggling lower, and then fired a full power gyaku tsuki reverse punch into the man's kidneys. The man seemed to implode, crumpling and attempting to turn at the same time. As he did so, he unwittingly brought his solar plexus into Caspasian's line of sight, receiving a second gyaku tsuki punch delivered with the same fist as the first blow. The two together turned the man into a useless heap slumped on the floor of the prompter's box.

Ghazali's furious voice screamed out above the stage. 'Get him, Kalkan. Then come and join me on the roof.'

Footsteps thundered across the floorboards and Caspasian knew they would soon find a way down to him. He tried to retrieve the pistol from the Turk he had just brought down, but it had tumbled onto the stage not down into the box. It remained infuriatingly out of reach.

He hunted around for a way out and located a flight of steps but as he started up them, another of the guards came pounding down. The man saw Caspasian just in time to prevent himself from running headlong into a punch. He jerked backwards and blazed off a shot at Caspasian's head. The bullet smacked into the brickwork inches from Caspasian's face. A razor-sharp fragment burst away and whipped past Caspasian's cheek with the ferocity of shrapnel.

Throwing himself back down the stairs, Caspasian dived for the ground, scrabbling away from more bullets that chased in his wake, each one closer than the last. With his back against a packing case, Caspasian braced himself for the impact of the next one. The firing pin clicked on an empty breech as the gun's mechanism spat out the last expended round. Caspasian's body reacted before his mind, jerking him to his feet and launching him at the surprised Turk, still fumbling to remove the empty magazine from the weapon.

Two stairs below the man, Caspasian grabbed him with one hand in the belt of his trousers and the other gripping the lapels of his jacket, lifted him bodily off the ground and propelled him downwards onto the concrete floor. He fell heavily, shaking his head to clear it. Before he could gather himself Caspasian was upon him. With his right foot, Caspasian threw in a mae geri front kick that took the Turk full on the side of the jaw. He saw the mouth jump sideways and the man collapsed unconscious.

Caspasian scrabbled to retrieve the pistol. Before he had gone down, the Turk had managed to get the empty magazine out of the pistol grip, but when Caspasian ran his hands quickly through the man's jacket pockets, there was no sign of a replacement. He cursed, hearing the footsteps of another man coming down the steps. A voice called out the name of his unconscious comrade, and Caspasian hurled the useless gun at the newcomer. It rang harmlessly off the wall and clattered down the steps. Two shots snapped at Caspasian, pursuing him through the darkness. He collided with an obstacle but found it to be a wooden panel. Feeling his way along it he came to a handle and opened it to find himself in the orchestra stalls. He slipped inside and hurriedly closed the door behind him before the shaft of light he had admitted to the darkness would betray him.

The stage above him was now empty. Voices echoing throughout the theatre told of the hunt for him, but of more concern to Caspasian was Ghazali's absence, knowing that he would be making his way to the firing point to engage the crowd with sniper fire.

He slipped over the top of the orchestra stalls and dropped down beside the front row seats. A box stood ten yards distant. Caspasian gathered himself and ran for it.

'There he is!'

Bullets tore holes in the crimson velvet of the seats beside him, the white cotton insides bursting out through the tears like instant rosettes. Caspasian measured his stride and launched himself over the balustrade, knocking aside the seats in the box and banging heavily into the door at the back of it. Still lying on the floor, he kicked out at the handle, bursting the door open and crawled through into the narrow corridor behind. Turning to the right, he hurled himself down the corridor until he came to the base of a steep staircase that led to the upper floors. With his back to the wall, he edged slowly upwards, taking the steps one at a time. He knew that at any moment someone would be coming for him from below but the last thing he needed was to run into another trap. Counting Kalkan and Ghazali, he reckoned that there were at least six men confronting him. For all he knew there might be more. He had to assume the worst.

Rounding a bend, he found himself at the top of the flight and facing an open bar area. The floor was covered with a thick red carpet of gaudy pattern and the cream paint on the walls was starting to flake. Elaborate cornices were painted in gold, and several heavily framed pictures, all popular reproductions, hung on the walls. There was one window to the outside world but it was shuttered, enough sunlight penetrating through the cracks around the edges to make all the details of the room visible while creating an atmosphere of oppressive gloom.

Caspasian took a step forward but the moment he transferred his weight to his front foot the floorboard beneath the carpet gave a resounding crack.

'Kalkan?'

The voice came from barely yards away, the far side of a pillar dividing the room. Caspasian grunted roughly, trying to bluff the man for just long enough to reach him. It was no use. The man's senses had already been alerted by the earlier shots and he was waiting for him. As his body appeared from behind the pillar, gun-hand first, Caspasian darted forward, covering the intervening space in a split second, feet gliding smoothly over the carpet. He lowered his centre of gravity, flexing his knees and investing his hips, thigh and leg muscles with strength and focus to produce a rock solid platform from which to operate. His hands came up and as the Turk raised the pistol to fire, Caspasian reached out and enveloped the man's wrist with a kake-uke grasping block.

With irresistible force Caspasian drew the man forward, unbalancing him. As the Turk staggered, bracing himself with his front leg against the strength of Caspasian's tug, Caspasian executed a de-ashi barai foot sweep. The Turk began to fall, but he was no fool and as he did so, instead of resisting further, he went with the momentum, launching himself into a forward roll that took him out of Caspasian's immediate reach. He started to recover, rising and turning to face the new onslaught which he knew would come. Caspasian's speed took him completely by surprise and before he could develop his guard, Caspasian was upon him. A gyaku tsuki reverse punch caught him behind the left ear and set his head spinning. The Turk attempted to shake it off but the blow had struck home. A second punch caught him in the side of the ribcage. The man felt one crack. Then another foot sweep took him down again and before he even hit the ground blows were raining down upon him.

Caspasian retrieved the man's gun which lay abandoned on the carpet. It was a .32 Ruby like Béranger's. With a shock Caspasian realised that it was Béranger's. He ran his hand over it, taking note. Paying homage. Grim determination flooded through him, renewing his conviction.

He checked the magazine and found it fully charged. Clicking it home, he snapped back the mechanism and let the spring take it forward, slotting a bullet into the breech and leaving the firing pin cocked and ready. The safety catch was set to fire.

Choosing the door on the far side of the bar, Caspasian moved towards it, pistol ready. A glass panel set high in the wooden frame showed the corridor beyond. It was empty. He eased open the door and slipped through. He had to get higher. That was where he would find Ghazali.

More stairs led up to the next level and Caspasian went for them. He knew that he was going to have to sacrifice stealth for

335

speed, but having a gun compensated. At least if he were to walk into a trap he would have a chance of shooting his way out of it.

The next second his theory was put to the test. He emerged onto the uppermost floor of the theatre. The seating had been removed and it looked as though it had not been used for some considerable time except as a storage area. Rolls of carpet, pieces of scenery, lighting equipment and trunk upon trunk of costumes were scattered in a haphazard fashion. As Caspasian peered over the topmost stair to review the next phase of his progress, a shot snapped close past his head. He made to go back down the steps but voices from behind told him he was caught in the middle.

A few yards away, a pile of trunks were roughly stacked. Taking a deep breath, Caspasian threw himself at them, blazing off rounds in the direction of the firer as he went. It was just enough to put the man off his aim, and by the time further shots cracked at Caspasian he was safely into cover. He sat with his back to the trunks, making himself as small as possible, and faced back towards the stairs, pistol ready, the body of the small gun couched in the cupped palm of his hand for support. Béranger's gun. Paul Béranger. His friend. The moment anyone appeared above the top stair, Caspasian was ready to blow them to hell.

Stairs creaked. From behind him a voice called out, but was met with silence from whoever was advancing up the stairs. Caspasian's eyes were fixed on the spot, expecting his target to appear at any second. When it did, his finger tightened on the trigger just as Ganga's face popped up and stared straight at him. Caspasian jerked his gun aside, just in time. Ganga grinned at him, realising how close he had come to receiving a bullet between the eyes. With sign language, Caspasian indicated that Ganga should fire a shot into the trunk beside him. Ganga brought up his rifle into the aim and complied. The shot smashed into the wood with deafening effect. Caspasian cried out, feigning a strike. There was a voice from behind him and the Turk moved forward to investigate. As he did so, Caspasian rolled out from behind the trunks onto his stomach, aimed and fired two quick rounds in rapid succession, both of them hitting the man in centre chest. The Turk's arms flew out to his sides and he was knocked backwards, dead.

Ganga came forward. 'Are you all right?'

'Yes, but where are the others?'

'Over there somewhere,' Ganga replied, indicating the opposite side of the voluminous theatre. 'We found your markings on Ghazali's map and when we drove up we saw Ghazali himself, Kalkan, and some other men on the roof. Kraus and the others went up the other side while I tried to make contact with you. We should have the Turks caught between us.'

'Come on then,' Caspasian said, leading the way towards a metal ladder that climbed towards a trap door. 'This probably opens out onto the roof. We've got to stop them!'

Sure enough, when he opened the trap door, dazzling sunlight burst into the gloom of the interior. Caspasian squinted into the glare and pushed his head and shoulders outside.

'Come and join us, Caspasian,' Ghazali said. He was standing less than a dozen paces away. Beside him, Kalkan and two Turks were guarding the Professor and Michelle. Kraus lay on the floor, unconscious, a savage gash on his forehead weeping blood onto the sand-covered surface of the roof. 'Your friends have already graced us with their presence. Presumably that Gurkha ape is with you?'

Caspasian eased himself up through the trap door and looked down behind him. There was no one there. He shrugged at Ghazali. 'Afraid not.'

Ghazali dismissed it. 'No matter.'

Kalkan relieved Caspasian of his pistol and then spoke urgently to the two Turks who jogged away to a door and disappeared back into the body of the theatre.

'We'll get him,' Ghazali said. 'In the meantime, you and your

337

friends can watch while we complete this part of our task. In fact, it couldn't be better. You can stand over there on the edge so the crowd will be able to see you when we shoot. It's a bonus I hadn't counted on. A British officer himself in charge of the machine gun. A nice touch, don't you think?'

Michelle went to assist Kraus but Kalkan grabbed her wrist, tugging her away. The Professor put his arm around her like a protective father. Kalkan started towards the machine gun which was set up near the edge of the roof, but Ghazali waved him back. 'Watch them. I'll do the shooting myself. I'm going to enjoy this.'

To his dismay Caspasian saw that the LMG was a British Lewis gun, a fully charged 47-round drum magazine clipped to the top of the breech. With a cyclic rate of 550 rounds per minute it would have a devastating effect on the marchers packed tightly together in the street below.

He was ushered over to join the others. Michelle came to him. 'We've got to stop him,' she whispered.

Desperately, Caspasian searched for an answer, but his eyes met Kalkan's and he knew that if he made the slightest move he would be shot out of hand. He was clean out of tricks.

'Ghazali,' he said. 'This is stupid. Why go to all this trouble? You've got the gold. Why not just take it and go? You don't have to do this.'

Ghazali was kneeling down beside the gun, checking the magazine. 'For an intelligent man you say some stupid things,' he said without looking round. 'If I had wanted to run off with the gold I could have done so at any point during the last ten years. No, my young friend. The future of my country is far more important to me.' He waved a hand at Kalkan. 'As it is to all of us. To every Mamluk that is waiting throughout the Levant for my signal.' He yanked back the cocking handle. 'For this signal.'

He lay down behind the gun and snuggled the butt into his shoulder. Down in the street below the marchers were passing beneath the theatre. Their foremost ranks were tightly pressed together and as he watched Ghazali take a bead on them Caspasian knew that he could not possibly miss. His fire would inflict slaughter as he intended. And there was absolutely nothing Caspasian could do to stop him.

The noise of the crowd rose up in a mighty roar of chanting. They had seen the British soldiers in the side street and some of the crowd were waving their fists at them while others urged caution and restraint. In a second, all of that would have been blown asunder and the country would have been set upon a new course.

A whistle came from the far side of the roof. Caspasian, Kalkan, the Professor and Michelle turned to look. As they did so, there was a flicker in the light, a rent in the sky above them that rippled through the air. For a second Caspasian thought of the iridescent flash of a kingfisher, like the one he had seen on the Nile steamer when standing with Michelle. Kalkan frowned, trying to recognise what it was. Caspasian dived for Michelle and the Professor, throwing them clear, the three of them going down in a tangle of arms and legs. Kalkan's gun came up, swivelling to face this new and unexpected adversary, just as the flying kukri scythed through the last yards of space, cartwheeling blade over pommel, and struck. The blade smashed edge-first into his sternum, driving in deep, the tip finding its way into Kalkan's heart. The pistol fell from his hand, clattering onto the roof as his fingers fussed uselessly at the blade lodged at his core. He took three faltering steps backwards, propelled by the massive force of the impact, and fell.

Ghazali looked round and took in the scene in a second. The machine gun was in his hands. He had time. Time both to kill the accursed meddlers and also to fire into the crowd below. He spun onto his feet, bringing the gun up as he did so. Across the rooftop he could see Ganga going for his rifle. Ghazali had only a second or two to act, but it would be enough. The gun in his hands was a Lewis. There was a full drum magazine on the top and he knew how to use it. A broad spread of fire would compensate for any lack of marksmanship. He would sweep up the lot of them. Mow them down. Cut them to ribbons. He could see Caspasian trying to shield the girl. He could see the Professor scuttling for cover that Ghazali knew his bullets would chew their way clean through. He could see the Gurkha sergeant unslinging the rifle from his shoulders.

Ghazali pressed the trigger and the gun fired. Starting from left to right he swept the roof top, first one way and then back again. Bullets intended for the marchers chewed and spat and bit their way through the scant bits of cover that were available. The bullets pocked the ground around the Gurkha sergeant's feet forcing him to dive for cover. They snapped at Caspasian and the girl, huddling pathetically on the floor, they sought out the Professor and chased him on his belly across the roof tiles. They blazed out across the rooftop in all directions and Ghazali exulted in the feeling of power it gave him. His whole body shuddered with the force of the shots. Buffeted by the recoils of the giant 29-pound monster, Ghazali spread his feet to steady himself. Bracing his right foot against a strut that protruded from the surface of the roof, he shifted his rear foot backwards. It pressed into thin air. Ghazali's heart lurched. He felt the shock of it in his mouth. The barrel of the big Lewis gun shot up towards the sky and involuntarily his finger squeezed off another burst. It jarred into him, countering his desperate moves to regain his balance. His face turned and he was looking out into space, staring down into the dingy alleyway that tracked along the side of the theatre. He dropped the gun into the abyss and his whole body convulsed in an attempt to get back onto firm ground. He was going to make it. His body bucked and weaved on the brink of the precipice. The edge of death. He flinched away from the drop, arms outstretched towards safety. His eyes followed them and all of a sudden he was looking into the cold, impassive face of Caspasian.

'Help me . . .'

From a position of perfect balance, Caspasian reached out, his hand open. Ghazali's fingers clawed towards it. Avoiding their grasp, Caspasian's hand closed into a fist and ever so lightly popped Ghazali on the chest. Ghazali's arms flew outwards and flapped like wings. His face went back, engraved with terror, and he fell.

Caspasian leaned forward and inspected the drop, following Ghazali's progress all the way down. Chief Superintendent Ghazali. Harry Ghazali. The Bey.

EPILOGUE

The sun would be up in a few minutes. There was not much time. Caspasian glanced back over his shoulder and peered down into the thin mist that was coagulating around the base of the Great Pyramid of Cheops in the pre-dawn coolness. His horse stood tethered in the care of a boy who gazed up at the climbing Englishman, amused at such extraordinary antics.

Caspasian turned again towards the summit, still several hundred feet above him. He scrambled up the next enormous block of stone, and then the next, score upon score of others stretching above him in a raggedly ascending staircase leading up into the darkness. The physical demands of the climb were an ideal tonic for limbs fresh from sleep and in need of a sharp awakening. Already Caspasian's lungs were hard at work, his breath starting to labour, sweat prickling down his spine. His hat had stuck to his forehead and he swept it off, scrunching it up and stuffing it in his belt. He ran a hand through his hair before turning again to the next stage of the climb.

As arms and legs worked, so too did his mind, running over the events of the past weeks. Throughout the Levant and in Turkey itself, the dismantling of the Mamluks was almost complete. Robbed of their leader and stripped of funds and weaponry, the organisation had rapidly begun to fall apart. Informants had come forward and the secret society was unravelling.

The Turkish intelligence service had been on to Ghazali for some time. One of their agents had attempted to contact the antiquities dealer when he had offered the fragment of parchment for sale. He had been close to making contact in the City of the Dead when Ghazali himself had surprised the dealer and murdered him. With the chance intervention of a British patrol, the Turkish agent, operating under cover, had been forced to run. But Ghazali's plan had also been foiled. He had been prevented from keeping the papyrus to himself. It had entered the public domain and, with it, the location of the lost city of King Menes and the Mamluks' cache of gold and weapons. It had become imperative for him to thwart the British and French expeditions, at least for long enough to enable the Mamluk assassination plot to come to fruition.

Caspasian had been out to the aerodrome to wish good luck to Professor Fenwick the day he had left once again for the ruined city. With proof of its existence and the backing of the High Commissioner himself, the Professor had experienced little difficulty in raising the necessary funds for a further expedition, this time to be mounted by air. It would also be an opportunity to retrieve the bodies of Béranger, Sir Hubert, Simonin and the others, flying them back to Cairo for a proper burial as instructed by their next of kin.

The Professor had been on good form that day as he and Caspasian had waited together for the plane to depart. He had thanked Caspasian profusely for everything he had done.

'I wouldn't even be alive if it hadn't been for you.'

Caspasian had shrugged, uncomfortable with the praise and not knowing how to respond. He had wished the Professor luck with the new expedition.

'Ah, but this is just the start,' the Professor had said. 'With luck, I will find a clue that will lead me to the location of the real tomb! Now that would be a triumph, wouldn't it? Perhaps you'd care to join me on that expedition, John?'

Caspasian had been spared the need for a reply as the engines had started up at that point, drowning further conversation with a throaty roar. They had shaken hands warmly and his last glimpse of the little Professor had been of a small hunched figure, incongruously dressed in Norfolk jacket and Palmerston hat, scurrying towards the aircraft, battered valise in one hand, rolled umbrella in the other.

Two days later he had been to Port Said to see off old Jacob. Private Jacob Doherty of the General Post Office Rifles, captured at the fall of Khartoum by the Mahdi's forces on 25th January, 1885. He had indeed, albeit unwittingly, saved the life of Mahmud's father who, from a debt of honour, had similarly spared Jacob's life. By the time of Omdurman thirteen years later, and the defeat of the Mahdi's forces by the British, captivity had already destroyed Jacob's mind. Along with the fugitives of the battle, he was spirited away into the desert, there to survive for another thirty years, his status slowly changing from prisoner to talisman.

The High Commissioner himself had seen to it that a place was provided for Jacob at an old soldiers' home in Aldershot. But there was one further piece of news that Caspasian had been able to deliver to Jacob as he prepared to go aboard the steamer bound for Southampton. A surviving relative had been traced. A younger sister and her family. Jacob had listened to her name dispassionately, giving no sign of remembrance. But as he made his way up the gangplank, Caspasian had seen the faintest light of recognition dawning on the old man's face and, with it, a broad toothless grin.

Caspasian was nearing the top now. He checked the eastern horizon and saw that the sky was separating itself from the earth, darkness fracturing from darkness as at the moment of creation. With a concentrated burst of energy he flung himself upwards, tearing his way over the blocks of stone in an effort to make the summit in time. He was there before he realised it, heaving his body up over one enormous slab and lying gasping for breath.

'Where have you been? I thought you weren't coming.'

He looked up and saw Michelle smiling down at him. She was sitting on the opposite side of the flat-topped summit, legs crossed, hands on knee.

Caspasian tried to reply but thought it best to wait for his heart rate to slow down. Instead, he rolled onto his knees and stood up stiffly.

'Do you think it'll be too misty?'

He turned to face the east and studied the changing sky. He shook his head, hands on hips, pulse gradually calming. Michelle patted the stone seat next to her. Caspasian moved across and slumped down onto it. He pulled his hat out of his belt and used it to mop his face. Michelle watched him and laughed gently. 'Don't say you're out of shape? You obviously need some exercise. Perhaps you should have gone back into the desert with the Professor.'

'*Pas du tout*. A nice quiet office will do me just fine.'

She regarded him doubtfully and screwed up her nose.

'Well, perhaps just for a while.'

'By all accounts you're not going to have your little office,' she said.

Caspasian beamed. 'News travels.'

'The High Commissioner told me. You're getting a rifle company again. Congratulations.'

'I don't think I'll have it for long though. Colonel Humphreys wants me out of the regiment. At least so long as he's there.'

'But the High Commissioner . . . ?'

'Has other things to concern him. There are weightier matters at the Residency than the career prospects of John Caspasian. It's one thing for Ganga to get posted back to a rifle company and for Bharat to get the job he always wanted.'

'Which is?'

Caspasian grinned. 'Officers' mess sergeant.' He chuckled. 'He's a lazy bugger and quite useless as a soldier but I have to admit that the mess hasn't been the same since he took over. The accounts are in order, the silver shines so you can see your face in it, and if there's the occasional discrepancy in the wines ledger, well, who cares?'

When he had finished speaking he suddenly noticed that she was not wearing the small leather pouch on her belt. He glanced at the ground to see if she had her bag with her. All he could see was a hat lying beside her on the stone.

'It's back in my hotel room,' she said, reading his thoughts. When she saw the expression on his face she smiled. 'It's all right. Perhaps it's time to move on.'

'Yes, but that's no reason to . . .'

'No reason to cling quite so tenaciously to the past, John.' She placed a hand on his wrist. 'Don't get me wrong. My family's memory is as dear to me as ever. It's just that . . . well, I've been thinking about what you said in the desert. About learning to live as a survivor.' She observed him closely. 'But I want to be even more than that. Neither ghost, nor survivor, but . . .'

'Normal?'

She held up her hands and laughed. 'Michelle Simonin, normal? Now there's a thought!'

Caspasian felt suddenly wonderfully happy. Although the sun had not yet risen he felt as if the two of them were already being illuminated by it.

'Since Émile died,' she continued, 'I have been thinking of lots of things. Many things have fallen into place, and some haven't. Most of all I know that I want to travel. For once I can go where I want, do the things I want to do, be with the people I want to be with. And I have the means as well.'

'Émile's money goes to you?' Caspasian asked, delighted.

'All of it. It's no fortune, but ample to allow me to do as I please. For the first time since . . . for the first time ever.'

'I can imagine how that feels.'

'Independence.' She spoke the word wistfully.

'Free,' Caspasian added.

She looked at him and smiled radiantly. 'As a bird.' A frown clouded her face. 'But I was sorry to hear about Kraus. I believe he's gone to Algeria.'

Caspasian sighed. 'Sidi bel Abbes. He's been posted to the headquarters in a training job for a while.'

'How do you think he'll like that?'

'Not very much.'

'*Le cafard*,' she said, nodding sadly.

'Kraus isn't the sort to let boredom get in his way. Personally I think he rather liked his recent flying experience. I wouldn't be surprised if he moves on from the Legion. The airlines are the thing of the future. There are routes opening up all over the world. They need men with the pioneering spirit and who better than Kraus, an ex-Legion sergeant?'

'I can think of one person,' she said.

Caspasian looked at her and noticed the glint in her eye. 'You've heard the rumour then?'

'Cairo's a small place. Nothing travels as fast as gossip. What's your version?'

Caspasian toyed with his hat in his hands. 'OK, then. When the Colonel told me he'd been ordered to give me command of a rifle company, he also said he was pulling out all the stops to get me transferred out of the regiment again. Apparently there's some new project in South America. Something to do with a new airline.'

'Aeroplanes?'

Caspasian grimaced. 'Airships. There's an ambitious plan to establish a network of routes right across the continent but there are problems.'

'I'm not surprised, what with the Andes and the Amazon in the way.'

'Not those kind of problems.'

'Oh?'

'Well, I've only heard the barest details so far, but it seems there's a complication with a revolutionary movement down there.'

Michelle stared at him wide-eyed. 'John Caspasian, can't you keep out of trouble for more than a few weeks at a time?'

She reached out and shook him lightly by the shoulder. He caught hold of her hand, pulled her towards him and kissed her. Michelle was still a moment and then returned his kiss, lips pressing firmly into his. He could feel her body against him and smell the scent of her hair.

All of a sudden, light reached out and touched them. From the far other side of the distant city, a single point of crimson fired across the intervening space and caught them unawares on the summit of the pyramid. Shadows sprung instantly from the tumbled stones around them, descending slowly down the enormous flanks of the structure. Eventually they would strike the desert floor, whereupon they would travel westwards across the plateau, heading ever further across the continent towards the ocean on the far side.

'Sunrise,' Caspasian said.

'A new day,' Michelle answered. She sat contemplating the sun, refusing to look away until her eyes could bear it no longer.

'When do you leave?' Caspasian asked.

'I have absolutely no plans whatsoever,' she replied. 'And it feels wonderful.' She took his hands in hers. 'Why? Do you have something in mind? Not another cruise on the Nile I hope!'

He laughed. 'No. Not that.' He checked his watch, then peered down the side of the pyramid where the mist was rapidly clearing, burnt off in the steadily rising heat. 'It's just that I know a place that serves the best coffee in all Cairo. Coffee and honey cakes.'

'Mm. I can't think of a better way to start the morning,' she said, glowing from within. 'And then what?'

'And then . . .' Caspasian mused, getting to his feet and holding out his hand to her. He grinned. 'I have absolutely no plans whatsoever.'